THE SHATTERED VIGIL

D0891111

Books by Patrick Carr

THE STAFF AND THE SWORD

A Cast of Stones

The Hero's Lot

A Draw of Kings

THE DARKWATER SAGA

By Divine Right (e-novella only)

The Shock of Night

The Shattered Vigil

THE
DARKWATER
SAGA

THE
SHATTERED
VIGIL

PATRICK W. CARR

BETHANYHOUSE
a division of Baker Publishing Group
Minneapolis, Minnesota

© 2016 by Patrick W. Carr

Published by Bethany House Publishers
11400 Hampshire Avenue South
Bloomington, Minnesota 55438
www.bethanyhouse.com

Bethany House Publishers is a division of
Baker Publishing Group, Grand Rapids, Michigan

Printed in the United States of America

Library of Congress Control Number: 2016942748

ISBN 978-0-7642-1347-2

This is a work of fiction. Names, characters, incidents, and dialogues are products of the author's imagination and are not to be construed as real. Any resemblance to actual events or persons, living or dead, is entirely coincidental.

Cover design by LOOK Design Studio
Cover photography by Aimee Christenson

Author represented by The Steve Laube Agency

16 17 18 19 20 21 22   7 6 5 4 3 2 1

To my wife, Mary:

The only problem with knowing I married "up" is conceding that you must have married "down." I'll try to bear up somehow.

To my four sons,
Patrick, Connor, Daniel, and Ethan:

No children ever inspired their father more.

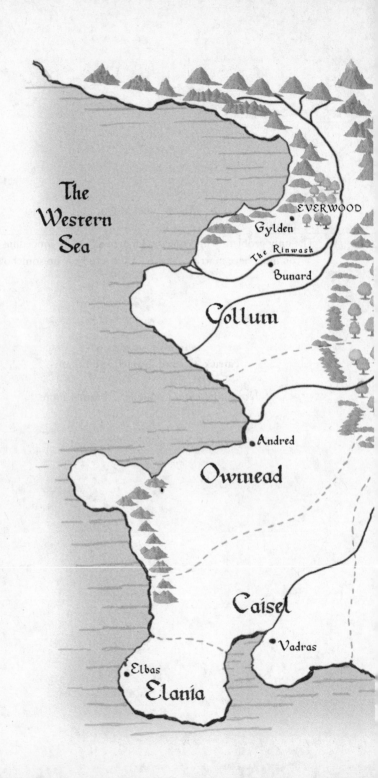

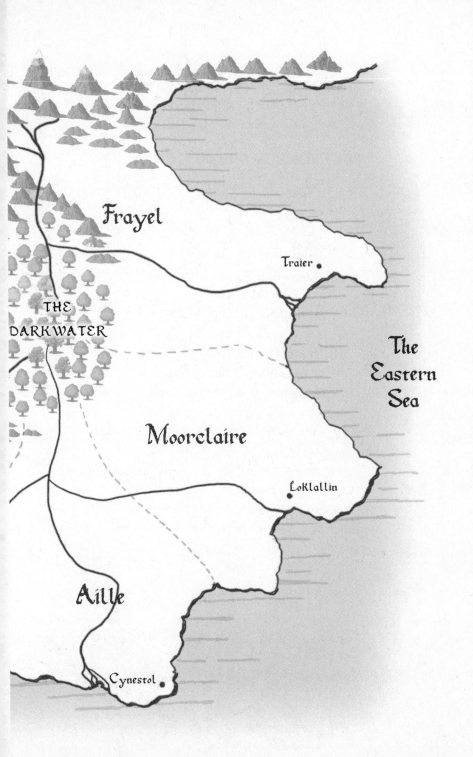

THE EXORDIUM OF THE LITURGY

The six charisms of Aer are these:
For the body, beauty and craft
For the soul, sum and parts
For the spirit, helps and devotion

The nine talents of man are these:
Language, logic, space, rhythm,
motion, nature, self, others, and all

The four temperaments of creation are these:
Impulse, passion, observation, and thought

Within the charisms of Aer, the talents of man,
and the temperaments imbued in creation
are found understanding and wisdom. Know and learn.

PROLOGUE

Darkness fell within the storyteller's room, the pain and light of day diminishing, though the heat remained, absorbed and surrendered from countless clay walls and tiled roofs. Nightfall. He relished the dying of the light, the way the sun that blinded him slid beneath the horizon with all the desperate clinging of a drowning child.

Somewhere within the confluence of memories within his mind a twinge of regret flashed through him like an unexpected strike of lightning. He ignored the stray emotion without so much as a grimace to mark its passing. Such vestiges of humanity manifested themselves less often as time passed, but the emotion served to remind him of his limitation and strengthened his resolve to conquer it. Until he could bend creation to his will, he would have to adapt. For now.

Rising from his bed, he removed the outermost cloth shielding his eyes from the unbearable brightness of day. The other, thinner cloth he left in place. It would allow him to function in the lantern-light of the expensive restaurant and tavern below, but there was another more important reason that had nothing to do with his disguise or the girl's expectations.

He grabbed the polished cane by the door and ventured into the hallway, thumping the wood on the floor with the regular rhythm of a blind man searching his way. The stairs had been split into sets of nine and he smiled. Of all those walking on the northern continent only he and another knew the import of that number, knew its importance in relationship to the other two mentioned in the exordium.

A pop and flare from the fire in the center of the room caught him by surprise, and he squeezed his eyes shut against the pain, his cane serving its pretended purpose for a moment. He took the shadowed table at the back of the tavern, the one most shielded from the fire and lanterns.

She came through the front entrance, as he'd instructed her, when the last ray of light had vanished from the spire of the grand cathedral. It was a trivial exercise, but it served to reinforce the unquestioning obedience he would require, and it provided the time necessary to arrive before her and prepare the wine. She noted the dagger he'd placed on the table before him but said nothing. Attractive, she responded to power and drink as courtesans and sycophants had responded for countless millennia, with near worship of those who exercised dominion over them.

"Greetings, Magden," he said with a self-deprecating smile. "Do you never tire of an old man's stories?"

"Never." Flattered to think that her presence pleased him so much, she laughed, gazing at him with . . .

Devotion.

Despite his intimate familiarity, the library here in Vadras, the chief city in Caisel, had proven difficult to penetrate—the sanctum where the priests stored the oldest writings even more so. In the end, he'd had to use a series of disposable intermediaries with instructions on which texts to find. Even then it had taken weeks to gather the names of those minor personages, individuals without fame or acclaim, who lived within the city and owned the particular gift he required.

A pure gift would have been simpler, the memories would have taken less time—the emotional responses more intense from the outset—but the end result would be the same. And for his purposes a partial gift served him better. Those with full gifts—in their arrogance they misnamed this parceling, this division, something so far less than what it had been—attracted attention. He required something less, a partial gift, whose owner moved freely and randomly through the city and court, one of the countless faces who'd left family and friends behind to make the journey to the second-largest city on the continent.

Someone whose disappearance would go unnoticed until it was too late.

Magden—he forced himself to remember her name only because it flattered her that he bothered to know it—leaned forward, anticipating his tale, her bare hand extended across the corner of the table, her offer implicit in the coy smile and tilt of her head.

"Tell me the story again." She smiled. "The one about me. You've never finished it."

"Well . . . " He lifted his hands. "It's a story of some depth."

She pouted. "But every night you start over at the beginning."

"The most powerful tales require an attention to detail seldom found in other narratives." He put a smile on his face but ignored the offer of her bare skin for the moment. Almost—almost she was ready. "Magden was born in the far north," he said, beginning the same story he'd told her several times each night for the past two weeks. "There, like here, she danced and loved, and the love of her life was Count Orlan, brother to the duke and the most handsome man in the city of Bunard."

His voice dipped, like the fall of notes from a mandolin just before the villain appeared on stage during a play. He paused, waiting for a sign that the story and the memories he'd planted had taken hold. It didn't take long. Her brows drew together and her face darkened, her expression becoming murderous, no longer the aspect of a girl hearing a story, but a lover longing for revenge—real revenge.

"Until he killed him," she snarled, her hand curling around the dagger, tightening until the blood drained from her knuckles.

Through the cloth that protected him from the stabbing glare of the lanterns he noted the pallor of Magden's eyes, the way their rich green, like spring grass, had faded to the barest hint of sea-foam, and he withheld a smile. "Until *who* killed him?" he prompted.

She didn't answer, and a look of confusion passed across her face as her mind attempted to reconcile false memories with real ones. He still had work to do.

"The peasant. Willet Dura."

He reached out to take her hand and dropped into a delve, where he strengthened the false memories of love and betrayal and the emotions of rage and revenge that went with them. Pausing in the flow of her memories, he stooped to take one of the brightest-colored threads, yellow bordering on gold, and merged with it, finding himself in a bright glade with Magden's father, where they played, their laughter as luminous as the sunshine.

With a twist of his mind, he destroyed the memory, pleasure at its loss pouring through him. He bent low to grab a score more, slashing them with his will until nothing remained. The most recent memories—those of the story he poured into Magden night after night—drifted by, dim and insubstantial by comparison.

Soon now. Soon those strands of recollection would be as strong and real and indistinguishable to Magden as her own memories. Soon they would be all she knew, all she was. At the last, he would destroy everything else.

Then she would be ready.

She left the tavern, and he made a mental check of the time. His next devotee would be coming soon. He smiled, filled with purpose, and one of the tavern girls smiled in response, an answering gesture to a kindly old man who told stories to some of the locals. He lifted his arm in a blind man's directionless wave, requesting another glass of wine.

There were hours of darkness remaining to him.

CHAPTER 1

Bunard, Collum
The first week of Queen Cailin's Regency

How many shades of fear were there? I sat within the Merum cathedral, surrounded by the dusty, unused opulence of a church that had survived millennia of war, internal and otherwise, with my hand inches away from another hue of dismay. The woman before me had a face I wouldn't have looked at twice out in the street or the marketplace, but seeing it now, I imagined that the pinched lines decorating her mouth and perpetual squint to the eyes—as if she were more attuned to anger and jealousy than sunlight—spoke of darkness within her heart.

Those eyes leapt at me as I entered the delve. Memories washed past me of life in the lower merchants' section, days filled with relentless toil as a tanner's daughter and then a tanner, mired in the stench of the craft and bereft of love. I swallowed my indignation at the unfairness of life.

Bronach's skin lay warm beneath my touch, despite the chill of her prison, and I hurtled through her memories without bothering to search for the moment she gave up on her life. Bronwyn and Toria Deel had made it plain it was not my duty to understand—only to judge.

The time for mercy had ended when the sun emerged from the darkness of Bas-solas ten days prior. But in truth, Bronach had already been judged by her actions. On the day of Bas-solas, the festival celebrating the death and rebirth of light, Bronach had taken a knife to her family. Then she'd taken to the streets.

13

I couldn't retrieve the memory of her face out of the myriad people in Bunard who'd tried to kill me that day, but there had been plenty of others who'd witnessed her killing frenzy, had seen her turn into something evil and unrecognizable. A sigh whispered from me. Since I was a reeve, the gift passed to me by Elwin as he died—a gift that imparted an ability to determine guilt without doubt—should have made me happier than this, but how long could I bear living those deeds as though I'd committed them myself? I wondered if the doors in my mind were secure enough to keep their memories in check.

I searched the recesses of Bronach's mind, floating through memories of slights and insults from other goodwives in the city, wives whose husbands honored their marriage bed. She had treasured every jibe, real or perceived, until fantasies of retribution had consumed her.

Tracing the threads of memory, I finally found what I sought—a black scroll, wrapped and sealed with thousands upon thousands of black strands connecting it to every memory that defined the woman.

The script upon it, black written upon black, remained unreadable. I opened it and tried to make sense of the flowing strokes of midnight, but the whorls and loops of writing looked more like a child's attempt at art than an alphabet. With a pang of regret, I took the scroll in my hands—noting the strangeness of having a sense of them within someone else's mind—and tore it to pieces, smaller and smaller, until those disappeared from reckoning. At each tear, a black thread tying the scroll to Bronach's past snapped, and a bit more of her mind—the essence of who she'd been—flared and disappeared.

I searched as I destroyed, seeking some clue to the truth of the Darkwater. How had the evil gotten free of the forest? But nothing within her memories yielded information or insight. I came out of the delve with a prayer on my lips for Bronach's soul, just as I had the others, that somehow her mind might heal.

"Come back to us, Bronach," I pleaded. Fear clenched my gut, and my silent plea to Aer continued.

The lamplight shifted over Bronach's shoulder, blinding me, and for the moment in which I tried to blink away the glare, I dared to hope this time might be different. It had happened before, once—it could again.

Her mouth gaped at me, slack and unresponsive, and her eyes had dulled. They might reflect the light, but they would never sparkle in it again. Slowly, as if to mock my prayer and fear, a bit of spittle gathered at one corner of her mouth and started to trickle down her chin.

"That's all, Willet," Bolt said from behind me. "You can't do any more today." A sigh of disapproval ghosted from him. "Five. And you shouldn't have done that many."

I stood as Bolt gathered Bronach in his arms to take her to the apothecary one room over where the broken were taken to find release. I snorted the word in disgust at myself. "Release."

"Willet?"

I looked at my guard, with his sandy blond hair going to gray and the light blue eyes that always shone as if he were looking into the sunlight. Not much got past him. Given his experience as a guard for the Vigil—the small group of gifted within the church who possessed the ability to see into the hearts and minds of others—not much would.

And now I was one of them, holding power within my hands that most men or women could scarcely conceive—power that would give kings dominion and lovers unimagined intimacy, ability that would give judges infallibility and confessors clarity. And I hated it. I answered as if my words could somehow cleanse me of Bronach's death and all the others condemned to their final resting place in the caves beneath Bunard. "It's not release," I said. "It's death."

I shoved Bronach's memories into the same room as the rest of those I'd delved that morning. A stab of guilt pierced me that I hadn't even given the tanner woman the dignity of putting her memories in their own keeping place within my mind. I'd dumped the last essence of Bronach into a common grave with all the others who had tried to kill me. Pellin had warned me of the toll keeping them would exact, but a voice in my head, my own, accused me of taking the last vestige of Bronach's dignity from her.

I couldn't disagree.

"What was she like?" Bolt asked. He knew the answer to his own question. He couldn't help but know. This was his way of affording the dead some final dignity. He always asked, and I always answered. As absolution went, it didn't mean much, but it was all he could offer and I took it.

Breath whispered from me in a long sigh. "Like all the rest. Her envy ate at her spirit year by year until that was pretty much all that was left."

"But why go to the Darkwater?"

15

I shook my head. "Those memories were wrapped within the scroll. I couldn't read it, but I'm hoping Custos might."

I'd stored the vision of the scroll in Bronach's mind with all the rest behind a door as secure and impenetrable as my thoughts could make it. Two weeks before, during the attack on Braben's Inn, I'd been trapped in the mind of a dying butcher, held there by dark threads as his life ebbed away from Bolt's knife cast. If I had still been within the delve while he died, my mind would have died with him. The encounter had managed to teach me caution and fear.

I pulled a shuddering breath into my lungs. How had power managed to make me so afraid?

Bolt's face might have been carved from living stone, but since he'd become my guard I'd learned to interpret the minute variations in his expression . . . sometimes. "Do you think the librarian will know something that Pellin doesn't?" he asked. "The Eldest has spoken of the script before. There's nothing written about it, not even in the Vigil's library in Cynestol. Don't you think the Vigil would have unraveled it by now? Pellin's had centuries."

Bolt's reminder of the longevity most of the Vigil would experience— as if they'd found the legendary third continent and its wellspring— brought a flash of heat to my face. I didn't want to be reminded how Elwin's gift had extended my own lifespan, thrusting a future upon me in which I would be forced to watch every friend die of age or war while I hardly aged at all.

I checked that thought. Friends came into a man's life and they left it—that was the nature of the world—but I'd had the opportunity for something more. Elwin's desperate, dying gift in the House of Passing had left me with two almost equally bitter choices. Marry Gael and watch her and my children age and die while I remained young, or grant her uncle, Count Alainn, his greatest desire and let her marry Lord Rupert.

"Don't remind me," I said, my voice tight. "And you're probably right. Still, it can't hurt to try." I paused to look around the room that had been set aside for the Vigil's grisly task. A few paces away, Bronwyn and Toria Deel—what remained of the true Vigil, along with Pellin and Jorgen—each delved one of the prisoners. "I need to get out of this room for a while." A thought occurred to me. "And the cathedral."

Bolt's face shifted into a look of mild disapproval, which was the same as saying that it lost whatever small expression it held. He could have given rocks lessons on how to be stony. "Are you going to see her again?"

He didn't have to say who *her* was—ever and always there would be only one. Gael. "No." I saw him relax, a minute shift in the set of his shoulders, as if he no longer anticipated drawing the sword at his side. "I haven't seen Ealdor since before Bas-solas." I sighed. "Pellin is going to send me from Collum once we're done delving everyone who went insane. I need to say good-bye."

He turned to signal Bronwyn, nothing more than a quick flutter of the fingers of his right hand and a tilting of the head, but I saw her rise and approach as if she'd been summoned. Her guard, Balean, shadowed her, protecting her against whatever threat might arise in a cathedral. My hackles went up. Pellin and Bronwyn were both old beyond belief. I didn't know just how old, but they accumulated their life in decades the way others numbered individual years. Neither of them trusted me for reasons I couldn't control any more than the color of my eyes.

"How do you fare, Lord Dura?" she asked. Not Willet or Dura, always Lord Dura. Lady Bronwyn never failed in the use of the title, a fact that had escaped my attention until I discovered her age. She and Pellin had been born in an older, more formal time. Even their speech carried hints of an accent that no one living would be able to identify, vestiges of the language all people had once spoken that had changed over the course of centuries.

"Well enough," I said. I briefly considered playing dumb and just as quickly rejected the idea. The events of the festival had taught me that I needed the help of others in the Vigil no matter how hard I might try to deny it. If trust could be established between us, it would be up to me to take the first step. "I'm going to visit a couple of friends, one here in the cathedral and another in the city."

She nodded in approval, but the corners of her eyes tightened just a fraction, giving the lie to her expression.

> *"Friends are bless and balm to me:*
> *One to mirror,*
> *Two for strength,*

Three to reveal what must be seen,
Four of us in perfect unity.
Different as we can be,
Yet we command eternity."

She nodded her head as if there were some particularly deep wisdom contained within the singsong that I couldn't fail to see with her. She didn't dispense children's rhymes as often as Bolt invented his own militaristic quips, but it didn't take a gift to see that she had spent quite a bit of time with them. I couldn't help but feel Bolt saw me as a raw recruit while Bronwyn looked upon me as an untutored schoolboy.

"Who are you going to visit?" she asked.

The directness of the question surprised me, but I stifled my initial response. I had no secrets from the Vigil. None. They'd delved me and those closest to me. If I attempted to dissemble or refused to answer, I would only give them cause to believe that the dark scroll, the vault, in my head had taken control of me at last. The irony would have been laughable were it not so incredibly tragic. I held the same scroll in my mind that I had been charged with destroying in those who'd murdered others during Bas-solas.

No wonder the Vigil didn't—couldn't—trust me. "Custos and Ealdor," I said.

She nodded. "I would like to accompany you, if you will permit it. The librarian is of particular interest to me."

The request was lightly made, at least by her tone, but I could see Lady Bronwyn steeling herself, a soldier shouldering an unpleasant duty. She, like Toria Deel and me, had spent days breaking the vaults and minds of others, and yet my intention to visit a pair of old friends elicited this reaction.

My stomach started a promenade around my insides, my fear fighting against my curiosity. Why did she want to come? She'd left the choice up to me. I didn't want company, but questions crowded my discomfort aside. As usual, my curiosity won without breaking a sweat.

"Of course, Lady Bronwyn. I will welcome your company."

CHAPTER 2

I worked my way through the halls of the Merum cathedral, gathering and replaying random memories as I went. Somewhere beneath me on the lowest level, Peret Volsk lay imprisoned. In the halls above him, scores of people were interred, waiting for the Vigil to break their vaults. Once we'd completed that task, I would leave the people of Bunard, with their familiar faces and handclasps.

Somehow, I couldn't see it as an adventure anymore. I'd be leaving behind my heart and soul, ripped from me in the person of Gael. Dark thoughts drifted through my mind. It would have been easier if she'd died during Bas-solas. I imagined myself riding out of the city, determined to exact vengeance on whatever power had been loosed from the Darkwater. The heels of our boots struck echoes from the floor, my thoughts influencing my feet. The pain twisted, accusing me. No, it would have been better if *I* had died.

It wasn't until we entered the library and I saw Custos across the massive domed hall that I realized the absence of almond-crusted figs in my pocket and a random book or scroll in my hand. As we drew nearer, Custos noted my empty hands as well. For a moment we stared at each other, unsure of where to begin without the customary props of our conversation. His gaze shifted to Bronwyn and her guard before returning to me.

"I'm sorry, old friend," I said as I showed him my empty hands. "I forgot."

His stricken expression cut me. Lines of grief put years on his face that didn't belong there.

"I'll go get them," I said. "Wait for me."

One of his hands, the fingers worked thin by incessant writing, waved my concern away. "It's not the figs, Willet. I've just received word there's been a fire in Caisel." Tears welled in his eyes. "Most of the library is gone. The brothers managed to save a few of the texts, but it will take lifetimes of copy work to restore it."

I had nothing to say. Books were more than Custos's life work; they were his friends. Hating the thought of adding to his pain, I put my hand on his arm. "I'm going to have to leave soon, Custos," I said. "I can't stay here."

His shoulders lifted a little before settling, and a sad smile made a brief appearance on his features before it too drifted away. "It's the unforgiving rule of history, Willet. Every book has its epilogue. I must say I've enjoyed this one more than any other."

I nodded, but inside a piece of myself seemed to break off and float away. "Is there some place private we can go that has ink and parchment?"

"Of course."

As he turned, leading us to the sanctum, Bolt leaned in to mutter in my ear. "This is another reason the Vigil lead solitary lives. How many times would you have to say good-bye to your closest friends before you decided you couldn't bear it anymore?"

"What about Toria Deel?" I asked, referring to the youngest member of the Vigil. From hints they had dropped, the Elanian was over a hundred, though she looked to be of an age with me or younger.

He dipped his head a fraction, as if I'd found a flaw in his argument. "Ah. She is more social than the rest, even more than Laewan was." A soft chuckle escaped him. "But she's Elanian," he said as if that explained everything.

I'd never been to the southernmost country on our continent, but I'd heard the tales from merchants of the fiery, dark-skinned, dark-haired southerners. At the time, I'd dismissed most of them, presuming it was the ale talking, but now I wasn't so sure.

Custos closed the door of the sanctum and led me to the trestle table in the center of the room, Bronwyn and Balean stopping with Bolt a few paces away. Along with the knowledge the librarian had given me on partitioning my mind, the domed room had been my means of survival weeks before, when Laewan had tried to break into my mind. I stored all of my memories in an exact replica of this sanctum within my head, safeguarding them against the enemy we faced.

"I need that mind of yours again, my friend," I said, taking up the quill and inkpot to draw the writing I'd seen on the black scrolls. My hand, more accustomed to a sword after years in the king's service than a quill, couldn't quite replicate the beauty of the flowing script I'd seen. I closed my eyes for a moment, recalling the exact appearance of the words that had been Bronach's death sentence, then transferred them to the paper before me. "Have you ever seen writing like this?"

I stepped aside as he leaned over the parchment to gaze at the whorls and loops that flowed across its width. I could almost sense his mind sorting through every book and sheet he'd ever read, searching for some connection, and amazement filled me again. Custos remembered every detail, down to the last word, and he'd consumed the contents of the cathedral's massive library.

But he straightened, shaking his head. "No, Willet, and what's more I've never even heard mention of such a script. Where is it from?"

Behind me, Bronwyn cleared her throat and Balean's posture shifted. I resisted answering.

Custos didn't possess the same ability to read people as he did parchment, but Lady Bronwyn hadn't been subtle. The librarian's eyes flicked to her before he spoke. "One of your, ah, associates, came to visit. They took the writing from Tiochus I showed you earlier. I think they meant to burn it."

For an instant, I could see anger flickering in the depths of his eyes. As keeper of the vast library in the Merum cathedral, Custos prized the writings that filled it above all else, tending and keeping them so that the knowledge contained within ancient and not-so-ancient texts would never be lost. The purposeful destruction of something as precious as a first-century writing on the gift of domere would be an act of apostasy to him.

Bronwyn's face softened. She stepped forward and laid a gloved hand on the librarian's arm. "Be at peace," she said. "The Vigil do not destroy the texts that they find regarding their gift. The loss of knowledge would hurt them as much as you. They are all tended and safeguarded."

Custos nodded, but an instant later I saw an expression dawn on his face that I'd never seen before. "All of them?" he said, his voice almost too soft to be heard. "How many? Where?"

She took a half step back.

Custos pursued her and reached out to take her hand, but Balean caught his wrist. "You have to let me see them."

Bronwyn started to shake her head, but before she could answer, I spoke. "You're right, of course."

"Have you gone daft?" Bolt said with a jerk.

Members of the Vigil didn't usually start to slip until they were very old, but I did a quick check to make sure my thoughts were still my own anyway. "I don't think so," I said, turning to meet Bronwyn's gaze. "It only makes sense. As far as I know, no one else in the world can do what Custos does." I waved my hand at the room around us, indeed, the entire library. "Who else can memorize so much?"

Bronwyn's eyes narrowed in thought. "He's memorized the entire contents of this room?"

I laughed, sweeping my arm to indicate all that resided beyond the door of the sanctum. "No, I mean he's memorized the entire library. All of it."

Custos met Bronwyn's gaze for a moment, then scuffed his feet like an embarrassed schoolboy.

I couldn't keep from laughing. "Whenever I visit, I pick a book at random and open it to some page Aer or chance decrees and read him a passage. The challenge is for him to finish the passage from memory." I laughed at the look on Bronwyn's face. "It's our game. The price if I lose is a packet of almond-crusted figs." I patted Custos on the top of his bald head. "I always go to the market first. It saves time."

Bronwyn shook her head. "There's no such gift, talent, or temperament that can do such a thing."

"Longevity doesn't equate with omniscience," Custos said.

"Perhaps people are more wondrous than you know," I added before Bronwyn could respond. "Come with me into the library for a moment."

Without waiting, I left Custos and Bolt in the sanctum with Bronwyn in tow. Balean followed, his posture vigilant as if he expected assassins to leap from the pages of some story and attack.

I paused to swing my arm in a wave that encompassed the entire library. "Choose anything. Book or scroll, old or new—it won't matter."

Her green eyes narrowed as she considered my challenge. "I've seen tricksters perform at nearly every court in the world, Lord Dura. You have no 'suggestions' or 'guidance' to offer on my random selection?"

I laughed. "I'm no magician, Lady Bronwyn. If you like, I will return to the sanctum and await you there."

She cocked her eyebrows at me, the look speculative. "No, Lord Dura. That won't be necessary." With half a dozen quick steps she moved to the nearest case and selected a book from the bottom shelf, then lifted it and blew, eyeing the displaced dust with satisfaction.

"No one has read this in a while, it seems." She smiled at me. "Shall we return, Lord Dura?"

My expression mirrored hers. "By all means."

Custos stood, a shy smile lifting the corners of his mouth as Lady Bronwyn stopped three paces short of where he stood and flipped the book open to a page near the end of the text. "How is the game played?" she asked me.

"I pick a random spot in the book or scroll, as you have done, and then I read enough of the book to distinguish it from any of the other texts in the library." I shrugged. "It usually doesn't take much, a sentence, two at the most."

Mild surprise wreathed her features, but now I saw genuine interest there as well, not just the appreciative disbelief people wore for the court magicians. Bronwyn cleared her throat and read. "'In the one thousandth four hundredth and sixty-fourth year of the coming of the exordium, we discovered—'"

Custos held up his hand. "'—gold in the mountains of the farthest north. We lacked the equipment needed to mine, but most of the men were unwilling to leave, remaining past the last day of autumn to pan the streams coming from the frozen wastes. I returned south, tracking my way through the ancient trees and rumors of the Everwood, leaving ahead of the winter. The men I'd come to think of as brothers, I never saw again.'"

Bronwyn, her mouth gaping, gazed at the age-spotted dome of Custos's head as he stared at a spot on the floor a pace or two in front of his feet. "Your pardon, honored librarian, I didn't bring any figs with me." She shook her head and lifted the book in her hand to trace a pattern on the dusty cover. "You are required. Who else besides those of us in this room is aware of your . . . " She paused, searching for a word. "Hmmm . . . " She clasped her hands. "I can't very well call it a gift or a talent, or even a temperament. You have an ability, Custos. Who else knows of it?"

Custos shook his head. "No one except those in this room. I was afraid they would take me away from my books."

I didn't need my gift to interpret the expression of ownership dawning on Bronwyn's age-lined face. "Welcome to the Vigil, Custos," I said with a smile. "May Aer have mercy on your soul," I uttered under my breath.

"It will be up to Pellin, of course," Bronwyn said.

I nodded, but I knew once Pellin accepted the truth of Custos's unique ability, he would welcome him.

"How many writings are there in this secret library?" Custos asked, peering at Bronwyn without fully lifting his head.

Bronwyn squinted. "I've never counted them, but the space required is considerable. Thousands, perhaps."

Custos's face filled with longing even as he nodded. "There would have been many at first, but as the gift supposedly died and then even rumor of it faded, the writings would have slowed to a trickle before they stopped altogether."

Bronwyn nodded. "True. I'll speak to Pellin at the first opportunity."

I caught Custos's attention and pointed to the looping figures I'd traced on the parchment. "But we have other matters to attend to as well."

Custos picked up the sheet. "Some things aren't learned from books in a library. I'll show it to some of the brothers who've traveled the southern continent. Perhaps they will be able to make something of it."

We looped our way back through the library and out into the stable yard before setting off for Ealdor's little church. It would be good to see him again, though I suspected he would still be mourning the loss of a portion of his flock. The slaughter of Bas-solas had taken a heavy toll on the lower merchants' section of the city, where his parish sat nestled against the river just across from the poor quarter.

I rode Dest through Criers' Square next to Lady Bronwyn, with our guards flanking us on the outside. We were twenty paces past it when I reined in, pointing to the intersection where representatives of the four orders of the church declaimed their interpretation of the exordium and the rest of the liturgy each day.

Something was wrong.

"What do you see?" I asked Bolt.

He gave me a facial equivalent of a shrug. "The usual. Each order has their crier on a stand, waiting their turn."

"That's what's wrong," I said. I pointed to the four men and women dressed in the color of their order, red for Merum, white for Vanguard, blue for Absold, and brown for the Servants. "Where is the speaker for the Clast?"

My guard searched the thin crowd. "Not here. Maybe they're taking the day off."

"Rabble-rousers don't usually do that," I said. "They don't like to give people time to reflect on how idiotic their arguments are."

"Killed during Bas-solas, perhaps?" Bronwyn asked.

I shook my head. "Along with all his cohorts? One can only hope. But what would that mean?"

Her stare became icy. "That they'd all been to the forest. I'll inform Pellin. I think he'll want to take a closer look at our friends from the Clast."

We continued through the nobles' portion of the city. The eccentricities of the Vigil took some getting used to, but the way Bronwyn peered at me, her green eyes sharp and intent like a bird's, put me on my guard.

"When was the last time you slept?" she asked without preamble.

I allowed myself half a smile. "Last night, of course."

"You know what I mean, Lord Dura."

I did, and the topic was one I took pains to avoid with the Vigil. They didn't view it similarly, however, and as I was the newest addition to the group, they seemed to think they could ask me any question they wished and expect an answer. Worse, they were right.

"I haven't been able to stay asleep since before Bas-solas," I sighed. "Bolt keeps me in my quarters and I catch a bit of sleep during the day when I can."

Her mouth constricted, compressing into a thin line of disapproval, accentuating the age lines surrounding it. "You can't go on like that indefinitely."

A fatigue so deep it felt as if it emanated from the marrow of my bones washed over me, and I pulled a length of chiccor root from my cloak and took a nibble. "No argument there. I imagine I will be able to sleep soon enough."

"How so?" Bronwyn asked.

I turned in my saddle to gaze at her. "Because it appears we've captured almost all of those infected by the Darkwater. There are only thirty or so left in the cells of the Merum cathedral. Pretty soon the last vault will be broken and the guards and apothecaries won't have to put the drooling idiots we've created out of their misery under cover of darkness. Bunard will have a night without murder, and then I will sleep."

I saw her stiffen, and Balean shot me a look that said he wanted to deliver some type of physical chastisement. "Your pardon, Lady Bronwyn," I said. "I know they went to the Darkwater of their own volition, but these are the very people I promised Laidir I'd protect." I said the king's name like a penitent flogging himself, trying to expunge my failure by reminding myself of it.

Bronwyn must have caught the shift in tone. "You did everything you could."

"Did I?" I shrugged. "We say that, but in my mind I can see a hundred things I might have done differently so that he might have survived that night."

Her eyes caught the light, the green iridescent in the late afternoon sun, and for a moment I saw the woman she must have been hundreds of years ago. "Missed opportunities and guilt are their own burden, Lord Dura," she said. "Beware of them. It's not just the weight of memories that can undo us."

I wasn't in a position to argue, and the sight of Jeb, the chief reeve, coming toward us scattered my train of thought anyway. The muscles in his jaws worked as if he wanted someone to try and take a swing at him so he'd have an excuse to pound them to a pulp. I put Dest in his path and dismounted.

"Good morrow, Jeb."

He stopped, and I heard the knuckles in his hands pop. "What's good about it, Dura?" He spared a couple of heartbeats to glance at Lady Bronwyn and our guards. "When are you going to get back to your job?"

Jeb didn't know what had happened to me or what I'd been doing for the past few weeks, so I couldn't really respond to his accusation. "Soon, I hope." Which was the truth, no matter how unlikely.

"Might as well be never, if it's not. *Kreppa.*" Jeb used curses the way most people use punctuation. "You'd think with a war every few years and the slaughter of Bas-solas, we wouldn't be so eager to kill our own."

I'd suspected my sleeplessness the previous night had been due to murder in the city, but having Jeb confirm it awoke a familiar hunger. "They'll stop in a few days," I said, "once the worst of the suspicions die down."

Jeb shook his head. "People are stupid, Dura. They'll suspect anybody." He looked over my shoulder at Bronwyn. "Go play the noble with your friends. Let me know when you get bored and want to do some real work again."

We crossed over the broad multi-arched bridge that led to the upper merchants' section of the city, the houses only a little less splendid than those of the lesser nobles.

The mention of Laidir, my dead king whom I'd failed, had served to sharpen my mind despite the fog of sleeplessness I wore. Something more than idle curiosity lay behind Bronwyn's request to accompany me to Ealdor's church, and judging by the way tension stiffened her spine as we drew closer, it wasn't a pleasant duty.

We continued on the main thoroughfare until we came to the bridge leading from the upper merchants' portion of the city to the lower merchants' quarter, and I could see the rear of Braben's Inn, where it backed up against the river. Longing awoke in my chest, and I faltered for a moment, considering a brief detour to indulge my selfish need for hospitality. Braben had always welcomed me, even after Laewan had tracked the Vigil to his inn and tried to burn it down. Braben's gift of helps must have included a large portion of grace.

We turned right to parallel the southernmost branch of the Rinwash, and two hundred paces later we stopped in front of a ramshackle parish church, the weather-battered emblem of the Merum order out front resolutely visible in defiance of time and elements. "You didn't want to come here," I said. "Why did you, Lady Bronwyn?"

Balean held out a hand to help her dismount, and she took a moment to smooth her skirt before answering. "Pellin ordered it."

"That's not much of an answer," I said. "After Bas-solas, I thought we were past the games we played with each other."

She gave me a sad smile that said she would have liked nothing better. I had the good sense at that moment to be afraid.

"I protested his order, Lord Dura," she said, "but he insisted. You perhaps know better than the rest of us how time can be an enemy. None of the Vigil has seen time as anything but an ally for centuries now. We are unaccustomed to haste."

Her tone, as if I were a wounded animal that needed calming, sent threads of fear up and down my spine. How much can a man lose? I really didn't want to know. "Why did he insist?"

Bronwyn took a deep breath. "The Eldest shares his counsel when he sees fit, Lord Dura, often keeping it to himself, but in this he was unusually forthright. He means you to be a member of the Vigil."

"That implies I'm not."

Her expression refused to settle long enough to convey any emotion I could identify. "There are . . . things within your mind that preclude us from taking you fully into our confidence, Lord Dura."

"Things." I wrapped my mouth around the unexpected word. "Plural. As in more than one."

"We need your services, Lord Dura," Bronwyn said, sidestepping the obvious question.

"Out of desire or necessity?"

She allowed herself a smile that fought the tension in her shoulders. "Necessity. It is that necessity that brings me here, to begin your healing. Your vault is beyond our power, but . . ." She spread her hands.

I stopped to look at the church, a bit more run-down than I remembered—perhaps more than a bit. "I don't understand."

Her mouth tightened before she stepped forward to take my arm in hers, like a grandmother offering her wisdom. "Come inside and you will."

CHAPTER 3

No candles burned in the small, gloom-filled narthex, the entry hall abutting the sanctuary, but that wasn't unusual. Most priests didn't hold mass until evening time, and Ealdor's parish, sitting as it did in the part of the city that had been abandoned since the last war had depleted Bunard's population, rarely had visitors.

But I'd never seen it looking this disused.

"What do you see, Willet?" Lady Bronwyn asked.

She'd used my first name, just my first name. I gritted my teeth against the answer, as if she meant some insult to one of the few men I could claim as friend. "It's a run-down church," I said, my voice sharp. "That's by Ealdor's choice. I've offered him money to fix it up, but he always tells me to save it for those in the poor quarter." I turned to face Bronwyn and her guard. Bolt stood off to one side, his face expressionless. "He's the best churchman I've ever met."

Bronwyn nodded, her eyes moist. "I don't doubt it, Willet."

"Why is it you people only use my first name when you're about to give me bad news?" The skittering sound of rodent feet came from my left. "You need to make up your mind—you're either beating on me like a cheap anvil or you're treating me like spun glass." My gesture encompassed the whole of Ealdor's run-down church. "Just what is it you want to see here?"

Bronwyn gave her head a little shake. "It's what we want *you* to see." She stepped past me, and for once, Balean didn't follow her. Instead he waited, looking at me with cold eyes. I stepped through the arch of rotting wood into the sanctuary. Bronwyn stood just inside, her expression unreadable. "Use the skills that made you a reeve," she said, pointing inside around the lofted space, "and tell me what's written here."

I hardly needed her encouragement. I'd been doing exactly that ever since we'd entered the narthex, but what I saw made my head hurt. The building, never well-kept, wasn't just decrepit, it was on the verge of collapse. Thick dust and bird droppings lay undisturbed on the pews and floor, and shafts of sunlight streamed through holes in the roof as big as my fist.

I opened my mouth to offer an explanation, some defense, but Ealdor wasn't here. And the sense that all men who've been to war possess—the one that tells them they're without hope or succor in the midst of battle, that they are irrevocably alone and lost—told me he wouldn't be here. I took a deep breath that carried the smell of roosting birds within it and forced the memories of the last war away. If I started down that road, it would be some time before my mind returned to the present.

Instead I concentrated on the footprints in the dirt and dust—my footprints, only mine—leading from the narthex to the crumbling altar and kneeling rail at the front of the sanctuary. Bronwyn had told me to use my skills as a reeve. I did so, coming to one begrudging deduction at a time. Since I'd last seen him, Ealdor hadn't walked from the altar to the entrance of the church, and no one from the outside had ventured in.

I set my jaw, refusing to come to the obvious conclusion, and followed my tracks with my head down, focused on each print like a dog on the scent as they led me to the altar. I didn't bother to ask whose or to lift my foot and check the sole. I knew the familiar track of my boots as well as the feet I put them on.

At the front of the church I stopped, pausing in the area between the last of the splintered pews and the steps leading up to the altar, the same altar where I'd performed mass in contravention of the rules of the Merum priesthood. Bolt didn't bother to accompany me there—there was no physical danger present. A single set of tracks ascended the steps to the altar to disappear behind it before leading to the confession rail and the side entrance.

I didn't have to go any farther; Bronwyn had accomplished her task. "There's no one here." I murmured those same four words over and again in a voice small enough to fit in the palm of my hand.

"This is the truth I would have waited to reveal, Willet," Bronwyn said.

Annoyed, I might have made some dismissive gesture with my hand, as if brushing away a fly. "Don't do that. Don't call me by my first name because you're afraid." The single set of tracks in the dirt and dust of the long-dead sanctuary held my gaze like some mythical wizard's spell. I sifted through every memory of Ealdor I could dredge to the surface of my thoughts. They seemed so real.

They were real, my mind kept telling me.

But the physical evidence of the church told me they couldn't be. While Bronwyn watched me, while our guards scanned for threats from voles or mice, I backed through the logic, trying with methodical desperation to reconcile my memories with the tangible reality that lay at my feet. They couldn't be resolved. I extended the logic a step further.

Nothing could be resolved.

Bronwyn came forward and placed a gloved hand on my shoulder. I could feel the touch, light as a bird, more as a sensation of warmth than the pressure of weight. Looking back and forth between the green of her eyes and the black leather of her glove, I shook my head. "I remember, *I remember*, Ealdor doing that exact thing countless times."

"But feel it, Lord Dura," she said. "I'm here now, and I'm real. Look at my tracks in the dust."

I shook my head. "It's not that simple. For all I know, you're the fantasy I've invented in my mind." I waved a hand at the run-down church. "Perhaps this is all a dream I've built to keep some truth hidden from myself." Unbidden, a memory of Calder came to me. We'd fought together in the war and had formed the friendship of men trying to survive. And we had—or mostly. After we came back to Bunard, Calder's grip on reality slipped a bit more each week until he couldn't see anything but the last battle. They found his body floating in the Rinwash a couple of miles downstream with a pike still locked in his grip. We buried it with him.

Bolt came forward out of the shadows. "He deserves to know the truth of your experience, Lady Bronwyn, and he's stronger than you think. Men are like swords, tempered by circumstance."

She nodded. "Very well. I can't prove to you what is real and what isn't. The nature of memory is fluid. Often when we delve a person, the memories we see are phantoms they've invented without realizing it, but to us, they appear as real as any other memory. When Pellin and the rest of the Vigil delved you, they believed Ealdor to be as real as you until Pellin came here to speak with him."

"You're not telling me anything I didn't already know," I said with a shake of my head. "I've seen reeves question a woman or a man, if you can call it that, *telling* them they had committed a crime, insisting that others had seen them do it." I swallowed my disgust. "I've watched simple tradesmen confess to something they'd never done, building a memory to match what they'd been told." I looked around the ruins of the church. "But that doesn't get me any closer to the truth."

Bronwyn still held my shoulder and I felt a gentle squeeze. "In my experience, one of the ways to know the difference between the truth and a lie is that the truth hurts more. Lies are easier to believe."

There, she had me.

I looked at Bolt. "It's not one of yours, but you should probably write that one down." Bronwyn's simple assessment had managed to cut through all of my internal wrangling with the merciless efficiency of a knife. Life was loss. Anyone that tried to tell you it was something else was lying. I took one last look at the church where I'd found comfort so often and resolved never to return. "I think I'd like to go now."

We stepped from the empty shadows of Ealdor's—or whoever's—church into the ruddy glow that marked the end of the day. The streets were already clear of merchants and hawkers, pickpockets and night women. Normally, they would be out for hours yet, filling the cobblestoned market street that ran the length of the city, trying to squeeze a bit more prosperity from spring and summer here in the north. I checked the rooftops as we went but couldn't spot any sign of what I searched for.

"They're up there," Bolt said, catching my inspection. "The urchins haven't seen anything since Bas-solas. Hopefully, they won't see or hear anything tonight either."

Fatigue as deep as the main flow of the Rinwash ran through me, slow, but massive, like the river in summer. I tried to remember what a real night of sleep felt like, an evening without murder. "I hope so. What about the villages?"

Bolt shook his head. "The same, nothing since the eclipse. Evidently, Laewan put everything he had into the attack. Perhaps this is all over."

I mulled that over for the space of an entire heartbeat. "You believe that?"

"Not really."

When our horses passed through the gates of the Merum cathedral, Toria and her guard, Elory, were waiting for us. The youngest member of the Vigil stood in the middle of the yard like a portent of doom.

We were halfway into dismounting when her voice, clipped and sharp as it always was now, cut through the background murmur of stable hands and tack. "There's something you need to see."

She turned, her hair momentarily flaring into the wind, and strode toward the entrance of the cathedral, her heel strikes loud against the stones. I saw Bronwyn raise a brow to her guard, surprised by Toria Deel's lack of deference.

The Elanian stopped before the wide double doors of the room where we delved and then broke those who'd participated in the attack. "I've had them brought here along with a healer."

"Brought who, dear?" Bronwyn asked. At her side Balean had shifted, angling his body toward the door, his hands beneath his cloak.

"Some of those we've broken." Without bothering to explain further, she opened the door to the right and slipped through.

I stumbled as I entered. Twelve men sat on stools, lined up along one wall, their mouths open and eyes staring at nothing, reflecting the emptiness within their minds. And they were all stripped to the waist.

Dark blotches, some as large as my hand or bigger, discolored the skin of every man, the deep red-and-purple colors lurid and painful in the fading light. I'd seen marks similar to those before on the backs of men who'd been beaten for disobeying orders, but those bruises had been red with the halo discoloring the skin around them from the impact.

"Why were these men beaten?" Bronwyn whispered. "Did Cailin order it? There's nothing they can tell anyone."

"They weren't, Lady Bronwyn," I said. "And if they were, I doubt they would need to be gathered."

Toria gave me a brief nod, but her eyes held too many emotions for me to sort them out. I wondered briefly if all Elanians were as inscrutable.

"Lord Dura is correct," she answered, turning from me. "None of these men have been mistreated in any way."

"Other than breaking their vaults and turning their minds into porridge," I said.

Before Toria could respond, Lady Bronwyn looked skyward and sighed. "Children," she muttered, "quick to anger and slow to forgive."

"It's not me he's accusing," Toria said to Bronwyn. "It's himself."

I cared even less for her insight than I did for Bronwyn's condescension, so I strode over to where the nearest man perched on his stool like an oversized bird. Bruises the size of my hand covered the front part of his torso. When I put my hand against one of the bruises and pushed, I could feel the grind of displaced bone. It didn't take a healer to see that he'd cracked several ribs.

No halo discolored the skin around the bruise. In spite of what had just occurred in Ealdor's church, or perhaps because of it, I found myself curious. The man before me had been in the fight during Bassolas but had managed to suffer an injury that couldn't be traced to the usual causes.

I looked at the healer, a tall man with birdlike eyes and gestures that noticed everything with quick darting glances. "Interesting. It's not from a hit or strike."

"Yes." He nodded, walking over to me with short, quick steps. "They are all like that."

I moved to the next man, who sported similar bruises on his torso, as well as a large discoloration on his left bicep. "I'm going to take a guess and say that this fellow was wrong-handed."

"Good, good," the healer said. "You have a temperament for observation."

"I'm the king's . . ." I said out of reflex before I could stop myself. Not anymore. Laidir was dead, slain by whatever had driven these men to attack us during the festival of light. The healer looked at me, his head cocked to one side, as if I'd become a puzzle to sort out. "I used to be a reeve."

"Ah." He nodded.

"But I've never seen an injury exactly like this."

"I would be surprised if you had," the healer said. "I've only witnessed them once or twice myself."

"When?"

"Years ago," he said in a musing voice, "a man was brought to me for healing. He'd been up in the mountains and had ventured out onto a stretch of loose rock that gave way. The slide took him to the edge of a cliff. It wasn't fast, but he fell and got trapped beneath a boulder." His dark eyes lit as he recounted the man's tale. "Ten feet from the edge, knowing he would die if he couldn't escape, he thrust the boulder off and rolled out of the slide."

He turned to the man in front of us. "His bruises and injuries looked exactly like that of these men. Their ribs were broken by their own exertions. The body is capable of extreme feats of strength, but the mind and pain limit them. In dire circumstances, such as the man in the rockslide, the limitation is removed—but this is the result."

I stared at the man on the stool. "You're telling me this fellow broke his own ribs."

The healer nodded. "All of these men did. Even were their minds hale and whole, these men would never be the same again. Bones, ligaments, tendons, and muscles are broken or shredded. If their minds weren't empty, they'd be screaming in pain."

They had been before their vaults were broken. Day and night, the lower levels of the Merum cathedral had echoed with screams I'd attributed to insanity. The Darkwater had broken their minds, and that had enabled Laewan to push their bodies past the breaking point, making them seem gifted. I felt sick.

"Thank you, Healer Daward," Toria said. "You've been most helpful."

He nodded, recognizing the dismissal. "Might I return later, Lady Deel? I would like to make some notations and drawings of these injuries."

Toria glanced at Bronwyn, who stared at the men, showing no sign she'd heard the question. "I will send word," she said.

She waited until the healer had left the room. "They're not gifted."

Bronwyn nodded. "No, but I'm not sure how this insight into our enemy helps us."

"That's because your battles have always been small and personal," I said. My guts tightened a bit more at the implication sitting on the stools. I gave the two women a small mocking bow. "Welcome to warfare, ladies. You hoped that this horror ended with Laewan's death, but I fear your true adversary is more powerful—and desperate—than you know."

"*Our* adversary," Bolt said behind me.

I nodded, waiting, but he didn't appear to be on the verge of saying anything more. "No quips or quotes?"

"Not this time," he said, his craggy face impassive.

I turned back to Ladies Bronwyn and Deel. "In order to get his men to fight like gifted, *our* adversary had to suppress the part of the mind that registers pain. But it's a two-edged sword."

"It's a rare blade that doesn't cut both ways," Bolt said behind me.

"It would be nice to know who we're fighting," I pushed.

Bronwyn wore an expression that would have looked more at home on her guard. "We're fighting the Darkwater, Lord Dura. You know that."

I nodded. "So I gathered, but the evil we've met walks on two legs and has names like Laewan or Barl or Bronach."

She grimaced, as if fighting against the coming words. "Pellin lost touch with Jorgen weeks ago."

"If we're lucky, he's dead," Bolt said.

I pointed to the men on the stools. "Do you think Jorgen helped Laewan do this?"

Bronwyn shook her head. "They couldn't have done this by themselves. The Vigil never had this knowledge. We're fighting an enemy who possesses a power we've never seen. We can manipulate memories, but this . . . ?" She pointed to the nearest man's bruises.

"Blocking their pain makes these men more dangerous," I replied, "but whatever we're facing, our adversaries can only use them in such a way once. Drive the body too far and you break it." I paused, waving at the collection of lost souls Toria Deel had gathered. "These were used up during Bas-solas. Now they need replacements."

"They need to find a way to get more people to the Darkwater," Toria said.

"And we have to find a way to prevent that," Bronwyn replied. "I will send a messenger to Pellin at once."

"Why not use the scrying stone?" I asked.

"Too risky," she said. "They are not all accounted for. Until we can get them replaced, we'll have to use more traditional means of communicating."

The hitch in her voice told me she'd left out more than she'd said.

CHAPTER 4

A week later I slept until daffodil-colored light came through the slit of the window that faced west in my room. I came to this awareness as I passed from sleeping to waking without the usual intermediate steps of consciousness where accusations waited to assault me. When I rolled away from the light, I saw Bolt sitting in the thickly padded chair a few paces from the bed, a worn book opened to the halfway point resting on his lap.

"It's finished," I said.

He nodded. "Here in the city, at any rate."

I thought about that. "They threw every man and woman under his influence at us. If any of them had slipped back to their village in the confusion, we would have heard about it by now."

"Probably." He marked his spot and closed the book, but I got a glimpse of the title before he put it away. *A History of Errants in the North*. It reminded me of how little I knew about my guard. "There's a messenger from Queen Cailin here to fetch you to the keep." A grin split his craggy face and the light blue eyes crinkled in amusement. Bolt's amusement usually tied itself to someone else's discomfort.

I glanced out the window. "How long has he been waiting?"

The grin deepened. "Since just after dawn."

I scrambled for my clothes, running through everything I could possibly say before I realized how clear my mind felt for the first time since Bas-solas. "Thank you for letting me sleep. I guess I needed it."

"Not much guesswork there," he grunted. "Some of the brothers were talking about laying wagers on when you would drop. Evidently there was quite a bit of interest in the outcome."

I grabbed a light cloak against the cool of the spring evening. "Funny. I hope you're not serious. Did the messenger say why Cailin wanted to see me?"

Bolt stood and fell in beside me as I made for the door. "No. You're to report to Laidir's study."

"That's no surprise," I said. "There are probably things—quite a few things—she'd rather not discuss in open court. Send the messenger back to the queen with my apologies. I'm on my way."

The tor lay directly north of the Merum cathedral, where I and the rest of the Vigil stayed while we broke the rest of those who'd been to the Darkwater. I wouldn't have been able to explain why, but instead of using the main access, I detoured around to the east to the prisons. This earned me a look from Bolt, but I had no answer for him other than my own curiosity.

"I miss them." I rolled my shoulders, though he hadn't said anything. "And I want to know what's been happening in the city to keep me awake at night."

"Ah." Bolt nodded, and his eyebrows might have dipped a fraction, or not. "Sooner or later you're going to have to leave your days of playing the reeve behind."

"Playing the reeve? You make it sound like I'm part of some troupe going from village to village and mumming for coppers."

"Compared to your responsibilities with the Vigil, you are."

"Doesn't every life matter?"

"Don't be stupid," Bolt said. "Strategically, some matter more than others, and you know it. You don't send a captain into the vanguard with his sword."

We entered the cavern at the base of the tor that comprised the station of the city watch. The blood from Laewan's attack had been washed away. Something so ethereal as human suffering barely registered on the cold indifference of the stone. I looked for Gareth but didn't see him. My former partner was no doubt somewhere within the city.

"You don't work here anymore, Dura," a voice growled behind me.

I instinctively moved away from the sound. Jeb didn't have a reason to cuff me upside my head with those obscenely hard knuckles of his, but Bunard's chief reeve didn't always need or want a reason.

Bolt laughed at me. Sometimes I wondered about the depth of my guard's loyalty.

"I hadn't seen anyone in the watch since Bas-solas," I said.

Jeb had seen action in two of the wars between Collum and Owmead and lived to tell about it, which made him either incredibly lucky or too mean to die. I didn't have much doubt about which. With his lantern jaw and a nose to match, his scarred head looked about as inviting as an axe and his knuckles were about as lethal.

And he hated those who used their abilities to take advantage of others through theft or worse, and when children got hurt or killed I'd seen a side of Jeb few criminals had the opportunity or desire to witness. Six years ago Jeb had caught a tanner in the act of taking another man's daughter for personal pleasure. The girl might have been all of eight. Jeb sent the girl home and then proceeded to beat the man to death with his fists. By the time he was done, the tanner's face resembled one of the discarded carcasses in his barn.

"Don't go all mushy on us, Dura," Jeb growled, his eyes narrowing. "You look worse than usual. You been night-walking again?"

I nodded, then shrugged as if I were changing the subject. "What's the city been like since Bas-solas?"

Jeb hawked and spat on the stone floor of the cavern. "Same as before. About what you'd expect from a bunch of stupid *kreppa*. So busy looking for scapegoats that they're killing each other over suspicion. None last night though. Maybe they're running out of people to blame."

"Any gifted?"

Jeb shook his head. "No, thank Aer." He clenched a fist and his knuckles made a sound like someone snapping chicken bones. "It's going to take some time to get my hands on the ones responsible. They're killing each other quicker than I can beat confessions out of them." He shook his head in disgust. "Some of us have work to do, Dura. Did you need anything more than just city-watch gossip?"

I shook my head. "No. Tell Gareth I was here."

We came out into the light and began the long climb up the heights. Even taking the steep stairs that cut across the winding road that circled up the tor took twenty minutes. By the time I got to the top levels of the keep my thighs were burning. It would take more than one night of undisturbed sleep to get back to normal.

I laughed at that thought. I didn't know what normal was anymore. We passed through the hall of remembrance, and I noticed the addition of weapons, the bloodstains on them still fresh, and nodded approval. Win or lose, glorious or not, the hall reminded all who came after of the price that had to be paid.

We ascended the main staircase and came out across from the throne room. Strains of music wafted toward us, but no laughter. The relative silence of the hall only served to emphasize its emptiness.

"There's a place I'd be just as happy never to see again," Bolt said.

I laughed. "I don't know why. I think most of our nobles would be falling over themselves to hire you after you dropped Lord Baine. For once, I wouldn't mind going back to court. I could enjoy an honest conversation with the other nobles without having to put my back to the wall."

"That's a serious mean streak you've developed there."

I nodded. "I was a lot nicer before I became one of the nobility."

We cut around, winding through the maze of hallways until we came to Laidir's study. My throat tightened around a dozen memories of my king, the man who'd raised me to the nobility and the closest thing I'd had to a father since my own passed.

And I was here to offer obeisance to his killer. I didn't regret sparing Cailin's life, but I hadn't expected her to survive the destruction of her vault. That made her the sole occupant in the category of those who had done so, much as I was the only one to carry a vault for an extended period of time and not go into a killing rage. No bonds of affection existed between the queen and me, nothing resembling the regard shared with Laidir. But I needed Cailin, needed to understand how she'd survived. Regardless of my feelings for her, she embodied hope.

The guards at the door, Carrick and Adair, nodded in recognition.

"Weapons," Carrick said, and watched as we emptied scabbards and sheaths until a small pile formed at his feet.

"Expecting trouble?" Adair asked with a frown.

"When I don't, I regret it," I said.

"'A wise man prepares for strife,'" Bolt quoted, "'while the foolish—'"

40

I put a hand on his arm. "We all know that one, and I've kept the queen waiting long enough."

"Not just the queen," Carrick said, but he didn't elaborate as he opened one of the vaulted doors.

I hadn't really expected anything to change in this place where Laidir had exercised the gift of kings and pursued the knowledge he prized in order to run the kingdom. Everything remained exactly as if he were still alive. Only the figure occupying the small throne between two more guards was different. That struck me as odd.

That and the fact that Gael stood by her side. Neither woman looked happy.

I stopped as if I'd run into a wall. "All of a sudden, I feel naked without my weapons," I muttered. I waited for Bolt's customary reply, some soldierly advice he'd make up on the spot and try to pass off as ancient wisdom. "Have you run out of proverbs?"

He shook his head. "Just the opposite. There are so many fighting to get loose that I can't decide which one to use."

"Approach, Lord Dura," Cailin said, her voice clear, confident. "Guards, you will wait for us without."

Niall and Ronit looked at each other before Niall, as dark as winter and nearly as warm, cleared his throat. Cailin glanced up at him and assayed the tiniest smile. "I am as safe with these men as I am with you."

They nodded and left, stepping around Bolt and me while I tried not to gape. After the door closed, I favored the queen with a bow, not the mocking kind I usually reserved for nobles. "My compliments, Your Majesty. I wouldn't have thought anyone could have captured their loyalty as utterly as Laidir, but I see I was mistaken."

Cailin's smile had faded, but she acknowledged the compliment with a gracious nod. "I have you and circumstance to thank for that. The tests are done. The priests have determined that the gift of kings has come to my son, Brod. I will serve as regent until he is old enough to take the throne."

She rose and came toward me with Gael trailing after her. "A man, Pellin, came to me in secret with the Chief of Servants the morning after the festival." Her eyes widened at the memory. "He tried to brush my hand with his." She wet lips gone dry. "Is it true? Not just some conjurer's trick? Can you see so much with a single touch?"

"Yes," I said.

She nodded, but I could see doubt behind her eyes. "And your contemporary, Laewan, was corrupted by the forest?"

"I never met him that I remember, Your Majesty," I said. "But I know what I saw at Bas-solas. Something evil has gotten loose."

"The Darkwater Forest is virulent beyond redemption or diminishment," Bolt said.

Cailin's eyes grew distant, and I wondered what other talents the queen might possess. When I'd delved her I'd seen an intellect few could match. "Always?" She gave a vague wave of her hand. "Everything has a beginning and an end even if we are often too timid to see the possibility of it." She sighed. "No matter. Is our immediate threat ended with Laewan's death? Has the forest returned to its prior state?"

I turned to Bolt, waiting for him to answer, hoping for some insight into the Vigil that Pellin and the rest refused to share with me, but I was disappointed. He shrugged and shook his head. "We don't know, Your Majesty, but with the death of Laewan, we've earned a respite."

Cailin cocked her head in thought. "Or the enemy's moves are hidden from you."

"Possibly," Bolt admitted. "With the cleansing of the threat in Bunard, the Vigil will be able to resume its duties policing the rest of the kingdoms."

I saw Cailin give a quick nod of acknowledgment, if not satisfaction. "Well then, to other matters," she said, turning her attention to me. "Lord Dura, I am reinstating your betrothal to Lady Gael."

Gael's smile, filled with triumph, lit the room, and for a moment I was tempted to believe that Queen Cailin could actually do what she said. An aching need hollowed out my middle, like a dagger cut that spilled my guts, overwhelming me with emptiness even as Bolt stirred in discomfort at my side.

"How is this possible?" I asked.

Out of the corner of my eye, I saw Bolt wince. "Wrong question," he whispered, but only I heard him. He wore his disapproval like a coat of mail whenever I tried to secure a future with Gael.

"Is it not enough that it *is* possible?" Gael asked me, her voice nearly as sharp as the blue-eyed gaze she favored me with. Even anger directed at me couldn't diminish the grace of her features. But instead of giving myself over to thoughtful consideration of them as I'd always done before, I found myself imagining them succumbing to the ravages of time while I remained unchanged.

I shook my head. "No, not anymore."

Gael came forward until we were close enough to touch, but she held her arms at her side, refusing contact. "You owe me an explanation, Lord Dura. If I have beggared myself to no end, I at least demand an explanation."

"Beggared?" *Oh, Aer, no.* "You've surrendered your gift?"

Bolt gave a small groan beside me but held his tongue.

Gael gave one sharp nod, her eyes no longer blue but slate, like clouds that carried lightning with them. "Was that not the plan? Uncle fought me, brought every lever to bear to force my marriage to Rupert, but I threatened to surrender my gift to his rival, church law or no, even if the crown threatened my banishment."

"And I would not have," Cailin said, "even though the church would have encouraged me to do so."

"The gift lies with my uncle now," Gael said.

"But Bas-solas," I mumbled, searching for some way to comprehend what had been done.

Gael cut the air with her hand. "You survived. That was all I needed to know. Most of my possessions have been sold, the remainder packed for whatever journey lies ahead of us. Us, Willet."

Bolt sighed, shaking his head. I turned to him like a drowning man reaching for a branch. "Is it forbidden?"

"Willet . . . " His voice rasped. "You can't seriously—"

"Is it forbidden?" I demanded.

His face closed, all emotion squeezed away until his countenance became like rock once more. "No. It is not forbidden." He nodded toward Gael. "But if you do not tell her, I will, though you may hate me for it."

My laughter sounded more like a bark. "I'm disappointed that you think so little of me. I *will* tell her," I said as I turned to confront the questioning in Gael's eyes. "Now.

"The gift that Elwin gave me, that the Vigil possesses, does more than allow me to see into the hearts and minds of others. It extends my life."

Gael's brows drew together in doubt or consideration. "How long?"

I shook my head. "I don't know, but Custos showed me two memories he had of Pellin that were thirty years apart. It was difficult to tell if he'd aged at all."

She turned from me to Bolt. "How old is he? How old are they?"

Bolt's mouth worked for a moment as if he couldn't decide whether to answer. "Pellin is over seven hundred years old, Bronwyn a bit less."

Gael's eyes narrowed. "And Toria Deel?"

My guard shrugged as if the question were unimportant. "About a hundred."

For some reason this last answer was the one that brought shock to her gaze. "She's a girl."

"Can't argue with you there," Bolt grunted. "But she's Elanian. A hundred years hasn't been long enough to take the edge off her temper."

Gael inched closer to me, her hand taking mine, but the gloves I wore prevented me from delving her. "You don't want to watch me grow old."

She hadn't asked, but I answered anyway. "We were supposed to grow old together, and it wasn't supposed to take most of a millennium for me to age."

"Does the prospect of being married to a crone unnerve you, Willet?" She smiled.

I shook my head, disbelieving. How could she possibly find this amusing? If we both lived to be a thousand, Gael would find a way to surprise me. But we weren't going to live that long. Only I. "Will you still be willing to take me to your bed when you've become old enough to be my mother?"

I saw her pause, her eyes fading from the color of flint, not yet turning blue. "Children?" she asked.

I nodded. "I've always wanted children, with you. As many as you would wish." I waved an arm at the stones of the tor that surrounded us. "Enough to fill a castle. Enough to see all the different facets of your beauty and personality and fire." My voice rasped under the strain like a saw through wood. "Would you have me bury you, my sons, my granddaughters, and all the rest of my descendants for hundreds of years? How much grieving do you think I can stand?"

"No." Tears gathered at the corners of her eyes, but they stayed there. She refused to blink them away. "No. We have a chance for love."

I nodded. "But how long will it last? Will you give up the children you've always wanted simply to keep me from grief?"

Gael stepped back from me, dropping my hand, and with that one movement it felt as if she'd pulled my heart from my chest and taken it with her. I shouldn't have been able to feel it. Why didn't I feel numb?

"Do not think this is over between us, Willet Dura," Gael said.

Somewhere in my chest, something fluttered and I felt blood move through my veins again as she continued. "The man who rescued himself from the Darkwater and saved Bunard from the slaughter of Bas-solas can find a way for us to be together."

Before I could respond, Gael curtsied to the queen and left, her footsteps coming more quickly until, at the last, she opened the door and ran away.

CHAPTER 5

I made my obeisance to the queen as quickly as protocol allowed, but it still took me three corridors and a set of stairs to catch up to Gael. If she wanted me to find a way for us to be together, I was going to have to dig my head out of the well of other people's memories I'd fallen into and resume the habits of the king's reeve. And there was one very large loose end I'd left dangling for too long.

I caught up to her and grabbed her by the arm, but when she turned she ducked her head, scattering tears across the floor. She didn't look up from the stones beneath us until she'd scrubbed each hand across her cheeks, pulling her shoulders back to face whatever I had to say.

"If you want me to find a way for us to be together," I said, "I'm going to need your help."

She nodded but I saw her eyes narrow in surprise. "That's a better response than I expected—and sooner as well. Name it."

I pulled a face and figure into my memory against the tide of everything that had happened in the preceding weeks, a young woman, hardly more than a girl, with raven hair and a dress that showed too much skin. "I sent Gareth to you with a message that I needed a serving girl working in the tor taken out of the city and hidden. Where is she?"

Gael shook her head at me, and a trapdoor opened beneath my stomach before she spoke.

"I don't know."

"Did you get the message?"

Gael nodded. "I sent Marya to retrieve her, Willet. I gave her enough

46

money to send Branna anywhere in the seven kingdoms. She took her out of the city and returned just before Bas-solas."

I nodded, trying to ignore the dip in tone and volume at the end. "Perfect. Let's find Marya and ask her where Branna went."

Gael started shaking her head before I'd finished. "She's dead, Willet. Marya died during Bas-solas."

I couldn't recall leaving Gael's presence or doubling back to retrieve my weapons from the queen's guards. Bolt didn't say much as we descended the tor back to the Merum cathedral, not that he had much chance. I chewed and gnawed imprecations most of the way. The only consolation was that with Marya's death, Branna was forever beyond reach of those who sought her. I turned my attention to the task Gael had laid upon me: to find a way for us to be together.

It couldn't be done.

For us to marry, one of two things would have to happen: I would have to surrender my longevity or Gael would have to acquire it. To accomplish the first I would have to die and then somehow come back to life after the gift had departed. For the second, one of the Vigil would have to bestow their gift on Gael. Neither option lay within my power.

Torchlight appeared on the streets as sunlight faded behind the western hills and the sky turned purple, then charcoal and finally black. Stars winked into view as we entered the courtyard, and a sliver of argent appeared through the peaks to the east as a gibbous moon ascended. My steps faltered, and I reached out to pull Bolt to a stop beside me.

"What?" he asked, his hand on his sword in anticipation.

I closed my eyes, listening. "Nothing. That's just it. No screaming, no killing, just the sounds of nighttime in Bunard—the way it used to be." Voices spilled out from the Eclipse across the way, and a sudden longing for hospitality and ale washed over me.

When we got to the Merum cathedral I kept going, descending the rise that encompassed the churches of the four orders to cross the broad arched bridge leading over one of the branches of the Rinwash River and into the nobles' section of the city. Behind their high walls I could hear snatches of music and laughter, carried to me on the air as it cooled. The tones sounded almost normal. Perhaps Bunard would recover after all.

"You can't mean to see her again," Bolt said.

I shook my head. "No." I had no solution to offer Gael, and seeing her would only remind both of us of a future we couldn't have. At that moment I might have taken a sword to Elwin myself. His gift had stolen my future. "I need something else tonight."

"Are you headed to the poor quarter?" he asked, his voice tight.

I frowned, though he wouldn't be able to make out my expression in the dark. "Why would I do that?"

He cleared his throat, coming as close to uncomfortable as I'd ever heard; if the sound of rocks grinding could convey such a thing. "Some men seek the comfort of a woman when their lives have taken a bitter blow."

Laughter caught me by surprise, and pig noises came out of my nose before I could get my mouth open. "You think I'm on my way to see one of the night women?" I wheezed. For a second I couldn't get my breath. "Do you have any idea what Gael would do to me if she found out I'd sought the arms of another?"

"Leave you?" Bolt asked. I couldn't help but detect a hopeful note in his voice, as if seeking solace for a price might not be such a bad idea after all.

My laughter took on an edge of hysteria. "I wouldn't get away so easily. The woman has claimed me. No, I would endure a mixture of kindness and anger along with a very real possibility of physical violence until I saw the error of my ways." My laughter subsided as the realization of just how much I'd lost hit me again. I shook my head. "I want to go to Braben's. I want to hear the warmth of simple voices with small concerns and the sound of wagers being placed on a game of bones." I shrugged. "Besides, I'm tired of wine."

We walked in silence until we crossed over the next bridge and entered the upper merchants' quarter. Foot traffic thinned, and for several stretches, Bolt and I walked alone on the street.

His arm caught me in midstride. "Stop," he whispered.

I halted, my weight forward on my feet and my hands on the daggers I kept hidden on various parts of my person, ears straining to hear. The clop of a hoof against stone sounded in the distance, came three more times before Bolt relaxed enough for us to continue.

We strode along the southeast arc of the city until we came within sight of the tavern at the north end of the lower merchants' section. A few scorch marks still showed where Laewan's men had attacked it, but light spilled through the clear windows overlooking the street. Through them I could see patrons talking and laughing by lamplight, the customary blur of features as usually seen through glass, absent. "Nice windows," I remarked.

Bolt nodded. "Pellin paid for them along with the rest of the repairs. His way of thanking Braben and apologizing at the same time."

I laughed softly. "You mean the church paid for them."

By the warm yellow light coming through the window, I saw Bolt's head cock to one side in dismissal. "It amounts to the same thing. The Merum have their Archbishop, the Servants have their Chief, the Vanguard their Captain, and the Absold their Grace. They all answer to the Vigil. Through the centuries, it's the one thing that's kept the church from dissolving completely." He stopped to peer over his shoulder into the darkness, listening. "Let's get inside."

I stepped through the door into brightness and warmth, my steps growing light, as if I were shedding weight as I went. The tavern wasn't quite filled to capacity—many in Bunard had yet to recover from the slaughter of Bas-solas—but those present, craftsmen and women and simple traders from near and far, enjoyed each other's company as if it were a balm to the soul. Braben owned a gift—a partial, or else he'd be a noble—of helps, a way of making everyone feel welcome.

"Lord Dura." Braben, a heavyset man with thick forearms and hands the size of plates, called my name from behind the bar. A few of the patrons turned in our direction, casting glances over their shoulder before returning to their own conversations. I searched Braben's expression for mistrust or anger. The last time I'd been in his tavern, I'd brought an attack that almost cost him his livelihood and his life. If anyone had a right to a grudge, he did, but all I saw in his face was the same welcome I'd always received—Aer bless him.

I pointed to an empty table close to an interior wall near the fire but away from the windows. I moved toward it, but I was three paces from the door when I realized I was alone. Behind me, Bolt stood in the entrance of the doorway facing out, as still and focused as a hound on the scent.

Gooseflesh raced down my spine until it hit my feet and I moved back to Bolt's side, my right hand palming a dagger inside my cloak in case I needed to make a quick throw. "What is it?" I whispered.

He gave me a brief shake of his head, as if he wouldn't or couldn't answer. I moved to the side and watched as his gaze swept toward each of the passersby outside the bar, focusing on them for a split moment before dismissing them as a threat and moving on.

With a last glance for the street directly in front of Braben's, he pivoted on one heel and stepped sideways away from the open door, putting the wall between the two of us and the open air beyond. "Let's have a seat."

I indicated the table I pointed at before. "Will that do?"

He checked over his shoulder and then back at the table and gave me a terse nod. "We may stay here tonight."

I put a smile on my face and didn't let it slip until we were seated and Braben's backside retreated from us after putting a pair of mugs on the table. "What in the name of all that's sacred is this about?"

Bolt didn't bother to look at me. He'd pulled his chair to the outside of the table and, despite the effort he put into striking a relaxed pose, looked like a coiled spring. "You've been in the Vigil for less than a month, Willet." His unblinking gaze, as tight as the rest of him, never left the door.

I snorted, yet I couldn't help but follow his example. No one entered or left the tavern and the street outside remained empty.

"Have you ever traveled beyond the confines of your city?" Bolt asked.

I laughed, but in the presence of his scrutiny it sounded both harsh and feeble. "You know I have, or do forced marches to the vale between Collum and Owmead to fight a war not count?"

He nodded as if I didn't have his attention. "They count, but you're talking, what, thirty or forty leagues? The northern continent is vast, and the world more so. It holds stranger things than you can know."

The dismissive tone, more akin to what I would hear from Pellin or Toria Deel, irked me. I leaned in close so that no one could hear what I said next. "Stranger than coming out of the Darkwater and sensing murder in my sleep?"

A ghost of a smile played across his face, but whatever kept his eyes glued to the door chased it away. "No, but there are still many things you haven't seen—me either, for that matter."

By the bar, people jostled and shifted, and a man turned to confront another, but there was nothing but empty space between them.

Or was there?

For the barest fraction of a heartbeat I thought I'd seen someone, a woman carrying ale tankards.

I looked away.

"Here! Watch where you're going!" a man growled.

I turned toward the disturbance, saw a man with his arm out grasping at air.

Bolt followed my gaze, his brow furrowing.

I tried to find the girl holding the tankards, but for some reason I couldn't seem to focus. I caught a glimpse of her four paces away, but my gaze kept sliding from her. A gleam of light off polished steel caught my eye.

Bolt stood, his sword leaping into his hand. "What do you see, Dura?"

I tried to point to the woman bringing ale to our table, but there was nothing there.

Two paces away, a man's elbow jerked as if hit from behind.

For a split second I thought I saw the woman coming toward me, but then the image was lost. Bolt put himself by my side. Part of my mind screamed at me to understand.

A gleam of light off polished steel?

A knife?

The whistle of air came, horribly close, steel coming for my throat. I threw myself backward in my chair and threw my dagger toward the sound. I didn't have time to ready the throw. The knife stopped in midair before falling harmlessly to the floor. Bolt leapt and slashed in the same motion but found nothing.

I caught an impression of her again, coming for my side, but I couldn't keep her in sight. Every time I blinked I lost her.

I kicked out with my feet and tried to roll under the table, but I was falling. I managed to squirm a pace away. Bolt straddled me, his sword weaving a net of protection over me that cut the air with high-pitched whines. But his head jerked back and forth, unable to see her.

I heard a footfall behind me and caught a hint of her again. Bolt shifted, aiming for the sound. Too late.

Something brushed my leg, and I threw my arms up to block a strike I couldn't see.

A dagger hurtled through the air and stopped two feet above my chest, then disappeared. Another followed the first, a bit lower.

A gurgling sigh preceded the thud of a body dropping to the floor, and I looked over to see a woman lying beside me on the floorboards, daggers in her throat and chest, her eyes wide with surprise.

Chaos erupted as a crowd of patrons tried to flee for the door at the same time. Chairs and tables were tossed aside, and from where I lay on the floor I could hear the thunder of boots rushing into the night. A few customers had drawn steel and were crouching behind overturned benches or trestles, their eyes showing white.

I rolled the dead woman over, searching her face. Nothing in her sightless gaze called to me, no hints of eternity or judgment, no longing in my chest to see what church and theology told me she should be witnessing right now. Her eyes, devoid of every last trace of color, held all the knowledge and allure of an empty glass.

I pulled the knives, recognized the workmanship. When I turned and scrambled to my feet like a scarecrow testing its legs, Rory stood at my side, his young face livid and angry.

"If you let some pretty thing put a dagger in your chest, what am I supposed to do for a home, yah?"

Before I could answer, he turned on my guard. Bolt stood looking at the woman's body as if she were an impossible affront, a negation of his skill that shouldn't exist.

Rory spat. "How could you miss?" He nudged the dead woman's leg with one foot. "Any boy or girl who's been with the urchins for a year could have taken her."

Bolt didn't respond at first, standing bemused, as if the dead woman had managed to cast a spell over him that persisted after her death.

Braben came over, his face filled with a mixture of sorrow and anger. I knew what he meant to say, so I held up a hand. Until I left the city, I still owned a minor title. Braben stopped, his head dipping in respect.

"Master Braben," I said, then stopped. Braben wasn't a peasant. He was my friend. "I'm sorry, my friend. I would never have come back here if I'd known this would happen. I will see to it that you're repaid for whatever business you've lost, for however long you've lost it." A sigh whispered across my lips. "And I won't come back until I can guarantee your inn peace. Your friendship deserves no less."

Rory cleaned his daggers on the dead woman's skirt and tucked them out of sight. Bolt lifted the body as easily as he would have a child's. Then he handed her to me.

"Why do I have to carry her?"

His mouth pulled to the side in disgust. "Because I can't guard you if my arms are full."

Rory snorted. "You couldn't keep him safe when your arms were filled with weapons."

Bolt's face darkened and he appeared on the verge of cuffing Rory across the head before he gave a grudging nod. "I can't deny it." His eyes narrowed. "If she's what I think she is, your youth is more of an advantage than you can know. We'll take her to Bronwyn for confirmation, but I think someone's made a dwimor."

CHAPTER 6

I wouldn't have recognized the word except for the knowledge Custos had given me. "Phantom?" I shrugged. "She looks real enough to me."

"It describes how they move, not what they are."

I flashed my reeve's badge at a squad of the watch and commandeered their horses for the trip back to the Merum cathedral, trying not to think about the dead woman or her blood. My cloak was covered with it. At least this time I knew where it had come from. Bolt's craggy face had shut as completely as a tomb. He hadn't said a word since we left Braben's.

I pointed to a side street. In the aftermath of Bas-solas, they were all brightly lit. "Shouldn't we avoid the open in case there are more?"

Bolt shook his head. "Speed is more important than stealth." He dug his heels into the flanks of his horse and began a trot that set my teeth to jangling.

Rory trailed us by a few dozen paces, his legs sticking out from the side of his horse and his hands holding the reins as if he were keeping serpents at bay, eyeing them as if they might decide to bite him at any second. But his expression didn't match his circumstances. His eyes were lit and avid with curiosity. Bolt reined in with a curse until Rory's horse caught up with ours.

"You're going to have to teach him how to ride," I said to Bolt.

He twisted in his saddle, and I saw a muscle in his cheek twitch. "Among other things. He's about to find out just how dark the world can be."

Rory had grown up in the poor quarter. Like a lot of the urchins, he'd been orphaned by circumstance or neglect and ended up making a living as a petty thief among the detritus of the city. Yet he'd survived and had even managed to wring a measure of success from his circumstances by finding other children likewise abandoned and bringing them together in a community, giving them a chance at life.

I guessed Rory to be about fourteen or fifteen—it was hard to tell. With decent food he might have been taller—he certainly would have been thicker. Growing up in the poor quarter had exposed him to the worst that human nature had to offer. Thieving, whoring, abuse, and neglect were the stock-in-trade for many who lived there.

I knew it, and more importantly, Bolt knew it. If something about the dwimor could shock his young apprentice, I wasn't so sure Rory should learn of it.

"Is it something he has to see?" I asked. Nominally, Bolt served me, but when it came to matters of training his replacement, I had no say.

For an instant that might have lasted a heartbeat, Bolt's expression softened. "He has to know." He paused, the muscles in his jaws bunching as if he were trying to keep from speaking. "I can't protect you from their like. If there are more of them coming for you, the boy's daggers are the only thing that might keep you alive."

I could hear him grinding his teeth, and he wore the expression of a man itching for a fight. We crossed the northernmost bridge over the Rinwash and turned into the Merum courtyard a moment later. The detachment of guards at the entrance, eight in all, stiffened at the sight of the corpse and drew weapons.

Bolt dismounted in front of the lieutenant in charge. "I need the ages of your men."

"Sir?" His eyes widened in the torchlight.

Bolt ground out a pair of curses that put steel in the man's posture before enunciating each word of his question as if the lieutenant were an idiot. "How old are each of the men you have with you?"

The man twisted, barking the order to report. Bolt listened, nodding as each man gave his age. I nodded in appreciation. They were all veterans, serious-minded professional soldiers, unlikely to panic, no matter the threat.

"Great," Bolt huffed. "They're all very experienced. Not a pink-cheeked recruit among them." He pointed to the nearest. "You. Run into the cathedral and bring three acolytes out here to help you keep watch tonight." He turned to Rory. "How old are you?"

The thief's shoulders made the trip to his ears and back. "Fifteen, I think."

"You think?" Bolt grated.

His tone slid from Rory's expression like water sliding from oil. "It's not like I had a big party every year on my naming day, yah?"

"Humph." Bolt turned back to the man. "Make sure the acolytes are fourteen or younger. Give them chiccor root, if you have to, but make sure they stay alert and keep watch all night. They're to yell and point if they see anyone approaching the gates."

The lieutenant cleared his throat. "Begging your pardon, sir, but that's our job."

Bolt's sword, useless at Braben's tavern, appeared in his hand, the point at the lieutenant's throat. "And you can't do it if you can't see them coming. Do you understand me, Lieutenant? Only the young can see them, or do you not know the rhyme from your childhood?"

Bolt ground his teeth at the lieutenant's blank stare, then started chanting in his gravelly voice.

> *"Facing east and turning west,*
> *Then scouting north and south,*
> *You can't see him or spot her.*
> *To find the ones who wear the wind,*
> *Go bring your sons and daughters."*

With a growl at the now wide-eyed lieutenant, Bolt announced, "We'll take her inside. Pellin and Lady Bronwyn will need light." His tone held all the warmth of granite in winter, but he took the woman who'd tried to kill me and cradled her in his arms as if he wanted to protect her.

Rory glanced up at the bell tower looming over us and gave his head a small shake. "I'll be returning to the poor quarter. Bounder will make a decent head of the urchins if I can keep him from being too aggressive with his thieving. Taking so much attracts attention."

"No," Bolt said in a voice that forbade discussion. "They will want to see you most of all."

Rory muttered something under his breath that I couldn't quite make out, but it almost brought a smile to Bolt's face.

We passed the assembly room where we'd broken the vaults of a fair portion of Bunard's inhabitants and entered the maze of halls that made up the living quarters of the Merum order, vastly reduced since the church had split hundreds of years before. I sent a pair of acolytes ahead of us, one to notify Pellin, Bronwyn, and Toria that we were headed to them with a dwimor, the other to fetch Custos. Pellin had yet to agree to Rory's and Custos's attachment to the Vigil, but he hadn't said no either.

Bronwyn's guard, Balean, stood at her door, sword bared with two white-robed acolytes facing opposite ways down the long hall. The one facing us pointed in our direction.

"I see two men and a lad about my age," he said. "The old one is carrying a woman. I think she's dead."

Bolt made an affronted sound in his throat. "The old one? Decades of service keeping the northern continent safe and that's the thanks I get, to have some drippy-nosed church boy point his soft hand at me and call me 'the old one'?"

Balean spoke through the wood of the door and it opened to reveal Pellin, Allta, Lady Bronwyn, Lady Deel, and her guard, Elory, in the room beyond.

Bronwyn motioned us in, but when she saw the expression on Bolt's face, her gaze darted away again. "Come in quickly. Balean, remain with the acolytes." Her lips tightened, and she reached up to brush one of the wrinkles that lay around his eyes. "Don't trust your vision—trust theirs."

Bolt put the body of the dwimor on a table large enough to seat eight. Without hesitation, Pellin put his thumbs on the dead woman's eyelids and pried them open. A sigh whispered from him. He turned to Bolt, his expression a mixture of curiosity and shame. "How did you know what she was?"

The anger I'd sensed Bolt harboring during the ride back to the cathedral surfaced at last. "The day after I challenged and was assigned to protect you, Cwellan took me aside and told me about every threat the Vigil guards had ever faced or ever might." Bolt's voice rose until it filled the room. "He made me repeat the list back to him until I could recite it word for word." He pointed to the dead woman. "Not once did *you* mention her kind."

Pellin and Bronwyn exchanged glances. "We didn't think it was needed."

Whatever Bolt wanted to say next, he swallowed and took a half step back, crossing his arms over his chest.

I went through everything I'd been able to surmise, deciding not to waste time having the Eldest confirm the obvious. Bronwyn didn't look very forthcoming; she'd gotten that tight-lipped cast to her face that said information would be hard to come by. "How is it done?" I asked. "And if it can be done, why wasn't it done earlier?"

"Still the reeve?" Pellin asked.

I nodded. "Ever and always," I said. "Though some of it seems to be wearing off. I have no idea where you've been for the last two days, for example."

Even Toria Deel, whose willingness to push the boundaries of respect rivaled my own, started at my comment, but Pellin didn't rise to the bait. "Do you suspect everyone, Lord Dura?"

"It's kept me alive so far."

"No one can fault you there," Bronwyn said. She made a gesture toward Toria, inviting her to look at the body. "Check the eyes, my dear. It's the only way to be sure."

The youngest member of the Vigil, other than myself, moved over to the table and copied Bronwyn's inspection from a moment earlier. "The irises are clear, like glass, but what does it mean?"

"It's a dwimor," Pellin said. "A person whose mind has been completely erased, or nearly so."

A sound came from Bronwyn's throat, and she swallowed against whatever memory or emotion caused her face to appear as if the dead woman might rise up and accuse her. "I haven't seen one in centuries."

I pulled in a breath as the reason behind the depth of Bolt's anger became clear. "Not since the Vigil made the last one."

Toria pivoted toward me, her anger as quick as a sword stroke. "Do you never tire of accusing us? You think *we* are responsible for this monstrosity?"

She would have said more, but Bronwyn cut her off, her voice all the more terrible for its quiet. "Lord Dura is correct. This is of our doing."

"What?" Toria asked, looking to Pellin for support but finding none. "That's impossible. I've read through the history of the Vigil countless times. Nothing even alludes to this."

Bronwyn sighed. "The Gift Wars were three hundred years and more in our past when I came to the Vigil, and in the foolishness of youth, I assumed nothing like that could ever happen again. Every nation on both continents had agreed to the proscription against gift-gathering." Her green eyes grew watery. "But it happened again. Not gathering, exactly, but to the same effect, as countries battled for the gift of kings." She shook her head. "You could have waded for days through the blood that was spilled. King Agin had gained control of the southern half of our continent." She fought whatever shame she felt enough to look me in the eye.

I recognized the name and suppressed a shudder. What kind of a man would deliberately plunge the nations into famine? "He tortured the kings into surrendering their gift to him and his siblings."

Bronwyn nodded. "We needed a weapon."

"So you made the dwimor—assassins that couldn't be seen."

She nodded, accepting the responsibility of her admission while Toria gaped, shaking her head as if she could restore her image of Bronwyn. "How could you conceive of such a thing?"

Bronwyn's chest rose and fell twice before she answered. "There, we were aided by the theologians. They pored over the exordium and the rest of the liturgy, searching for anything that might help us. It was Alor, a young Merum priest, who first thought of the idea. He'd read that passage in the fourth book that spoke of seeing a man for his gifts and talents and temperaments instead of his appearance." A hint of a smile played across her lips at some portion of the memory. "We tend to think so rigidly about the world around us, never suspecting there are wonders right before our eyes. Alor was one of those who saw wonders everywhere he looked. I still remember his smile, the way it lit the space around him. He was the one who argued that if you could empty a man of everything that defined his personality he would be almost impossible to see. He said the inspiration came from the child's rhyme." She looked at us. "You know the one—'Who will be the king's best man, filled with his desire? Empty him out and fill him up, full of fateful fire.'"

Bronwyn's thin shoulders lifted a fraction before settling back into place. "We scoffed at him at first, but necessity is a slow, implacable torturer. One by one we went back to the liturgy and reread the verses Alor claimed for his justification."

> *"You will know a man by his character,*
> *A woman by her nature.*
> *As the fruit reveals the tree,*
> *So the deeds reveal the mind.*
> *Thus will the sons and daughters of men be reckoned.*
> *Thus will they be seen by others."*

Toria's face went stiff with disapproval. "It had to be done by the Vigil. No other gift would allow you to empty a man." She pulled a breath, her chest working as if the air had become too thick to breathe. "And you forced men into giving up themselves so that they could kill."

Pellin shook his head but gave no other sign that he objected to Toria's accusation. "We were desperate. Winter was coming, and Agin had us pinned in the north. We were about to lose half our army to starvation. Our ranks were filled with men and women who'd lost everything to that butcher. We asked for volunteers. Even after we explained what would have to be done, we turned them away in droves."

"You appealed to their vengeance," I said. What did I feel? Wonder? Disgust? It was hard to tell. "How was it done?"

He might have misunderstood my question, or the momentum of his memories might have been too great for him to break, but he continued as if I hadn't spoken.

"We chose six. Two each for Agin, his brother, Baelu, and his sister, Ceren." Pellin shook his head. "We were clutching at straws and had no idea what to expect, but we succeeded."

Bronwyn took up Pellin's narrative. "In the end we had half a dozen assassins you couldn't see if they stood right in front of you."

To one side, Bolt's scowl deepened. I stopped Bronwyn, the hitch in her voice telling me what she would hide even now if she could, but it needed to be said, though she might hate me for it. "And how many men and women did you ruin before you were able to get those six?"

Toria's head whipped to look at me, and the color drained from her dark skin. She swallowed as if she might puke any second. "Oh, Aer."

Tears gathered and spilled from Bronwyn's eyes, following the wrinkles in her skin down her cheeks.

"Dozens," Pellin whispered. "So many."

Bronwyn squeezed his arm, then looked up at me. "Pellin quit after his third attempt, but Cesla argued that we had to continue. The Vigil nearly broke."

"Tidrian should never have allowed it," Pellin said.

Seeing my look, Bronwyn sighed. "Tidrian was Eldest then. Perhaps that was a mistake. Formona might have been a better choice, but she grew distrustful of the gift as she got older. By the time war came to the continent Tidrian and Formona alone carried more than two centuries. Jorgen was even younger in the power than I."

"Tidrian put it to a vote. Elwin sided with Cesla"—she shrugged—"as he always did, and Jorgen as well. Pellin and I sided with Formona."

I shook my head. "You voted?"

Bronwyn gave me a slow nod. "Deadlocked, Tidrian had to make the decision he'd tried to avoid. Formona's voice, as the next oldest, should have carried more weight."

"Cesla was ever persuasive," Pellin said.

Bronwyn looked at him as if she might offer some word of comfort but turned back to me a moment later. "Tidrian refused to aid in the creation of the dwimor, citing age and fatigue, but Formona claimed it was his way of offering a compromise. He didn't expect Cesla to succeed without his or Formona's aid, but they underestimated his strength in the gift. Cesla, Elwin, and Jorgen continued undaunted." She swallowed thickly. "Somewhere in north Owmead there's an unmarked grave with the bodies of all the failures in it."

"They paid a price," Pellin said. The eyes of the dead woman held him transfixed, and I wondered if he searched for some forgiveness or absolution there. "Creating a dwimor was far more costly than a delve. For each attempt, Cesla, Elwin, and Jorgen used up a part of themselves. My brothers and I were of an age at the beginning of the war, our birth difference minuscule as the Vigil reckons time, but by the end, they were older." He sighed. "They paid." He shook himself. "With a single month of stores left we sent out the six, three women and three men, emptied of everything that made them human. They retained enough knowledge to eat and to kill those whose images were put into their minds."

"The scrolls say Agin and his kin were killed by their generals in a squabble for power," I said.

Pellin sighed. "For once, we didn't have to alter history. No one gave credence to assassins that couldn't be seen. The southern armies fell into chaos after Agin's death, and we poured out of the north. The church issued the decree that whoever held the gift of kings at the dawn of the new year would be king over whatever territory they held. We lost almost as many people to the bloodshed as we would have to the famine."

Pellin fell silent.

"Why could I see her?" Rory asked.

Bronwyn's expression became wistful. "You're young. The expectations and presumptions you hold within your mind are less rigid than those of someone older." Her voice dropped into a lyrical cadence. "'And a child shall see and provide the way.'"

I knew the quote as I'd known all the others from the time I'd spent preparing to become a priest. "That's a bit out of context."

"Is it?" Bronwyn asked. "Who's to say what circumstances Aer foresaw when He inspired the writers of the liturgy? It's confirmed Alor's insight, has it not?"

I laid questions of inspiration and interpretation aside. The blood on my hands from a decade ago had put the priesthood beyond my reach, and more pressing matters required my attention. I pointed at the body of the woman with the colorless eyes.

"Why were we able to see her after she died?" I asked.

Pellin shrugged. "Her body became a thing, like a chair, or a book, or piece of parchment. Without her life and twisted mind to sustain her, it became nothing more than an object."

"When was she made?"

Bronwyn shook her head. "It's impossible to say, but it's unlikely Laewan had the ability to create her."

Toria nodded. "He was newer to the Vigil than I. Neither of us could have known it was possible." Her voice turned to steel. "You lied to me." Neither Pellin nor Bronwyn answered.

"So . . . " I sighed. "It is as we feared. It's not over. Whoever was ultimately behind the madness of Bas-solas will look to strike again."

"It's possible that whoever turned Laewan could have taught him the means of creating a dwimor," Bronwyn said.

Pellin's mouth tightened, and he shot a quick glance at me before he nodded grudgingly. "If any of you venture from the cathedral, take a pair of acolytes with you. The younger, the better." He sighed as if he'd been forced to shoulder a burden he'd been trying to avoid. "This strengthens my fear that Jorgen has been turned." He caught my gaze and held it. "One thing we have in our favor is the amount of time it takes to create a dwimor. Cesla or Elwin working through sunrise and sunset could only produce one every five days, Jorgen more than twice as long."

"Produce?" Toria's mouth twisted around the word as if it tasted of myrrhen root, and she pointed at the dead woman on the table. "You're talking about a person, a living being, and you make it sound like you're a cobbler trying to rush a new pair of boots."

Pellin took the assault without defense, nodding, but Bronwyn wasn't immune to the accusation. It was clear everything Toria Deel said hit her with almost physical blows. "You weren't there. We were about to lose the whole continent." She turned to the body. "Agin's depravity ran so deep. Thousands volunteered. Even at that there were only a few we could use."

"The ones with a particular gift?" I asked without knowing precisely why I did so. Something in the ancient children's rhyme tugged at me, a connection I couldn't quite make, but Alor's intuition explained Bronwyn's penchant for quoting children's rhymes at odd moments.

Toria must have seen more clearly than I. "Aer help us—they were all priests."

Bronwyn shook her head. "Not all of them. People were less—" she paused to hunt for a word—"categorized in that time, but in the end every assassin we successfully created held a gift of devotion."

CHAPTER 7

Pellin left us soon after, claiming a prior engagement and leaving Bronwyn, Toria, and myself to sort through the assassin's clothes and search her body for marks, scars, or tattoos that might give us some idea who she'd been before she became a tool for someone else's hatred.

"Look again," Bronwyn said. "There has to be some connection between the dwimor and its target. Agin had killed so many that it was easy to find those who hated him."

"You shouldn't have done it," I said. "You took their gift of devotion and twisted it into a tool for revenge."

Bronwyn met my gaze for a space of time that was just long enough to show me the depth of hurt my words caused. "It wasn't up to me, Lord Dura. I had no authority—Pellin and I fought it as best we could." Her face twisted into regret all the same.

"Their relationship never recovered." I said. "Cesla's and Pellin's, I mean."

Bronwyn gave me a slow nod. "Bolt keeps reminding me how quickly you see to the hearts of others. No. It didn't." She flung up a hand. "Pellin insisted we were using evil to fight evil. He said if Aer wanted to keep Agin from power, then a better way would present itself. After his brothers mocked him for the convenience of his beliefs, Pellin disappeared into his books, searching for an alternative he never found. Cesla and Elwin had always been the closest of the three, but the making of the dwimor widened the gap between Pellin and his brothers until it became a chasm. In the centuries since, they hardly spoke." Bronwyn pointed to the body of the woman. "The dead teach the living, as the healers say. Now, please, look again."

I avoided rolling my eyes, just. This same request had been issued half a dozen times already with the same conclusion—I didn't know her. She was small featured in a way that might rouse protective instincts in a man, and she had legs that showed the musculature of someone used to physical exertion, but without the thick-bodied appearance of a common laborer. This coupled with the lack of calluses on her hands meant she was no farmer's daughter, perhaps a dancer.

I didn't know any dancers.

"Try sifting through your memories, Lord Dura," Toria said, "as if you were delving another. Let them flow past you in succession from new to old until you see her."

I squeezed my eyes shut so neither of the two women could see the expression I really wanted to wear. "All right, I will. Again."

My life flowed past me, but the gift I'd received from Elwin along with the insight I'd gotten from Custos did nothing to bring memory, meaning, or purpose to the dead woman's face. I couldn't help but sigh. Ealdor's memories had seemed as real and tangible as all the rest. I sat in silence with my eyes closed until I couldn't go back any further, until the day I emerged from the Darkwater Forest. The hole in my memory, a blank wall where feeling and recollection should have been, refuted my attempt to see into it. I skipped back to the battle and continued back until I reached my early childhood, where memory frayed into a chaotic sea of impression and want and little more. "There's nothing there." I shrugged. "We never met."

"Her features resemble those from the south," Toria said. "Have you ever been to Caisel?"

"No. I think I'd remember that. I've never been south of the Blood Vale between Collum and Owmead."

"Unless, of course, you *can't* remember it," Toria said.

Only the slightest hint of accusation accompanied her words, which in itself qualified as a minor miracle considering the enmity that had accompanied our initial meetings. It put my hackles up anyway. I knew what had to be coming next, and sure as the sunrise, Lady Bronwyn didn't disappoint me.

"True," Bronwyn said. "I suppose you might have met this woman in the Darkwater Forest or, more likely, on one of your night walks. It's a shame Rory killed her. If we could have delved her, we might have seen not only the connection to you, but also who twisted her this way."

"Does there have to be a connection?" I asked.

That drew her up short, and she considered the idea for a moment before shaking her head. "Probably not, but it would take longer. Pellin might know."

"Where did he go?" I asked. The Eldest of the Vigil had made himself scarce since the day after Bas-solas, leaving the rest of us to do the heavy lifting of delving everyone we'd captured. Even the appearance of the dwimor had failed to engage his attention for more than an hour.

Toria Deel took a half step back, her expression blank as new parchment. Bronwyn lifted one shoulder and let it fall. "The Eldest requires some measure of solitude. He is seeking . . . an alternative."

Toria Deel nodded in understanding, but I had no idea what Bronwyn meant. "To what?"

She took a deep breath. "He hopes to avoid involving the heads of the church. Circumstances are different now. Even the appearance of weakness on the part of the Vigil is disastrous."

I shook my head and she turned to face me, her lips tight with annoyance. "The death of Laewan has put him in an awkward position. Laewan's gift has gone free."

"You hope," I said.

Bronwyn and Toria both started at that, then nodded. "Yes," Bronwyn said. "Desperately. Before Cesla's death the gift hadn't gone free in centuries. Finding a free gift takes organization and discretion of the highest order."

I could have pitied the Eldest in that moment. "For the second time in ten years. That's not nearly long enough for people to forget that Cesla's gift went free as well. And . . . there is still Jorgen's silence to consider." There were no easy answers to that concern.

"Thus our problem," Bronwyn said. "The four orders are uniquely equipped to help us investigate anyone who shows signs of receiving the gift of the Vigil, but we have failed to find Cesla's gift in all these years, and now we're asking them to be on the lookout for another." Her lips thinned into a line of disapproval that Toria mirrored. "They are calling Pellin's ability to lead the Vigil into question. They've agreed to aid us, but the Archbishop of the Merum has suggested bringing the Vigil under control of the church."

"Humph," I said. "And I bet he's offered to shoulder the responsibility of overseeing us. That's very noble of him."

Bronwyn nodded. "At this point, the infighting between the Merum, the Servants, the Vanguard, and the Absold is the only thing allowing us to remain independent of their control."

Toria nodded. "It's not inconceivable that, if they managed to find the gift, they would hold it hostage."

"Cesla, Laewan, and Jorgen." I recited the names of men I should have known, other members of the Vigil. "You're down to four." I shook my head. "Ten years ago, in the war between Collum and Owmead, the enemy was more than happy to trade losses with us. They outnumbered us two to one. You can't win a war of attrition."

"You?" Toria Deel threw my words back at me like a gauntlet. "Do you refuse to count yourself among us?"

I pointed to the body of the woman behind me. "I seem to be numbered with you whether I will or no, but we both know that I'm not truly part of the Vigil and can't be while I have this." I tapped my head with one finger.

I turned and pulled the sheet up over the nearly naked woman's body. Her skin had already started to purple, and other, less savory, processes would begin at any time. "Assassin or not," I said, "she needs to be tended to."

I'd already turned away when a thought struck me, and I pivoted on one heel. "Never mind. I'll take care of her myself."

Pellin woke from a rare afternoon nap in his quarters four hours before sunset without checking the clock candle on the mantel over the fireplace to tell him this was so. The rhythm of his day, established through uncounted years of repetition, couldn't be thrown off by the temporary disruption of the troubles here in Bunard.

An openmouthed smile of disbelief pulled his lips to one side without his intention. Troubles? Disaster was more like it. Yet the Vigil remained, and the most immediate threat to its survival had been defeated, at least temporarily.

On the edge of his vision, Allta entered his sleeping quarters from the anteroom where he'd kept guard along with a rotating shift of Merum acolytes, young men accustomed enough to the sleeplessness of their prayer vigils to maintain watch on the locked door to the Vigil members' quarters.

"Ignorant," Pellin said, dispensing with every word that he would have used to begin this conversation at a later hour except the most important.

"Pardon, Eldest?"

His need for clarification demonstrated another difference between Allta and his former guard. Bolt would have made the connection between Pellin's limited speech and their present circumstances. Pellin sighed. Perhaps if he spoke through his misgivings, he or Allta might find some clue in them.

"We are ignorant of our ultimate enemy," he began. "The Vigil has stood watch over the Darkwater Forest for uncounted centuries, maintaining the sentinels, tracking down the rare exception to the ferocity of their watchfulness, and dispensing our ultimate justice to the kings and queens and the heads of the church. On the southern continent our counterparts do the same for the Maveth Desert."

"Yes, Eldest." Allta nodded without adding anything more.

Pellin restrained a sigh. "And the rhythm of our appointed task never changed, never altered. The Gift Wars came, the northern church split into pieces, and then the Wars for the Gift of Kings came. Through it all, the Vigil dispensed justice as best we could and intervened when we had to, but the ultimate task never changed." He turned to face Allta, hoping the discipline of conversing would unlock something in his mind. "We patrolled the forest, trained untold generations of sentinels, and broke the vaults of those rare exceptions who slipped through the net. Do you understand? It was always the same."

His guard nodded. "And now it's not."

Bolt might have answered the same. "And when did it become different?" Pellin asked without expecting an answer, because it predated Allta's service. "Ten years ago." A moment passed as the sky outside the narrow slits that constituted his windows faded to dun. "Come, my friend, you've overheard enough conversations to fill a library, and we never bring guards into our service who lack a certain mental acuity."

"Cesla was killed," Allta said. Even though it had happened prior to his service, a look of frustrated need for revenge darkened his features.

"Yes." Pellin nodded. "But something else happened then as well, something we might look upon as rare and wondrous. A man emerged from the Darkwater, a man with a vault who managed to live a life free from the mindless rage every other survivor exhibited."

"Eldest?"

"Too many questions," Pellin murmured. "We don't know the timing between Lord Dura's miraculous survival and Cesla's death." He shook his head. "And we don't know what the Darkwater *is*."

"The liturgy proclaims the Darkwater as the dwelling place of man's sin," Allta said as if that settled the matter.

"Yes, yes," Pellin nodded. "And it's easy enough to believe, but that gets us no closer to understanding its more fundamental nature. Why do those who venture within its poisoned borders go insane? Why and how does it grow? Why has its nature changed now, after thousands of years, and what do the death of Cesla and Willet Dura's strange survival have to do with it?"

Pellin sighed. "I'm afraid there's only one way to know. One of the Vigil will have to enter the forest. Somewhere within the boundaries of those twisted trees lies the truth."

Allta shook his head. "The forest can't be searched, Eldest. West to east, it is eight days across, even more from south to north."

He didn't, couldn't, answer his guard's objection. Allta had stated a fundamental truth and one the Vigil had fought for thousands of years. In fact, the liturgy commanded complete, unquestioning avoidance of the forest, and nothing in their collected writings gave more than the barest hint of the "why" behind its evil.

But the liturgy had never hinted at a man like Willet Dura, either. Everyone who spent a night in the forest went insane. Everyone, the liturgy said—and thousands of years of evidence confirmed it. Pellin took a deep breath, trying to loosen the knot in his chest. Many of the mathematicians of Moorclaire would love Willet Dura. With their passion for proof and counterexample they would latch onto him as a refutation of the entire liturgy; a man who lived.

He suppressed a shiver. The Vigil's gift, domere, the gift of judgment, had come to Dura from his dying brother. With a mental wrench that almost hurt, Pellin forced himself to look for advantages in the contradiction that was Willet Dura. Surprisingly, he found one. Who better to investigate the depths of the Darkwater than the one man who'd already survived it?

"Eldest?" Allta's voice called to him.

His arms jerked like a man on the edge of sleep, and he turned to see his guard nodding toward the lowering sun outside the window. "Ah, I see it's time to depart while we still have light. Thank you."

Five minutes later, not nearly enough time to mark by the movement of the evening sun, they were admitted to the cathedral of the Pueri, or the Servants, as most people referred to them. Pellin stifled a centuries-old regret at the split of the church. Barely a score of years after the north-south split between the continents, led by the priest, Maren Wittendor, the Servants had been the first to split from the Merum. The Absold and the Vanguard had split soon after.

As they entered the open doors of the cathedral, a brown-robed priest came forward to greet them, the symbol of his order, a hand supporting a foot in the pose of ceremonial washing, stitched into the left side of his robe, just over the heart.

"How may I serve you?" The man bowed, reciting the ritual greeting. He straightened almost, but not quite to the point of meeting Pellin's gaze, instead selecting a spot somewhere in the middle of Pellin's torso so that his head remained bowed.

Pellin dug into the interior of his cloak, feeling for the symbol of office he carried with him. Four such were grouped together at need, and his hands roamed over each in turn until he felt the familiar contours of the foot-in-hand beneath his fingertips. He pulled the silver medallion that identified him as a Servitor of the order, one level below the Chief of Servants herself, and showed it to the priest.

"My name is Pellin, and I have tidings for the Chief," Pellin said from within the hood of his cloak. "Would you be kind enough to show the way?"

"Of course," the priest nodded, and his head resumed its lowered posture. Like most of the servants, his hair was bowl-cut, in strict avoidance of the current styles, short or long, that predominated in the court or the social circles of the merchants.

Unlike its Merum counterpart, the Pueri cathedral had been built along remorselessly uniform lines and right angles. After the sanctuary, every corridor was identical to the one before, and every office, regardless of the relative importance of its occupant, held the same amount of space. The priest guided them to the back of the cathedral, to the last door. Even here, the Chief of Servants' office occupied no more space than the myriad of those who reported to her. The only concession to her importance was the presence of the woman who sat at a broad table outside the door, a woman unknown to him.

Every prison had its keeper.

The priest bowed. "Secretary Iren, Servitor Pellin has a message for the Chief of Servants."

Unlike the priest, the woman at the table had no difficulty meeting Pellin's gaze, or attempting to. His hood had been pulled forward far enough to allow little more than a hint of his face. She stood, and Pellin resisted the urge to gape as her head continued to ascend until she could have looked Allta straight in the eye. "Servitor Pellin." Her lips framed the title, shaping the sound, testing it. "Thank you, brother. You may return to your duties."

She waited without moving toward the closed door behind her until the priest had moved well beyond earshot. "I'm familiar with all of the Servitors of our order. I don't recall your name being among them."

Pellin bent slightly from the waist. "I'm not, strictly speaking, a member of the order of Servants."

The woman's features, already sharp beneath her iron-gray hair, hardened until they became positively chiseled. "I believe I just said that."

Within the confines of his hood, Pellin smiled. "Yes, well, names open doors, as they say. Perhaps you could mention mine to the Chief and let her decide whether or not to see me."

The woman shook her head. "I'm afraid not. The Chief is occupied with other matters at the moment, and I'm not inclined to interrupt her for a liar with a convenient piece of silver."

Pellin's smile evaporated. "Allta."

The tone communicated all that he'd intended. The woman turned to face his guard, and Pellin watched as she blinked, her eyelids closing for a fraction of a heartbeat. When they opened, the tip of Allta's sword rested against the pale skin of her neck without drawing blood.

71

"I assure you, Secretary Iren, I merely wish a moment of the Chief Servant's time. If she has no desire to see me, I will be happy to depart." Pellin moved around the table and knocked at the door. "I won't even enter unless invited."

A voice called from within, inquiring, then again, but Pellin ignored it, moving to rejoin Allta, who still held Iren at swordpoint. "You can put that away now."

Allta sheathed the sword and resumed his pose of relaxed vigilance just before the door opened to show the wizened features of the Chief of Servants.

"I said I didn't want to be interrupted. What do I have to do, Iren? Wait until the Final Call for you to—"

She stopped, taking in the presence of Pellin, but more importantly, his guard, standing outside her door. One of Iren's hands traced a line along her throat and then waved at the air where Allta's sword had been.

"Ah, thank you, Iren," the Chief said, opening the door the rest of the way and stepping to one side. "Gentlemen, please enter. How may I be of service?"

Pellin stepped around the secretary's table, pausing just long enough to speak to the secretary once more. "Thank you for your service, Iren."

CHAPTER 8

"What's this about, Eldest?" the Chief asked once the door was closed. While her office was no larger than any of the others within the cathedral, it did boast comfortable chairs. Pellin seated himself within one as Allta stationed himself in front of the locked door.

"I need to speak with the heads of the orders, Brid," Pellin said without preamble. "By now they've all gotten some version of what's happened here, and this isn't something I can address with messenger birds."

Brid Teorian, Chief of Servants, stepped around Pellin, avoiding the chair by his side to seat herself at her desk. She leaned forward resting her elbows on the burnished wood, a soldier holding her shield.

"In truth, I'm pleased you sought me out, Eldest," she said. "The heads of the other orders are concerned by the events here in Bunard, and an explanation, which some say is days overdue, would go a long way toward ameliorating their worries. They've demanded an immediate audience."

Pellin nodded while his mind raced. Those who'd given their lives to the church rarely used confrontational language. It went against all of their religious and academic training. Any other time he might have found the sudden departure refreshing. "I understand. My apologies, Chief, if the duties of my office have kept me from offering the timely communication the heads of the other orders require." He paused to smile. Bolt used to tell him he didn't smile enough. Cesla and Elwin had been better with people. "Perhaps we can offer the heads of the

73

other orders the reassurance they seek even now." But as he said this he winced inside at the irony. They would be anything but reassured.

The Chief of Servants nodded, then reached inside the brown robes of her office to pull out a gold-braided chain with a silver wire-mesh cage dangling at the end. The construct was approximately the size of her age-spotted hand, but only half as thick as it was wide. Within the woven basket a diamond with a faint pinkish hue had been mounted, its main facets at right angles to each other.

Without ceremony, Brid Teorian placed the stone on the desk, halfway between herself and Pellin. Turning the cage slightly to face one of the facets directly, she paused to clear her throat. "Within the charisms of Aer, the talents of man, and the temperaments imbued in creation are found understanding and wisdom. Know and learn."

Pellin shook his head as they waited for the heads of the Merum, Absold, and Vanguard to answer the call. It had been mere weeks since the last such call, when he'd sat in this same office to inform the four arms of the collective church of Elwin's death and his own elevation to the status of Eldest. Hard questions then would certainly lead to harder questions now.

After a moment, a deep voice called from one of the facets. "I am here." Pellin recognized the voice of Collen, Captain of the Vanguard, who currently resided in Loklallin, the chief city of Moorclaire.

They waited for the space of a score of heartbeats, and the Chief of Servants leaned forward and recited the ending of the exordium once more.

A young woman's voice came from a different face of the diamond. "I crave your pardon." Pellin recognized Hyldu, Grace of the Absold, responding from the city of Andred in Owmead.

Across from him, the Chief of Servants momentarily appeared as if she were trying not to roll her eyes. "Greetings, Grace," she replied. "No pardons are required. We are still waiting for the Archbishop to join us." She paused, then recited the coda to the exordium again.

"Know and learn," a man's voice responded. Not so deep as the Captain's, it carried undertones of effort, the discernible whisper of the aged working to make themselves heard. Archbishop Vyne of the Merum had endured in his office, headquartered in Cynestol, the chief city of Aille, longer than expected.

Pellin waited until Chief Teorian nodded her permission to speak. "Greetings, Archbishop, Grace, Captain, and Chief. This is Pellin, Eldest of the Vigil."

Clamor erupted from the stone as three voices vied for attention. Pellin sat without responding, waiting for the outcry to collapse under the weight of his silence, before answering. "Your pardon, esteemed leaders, but the restraints of our communication keep me from answering all of your questions at once. Perhaps, if you will allow it, I can apprise you of recent events in general before we begin the process of satisfying your queries in particular."

"Please," the Archbishop said, "continue."

Pellin pulled a breath that held the distinctive flavor of parchment and ink and settled himself into the comfort of the head servant's chair. The recounting would take a while. "With your pardon, Excellencies, I'm going to begin ten years ago with two events that happened in close chronology. I can't tell you which happened first, and I have no evidence to present that the events are related, though I believe they are. You may recall the drought that came that year and that Collum and Owmead were engaged in one of their not-infrequent wars over the Syfling Vale as a result of it. That year also marked the passing of the Eldest of the Vigil, Cesla."

"Collum and Owmead have fought over the vale for centuries," the Captain said from the diamond. "What possible relationship could there be with his death?"

Pellin nodded, grateful for the interruption that gave him an opportunity to gather his courage. Not since the Wars for the Gift of Kings had such transparency been required of the Vigil. He was no fool. Those in power often claimed to desire information, but most preferred to live in the comfort of their ignorance—a protective skin that Pellin was about to strip away. "A man, a soldier in Collum's army, came out of the forest after spending at least a full day and night there. I say at least, Excellencies, because that portion of his mind is still closed to us."

He had suspected another outburst at this point. From the poorest farmer to the highest noble, the implications of living with the taint of the Darkwater for ten years would have been shocking, nearly unthinkable, but plain. It had never happened.

Pellin lifted his gaze from the scrying stone to see the Chief of

Servants waving her hand in tremored circular motions, bidding him to continue, and for the next hour he shared the sequence of events of the last decade in as much detail as he could, noting as he went those areas that he knew to be fact, those he could reasonably infer, and those that were speculation. When his narrative carried him to the events of the past week, he almost stopped, his heart working against the constraint of his ribs and his hands strangling each other, appalled at what he meant to reveal. But he needed the full measure of their aid—couldn't chance not receiving it. Against the weight of bile that threatened to fill his throat, he told them of the attack of the dwimor and Jorgen's probable hand in creating it.

Pellin leaned back in his chair, waiting for the flood of questions that must surely come. He wasn't disappointed. Any one of them could have been a grandson or granddaughter with a significant number of *greats* in front to him, yet they badgered him as though he were a stubborn schoolboy, ferreting out details of inconsequence, framing questions as accusations in their shock and anger.

Two hours later, with little additional information to show for it, Brid's office stilled. Pellin offered nothing further, and the facets of the scrying stone ceased their resonance, falling silent under the weight of the Vanguard's anger, the Merum's disbelief, and the Absold's despair. Across from him, the Chief of Servants gazed at him from within the depths of her birdlike brown eyes.

"Four." The Captain of the Vanguard's voice came from the crystal uncounted moments later. "With the loss of Jorgen to the evil of the forest, the Vigil of the north is reduced to four."

"If," the Archbishop said, "you believe Willet Dura to be trustworthy."

"The gift came to him," the Absold said, but her voice trembled, carrying more pleading than assertion.

"Perhaps it would be best if Lord Dura is placed under guard until the current problems within the Vigil have been resolved," the Archbishop said.

"Questions of Willet Dura's fidelity will have to wait," the Chief of Servants stated. "Our primary question remains: How is the church to safeguard the gift and survival of the Vigil?"

Pellin concentrated on remaining still. In the convoluted language of the clergy, Brid's question assumed the Vigil would come under the authority of the orders of the church. Assumed it! Perhaps he misheard or the Chief misspoke, but it would be a very short step from their suggesting Dura's imprisonment to demanding his own. If the heads didn't currently entertain the idea of bringing the Vigil under their direct control, it was vital he not inadvertently suggest it.

"To whom shall they report?" the Captain asked.

Pellin almost smiled. Through its long history, the Vigil had always been autonomous, the last defense against possible corruption of the church, even before the split. Questions of authority and hierarchy within the church took years to settle, even for minor concerns. The wrangle over who would command the Vigil might take decades to settle.

"As the Eldest has unfortunately confirmed for us, there are now only four members of the northern Vigil," the Grace of the Absold said. "Whether by coincidence or the will of Aer, I propose apportioning the resources of the Vigil to each order to safeguard the gift."

Pellin's complacency vanished between heartbeats as the heads of the other orders voiced their assent. Aer save them, what had he done? In his attempt to secure the orders' aid, he'd scared them into unimagined cooperation.

He leaned forward toward the stone. "With all due respect, your Excellencies, I believe the most important task for the church is to find Jorgen as well as those gifts that have gone free."

"To what end? We've been unable to find Cesla's gift for the last ten years, Eldest," the Captain asserted.

"It's not unusual for the gift to go missing for such a length of time," Pellin replied, wincing at the undercurrents of defiance in his voice.

"Regardless," the Archbishop said, "it would be folly to assume that the new owners of the gift will fall into our lap simply because we need them."

"Jorgen is another matter," the Grace said.

"Yes," the Chief of Servants nodded. "This one presents a more immediate concern. If he continues to send these dwimor against the Vigil, he alone could wipe the gift from the northern continent. I think a formal writ of anathema with a sizable reward for his death is in order."

"Do you think he can be found so easily?" the Chief of Servants asked.

"Perhaps not," the Archbishop said, "but if Jorgen is worried about keeping his head, he might be too busy hiding to create more assassins."

The sound of the Archbishop clearing his throat emanated from the crystal. "Perhaps it would be better to finish our discussion without commandeering any more of the Eldest's time."

Pellin listened to the quick assents of the other heads in disbelief and for a moment considered delving the Chief of Servants, but such an act without permission would be tantamount to an accusation, and he had none. Nevertheless, as she stood to signal his dismissal, the realization that he had been nothing more than an unwitting player on the stage for the last two hours wouldn't leave. Their cooperation with each other had been too easy, too familiar, without the endless debate that customarily accompanied even minor decisions.

He left the Chief's office in a daze, retracing his steps back through the Cathedral of Servants and out toward the broad plaza of Criers' Square with the mechanical steps of a child's wind-up toy. Engrossed in the catastrophe and his failure to avert it, he failed to notice that night had fallen until Allta jerked him to a stop, forcing him to see the lamps.

"Eldest, we have no acolyte."

Allta drew his sword, and they retreated into the safety of the Servants Cathedral. Pellin approached a robed servant standing just inside the narthex. "Brother, my servant and I require an escort back to our lodgings for the night."

The brown-robed priest cast a look toward Allta, who stood just inside the entrance, two hands taller and broader than most men and holding his sword with the deadly familiarity of those who live with the weapon in their hand.

The brother's blond eyebrows rose. "You need an escort?"

Pellin forced a smile and nodded. "Despite appearances to the contrary. My guard and I are both suffering from a temporary lack of visual acuity and would earnestly appreciate assistance."

The brother locked gazes with Pellin, squinting in an obvious attempt to verify his claim. With a shrug that communicated more doubt than certitude, he bowed from the neck. "I will serve you."

Pellin worked to keep his smile in place. For the second time he flashed the silver-worked medallion showing a hand holding a foot.

"Ah. Yes. Well, you are certainly welcome to come along, but I have found that young eyes are the best. Would it be possible to have an acolyte accompany us?"

The look of suspicion remained, but the brother nodded and disappeared into the recesses of the narthex to appear a moment later with an acolyte of perhaps twelve or thirteen, a dull-eyed boy who exhibited little interest in his present circumstances.

"This is Rundor," the brother said.

Pellin bowed his gratitude. "Thank you, brother. We'll send him back to you once we reach our destination." He waited until the brother retreated to the hidden safety of the cathedral's narthex, leaving the three of them alone at the entrance before addressing their guide. "Tell me, Rundor, how good is your eyesight?"

The boy stared at him openmouthed without answering, blinking slowly to keep pace with his sluggish thoughts.

Pellin backed away and held up two fingers. "How many do you see?"

Rundor's thick brows lowered in concentration, an expression that communicated no small amount of discomfort. "Two."

"Wonderful," Pellin exclaimed, putting an arm around the boy and leading him across Criers' Square. "Here's what I want you to do. Do you see the Merum Cathedral over there?"

Rundor nodded.

"Excellent. That's where we're headed, and it's about two hundred paces away." They took a few more steps while Rundor did his best to digest this information. "If you see anyone coming toward us, Rundor, anyone at all, I want you to point at them. Do you understand?"

Rundor nodded and lifted his hand and pointed at the empty expanse of Criers' Square in front of them.

Pellin bowed his head in frustration. He would have to find an even simpler way to explain. "Very good, Rundor, but don't point until you actually see someone."

The boy nodded, his arm dipping a fraction before raising it again to point. At the same spot.

Pellin sighed. "I think we need—" His head snapped to a hint of shadow, a ghost of movement at the edge of his vision.

Too many things happened in that instant—a whisper of displaced air; Allta crashing into Rundor, who tumbled into Pellin; the sound of meat being cut as a knife blossomed in Rundor's side; Allta drawing his sword to fight something they couldn't see.

Pellin stooped to pick up the boy, his back and knees screaming at the abuse. "Quickly, back to the cathedral!"

Then he heard footsteps, the strike of a bootheel directly in front of them without an apparent owner, and Allta began yelling for the city watch, his sword cutting the air everywhere at once.

A hint of shadow in the dark, black on black from the guttering torches, moved across his vision. Allta cocked his head listening, straining to hear over the sound of his sword cutting air, his weight forward on his feet, ready to spring.

The hiss of a blade, not Allta's, came from their left. Quicker than thought, his guard leapt toward the sound, and Pellin winced at the *chunk* of steel biting into flesh. Allta backed away, weaving broad figure eights with his sword, free arm clamped against the wetness spreading along his side.

"Stay behind me," Allta growled, backing toward the cathedral.

Shifting the boy, Pellin searched his cloak for something, anything that he might throw at their attacker, any object that would reveal his position or at least blind him momentarily so they could run. His hand closed around one of the medallions, and when Allta's head jerked to the left, he threw, but the symbol of office disappeared into the darkness to clatter against the stones.

Allta gasped as the assassin found an opening, and more blood worked its way down his leg. Pellin looked behind them. Twenty paces separated them from the gates of the cathedral. Rundor whimpered into Pellin's cloak.

Pellin stumbled, buckling under the weight of the acolyte. Fifteen paces separated them from safety. Across the square, booted feet came running, but they were hundreds of paces away. They'd never make it in time.

He tripped under the boy's weight. It was no use. He couldn't get both Rundor and himself back to the cathedral. "I'm sorry, lad," Pellin said as he laid the acolyte on the stones as gently as he could.

CHAPTER 9

Jeb looked at the body of the woman, his face wrinkling at the sight of her mottled skin. "She's a little overdue for burial, Dura," he growled.

I nodded. "I'll have her taken to the gravesman once we're done." I chose my next words with care. "She came for me in Braben's. I'm not sure how she did it, but she had that knife on me almost before I noticed her, and I've been more than a little watchful lately."

"You think she's one of Orlan's?" Jeb asked.

I cocked my head to one side as if considering the idea, but inwardly I ground my teeth. Jeb had completely missed the hint. "I'm not sure. But you told me that you had a bunch of unsolved murders, and I wondered if there might be a connection."

Jeb stared at me as if I were hard of hearing. "And how would we know that, Dura? I have no witnesses, as in none."

I knew what I wanted to ask and knew just as certainly I couldn't ask it. How would I explain to Jeb that his only possible witnesses would be children? "Did you try the urchins?"

Jeb fished into his pocket and tossed me the token I'd given him. "Their new head, Bounder, knows me a little too well."

Sometime in the past, Jeb had probably put his fists to use on the thief. Now that Bounder headed the urchins who chose to stay on the streets, no token or bribe would be enough for Jeb to enlist his aid. I sighed. "With your permission, I'd like to take a look around."

Jeb shrugged, turning away from the dead woman, his interest gone. "It's about time you started to make yourself useful again. See Gareth on your way out. He's got a list of every murder since Bas-solas we haven't been able to solve."

I left the quarters of the city watch and came out into dusk. Bolt took one look at the sky and commandeered one of the watch to take care of the woman's body. I knew better than to argue the point. Since Bas-solas, my guard's one nonnegotiable point was being out after dark.

Pounding at my door scattered my thoughts like water on a hot skillet. Before I could lift my gaze from the ficheall board, where I had just started a game with my guard, Bolt had left his seat and drawn. A second knock, followed by the sound of Toria's panic-stricken voice, brought a throwing dagger into each of my hands. I nodded to Bolt, who opened the door but kept his foot wedged against it just in case.

For once, the gaze Toria directed at me lacked the suspicion or resentment it usually wore. "Pellin's been attacked." She disappeared from the doorway quickly enough to seem gifted, leaving Bolt and me to run after her and her guard.

We followed her around the corner and wedged our way through a small crowd of healers at the door of Pellin's quarters. One of the women at the door wore the embroidered sigil of an apothecary. I swallowed against my worst fear and followed Bolt as he pushed his way through the mass, shoving and scattering bodies without apology or comment.

Inside, three men were being examined by healers in Merum red and the drab brown of Servants. Pellin and an adolescent lay stretched on the large table, tended by a single healer, and though their color could have served for linen, they were conscious.

Allta was another matter. A swarm of healers surrounded him, preventing me from seeing the extent of his injuries, but more than once I heard someone asking for pressure, and there were enough needles and thread in evidence to weave a tapestry.

Bronwyn stood at Pellin's head, scolding him, her face set against eventualities she didn't want to contemplate.

"Give over, Bronwyn," Pellin said. "If I were going to die I would have brought someone in." He cut his eyes to Bolt and gave his head a small shake. "Check on Allta and Rundor."

Bolt nodded and withdrew.

In the last war, I'd learned about all the ways men and women deal with fear in the midst of fighting. Most of them resembled some version of Bronwyn, who fought against its debility, or Toria, who channeled it into fire. Oddly, it was those like Toria who ended up dead, so caught in the rage of the moment they couldn't safeguard themselves.

"Toria Deel." Either she didn't hear me or tried to ignore me. "Toria," I said a bit louder. Her head snapped up at the absence of her last name, and I held up both hands. "My apologies. I needed your attention." I pointed at the door. "There are no children here, and the door is open."

Her eyes widened, and she snapped her fingers. "Elory, bar the door and send some of those hangers-on in the hallway for a pair of acolytes." She gave me an expressionless nod.

"The boy's going to have a nice scar, but he'll be up and about in a week," Bolt said, as he returned to stand by Pellin's side. "The dagger didn't hit anything vital."

Pellin nodded. "That's well. I still owe the Chief of Servants some recompense, but less than if he died." He bit his lower lip. "Allta?"

Bolt shrugged. "The healers have stopped the worst of the bleeding, but he left a trail of blood a blind man could follow. The healer from the Servants gives him one chance out of two, the Merum a bit less."

Pellin nodded and sighed in relief. "That's well."

I gaped. "What's well about it?"

Before I could say any more, Bronwyn leaned over to whisper in my ear. "They do not understand the depth of his gift. He can survive more grievous wounds than another man, and he will heal more quickly as well." Allta's soft snores seemed to confirm Bronwyn's reasoning.

We waited until the healers had finished their embroidery and bound Allta's wounds with oil cloth infused with goldenseal and comfrey. They left, supporting Rundor's weight between them, and we helped Pellin to a sitting position. Toria locked the door, and Elory remained in the hallway, flanked by Merum guards and four acolytes.

Bronwyn waited, face composed, until the door closed, then wheeled on the Eldest. "What stupidity compelled you to remain outside the cathedral after dark—and why, in the name of all that's holy, did you stay with Allta during the attack?" Her voice rose in pitch and volume until Pellin winced. "Do you not know who you are?"

"Give over, Bronwyn," Pellin said. "We had the boy with us."

"In the dark!" Bronwyn's voice cracked under the strain. "Why didn't you stay with the Pueri until dawn?"

"I didn't expect an attack," Pellin said, "and even if I had, I would have tried to return. As for why I didn't run, Rundor took the dagger meant for me. Allta was otherwise occupied and I wasn't strong enough to carry him back to the cathedral. After I set him down, I stayed on the ground, throwing dirt and sand until Allta knew where to strike."

"Clever," Bolt said. "He couldn't see the assassin, but he could see the sand bouncing off of him."

Pellin nodded. "It was a close thing, even so."

Toria nodded, but Bronwyn didn't appear ready to surrender her anger. I'd seen this reaction before as well. Some people hated the feeling of being scared even more than the cause. "You put the Vigil in jeopardy. Let me be clear, Eldest—I will not take the mantle. I will submit to the next in line."

Toria's eyes widened at that.

"What was so important that you had to return to the Merum cathedral tonight?" I asked.

Pellin took turns looking at the three of us who shared his burden. "I've made a grave mistake. I thought that a dose of uncharacteristic honesty would be the simplest, most effective way to secure the church's help in finding Laewan's gift." He shook his head. "But I scared them into unexpected cooperation. The heads of the four orders are of one mind. They've decided to bring the Vigil under their authority. Each of us will be assigned to a different order of the church."

For some reason he avoided looking at me as he said this.

Bronwyn and Toria's voices mixed in anger with Bolt's and even Balean's. Their denials and imprecations against the heads of the orders filled the room until Pellin raised his hand, calling for quiet.

I couldn't help myself. I laughed.

The rest of the Vigil looked at me as if they were certain the walls within my mind had collapsed and I'd lost myself to the senility that overtook some of the Vigil in the end. Even Bolt wore surprise on his craggy face.

I swallowed the last of my black mirth and pointed at the Eldest. "Don't you see? He means for us to run. Why else would he rush back tonight?" I caught Pellin's gaze. "First light, I take it?"

The women's stares drifted back and forth between Pellin and me. "Allta's injuries present something of a problem," Pellin said. "And somehow we need to get the Merum Archbishop to send us the rest of the apprentices from Cynestol now that Peret Volsk is unable to fulfill his duties."

Toria jerked in hurt and surprise. "Eldest, none of them are ready." Then she looked at me. I didn't have a clue why.

Bronwyn gaped at Pellin as if the man on the other end of the conversation had become strange to her. "They're children, Eldest."

"They're needed," Pellin said. "With the loss of Peret we have no apprentice at hand if one of us should fall."

For the first time since I'd become part of the Vigil I saw defiance in Bronwyn's expression. "No, Eldest. The oldest doesn't even own a score of years. You would crush them under the weight of the gift, and sending the request to Cynestol is pointless unless you mean to assign an apprentice to each of us."

Pellin's voice crackled through the air. "That is exactly what I mean to do. The dwimor pose a threat our guards can't combat, but we can prepare." His voice stilled. "Since our guards can no longer protect our safety on their own, we must each have an apprentice ready to receive our gift. Our guards can train them in the sword as we travel our separate ways."

I shook my head. By the looks Toria and Bronwyn exchanged with each other, they saw the flaw in Pellin's desperation as easily as I did. "You don't need apprentices," I said. "You need thieves, young thieves."

Toria gaped at me, but I saw a ghost of a smile flit across Bronwyn's face.

"Four of them have already proven themselves against the enemy, Eldest," I said. "And not only are they young enough to see a dwimor, they're skilled enough to fight them."

Bronwyn nodded, but Pellin spluttered at the suggestion, his expression twisted in repugnance.

"There is another advantage to using the urchins, Eldest," I said.

Pellin threw his question at me, forced and clenched like a fist. "And that would be . . . ?"

"If you use Rory, the Mark, Fess, and Lelwin and we lose one of the guards, they can accept their gift as well," I said. "During Bas-solas they were nothing short of astonishing."

"You've yet to voice your opinion, Toria Deel," Pellin said. "Are you in agreement with this insanity?"

She nodded once before she spoke. "It addresses our needs, Eldest." She paused to give me a stare that mothers taught their daughters in order to make men uncomfortable. "No one presumes it to be anything more than temporary, a precaution against the worst case."

"I've seen too many worst cases come to pass already. Aer forbid the next generation of the Vigil should be composed of beggars, larcenists, and thieves," Pellin snapped. "Or does the possibility of turning the most precious gift of Aer over to such not bother anyone besides me?"

Bronwyn jerked forward and poked her finger at Pellin's chest. "Perhaps you need to go a bit deeper into your theology, *Eldest*. Since when has a gift of Aer come to anyone who was worthy? Those *beggars and thieves* saved our lives. If their code of behavior is not so in keeping with doctrine, what would you have them do? Starve to death so that they can die clean and virtuous in the eyes of the church?" She drew breath to go on but never got the chance.

"My apologies, Lady Bronwyn," Pellin said. "You are right, of course." His tone turned rueful and amused. "As Toria Deel said, it is only a temporary precaution. Which of our prodigies do you wish to take under your wing?"

"Fess," Bronwyn said without hesitation. "He's having some, ah, difficulty adapting to life off the street, anyway."

"Ha," Pellin said. "You probably mean he's been swindling acolytes from the four orders out of their market money in his spare time."

Bronwyn shrugged. "You know as well as I do that some men aren't meant to be merchants, Eldest."

"Yes," Pellin drawled. "Obviously. Toria Deel, which of the urchins do you wish assigned to you?"

She glanced at me as she leaned forward to answer. "Since Rory is already in training to be Bolt's replacement, I think I would like to have Lelwin as my apprentice. She has a turn of mind that I find intriguing."

"Which leaves Mark to be my apprentice," Pellin said, "or *the* Mark as he likes to call himself. Wonderful. I shudder to think of the opportunities that little urchin can contrive, given access to the courts of every kingdom on the continent."

I saw Bronwyn struggle to keep the smile from her face and voice, and fail. "Think of it as your penance, Eldest, for disdaining the least of us."

The Eldest cocked his head to one side. "I hope I have the opportunity to pay it." He looked at me. "Will the urchins agree to this, Lord Dura?"

I smiled. "They will if you make it worth their while."

Pellin looked around the room, his gaze speculative. "The church will use tonight's attack to support their argument for bringing the Vigil under their direct authority."

There's a look a man gets when he's about to disobey a direct order, a hardening of the jawline and an unblinking squint to his gaze. I'd seen it a few times in the war. Pellin wore that look now. "We're going to have to leave the city before the heads of the orders think to take us prisoner. I believe Lord Dura will have a bit less freedom than the rest of us."

Toria glanced my way. "Why?"

Pellin nodded at me. "I told them nearly everything. The Archbishop suggested putting you under guard." He sighed. "The Merum are very traditional in their approach. Anything outside of their liturgical definition tends to be viewed with great suspicion, and you're about as outside the experience of the church as it's possible to get."

Something cold settled into the pit of my stomach. "If they want me dead, putting me under guard is the best way to do it, unless they intend on recruiting children to stand watch over me. If another dwimor comes, it will be like killing pigs in a cage."

"How much time do we have, Eldest?" Toria asked.

Pellin glanced toward the sleeping form of Allta, his gaze filled with possibilities. "Perhaps a bit more than we might have had otherwise. Allta's injuries are grave." He nodded. "Very grave. On any other man, they would take weeks to heal, possibly months. Yes, it will be some time before my guard is able to resume his full duties. As long as the Chief of Servants believes that I'm tied to Bunard, we rob the church's discussion of urgency."

He looked at Bronwyn and Toria. "But it's foolish for us to remain together. I want the two of you to take rooms at different inns in the upper merchants' quarter, but don't leave Bunard just yet."

Toria's brows lowered. "Eldest?"

"I'm waiting on a messenger from the southern continent," Pellin said. "I wrote to the head of the southern Vigil several months ago, requesting he send a set of scrying stones as quickly as possible. They were supposed to arrive before Bas-solas, but storms in the Western Sea delayed them."

"You knew Jorgen was corrupted?" Bronwyn asked.

Pellin shook his head. "No, but I allowed for the possibility. After he and Laewan went missing, I also sent messages to the sentinel trainers in each kingdom, telling them to move, to avoid any of their previous bases." He sighed like a man with too much weight on his chest, and I saw him finger a pocket within his cloak. "Until all of our stones are accounted for, we dare not trust using them."

"And you've already used them to trick the enemy once," I said. "It's doubtful such a ruse would work again."

Pellin nodded. "Agreed." He looked around the room. "I think we're about done for the evening."

I was the first to rise and take my leave. Bolt followed me out the door.

CHAPTER 10

Pellin waited until the door closed behind Dura and Bolt before he spoke again. "Lady Bronwyn, Lady Deel, a moment more, if you please."

Toria turned to him in surprise, and Bronwyn glanced at the door Willet Dura had just exited before she turned her gaze back to him.

"On second thought," Pellin began, "I think it would be better if we made such preparations as we can and left Bunard tonight."

"Since Lord Dura is not among our company at the moment, Eldest," Bronwyn said, "I can only conclude that you mean to leave him behind."

Pellin forced himself to respond to the words instead of the disapproval in her tone. "That is exactly what I mean to do."

"When the Chief of Servants finds us gone, Eldest, she will surely take Lord Dura into custody," Toria said.

Pellin nodded. "And if we do not leave this very night, then she will scoop all of us into her net like a school of fish who are too ignorant to scatter from the threat of capture." He sighed. "I thought to surprise the Chief with my visit, but their conversation, while masterful, held too many hints of prior preparation." He held up a hand to forestall Bronwyn's objection. "And in the unlikely event it was not rehearsed, our need for escape becomes that much more urgent. The church means to take direct control of the Vigil."

"I fail to see how running away in the middle of the night does anything more than delay the inevitable," Bronwyn said. "The heads of the orders will have our likenesses distributed to the outlying cities and villages, and sooner or later we will be in that net you spoke of, caught singly, but caught nonetheless."

"Should we not all remain here?" Toria asked. "We have a better chance of exerting our influence over the Chief of Servants if we are united. 'A cord of three strands . . .'"

Pellin shook his head. "Jorgen knows where we are. As Bolt would say, 'Better to be a moving target than a sitting one.'"

"But you're leaving him behind, Eldest, along with Lord Dura," Bronwyn pointed out.

"Lord Dura cannot aid us in what we are about to do. If his vault is a window to the evil of the Darkwater, we cannot afford to take him with us or allow him to know where we're going."

Bronwyn shook her head. "Hard duty, Eldest. I believe he would have agreed had you taken him into your confidence, instead of tricking him."

At Pellin's glare, she closed her eyes and nodded. "And what are the rest of us to do?"

He took a deep breath. They weren't going to like what he was about to suggest. If he could have, he would have waited. But the truth was they were never going to like it—no matter when he ordered it. By heaven's gate, he didn't like it himself. "I will contact the rulers of the kingdoms bordering the Darkwater. Perhaps I can barter for our freedom, convince them of the importance of our task." He put as much certainty into his expression as he could, tried to mold himself into a memory of Cesla—so sure, so certain.

It didn't work. Bronwyn's eyes widened in shock, and Toria stared at him as if the walls of his mind had given way and insanity had taken him at last.

"Are you mad?" Bronwyn finally said. "You'll start a war between the rulers and the church."

Toria's head twitched back and forth in disbelief. "Eldest, if we seek the aid of the kings and queens, we will be forcing the church to take action. By making us the prize, you're risking a war that could last for decades."

Pellin shook his head. "Not *we*—I will seek their aid. If we cannot stay free from the imprisonment the orders will enforce upon us, our world won't last a decade. The church is more concerned about safeguarding our gift than meeting the threat. I need not ask directly for the protection of the nobility, I merely need to be seen in their courts," Pellin said. He hoped to Aer it was true. "The church doesn't want war any more than the kingdoms do."

Not entirely certain of his argument, he continued. "I will begin in Owmead, in Rymark's court." It was clear that Bronwyn was not impressed with that idea either, but what else could he do—Andred was the closest capital city.

"Really?" Bronwyn asked. "King Rymark fancied himself the next emperor for years. Do you want to walk into his court and imply that you're willing to provide him access to your gift in exchange for your freedom? What will a man with that kind of ambition do?"

Pellin considered her counsel and saw the wisdom. "Your point is taken, Lady Bronwyn. I will avoid Owmead for now, travel instead to Vadras—King Boclar should be more amenable to our goals. On the way I will check in with Owmead's and Caisel's sentinel trainers.

"Toria Deel, I want you to search out the truth behind the Clast. Perhaps their disappearance after Bas-solas is nothing more than a coincidence, but I doubt it."

He returned to Bronwyn. "I want you to patrol the villages bordering the Darkwater. The enemy's defeat at Bas-solas means they must create reinforcements. To do that, they'll have to find a way to lure others into the forest. Do whatever it takes to stop them. I will ask the sentinel trainers to send you reinforcements."

"Should we not search for the gifts that have gone free?" Toria asked.

"I pray the heads of the church will find the ones who hold them."

"Ones they will surely keep hostage," Bronwyn said.

"I hope not," he said, "but the possibility cannot be discounted. Regardless, we must leave the search in their hands."

He moved against the pain of his wounds and retrieved a map from a richly polished desk drawer. "I will leave word for the scrying stones." His finger drifted along the seamed and stained parchment showing the kingdoms of the northern continent. "Let us agree to meet in four months." He pointed. "Here at the village of Edring."

"So close to Cynestol, Eldest?" Bronwyn asked.

"We should be safe enough, and we may need access to the library."

CHAPTER 11

The second month of Queen Cailin's Regency

I woke in the familiar rooms I'd occupied for months as King Laidir's reeve, checking to see if Bolt stood over me this morning, covered in sweat because he'd fought to keep me from wandering the city. Today only the sound of my breathing greeted me. Even if there had been a killing, the Chief of Servants had no intention of letting me investigate, claiming I was too valuable a resource to be risked.

And too much of a risk to run loose.

She hadn't taken kindly to me pointing out the contradiction in her arguments. I went into the anteroom and found Bolt there, seated with Rory, both of them staring at the ficheall board as if they could will the pieces to life. In the month of my imprisonment, Rory had exhibited a surprising patience for the game, an ability to concentrate for extended periods that had abandoned me.

Bolt glanced up from his contemplation of Rory's gambit. "You look like something the cook should have thrown away."

Even on the nights no one died, I still struggled to find rest. "I keep looking over my shoulder, even in my sleep, waiting for the church guards to put me in prison or a dwimor to come for me. I can't decide which would be worse."

"Dwimor," Rory said as if the statement hadn't been rhetorical. "It's always worse to have someone kill you than put you in prison."

"Sense," Bolt said. "Better the healer than the gravesman."

"Thanks, I'll commit that one to memory. You're not the one who has to talk to the Chief of Servants every other day, trying to convince her you're not evil incarnate walking the streets."

"I don't see why you're worried, yah?" Rory said. "You're still free, sort of, and maybe they've given up on dwimor after the first two failed."

I looked out the window, where the sun had already crested the mountains to the east and had begun the serious business of turning Bunard into a sweltering, humid mess of sweating humanity. "Who's 'they'? And if they're not making dwimor, what *are* they doing?"

"Jorgen," Bolt said.

"And hopefully only Jorgen," I said. "But what happened to him?"

Bolt bent his attention back to the game of ficheall. "When we catch him, I'll cut the answer out of his hide for you." He captured a piece and set it to the side of the board. I could hear Rory swearing under his breath from across the room.

"If we get the chance," I said.

Bolt shrugged. "Things could be worse."

"I hate it when people say that," I said. "It's like daring Aer to prove it."

The sound of someone pounding on the heavy wood planks with what sounded like the hilt of a sword punctuated my reply.

Between one blink and the next, daggers appeared in each of Rory's hands, and Bolt drew his sword despite the evidence of sunlight outside the window. He opened the door and stepped back, giving himself room to parry.

Jeb stood between two guards dressed in the plain brown of the Servants—though *guards* was overly generous. Servants didn't go about armed except in extreme cases that warranted self-defense. Two more flanked them a few paces back, holding Jeb's sword and dagger. The fact that Bolt could have cut through the four men with scarcely more effort than it took to draw his sword was supremely unhelpful. He seemed even more disinclined to hurt Servants than he had Merum.

The chief reeve had his hand raised, and he regarded the open door with a look of mild disappointment. Knowing Jeb, he probably wanted to put a few more dents in the oak with his knuckles. He shot a look at the men who shadowed me everywhere. "What's the matter, Dura, you force yourself on some Servant's daughter?"

Normally, Jeb would have laughed at his own jibe, but the thrust lacked his usual enthusiasm for other people's misfortune. The guards moved to accompany him into our rooms, but Jeb slammed the door. "I'll let you know if I need you," he muttered, despite the fact the guards were now on the other side of the door and couldn't hear him. He took a look at Rory, and recognition flashed across his gaze. "Can't say your choice of companions has improved overly much, boy."

Rory shrugged. "Tough times, growler, call for tough choices, yah?"

Jeb laughed. "I like this one. He's honest."

"Did you come here just to insult me, Jeb?" I asked. Fatigue and tension made my voice sharper than usual.

"What's the matter, Dura?" Jeb mocked. "Night-walking again?"

I didn't bother to answer. It wasn't my favorite subject.

As quickly as someone turning a coin over, Jeb's demeanor changed, becoming diffident, almost shy. "Actually, Dura, I came for your help. Two weeks ago there was a murder in the lower merchants' section just after dusk, a young woman, eighteen or so, pretty little thing. At least, she was before whoever killed her did some knife work on her."

I shook my head. There was no reason for Jeb to come to me on this. We were well into harvest season. The lower merchants' section would have been bulging with sellers and buyers throughout the day and a couple of hours afterward as people finished business and took to the inns and taverns. "What about the witnesses?"

Jeb chewed on his lip for a second before answering. "That's just it, Dura. There weren't any—at least not any that saw the killer, though plenty of them told me they saw the girl bolt out of the Hawker like she had death himself chasing her." His voice dropped into a raspy tone that he got when he was irritated and wanted to hit something. "A couple of the witnesses said they saw the girl bleeding as she ran out."

My stomach dropped a few inches at the same time as my blood froze. No witnesses in broad daylight. Dwimor. I had to get out of that room.

Jeb didn't miss my reaction. "Right." He glanced at Bolt. "This is your kind of mess, Dura."

"Who was she?" I asked.

"Viona Ness, a daughter of a minor noble. I wouldn't have known that except she was wearing her family ring. Got cut down in broad daylight on a busy street."

His expression darkened. "Nobody remembers seeing anything. It took me well over a week, but I found a witness—an urchin—who actually saw the killer." His shoulders inched up toward his ears and then lowered again. "But no magistrate would ever accept her testimony."

"I didn't think the urchins were talking to you."

"They're not, at least not when they're all together."

"Why would you need me, and what's wrong with her testimony?"

He darted a look at my guard, and I could see suspicion writing itself across the sharp angles of his face. "You'll understand when you see her." He jerked his head toward the door, and his face took on a look that on anyone else I would have called protective. "We can't bring your friends out there. She hates crowds, and anything more than two or three people qualifies."

I shook my head. "That's going to be a problem," I said. "I'm under the equivalent of house arrest. The Chief of Servants thinks I might be a threat."

Jeb shook his head. "Stupid."

I nodded. "I think so too."

"Not her," he growled. "You. You've got the fastest sword in Collum playing ficheall in your rooms, and you're telling me you can't leave."

I shrugged. "He has this thing about killing people he doesn't have to."

Jeb shook his head. "Who said anything about killing?" He backtracked a couple of steps and opened the door, pointing at me. "Gentlemen, as chief reeve it's my duty to inform you that Willet Dura intends to escape your oversight and go into the city."

Four guards with shoulders the size of blacksmiths' crowded into the room. Jeb gave me a wicked grin and proceeded to punch each man over the ear with his fist, the sound identical to a farmer rapping on a ripe melon. The men collapsed to the floor as if their bones had turned to water.

"There," Jeb smiled at me. "Problem solved. If we hurry, we can be out and back before they wake up."

"Are you insane?" I gaped. "Do you know what the Chief of Servants is going to do to me when she finds out I've escaped? I'll end up behind bars in the Merum cathedral."

I might as well have been talking to the unconscious guards for all the effect my words had.

"The damage is done, Dura," Jeb said. "You can sit and wait for them to wake up and try to convince them you stayed here the whole time, or you can use the opportunity to find out what's going on."

I turned to Bolt for support, but he'd already risen from his chair, leaving his game to move past me. "'If you've got no retreat, you might as well charge.'"

I shook my head. "That's not really one of your best."

He shrugged. "It's all I could think of."

We made our way to the lower merchants' quarter at a brisk walk. I didn't fancy riding out on horseback and making myself that much easier to spot. I took a moment to savor my freedom, taking in the smell of food from the marketplace, aromas that never drifted into the enforced hospitality of the tor, but every few minutes I checked over my shoulder for pursuit.

"Relax, Dura," Jeb said. "Even if they wake up and find you missing, they won't know where you've gone."

I nodded. "And that, more than anything else, is likely to set their teeth on edge."

We crossed over the bridge from the upper merchants' section of the city into the sprawl of the marketplace. Hawkers vied for our attention, and wagons and carts competed for space as farmers and teamsters loaded or unloaded goods. Rory ranged out ahead of us, gazing into each of the shadows between buildings that leaned on each other for support like drunks.

"Before Bas-solas, it wouldn't have taken me more than a couple of minutes to find an urchin," he said. He cast a glance at Bolt and then me. "The bargain took about three-quarters of us off the streets." He pointed. "This way."

We took a right-hand turn into an alley cast in gloom from the lean of buildings overhead. I recognized it as one I'd made a point to avoid in the past. Bits of raw sewage ran beneath our feet. When Rory pulled his daggers, Jeb and Bolt drew swords.

Twenty paces in, a shadow separated from the wall on the left and a rangy youth nearly as tall as me with red hair and a puckered scar where one of his eyes should have been stepped toward Rory, his hands not quite visible at his sides.

"You bring growlers into the poor quarter to finish the last of us, Rory?"

Rory shook his head. "They aren't what they look like, Clubber. No one's trying to finish off the urchins, yah? We need to see Bounder."

I'd seen older versions of Clubber before, cutpurses who made their living knocking people unconscious. Most of the time, their victims woke up after a couple of hours with a lump on their head and their purse missing. A few times the strike went hard and the watch was called in to investigate the death. That's when Jeb's fists came in handy.

Clubber was old enough and big enough that he wouldn't be with the urchins much longer. He didn't have a good end waiting for him.

When Clubber didn't bother to move, Rory stepped forward, moving within reach of the taller boy's arms, but I didn't have any fear of Clubber doing any harm. If he tried to put one of his knockers upside Rory's head, Bolt's apprentice would turn him inside out before he could count to one. But that would scuttle any chance of getting to Jeb's witness.

Clubber must have sensed something in Rory he didn't want to see. He jerked his head in acquiescence and turned to lead the way to a building that looked a little more stable than the rest. We descended down a set of stone steps on the verge of rocking loose from their setting and into a large cellar that might have been used to store roots or even wine a couple of centuries ago.

A few urchins, nothing like the number before Bas-solas, slept in gloom alleviated by a pair of candles. Bounder stood waiting for us, his face anything but welcoming at the sight of Jeb.

"I need to see the girl again," Jeb said.

Bounder's smile could have frozen water. "I don't know what trick you pulled to get her to talk to you, growler, but information has a price, and you didn't pay it."

This much I knew by heart from my dealings with Rory and Ilroy before him. "I'll pay it," I said.

Bounder laughed at me. "Well now, it's going to cost you double, eh? Once for yourself and once for the growler there."

I nodded. At that point I would have paid all the coin I had to get to Jeb's witness. "Agreed."

Bounder must have realized his mistake because his smile turned sick at the thought of the money he'd left in my purse. I needed his aid, but more importantly, I needed his goodwill. "I'll pay you up front, Bounder, and if I find the information useful, I'll throw in another half crown on top, but I don't have a lot of time to waste here."

He turned toward the exit. "We've got her in the lower merchants' section today, just off the market street. We have to keep moving her. She keeps wandering into the shops and inns. The owners don't mind her on the street, but they don't want her begging inside." He shook his head. "If you can call it that."

We retraced our steps back out into the open air, and fifteen minutes later we stood in front of a girl who couldn't have been more than six or seven. Something reached into my chest and stopped my heart at the sight of her.

I turned to Bounder, who shrugged. "We've never gotten a name out of her. One of the urchins called her Lytling and the name kind of stuck."

The name meant *unimportant*. I couldn't argue the interpretation, but my estimation of Bounder slipped a couple of notches. He would never be the leader Rory had been. "Disgusting," I muttered softly, but Bounder heard me anyway.

"It's not like she understands. She's never answered to that or anything else."

Lytling sat huddled on the market street, curled into a ball passersby wouldn't notice unless they tripped over her. Dried sweat had plastered her blond hair against her skull, and her green eyes darted, her unfocused gaze landing on objects, animals, or people without finding purchase. Dirt and holes marred the simple linen shift she wore, and new cuts and old scars laced the soles of her bare feet. I'd never seen a child so utterly bereft of humanity.

Her blank gaze shifted from Bounder to survey the rest of us, sliding away as though we possessed all the animation of the buildings in the background—but when it landed on Jeb, the little girl stood. Without acknowledging she'd seen him, she rose and walked on her skinny legs to where he stood in the back of our group, staring at the ground as she tugged on his cloak.

In that instant, the barest moment it took for the chief reeve to bend down and lift the girl in his arms, I saw something blaze forth in Jeb's face that was too bright to look at. When she nestled, squirming, into the crook of his arm, I hoped for a moment that she might speak, but she never blinked or gave any other sign of awareness.

"Greetings, little one," he rumbled.

"This is your witness?" I asked.

He nodded. "I told you no magistrate would hear her testimony. She doesn't speak."

I wondered if the strain of two wars, being chief reeve, and the slaughter of Bas-solas had done something to him. A lot of the veterans heard voices when they came back from the war. Sometimes they were able to ignore them until they faded, but sometimes the voices wore them down, growing louder until that's all they heard. "What did you hear, Jeb?"

He must have caught something in my tone. "I'm not crazy, Dura. I have two witnesses who saw her being led away from the scene of the noblewoman's murder just after it happened. She saw who did it."

I shook my head. I'd dealt with any number of broken children and even more adults in a similar condition. Even Myle, Gael's alchemist, as lucid as he was, would be difficult to question, and anything he told me would have to be confirmed. Lytling had retreated so far into herself, communication was impossible. I shrugged and started to peel the gloves from my hands, trying to make the motion as casual and inconspicuous as possible.

Bolt caught the movement and leaned over to whisper in my ear. "Don't bother. It's been tried before. Children of trauma don't store their memories the way normal people do. You won't be able to piece anything together."

"Is it dangerous?" I whispered back.

"No, but it's disorienting for a while. Trust me."

Hopeless or not, I needed to see into the child's mind, but she recoiled from me when I took a step in her direction, and that settled the matter. I put my gloves back on. I straightened and turned back to Jeb. "I'm not saying she didn't see it, Jeb, but how is she going to tell us about it if she won't speak?"

A look usually reserved for proud parents dawned in Jeb's eyes.

"Watch." He set Lytling on the ground and knelt, crouching, so that his head was on a level with hers. Reaching into his cloak, he pulled out two sheets of folded parchment and an artist's charcoal stick. Speaking softly so that his voice sounded like the buzz of a giant bee, he put one sheet and the stick in the girl's hands. "Little one, can you show me the person who died?"

She didn't acknowledge Jeb in any way a normal person would, eschewing even the usual nod of the head, but after a moment she backed the parchment with the piece of wood and began a series of sweeping strokes across it in a steady hand.

Jeb straightened. "It took me a while to find the right questions—a whole week, actually. This will take a while."

I checked the area for Servants and soldiers. "I hope we have it."

Minutes passed as we stood just off the market street waiting for Jeb's witness to finish her drawing. Twice I tried to sneak a peek at her parchment, but each time she would huddle over her work, blocking me.

"You're only slowing her down, Dura," Jeb said. "Be patient."

After perhaps half an hour, she lifted the charcoal stick and held the parchment out to Jeb without looking at him. Jeb took it in his scarred hand, his movement as slow and gentle as any I'd ever seen. "Thank you, little one."

The figure he showed me depicted a young woman, probably in her late teens, on the ground, her limbs splayed with her dying effort as she tried to crawl away from her own pool of blood. Lytling had shaded the eyes with the charcoal stick and I instinctively knew they had been a rich green, but they wore the horrified expression I'd seen in the war, the look of men or women who knew they were heartbeats from their last breath. Gaping cuts had sliced through the clothes, showing pale skin through the holes in the fabric. A long slice had parted the soft flesh of her throat and a trickle of blood collected into a small pool beneath on the ground. Everything from the cut of her clothes to her hair had been rendered in detail fine enough for me to recognize her if I saw her on the street.

"That's exactly what I saw, Dura, even down to the cut of her hair," Jeb said.

I nodded toward the girl by Jeb's feet. "All right, she was there. How does that help us?"

Jeb knelt again as he gave Lytling the second sheet of parchment. "Little one, will you draw the person with the knife for me? The one who cut the girl?"

She paused, and I saw her eyes darting before she started drawing, her unfocused gaze appearing to stare through her makeshift canvas instead of at it. I settled myself to wait, but in half the time it took to produce the first drawing, Lytling finished, holding the second sheet out to Jeb.

"She did this for me before, Dura, but I thought you'd need to see it done," he said, his gaze darting to Bolt then back again. "Viona was a noble's daughter, but the castellan is out of his depth. I think this is more the kind of thing you deal with now."

He held the sheet out for me. The likeness on the drawing wasn't anybody I recognized, the face and hair such that he wouldn't stand out in any kingdom of the north. But instead of drawing the entire figure, as she'd done with the victim, Lytling had sketched the barest outline of the man's torso and left everything inside blank.

And the eyes were completely colorless, devoid of any shading at all.

I handed the drawing to Bolt. "Anyone you recognize?"

He shook his head. "No."

CHAPTER 12

When we turned to leave, Lytling dropped her stick and clutched Jeb's leg, her face still blank as the parchment she'd been given, but tremors ran up and down her arms. He snatched her up and held her close, murmuring comforts into her ear in his raspy voice.

Twice I saw him try to disengage, but each time Lytling clung to him until he relented. I would have laughed if I hadn't been afraid of crying when I opened my mouth. The toughest man in Collum had just been completely and utterly conquered by a six-year-old orphan.

"I promise I'll come back," Jeb whispered into her hair. He reached up to pull one of her arms free of his neck. "I always come back."

Lytling dove headfirst into his chest, as if she could become part of him, the charcoal stick and parchment falling to the ground.

"Why not take her with you?" Rory said.

Jeb looked at the thief, his expression filled with too many emotions to sort out, but he threw his answer at me, as if I'd laid a penance on him. "What kind of home would that be, Dura? Living with the chief reeve, a scarred soldier with a rasp for a voice?"

Rory's question must have strengthened some resolve within him. In a single fluid motion, Jeb pulled her loose and set Lytling on the ground where she stood with her empty arms and vacant stare.

"Let's go, Dura," Jeb growled in time to the pops of his knuckles. "We've got a killer to catch. Reeve's work is no place for a child."

He turned away and headed back up the street, his back rigid against our condemnations or his own. Bounder took Lytling by the hand and led her back to her spot on the street, her begging bowl by her side. Before we left, Bolt put a silver half crown in it, but his motions didn't look normal. Not quick or smooth or gifted, the way they usually looked. They looked brittle. I had no idea what memories of his son, Robin, must be going through his head. I didn't want to know.

Bounder pocketed the coin and shook his head at Bolt's dangerous expression. "She doesn't really bring anything in." He shrugged. "Whatever ends up in the bowl is gone by the time we come back for her."

We caught up to Jeb a few seconds later, his long strides eating up the distance as if he couldn't wait to get away, the sharp profile of his face set toward the keep like the rudder of a boat. "What kind of life would that be, eh, Dura?"

I assumed the question was rhetorical, but after another six strides Jeb turned and caught my arm in a grip that I'd feel the next day and thrust his hatchetlike face down toward mine. "*Kreppa!* I asked you a question. What kind of life would that be for her?"

I pulled my arm away. "Not much, Jeb."

He gaped at me as if I'd punched him in the gut, but I didn't stop there.

"What do you want me to say, Jeb? That you'd be the world's best father? That a reeve with a voice like a saw going through wood could raise a little girl and love her like a real parent?" I swallowed against what I was about to say. "Do you really think someone who uses their fists for a living could be gentle and kind enough to love a child who's so broken she can't even speak?" I yelled.

I saw Jeb clench his fist as my words punched a hole through the armor he wore and into his heart. Any second now, he'd take a swing that would put me down for half a day, if I was lucky. I took a breath, met the passion of his gaze with as much as I could muster of my own. "Well, *I* think so," I said.

He spun away from me almost before I caught a glimpse of his face crumpling. We watched him sprint back to Lytling, his strides eating the ground, and scoop her into his arms. Even from here we could hear him uttering comforts to Lytling as he stroked her hair.

He didn't make any move to rejoin us, and the clock in my head told me I'd run out of time. By now the men Jeb had put down would have woken up from their involuntary slumber and notified the Chief of Servants of my absence. She'd have me hauled in and questioned. Of course, she'd probably offer me a cup of tea before she made my life unpleasant. Servants were unfailingly polite, no matter the circumstances.

What I needed was my independence, and being escorted everywhere by a quartet of brown-robed guards who didn't even bother to carry swords didn't qualify. If I could get to Custos, I might be able to give the Chief of Servants enough information to convince her to let me keep my freedom.

We moved off the main thoroughfare and came back to the Merum cathedral using the side streets, sneaking into the library before the swarm of brown-robed priests across the way could see us. "Maybe we'll get lucky and they won't think to look here," I said.

"You don't strike me as the lucky type," Bolt said.

Given the events of the last few months, I was hardly in a position to argue.

"We have a saying in the urchins," Rory said. "'A man makes his luck.'"

"I like that one," Bolt said. "We'll probably have occasion to use it again." He regarded his student with something more than just his usual professional interest. "Do you have any more sayings?"

Rory shrugged. "Lots."

"Great," I muttered, "he's one of you."

I found Custos in a back corner thumbing through a book of children's rhymes, turning each page after the merest glance. To the casual observer he would appear to be idly scanning the contents, perhaps searching for some verse or limerick of interest. Only I and a few other people would know that Custos was actually memorizing the book.

A thought struck me. "Why are you doing that?"

He raised his head, noting our presence for the first time. "It's a volume I've never seen before. Lady Bronwyn sent it along with a note asking me to commit it to memory, but she didn't tell me anything else about it." Custos gave me an owlish blink to accompany a smirk. "I think it's from their secret library we spoke of earlier." He closed the book, his thumb marking a spot a little over halfway through. "She's asked to delve all my memories of children's rhymes when next we meet." He ducked his head, embarrassed. "She and Pellin have thought up all sorts of uses for me it seems."

I laughed. "No one is surprised but you, my friend. I need your help."

Custos reached into his faded red cassock and pulled out a hawk feather to mark his place before lifting his head to smile at me as though I'd given him a packet of figs. "Do we need someplace more private?"

I shook my head. "No, not yet anyway. Is the name Viona Ness anywhere within that head of yours?"

He stilled for a moment while I imagined him reading through thousands of works with the speed of lightning. After a moment he nodded, and his gaze stilled. "She's not in the library." He shrugged. "At least not anymore." He pointed to the east section. I didn't see him over there very often. "Viona Ness is the daughter of a minor noble allied with the Deor family."

"Was," I said. "She was killed two weeks ago." I searched my memories of court for them. It didn't take long. My recollections of the throne room were few in number and dominated by the efforts of the Orlan family and its allies to humiliate or kill me. "Tell me about them. Jeb says she wasn't on the rolls of the gifted, but I thought you might know better."

Custos shrugged. "They have a gift of craft that, like all the other families, runs pure, but what makes them noteworthy is their talent set. It's an unusual combination for a family within the city."

Something in my gut told me Custos was about to tell me something important. "What is it?"

"Nature," he said. "By all accounts the talent is so strong in the Ness family, the church has tested them to see if there's something else going on there."

"Gift stealing?" Bolt asked.

Custos shook his head. "Though they never came right out and said it, that was the implication, but there's no gift that mimics the talent they have with animals."

I thought of Timmis, Braben's stable hand, with his gnarled hands and missing teeth and how horses he'd never seen before sidled up to him like a long-lost friend. It was touching to see, but more than a few stables boasted men or women with the same talent. "Why would that put the church on guard?"

He grimaced. "In the Ness family, it behaves more like a gift. When everyone in the family showed that talent for animals, the priests started to wonder."

"And what did they find?"

Custos shrugged. "Nothing, my boy. Of course, the fact that the Ness family income is modest in comparison to most of the nobility didn't hurt."

Rory nodded. "Why steal a gift if you can't make money with it?"

"Fair enough," I said. "The church found something unusual and came up with nothing other than the fact that the Ness family is unusual." I shot a look at Bolt. "Do you know why Viona was taken out of the library records?"

Bolt shook his head as Custos answered for him. "She withdrew from the family about two years ago and left the city."

For a moment, I wondered if I'd heard him right. "She surrendered her nobility? Was she firstborn?"

Custos shook his head. "No, fourth in fact." He gestured at the library. "She's not even here anymore," he said, his voice subdued.

I understood. To Custos, it was if Viona had more than died. Even her life had been erased. "Think, Custos. Is there anything else that might make Viona important?"

He could have answered me right away, but out of deference, I saw him run through all the information in his head again. "No. I'm sorry, Willet."

I gave his shoulder a squeeze. "Don't be. You gave us more than we had before. I think we'll wander down into the city and see if we can find out why she wanted her name erased from the family record."

We left the library and made our way down to the nobles' section of the city. It didn't take long to find the Ness family's estate. They lived in a fairly modest granite house on the edge of the river. I was more familiar with the Alainn family, so it surprised me that there were no armed guards at the gate, only a servant who appeared as thoroughly bored as only a man on sentry duty can. When we walked up, he looked at us as if we'd lost our way and had approached him by accident.

"Good morrow," I greeted. "Would it be possible to see Lord Ness?"

He stared at me before nodding, his face slack with surprise. "Possibly. May I tell him the purpose of your visit?"

Jeb or a member of the castellan's staff had surely been here before, to tell Lord Ness of the death of his daughter. I doubted he wanted to hear about it again, but I couldn't think of any other plausible reason to visit him. "Just tell him Lord Willet Dura is here to see him."

The servant's eyes widened as he looked at me, and I could have sworn a smile had begun to surprise the rest of his face as he nodded and turned away.

"Just once, I'd like to just have someone nod and say 'Certainly, Lord Dura, I'll just be a moment,' or something like that."

Bolt laughed. "You're famous. You should be happy," he said in an overly bright tone of voice. "You've given that man something unusual to talk about for days on end. He can tell all the other servants that he got to meet the king's hired killer, the man who killed Count Orlan and lived to tell about it."

"You're mocking me."

My guard nodded. "Yes. Yes, I am."

The servant returned and led us through a long hallway filled with paintings of animals depicted in colors no one would find in nature. Instead of turning into the audience room, the servant took us through another long hallway leading toward the back of the Ness estate, glancing over his shoulder every fourth or fifth step, as if he expected me to fly into a rage and start killing everyone present.

It was a relief when we came out onto a wide shaded patio at the back of the house on a slope overlooking a branch of the river. In a broad green space a young man worked with a heavy-chested dog with short tan fur, taking the animal through a series of exercises and praising the animal at frequent intervals. Lord Ness came forward to greet us without extending his hand, his arms tucked behind his back. I bowed, taking care to incline my head more than custom and respect demanded. "Lord Ness, greetings. I'm Willet Dura."

Ness acknowledged me with a curt nod. "I know who you are." His gaze slid from me to Rory and then settled on Bolt. "No one ever bothered to ask the right question."

I followed his gaze, which weighed and sifted my guard with all the feeling of a baker weighing out flour. "Lord Ness?"

Ness looked at me in irritation. "I rarely go to court, Lord Dura. I find the company of the animals I train here and on my holdings to be preferable to that of nobles. You can see the fruits of our effort in the best-trained animals in the kingdom." He pointed toward the young man and the dog, giving me a tight-lipped smile that didn't even come close to touching his eyes. "I try not to traffic in snakes."

I smiled. "We have that in common, then."

He didn't appreciate the comparison. "Lord Dura, let me be blunt. You went to court, offended a powerful family and your guard there dispatched his man, his gifted man, after a single touch of blades." He shook his head. "And no one thought to ask how a minor lord, the most minor lord, comes to hold the leash of such a guard. As I said, I don't go to court often, but I was there the night you assassinated Lord Baine." He shrugged, his face emotionless. "And now you're here to talk to me about my dead daughter."

This wasn't going well. "I can assure you, Lord Ness, I had no intention of challenging or being challenged that night. As for my guard, he is a friend, not an animal I hold on a leash."

His eyes narrowed. "And there you betray yourself, Lord Dura. The leash is for guidance, and animals can be far better friends than people."

He turned away from me for a moment, but not before I heard him murmur to himself. "Even family."

In front of him the young man whistled a short command and the dog returned to its kennel with unquestioning obedience.

"That's why I'm here," I told him. "I would like to find those who killed your daughter and bring them to justice."

Ness shook his head. "The castellan's men are investigating, Lord Dura. Your services are not required."

I waited for him to say more, but he continued to gaze at his garden and the dogs cavorting in it. I needed a way to break through the wall he'd put up. "The castellan's men do not know the city as well as I, Lord Ness. Would it not be better to have as many men trying to catch Viona's killer as possible?"

His shoulders dropped from their defensive position, but he shook his head in denial. "Lord Dura, my daughter left to pursue some unknown ambition over my objection and without my permission. I hadn't seen her in two years before they brought me to look at her body." I could see the muscles in his throat working to push the words out. "If you catch the killer, will that bring her back to life, back to her home?"

"No."

"Then what is the point, Lord Dura, of your investigation?"

I hid my hands behind my back and stripped off my gloves, tucking them into my belt as I answered. "The dead demand justice from the living. You don't wear the grief of a man who's lost his daughter."

His eyes narrowed at me as if I'd slapped him. "Is it justice for my daughter you are after, Lord Dura, or is she just a plank in a scaffold, a clue that might reveal some bigger threat?"

I had nothing to say, and Ness pulled air into his lungs as if breathing had somehow become difficult. "Viona died two years ago when she disappeared."

If I'd been a horse, my ears would have swiveled forward. "She disappeared?"

He turned away from me. "Very well, Lord Dura. If it will hasten your departure, I will tell you everything I know. After Viona disappeared, the castellan's men scoured the city for her for weeks. No trace of her was ever found. She'd vanished like the summer mist. Then a week ago, the castellan shows up with her family ring, the blood hardly dried, to tell me she's dead, cut down here in the city, probably by one of those pickpockets you have a reputation for favoring." He cut his eyes to Rory, who somehow exuded *urchin* despite the clothes and haircut Bolt had given him.

Ness looked at me. "Now, will you go?"

I nodded, but asked him another question anyway. "Lord Ness, before Viona disappeared, did she seem different to you?"

He eyes narrowed into a withering expression. "You've never had a daughter, Lord Dura. Viona was sixteen. She became different every morning and sometimes at noon and sunset as well."

I shifted my feet in preparation to leave. "Did you plan to give your gift to her?"

Ness shook his head. "No, Kyran is firstborn, but Viona's birth and talent would have served her almost as well. Animals loved her."

He turned away from me, and I motioned to Bolt and Rory for us to leave, but after a couple of steps, I asked my last question, the most important. "Lord Ness, I can see you loved your daughter, and I believe she loved you, but why would she visit the ministry to erase her name from the family record before she disappeared?"

He looked at me as if I'd become strange, shaking his head. Then he got angry. "She would never do such a thing, and those who did should be taken to account." His voice quivered. "Viona was bright and shining and precious to all of us."

I had what I needed and turned to leave. After a half dozen steps, Ness called out to me. "Lord Dura, do you care about my daughter?"

"I'm the queen's reeve, Lord Ness." I let a trickle of the anger I felt at Viona's death seep into my voice at last. "My job is to bring justice."

He pointed at me. "Then find the man who tried to erase the memory of her."

CHAPTER 13

I already knew where to look, but I didn't say anything until we were back on the street that ran in front of Ness's estate. I moved to one side of the entrance and waited.

"The browns could come any moment and scoop you up, you know," Bolt said.

I shook my head. "I doubt they're going to be looking overly hard in the nobles' quarter," I said. "Especially not on a side street tucked against the river. We have some time."

"For what?"

I saw what I'd been waiting for just before I heard the footsteps. "Him," I said.

The young dog trainer turned the corner at the far end of the estate, then started as he saw us waiting for him, his steps faltering. I watched him approach, his head swiveling to check behind him as he came.

"Kyran," I said.

His eyes widened, but he shook his head. "Leary. Third born."

Away from his dog, Leary looked more like a frightened boy than a trainer. I didn't want whatever doubts or fears he obviously harbored about speaking to us to overwhelm him, so I came to the point. "Tell us about Viona, Leary. Tell us about your sister."

He jerked, hearing some insult to his father I hadn't spoken. "Everything Da told you was the truth." He shrugged. "But Da didn't know Viona as well as he could have, or maybe he did, but didn't want to see it."

"What do you mean?"

He shrugged. "We love being around animals. It's a family trait, but from the time Viona was a girl it was more than that. People made her uncomfortable." He looked away at nothing. "Even family."

"Except for you," I said.

Leary nodded. "It got worse as she got older." He sighed. "And then she grew up and things got really bad."

I nodded. "She became beautiful."

"Worse than that," Leary said. "She was stunning. It wasn't as though father made her go to court very often. He doesn't care for it himself, but there are expectations even for the minor nobility to appear at least twice a year."

I didn't have to imagine the effect Viona would have had on court. The appetites of many of the younger nobles were well known. "Did someone ask for her hand?"

Leary jerked and then bobbed his head. "She refused to go back."

I knew what was coming next. I'd heard the same story any number of times, though the names changed and the characters dressed a little differently. "Viona and your father argued."

But Leary shook his head. "No. Father told her she didn't have to marry." He lifted his eyes from the ground to look at me. "But he couldn't keep the suitors away. Then she came to me one night and said she was going away, said she'd found animals to train and wouldn't have to deal with court or the men there. That was two years ago."

He fell silent, but I had the impression there might be more. "And you never saw her again?" I prompted.

Leary didn't even come close to looking at me, and I had to strain to hear him as he talked to his feet. "I did. Every few months I'd get a note to meet her in the lower merchants' quarter. She always wore peasant clothing and she'd cropped her hair."

I saw tears hit the ground beside Leary's feet and his chest heaved.

"But she was more beautiful than ever," he said. "She glowed." Leary shook his head. "You won't tell Father, will you?" he asked. "That I would see her?"

With an internal wince, I pulled the glove from my right hand. The walls in my mind felt secure, steady after weeks of rest from delving people, but there were so many doors. So many.

Leary still had his head bowed, waiting for some assurance from me. Quite possibly, he'd told me everything, but I couldn't take the chance. Some facet of his memories might tell me why a dwimor had elected to kill the last-born daughter of an insignificant noble. He had his hands in his pockets.

"No, lad," I said reaching for the skin exposed on the back of his neck. "I won't tell."

My vision fell through his hair and into his mind, my gift burrowing a tunnel into his head. I lost my sense of self on the way, until I became Leary, a contented young man who loved animals—the third son of Lord Ness, my father and a minor noble who loved me as well.

I sifted backward through memories, their colors and scents and sounds calling to me until I came to the surprise of Viona's parting. I needed to see this in order.

"Where are you going?" I asked as I stood in the entrance to her room. A crescent moon hung outside the window over the mountains to the west. Dawn was still two hours away.

She jerked, looking at me, and for a moment her eyes darted to the bed where she'd piled sturdy, functional clothes and boots, the garb she wore as she trained or tended our animals. "I'm leaving, El," she said, using the pet name she'd used for me since she'd first learned to talk. "I've got to get away from here."

I shook my head. "But why? Father says you don't have to take a husband. You don't even have to see the suitors, if you don't wish."

She shook her head, and the wealth of deep chestnut hair cascaded around her shoulders like a waterfall, framing her flawless features. "I'd still have to make the required appearances at court."

"So?" I asked.

She turned to face me, her sea-green eyes that completed her perfection resolute. "So how long before someone makes father an offer he can't refuse, El? We're one of the poorest families at court. Nearly every merchant in the upper quarter has income greater than ours. Laidir is a good man, but he doesn't have a passion for dogs like some of the other rulers. Without his patronage, the other houses have little need to curry favor with us."

"But you can't just run away."

She looked away from me, stuffing clothes into a canvas bag, but not before I saw something in her countenance catch fire and burn like a torch. "I'm not. I've been offered a job, El—training animals. And I've seen them. They're *beautiful*."

"All animals are beautiful, Viona," I said. "Stay with us."

But she crammed the last of her clothes into the bag. For a moment she paused, looking at the family ring on her hand, a heavy wolf's head worked into silver. She buried her head into my shoulder before she drew my head down for a kiss she planted on my cheek. Then she slung the bag over her shoulder and left.

I sifted through memories, reading each note asking to meet me in the poor quarter, but other than those simple requests there was nothing that might indicate where she'd been or what she might be doing.

I came to Leary's last memory. I crossed over the bridge of the Rinwash leading into the lower merchants' quarter, searching for Viona. She would be waiting for me at the Hawker, the broad, low-roofed inn where most of the merchants met after they'd closed their meat or vegetable stands for the evening.

Then I heard screams that cut their way through my heart. I ran, yelling and cursing at the people in my way toward the sound as the cries became weaker. I turned the corner into chaos as people ran in every direction, fleeing mindlessly like animals running from a fire. A knot of men and women huddled around a figure slumped on the flagstones. I pushed my way through, following a trail of blood, and saw Viona's body, her eyes glassy and staring through me. Rents in her clothing showed the indignity her killer had visited upon her, deep slash wounds visible on her neck, back, and arms. The world turned to fire in my mind.

I pulled out of the delve, struggling to separate my thoughts from Leary's last memory of his sister. More than anything, I wanted to shove those images away, lock them behind a door within my mind, and never let them out again, but something in Leary's last meeting with his sister struck me wrong and I was going to have to keep the memory in front of me until I could figure out just what. Worse, I had to find Jeb.

"We're going to find the people who killed your sister," I said, speaking to Leary's bowed head. "She will get justice." I couldn't tell if he heard me or not. He didn't nod or speak before he turned and ran back toward the alley that bordered his father's estate.

"What did you see?" Bolt asked me.

I sighed. "Mostly what you'd expect, but there was something strange about her death I can't put my finger on." In my mind I stared at the image of her dead body, the knife cuts in her clothing showing pale, perfect skin sliced open by the assassin's hatred.

Shaking my head, I set my face toward the tor that loomed over the nobles' section to the northwest. "We have to get to the tor. I need to talk to Jeb."

Rory shook his head at me. "You can't go back there, yah? The browns are going to be looking for you all over the place."

"The boy's right," Bolt said. "If you show your face, they'll surround you with so many Merum guards you'll be lucky to see the light of day again."

I checked the sun. We had perhaps two hours of light left. "Then we'll have to wait until dark so that we can sneak past the cathedrals."

"I don't fancy trying to fight a dwimor in the dark," Bolt said. "Pellin and Allta were lucky in the extreme to survive that attack."

I flexed my hand, sliding the thin leather glove back over the exposed skin. "I have to delve Lytling. Her mind holds the key."

Bolt shook his head at me. "It's pointless, Willet. She doesn't see the world normally anymore. You won't be able to make sense of what you see in there."

I nodded. "So you told me before, but I have to try."

Chapter 14

We stopped at an inn on the merchants' side of the Rinwash, where I sat drinking overpriced ale and thinking. I assumed Bolt and Rory were doing the same thing. They sat across from me in silence.

"She might not be important," Rory said at last. "Sometimes one of the urchins sees something they're not supposed to: a bigger crime, one trader swindling another. Once, during the winter, I slipped into a merchant's to steal a few bolts of wool. He'd just bought it from a seller from Gylden. Only the man wasn't from Gylden, and he wasn't a merchant. The first layer was wool all right, but beneath that it was cheap burlap." He leaned back and lifted his tankard. "The fake merchant would have killed me for what I'd seen."

I thought about that. I'd witnessed as much in my own experiences as reeve, and it seemed possible in this case, but in my gut it didn't fit. "She ran out of the Hawker. I don't know much about them, but the dwimor seem to ignore everyone except the one they're supposed to kill."

Bolt nodded. "She was young enough to see it. So, she saw it and tried to flee and it ran after her. If it was there for someone else—"

"The dwimor would have let her go," I finished.

"If they behave the same as they did before," Bolt said.

I tried not to think about all the ways they might be even more dangerous now that they were coming from whatever evil had gotten loose of the Darkwater. We drank our ale in silence, watching the door for church guards of any color as we waited for dusk.

The sun was just a sliver of orange-tinted crimson when we came around to the tor on the eastern side. I didn't use that entrance much since it wasn't located near my quarters or the guardroom where the reeves worked. My hope was that the church guards would be too busy keeping an eye on my usual haunts to cover the unfamiliar places as well.

We stood in the shadows of the trees and checked the alley that ran west to east toward the tor on the north side of the cathedrals. A mix of church guards wearing red, brown, blue, or white patrolled the walkway.

"Why can't anything ever be easy?" I asked no one in particular.

Bolt and Rory both took this as an opportunity to quote some adage from their past that I found to be totally useless. "All right," I said, looking at Rory. "The tor's guarded. How do I get in?"

Rory smiled. "Join the urchins and after a few years of training you'll be able to go anywhere you like." He looked me up and down. "Provided you lose a few spans of height and about a hundred pounds."

"Nice. What about you?" I asked Bolt. "There's at least one dwimor out there somewhere, and we don't even know who they're hunting. Are you ready to use your sword yet?"

He shook his head. "The proscription against fighting the church isn't some guideline. It's carved in stone and with good reason. The Vigil has maintained its autonomy for centuries by voluntarily submitting to the oversight of the church, limited though it may be. If they start to view us as the enemy, that's finished."

"Take a boat to the north side," Rory said.

I looked at Bolt. "That might work. The docks are right up against that side of the tor. Nobody uses that entrance except the supply masters."

Bolt strode forward from the shadows with his head down and checked the branch of the Rinwash that separated the cathedrals and the tor from the nobles' section. He paused to chuck a few rocks into the water before he returned. "No barges are headed this way and the water sounds pretty deep here."

I nodded. "It would be. It's the last moat in the city."

Rory shrugged. "We'll just have to swim."

"He can't swim," Bolt said, pointing at me.

Rory stared at me as if I'd disappointed him somehow. "What kind of a man spends his life on the river and never learns how to swim?"

I tried to stare down Bolt's laughter and failed. "You two were made for each other," I grumbled.

After he and Rory collected themselves, I saw Bolt shrug. "Well, it's time for your first lesson. Let's go."

"No." Memories of my last foray into the river were still too vivid. I'd almost drowned.

Bolt pointed. "This is our best chance. The flood wall will hide us from the patrolling guards, and we've only got to cover a few hundred yards."

"It might as well be a few hundred miles," I said. "Is there something about 'I can't swim' that I need to explain? Even if the guards don't see me, they'll hear me screaming for help."

"I'll show you," Rory said. "There's a stroke the urchins use to move quietly across the branches of the river. It's not fast, but it's easy to learn and it's quiet."

"'And a child shall lead the way,'" Bolt quoted the liturgy.

I shook my head. "Yes, that's perfect. Now you're borrowing your proverbs from Toria Deel."

In the end there was nothing for it but to swim. We found a spot out of sight of the patrolling guards, who obviously didn't think I'd be mad enough to try to escape by swimming, and slipped into the river.

"Stay close to the wall," Rory said. "The current won't be as strong there. Now, move like this." I watched as he stretched out both arms over his head and brought them down to his side as he executed a relaxed frog-kick, gliding forward through the water for a couple of yards. He didn't stroke again until he had almost come to a stop.

I swallowed my fear and tried to copy him.

"Don't fight it, Willet," Rory said. "The water will help you if you let it. Try to keep a lot of air in your lungs. It will help you float."

Stretching out my arms, I kicked again.

An hour later, with my shoulders burning and my lungs set to explode, we clung to the stone pier that butted up against the north face of the tor. Men worked by torchlight to unload a barge, moving like phantoms in the flickering shadows. Smells of pelts and seasoned wood drifted over us.

With my arms shaking, I pulled myself out of the water and stood at the end of the quay, wheezing like a horse. The men at the entrance wore the king's livery and vigilance, but there were no church guards with them. I heard the sound of swords being drawn while two more approached with their pikes leveled.

"Leave your hands at your side and approach to be recognized," one of the guards commanded.

"That's the crux of the problem," Bolt muttered.

We stepped forward into the orange circle of light cast by their torches, and I saw the guards' faces open in recognition.

"Lord Dura, what were you doing in the river?"

There didn't seem to be anything to gain by being less than forthright. "I'm trying to run down a killer."

All four guards snapped to attention, their eyes darting. Laidir's death had left a stain on the guards' reputation that would be a long time in cleansing.

"I don't think the killer is in the tor," I said, "and I don't think he's after the queen, but I needed a way to get into the tor without being seen." My tunic made sucking sounds as I pulled it away from my skin. "Thus the river."

They didn't move.

"Gentlemen," I said, "I'd really like to be about my business as reeve."

The guards nodded and pivoted out of the way.

We entered into the cavernous space of the tor's storerooms, where men moved by flickering torchlight to organize the latest load of supplies to come downriver. Rory looked around in shock. "Is this place ever left unguarded?"

I shook my head. "No, and there are no windows or other entrances from the outside."

"Pity," he said. "I could have kept the urchins fed and clothed with no trouble at all, and no one would have ever missed it."

I shook my head as we walked past a small mountain of wool. "I wouldn't count on that last part. The chamberlain doesn't draw much attention to himself, but very little gets past him."

"We don't have much time," Bolt said. "As soon as they change the guard at the dock, word of your presence in the tor is going to spread. Coming out of the river like some mythical sea monster is a good way to engrave yourself on the guards' memory. It's not like they get the chance to talk about their work very often."

Rory looked at me. "Why didn't you tell them to keep quiet?"

"Because that would have been the surest way to draw even more attention to us."

"'Three men can keep a secret if two of them are dead,'" Bolt quoted.

"I like that one," Rory nodded appreciatively. "We have one like it in the urchins: 'Share a secret, lose a life.'"

Bolt winced. "Is everyone in the urchins as grim as you are?"

Rory nodded. "Pretty much."

I picked up my pace until we were almost jogging. "If we hurry, we can be here and gone before any of the church guards know about it."

Jeb's quarters were two levels over the main guardroom. We ascended a narrow flight of stone stairs and made our way to the south end of the tor. Rory went first as we left the relatively deserted north end and encountered pockets of servants and minor functionaries whose tasks kept the kingdom running.

Twice Rory flashed a hand signal behind his back sending Bolt and me scurrying into hiding. By the time we reached Jeb's apartments, my heart had resumed the furious pounding from the river.

I balled my fist and knocked softly, hoping. "He might still be in the guardroom," I said. "We can't go there."

I waited a moment and knocked again, then started backward reaching for my dagger as the door flew open. Jeb's chin preceded the rest of his face out the door, but when he saw me, some of the tension went out of him. "Dura. Should have known it was you. What do you want?"

"I need to see Lytling."

His brows dropped low enough to turn his eyes into slits. "That's not her name, Dura. Don't call her that again. Her name is Aellyn." I couldn't see both hands, but I heard a popping noise.

"Is she here, Jeb?"

He nodded. "She's sleeping, and you're not going to wake her."

I looked at Bolt. There wasn't going to be any way for me to do this without arousing Jeb's suspicion. He liked to use his knuckles to get the truth, but he wasn't stupid. My guard's shoulders lifted and dropped back into place.

"That's fine, Jeb. I don't need to."

He still looked on the verge of refusing, but I could see the beginning of curiosity undermining his defiance. "If you hurt her, Dura, I'm going to be angry."

His quarters weren't large, only two small rooms, but anyone who didn't know better would have thought Aellyn had been living here her whole life. Jeb led us through the chaos of his belongings in the outer room to what should have been his bedroom. Here, everything had been ordered, but a rag doll, its middle creased by repeated hugs, lay at the foot of the bed, and a set of clothes in Aellyn's size had been laid out across the straight-backed chair.

The girl herself slept curled beneath a blanket, dwarfed by a bed built for an oversized reeve, but I could see the impression of Jeb's head on the pillow next to hers and in the wrinkles of the blanket.

"How long did it take you to rock her to sleep?" I asked.

Jeb sighed. "A couple of hours. Every time I tried to get up, she plastered herself to me like a leech." His face darkened to a shade usually reserved for thunderclouds. "If I ever catch up to the people responsible for this, I'm going to turn their name into a curse."

I pulled my glove off and moved around to kneel at the far side of the bed, careful not to bump it.

"Dura," Jeb warned.

I nodded, looking at him and hoping that he wouldn't ask me to explain. "I need to see what she knows, Jeb." By the door, Bolt sighed, but I couldn't tell if it was resignation or disapproval. I reached out to rest my fingers on Aellyn's arm, and Jeb's room disappeared.

Shocks and jolts hit me, body blows from an invisible fist as her memories poured into me. But there was no flow, no coherence or chronology to the images I saw. Aellyn's memories didn't connect to each other in strands but surrounded me, instead, as a cloud. If I hadn't been so desperate, I would have broken the delve. Aer, help me, I pushed myself forward into her broken mind.

Flashes of light like bursts of solas powder hit me as I fell and became the memories I saw. A man stooped to place a coin in my begging bowl, then turned to leave. An instant later I saw him approaching from the opposite direction, his eyes looking at my torn shift. Without transition he appeared fifty paces away, his back to me, not looking back.

I sat in the urchins' hovel at night, my eyes closed, eating to fill the hole in my stomach, images flashing past. Bounder led me away from the merchants' quarter. Men approached me where I sat at the edge of the street. I was walking alone away from a farmhouse, my steps too small to take me anywhere.

A tall man with a rough voice lifted me into his arms.

A tall man with a rough voice held me close, protecting me.

A tall man with a rough voice folded my hand inside his.

A tall man with a rough voice put a charcoal stick in my hand.

A tall man with a rough voice lifted me into his arms.

A tall man . . .

In the part of my mind that wasn't the broken child, I pushed again, trying to make sense of Aellyn's memories, but the threads were broken. They didn't lead anywhere—they floated in her mind like twigs suspended in water, neither leading forward to any future nor back to any past. Without a way to move in time, I had no way of finding the memories I needed. I floated up within the drift of memories, dots of color, not threads, that flowed past.

Then I saw it, a scroll at the bottom of Aellyn's mind, dark and heavy, an anchor that dragged on her soul. It wasn't the black obsidian color of those that had been to the Darkwater, but a charcoal gray instead. I dove back into the debris of her past, struggling to get to it, but the multi-colored flashes of remembrance buffeted me, turned me around, taking my sense of direction, and I lost my way.

I came out of the delve to see Aellyn on the bed in front of me, curled and sleeping, her fist close to her mouth as if she might start sucking her thumb at any moment. Bolt and Rory looked at me in expectation. Jeb's gaze shifted back and forth between us, failing to find purchase.

"What happened to you in there, Dura?" I heard Jeb growl. "What happened in the Darkwater Forest?"

"I wish I knew."

In her sleep, Aellyn turned toward the sound of Jeb's voice and her arms reached for him. A moment later her eyes opened and her fingers curled and opened again. I waited for the growl of Jeb's anger, but it never came. Instead he sat on the edge of the bed and scooped Aellyn up from her blankets and held her close. She nestled into his arms, and I watched as her gaze darted back and forth around the room, making more of those disjointed threads of memory that led nowhere.

"What did you see?" Bolt asked. Evidently he'd decided to abandon his pretense.

"Nothing useful," I said. "Her memories are fractured into such small pieces of time that she doesn't have a sense of her past." I didn't mention the scroll. I didn't want to know what had been done to her to make her create a vault, and at the moment I had no way of getting to those memories to see if aiding her was even possible.

I kept my distance from Jeb and the girl, thinking. "I wish Pellin or Bronwyn hadn't left," I said to Bolt. "I'm out of my depth."

"They often felt the same way."

I sighed. "That's disappointing. I'd like to think this gets easier over time. She had to pull those memories together to draw those two pictures." I gestured toward Aellyn. "There isn't any way she could have done it if her memories are fractured *all* the time."

I had assumed Jeb was focused on Aellyn, wasn't listening to me, but a moment later he lifted his head and sought my gaze. "Do you want to tell me what you're talking about, Dura, or are we going to play the guessing game?"

I pointed to the girl, balled up and snuggled against his chest. "Aellyn doesn't remember things the way normal people do. For most of us, our memories are like threads in a river, leading back to previous events. Pick a spot on a thread and follow it one way and you go back in time; go the other way and you go forward." I shook my head. "Aellyn's memories don't connect to past or future. They're disjointed images that have no context."

Jeb's face darkened. He'd seen enough of what the war had done to a lot of men and women who only looked like they'd survived it. He knew the cause of Aellyn's fractured mind. "Do you know who caused it?"

I shook my head. If he ever caught the people responsible, he'd beat them to death. Under the circumstances, I might watch and applaud. Wispy tendrils of an idea coalesced into awareness. "No, but I think there might be a way to get to the information I need, and it might help her piece her mind back together."

I looked around the room and spotted a charcoal stick, parchment, and drawing board on a small round table next to a broad chest. I brought them over and put them in Jeb's free hand. "Ask her to draw again, the same thing you asked before, but I need to see Viona before she died. I need to know what she looked like as she ran from the Hawker."

His eyes narrowed, but a moment later he accepted the implements and set Aellyn upright on his lap. "Little one, would you draw the woman who died again? Would you show me the way she looked as she ran out of the inn?"

She accepted the tools that allowed her to speak to the present, her eyes darting. For an instant, she reminded me of Custos searching the contents of an entire library kept within his mind. I stored that impression away. Perhaps there might be a way to heal Aellyn someday.

The charcoal made scratching sounds on the parchment as she drew. Carefully, as though I were trying to sneak up on a grazing fawn, I inched forward until I came within reach of her bare feet. Without haste or hesitation I stretched out my hand to touch her sole.

And there was Viona, looking behind her in terror at a man no one else but Aellyn seemed to notice. The memory didn't move, but I found I could move within it, shifting through the figures as though they'd become statues. It appeared the assassin had come for Viona through the back door by the kitchen and he was in the midst of shifting to avoid bumping into patrons by the bar. His hands were empty, but his eyes held surprise.

Viona had a short dagger in one hand—blood streamed down the other one.

CHAPTER 15

I came out of the delve, leaving memories behind that were nothing more than bits of shattered glass in her mind, but before I left I looked back and saw the strand of memory she'd held, healthy and intact, extending back and forward in time. I stepped back from the bed to see Aellyn bent over her parchment, focused on re-creating the image she'd seen. Time passed, kept by the sound of charcoal strokes against the parchment. I knew what I'd seen, but it only made sense to a point. I had everything I could get from Aellyn, but I waited for her to finish.

I didn't have Pellin's, Bronwyn's, or even Toria's experience with all the facets of brokenness that walked around on two feet, but it seemed to me that there might be hope for Jeb's newfound daughter. When she finished and held the drawing out to Jeb, it showed a part of the image I'd seen within her mind, a view of Viona Ness fleeing from the Hawker, blood pouring from her hand.

But now I knew the context.

Jeb looked at me, his voice the soft rumble of a mountain as Aellyn burrowed back into the safety of his embrace. "Did you get what you needed, Dura?"

I nodded, accepting the drawing he offered. "I don't understand it yet, but I got it. Get her to the healers, Jeb. Go to the Servants. The browns did the best with those of us who made it back from the war."

He scowled, but his voice remained soft. "I don't like church people. I'll take care of her."

125

"This isn't about what you like—it's about healing her mind. The Servants are the best healers in Collum."

He shook his head. "I've seen what they do to patients like her. They'll take her off someplace quiet and fill her with potions anytime she even looks like she's upset. Away from the city." He might as well have said "*away from me.*"

I put my hand on Aellyn's shoulder. "You may have to go with her, but I won't let them take her from you."

Jeb shifted on the bed to look at Bolt. "He can do this?"

Bolt nodded. "Not all by himself, but yes."

After a moment Jeb gave me a grudging nod. "If it means keeping her, I'll leave the city. Gareth's a good man. He can be chief reeve in my stead if they need to take Aellyn someplace away from Bunard."

"And take plenty of parchment and drawing sticks with you," I added. "It's the key to piecing her memories back together."

We walked away from Jeb's quarters in the tor, my feet wandering the hallways without a destination as I tried to make sense of everything I knew. I couldn't make the pieces fit. Without warning, Bolt's hand knotted in my cloak and pulled me back into a storeroom where the three of us stood, hardly breathing, as the sound of boots grew nearer and then fainter. The scent of onions and turnips hung heavy in the air, and in the half-light from the torches in the corridor, I could see burlap bags piled close to us.

Rory snuck a glance out the door at the retreating figures. "Merum."

Bolt grunted. "The guards at the back of the tor have gone off duty. They're probably all filled with ale someplace with their tongues wagging." He looked at me. "You need to learn discretion. You can't do this if half the guards in Bunard look at you as a form of entertainment."

"Entertainment?"

He nodded. "You leave a trail of chaos a mile wide in your wake, Willet."

Rory laughed. Usually the sound of a child's laughter is joyful and comforting.

I shook my head to clear the distraction of the guards searching for me. The pieces to Viona's death were in my mind, and I needed to make them fit. For almost the past year and a half I'd developed a habit of talking through my thoughts whenever circumstances had me stumped. Longing opened a desperate hole in my chest. I wanted more than anything to do that again. "I need to see Gael."

"This isn't exactly the time for romance," Bolt said.

I shook my head. "The first time I met Gael and her sister at court, they introduced me to their 'game.' They would look at a noble or servant and with a single glance unravel their circumstances and past." The image of Viona Ness I had painted in my mind troubled me, and I couldn't understand it. "She helps me think."

"I'm sure," Bolt said. Rory's laughter didn't help. "But we may not be able to get out of this room, much less the tor."

The guards would be looking for all three of us. At least, I hoped so. I dug into my purse, pulled out a pair of silver half crowns, and handed them to Rory. "I want you to bring the first servant you find who's close to my size. If he asks—no, when he asks—for more money, tell him it's waiting for him here." I sighed. "People say servants are invisible. We're about to put that to the test. The last time I tried it, it didn't work out so well."

Rory nodded. "From what I heard, you went out of your way to throw wine on Duke Orlan." He unclasped his damp cloak and let it drop to the floor.

As we waited in the darkness of the storeroom, I sifted through the facts, rearranging them like mismatched puzzle pieces. Viona had been attacked and killed by the dwimor, her body found in the street a few dozen paces away from the Hawker. Jeb's other witnesses had seen her running away, even if they hadn't been able to see the man who killed her.

I'd hoped Aellyn's memories would explain why the dwimor had targeted a shy, introverted daughter of a minor noble, but nothing fit. Even the memory of what happened in the tavern seemed at odds with itself. Viona had her dagger out, running from the dwimor across the room.

"How did she get away?" I muttered, but my voice still sounded loud in the silence.

"Willet?" Bolt asked.

"The image in Aellyn's mind doesn't make sense," I said. "Viona was already bleeding when she ran from the tavern. The dwimor had already laid her arm open, but the image in Aellyn's mind shows Viona at the door with the dwimor on the opposite side of the room."

"Second attacker?"

I pulled up the image in my mind, moving among the figures as if I were walking among statues, but nothing about any of them indicated malice or even awareness. "No."

"The girl's mind is broken, Willet," Bolt said. "She's not a reliable witness."

I wasn't convinced. According to Jeb, his adopted daughter had a perfect ability to re-create what she'd seen. That led me to believe Aellyn's memories and drawings were the only reliable witnesses I had.

"You've never seen or heard of Viona before?" I asked. "She's not associated with the Vigil?"

"No," Bolt said. "Maybe the dwimor was there to kill someone else and killed Viona because she'd spotted him."

I nodded. "Perhaps, but the dwimor that came after me didn't behave that way."

"She never had the chance," Bolt said. "Nobody saw her before she had a couple of marks on you, and Rory had a knife in her before she knew he was there."

There was a soft knock on the door before it opened to reveal Rory standing in the dim light of the hallway with a servant in a red vest over a white linen shirt, his eyes darting, searching for discovery.

"Do you know who I am?" I asked him.

He bobbed his head. "Aye, you're Lord Dura." His gaze drifted across mine at intervals before returning to the floor.

"Perfect," I said. "What's your name?"

His head dipped again. "Stefan, my lord."

"I need to switch clothes with you, Stefan," I told him. "I've got some people looking for me in the tor, and I'd rather not be found just yet."

He shifted his feet, clearly uncomfortable with the idea. "Um, you're not planning on killing anybody, are you, my lord? I could get in powerful trouble for helping you kill someone you're not supposed to."

I shook my head. "I just want to leave the tor, Stefan. I don't even want to draw my sword, which is why I want to switch clothes with you. If you look at it that way, you're helping to keep the peace."

He gave me another of those fleeting glances and spared a second one for Rory. "He said you'd pay another pair of half crowns if I agreed."

I pulled the coins from my purse and put my hand in the light so

Stefan could see them. "And he was correct, but I should apologize in advance. My clothes are a bit damp."

His eyes were still on the money I held as he unlaced his vest. "No need to worry about that, Lord Dura."

I waited until we'd finished our swap before turning to Bolt. "You and Rory take Stefan back toward the north pier. Avoid detection as long as you can. I'm going to try and walk out the front gate. I'm hoping they won't expect that."

"What do you want us to do when they see us?" Bolt asked.

I thought about that. "Run, but don't make them mad enough to pull weapons on you."

Rory snuck a glance into the hallway. "It's clear."

"Luck," I said. "You know where to meet me if you get clear."

I picked up a sack of onions, threw it over my shoulder to help obscure my face, and started for the front of the tor with my head down. Church guards in red passed me by, their gaze sliding from me after seeing my uniform. No one asked to see my face or whether I'd seen the men they were looking for. Menials weren't seen and didn't see.

When I was too far away from the storerooms to maintain the fiction of bringing supplies to the kitchens, I left the bag of onions in a closet and made my way toward the front gate. I felt exposed without them and my fingers twitched as I searched the hallways for something, anything to carry to help me escape notice.

But for once, luck seemed to be with me. The men on guard duty seemed more interested in looking for their relief than searching for three sodden river rats. I waited just inside the main entrance, busying myself with pretend tasks that kept my face hidden, until a squad of guards approached.

When the conversation turned from three people the church wanted to find to the destination for the night's libations, I walked around the knot of guards with my head down and kept going until I caught up with a rickety farmer's cart waiting to head back into the city. Bending low, I crawled underneath to clutch the splintered frame, my arms straining, until it crossed the bridge into the nobles' quarter.

Aer must have decided to bless me, because the wagon stayed intact and when it slowed to take a turn in the road, I dropped and rolled to safety. Ten minutes later, I stood at the gate to Gael's estate—or more accurately, the estate of her uncle—my livery dirty and torn.

The guards at the gate, a pair of furloughed soldiers named Aran and Gilliam, knew me, knew I still retained, however temporarily, my title. They barred me from entering anyway. Gael's uncle had tried to scuttle our engagement, seeking the wealth that would come from aligning his niece's gift to a profitable house from one of the southern kingdoms.

He hadn't appreciated Gael's response to his attempt to marry her off to Rupert, Kera's grieving suitor. Gael had done the unthinkable; she'd passed her gift to her uncle, destroying his hold over her. He'd never imagined she would voluntarily surrender her status to marry an ungifted, barely titled man like me.

"Please inform Lady Gael that Lord Dura requests an immediate audience, if it suits her," I said. I stood on the street as if I belonged there and tried to avoid looking guilty.

The guards exchanged a glance before turning their attention back to me. Aran licked his lips before ducking his head to speak. "Begging your pardon, Lord Dura. We've been forbidden to allow you onto the count's estate."

I heard the other guard mutter something under his breath with the count's name attached that didn't sound very complimentary. "Are you forbidden to take messages to Lady Gael from me?"

Both guards nodded, but it was Gilliam who spoke. "Aye, Lord Dura. Our esteemed employer has made it clear that he hasn't hired us to think but to follow his orders to the letter." He paused to give me a direct look. "To the letter, Lord Dura. No more. No less."

I smiled and gave Gilliam a bow of thanks. "I knew men like that, officers, in the last war who wouldn't trust their subordinates to think. They usually ended up face down in the mud. So, the count's orders forbid you from taking a message to Lady Gael."

They both nodded. "That is so," Gilliam said.

"Are you forbidden from taking a message from me to any of the count's servants?" I asked.

Gilliam shook his head. "No. Evidently the count can't conceive of a situation where a noble would desire to engage a servant in conversation."

"Well," I smiled. "Would you please tell Marya—" I stopped. Marya

130

had died during Bas-solas. "Would you please tell Padraig that I am at the gate and wish to speak with him?"

Aran nodded, winking. "Is the message of a private nature, my lord?"

I shook my head. "Not overly so. I see no reason to disturb the count, but if other members of his household are present, I don't mind if they overhear my request."

Aran and I exchanged bows, and he turned to make his way up the cobblestone path that lead through the manicured gardens to the count's estate. I spent the next ten minutes trying to ignore the itchy feeling between my shoulder blades whenever I heard hooves or boots on the street behind me. The church guards searching for me in the tor would figure out I wasn't there any minute now, if they hadn't already.

She came around the side of the house at a run but stopped short of falling into my arms, her eyes darting briefly to Aran and Gilliam. "Padraig sends his regrets, Lord Dura, but he is unable to meet with you at present." Her mouth turned up at the corners and her voice dipped into a register that made my knees wobble. "Is there any service I can render in his stead?"

I'd forgotten how much I'd missed just being in her presence, reveling in her challenging banter. She always won these little contests of wits. Gael was, after all, smarter and cleverer than I, but no man savored his defeats more than I did.

I let my gaze drift down to her feet and back up again. "Not *precisely* in his stead," I answered. With a sigh, I brought myself back to the duty that brought me here. "But I do need your help."

"Come, Lord Dura." She nodded. "The storehouse will give us privacy."

CHAPTER 16

We kept close to the walls of the mansion to avoid being inadvertently spotted by her uncle and came into the storehouse where Gael and Kera had practiced their craft, designing clothing that made the pair of women the center of attention each time they came to court. Then Kera had died, killed by a wasting disease.

The door to Gael's office had barely closed when she came into my arms, her lips finding mine, and I felt a knowledge of her that had nothing to do with my gift, had no part of delving. Her kiss communicated love and fear and tension as her hands crept up my back to lock in my hair. When we parted we stood forehead to forehead, not speaking.

"Why did you take so long to come to me, Willet?"

I shook my head, unwilling to break contact just yet. "The Vigil has been brought under the direct control of the four orders of the church. The Chief of Servants decided the best way to safeguard my gift was to keep me under house arrest. Jeb bought me a temporary furlough by virtue of his fists. Any moment now they're going to find me and put me someplace more secure."

She stiffened, a prelude to the blaze of temper that would surely come next. "So you save the city from disaster at Bas-solas and this is your reward."

I lifted my hand to tap my temple. "They don't know what to do about my vault. Maybe if I were in their boots I would do the same thing."

"Don't make excuses for them, Willet," she said, clipping her words. "You would do no such thing. Why did Jeb come to you?"

I took a step back so that I could bring her into focus. "There was a murder two weeks ago, the kind of thing I'm more likely to run into now than he is." A bit of the color drained from her face, but her mouth firmed and she nodded, once. "What can you tell me about Viona Ness?" I asked.

Her brows, dark and perfect like her hair, drew together. "I heard about her death, but I barely knew her. She seldom came to court, and when she did, we didn't speak. Men certainly seemed to favor her, as I recall."

"She was killed by a dwimor, an assassin that can slip through a crowded room without anyone seeing it." I shrugged. "Except for the young. It seems the older you are, the harder they are to see. The only witness to Viona's murder is a girl of six whose mind is so damaged she has to draw pictures to communicate." I took a deep breath. "Gael, you and Kera used to play your game of looking at people and working out their past. There's something troubling me about her murder, and I can't figure out what it is."

When she nodded at me to continue I told her everything I could think of. No detail was too minute or trivial to include, everything from the tiniest stroke of Aellyn's charcoal pencil drawing to the vision I'd seen in her head.

When I was done, Gael paced the room, thinking, while I waited for her to see what I couldn't. Twelve times back and forth she walked. Then she stopped, staring at the floor. "Her wounds."

"What about them?" I asked.

"Describe what you saw from the girl's picture again."

I pulled the image—put it at the front of my mind so that I could close my eyes and see it without distraction. "There are rips in Viona's clothing, and through them I can see deep knife wounds, the skin pale on either side of the cut."

"Is the blood keeping you from seeing the wound?"

I looked at each in turn. "Not so much. There's a little on the fabric of her shirt, but . . ." I stopped as I realized what I was saying and opened my eyes to see Gael looking at me.

"There's not enough blood," I said. "Not anywhere close to enough."

Gael's eyes narrowed. "The dwimor didn't mark her after the first wound."

"No," I shook my head. "He never marked her at all. In Aellyn's mind I saw both Viona and the assassin in the Hawker. Viona was already at the front door and the assassin was back by the kitchen. She held her knife in her right hand and her left was covered in blood. It's long odds to think the dwimor could have gotten lucky enough to cut just the inside of her wrist if she tried to defend herself."

"Viona killed herself," we said at the same time.

I pushed myself off the table I'd been sitting on and walked the length of the room as the pieces of Viona's death finally slipped into place. "Viona was sitting in the Hawker waiting for her brother. She saw the dwimor enter the tavern by the kitchen and something in the way he moved, the way people looked through him as if he wasn't there, alerted her. Instead of fighting or screaming, she opens her wrist."

"But why run?" Gael asked. "At that point, she was dead already."

I could only think of one reason. "To keep herself from talking." I brought my fist up to my head. "I'm a fool. I kept returning to the thought that Viona was incidentally killed by the dwimor because he realized she could see him—but the truth was more basic. The assassin was after her—and, what's more, she realized it." I looked at Gael as a knot of steel began to form in my chest.

"But how would she have known what to look for?"

"Pellin would have warned the sentinel trainers of his concerns—maybe not about dwimors specifically, but to be careful, on the lookout. They would have been watching for trouble." I took three steps and brought Gael into my embrace, my hands coming up to cup the deliciously soft skin of her face. "You are a treasure." Even as I said it, a twinge in my gut rebuked me. *And how can you take her to wife if you're practically immortal?*

I turned toward the door. "I have to find Bolt. I need to know what's going on with the sentinels."

Gael looked at me, tension in her brows for a second before she came to the same conclusion I had.

"That *has* to be it," I said. "What other use would the Vigil have for a girl who loved animals so much that she preferred them to people?"

We strode through the storehouse back toward the front of the estate and stepped through the door and into the night . . .

Right into a pool of torchlight. Eight fully armed men wearing

Merum red ringed us, the man on the far right wearing a captain's badge. Behind them stood the four Servants Jeb had put down. One of them had a bandage circling his head. And farther back—out of reach, of course—stood Gael's uncle, Count Alainn.

"There you are, Captain. As promised," the count said before turning his attention to Gael and me. "It seems you've run afoul of the church, Lord Dura." He smiled. "I think perhaps a petition to the queen might be in order." Shadows from the torches danced on his face. "Surely Her Majesty will see the necessity of nullifying your betrothal now."

I took the opportunity to remind myself that not all evil comes from the Darkwater Forest. Perhaps not even most of it.

"I can see how a person with your lack of character and limited perspective might see it that way, Uncle," Gael spat.

"Do you know why I keep you around, niece?" the count said with a smile.

"Because even with the gift you have no talent for business or negotiation?"

The count's vindictive smile soured. "I keep you here so that I can watch your dream of being married to him die. Your presence is suffered precisely because I know that Lord Dura will wind up dead or imprisoned and then the queen will be forced to endorse the marriage for you that I had arranged for Kera."

I looked at the men around me. I would have laughed except the count was almost certainly correct on all counts. Especially the part about prison.

"Captain," he said, "I would take it as a courtesy if you could take him off of my estate now."

I squeezed Gael's hand. "Find Bolt or Rory. Tell them everything."

The walk back toward the tor took longer than I expected, or maybe time only seemed to slow because my mind kept racing to find a way out of my predicament. Viona's death carried implications for the Vigil that I needed to explain to Pellin, Bronwyn, or even Toria, but I had no way of knowing where they were or how to communicate with them even if I did. The scrying stones were useless, undermined by betrayal, and I had no hope of getting to messenger birds while the church had me under lock and key.

We trooped through Criers' Square and turned left at the far end, away from the House of Servants and toward the Merum cathedral. The captain didn't speak to me at all as we entered and descended toward the lightless halls just above the river. Torchlight flickered on the rough granite that formed the cells. A brother passed us going the other way, holding an empty tray, and unbidden, a memory arose in my mind.

The prisons weren't empty.

I spotted hands sticking out through the bars of one of the heavy doors a bit farther on, and when the captain stopped short, I continued for a few steps until I stood before the door opposite. With a shrug, the captain came forward to meet me, opened the door to the empty cell, and waved me in. I waited within the growing darkness until the footsteps receded beyond hearing. When all sound and light had faded, the prisoner in the cell across from mine deigned to break the silence.

"Welcome, Lord Dura, to my home."

I knew the voice even if I couldn't see his face.

Peret Volsk.

CHAPTER 17

Peret Volsk, one-time apprentice to the Vigil and next in line to receive the gift of domere from Elwin, had betrayed the ideals he'd claimed to serve. All done in the name of love, of course. He'd allowed attacks on Bolt and me that nearly resulted in our deaths in the hope I would be forced to pass the gift on to him and he could live for centuries in perfect communion with Toria Deel.

Without scrying stones or colm messenger birds, I had no access to the other members of the Vigil. That I should find myself imprisoned across from the only other man or woman on the northern continent who might be able to shed light on the meaning behind Viona's murder was a miracle. I pulled a prayer of thanks from my memories as a postulant in the priesthood and fumbled my way through its unfamiliar cadences. I was more accustomed to saying the antidon for the dead.

"What, no imprecations?" Volsk asked. "No threats of retribution? No earthy soldier's curses, Lord Dura?"

"I need your help," I said.

Weak laughter somehow made it the distance from his cell to mine. "At the risk of sounding condescending, I have to point out that I'm not exactly in a position to render aid. Else, I would have freed myself long ago."

"It's not freedom I want."

"Strange how my viewpoint of time has altered since my imprisonment," Volsk said as if he hadn't heard me.

"I said it's not freedom I want."

"Once I believed that only centuries with Toria would suffice." He sighed. "Now I know better, all thanks to a prison cell four paces wide and three paces deep."

"Will you help me?" I asked, half expecting him to talk through my question as before.

"Why should I?" The tone of his voice sharpened from its blunt abstraction into focus.

"Why shouldn't you?" I retorted. "What else is there for you to do except recount the measure of your cell?"

He surprised me with a soft chuckle. "In truth, four by three paces is a forced approximation. I've been considering different possibilities of measuring it more accurately. Would it surprise you to learn that my teachers in Cynestol considered me talented in the mathematicum? For example, I could verify its rectangular shape by measuring the diagonals. Of course, that would have to be done quickly while they're bringing me my meals. But once that had been accomplished, it would be possible to use the sum of squares technique to refine—"

"They're going to come for me," I said. "I don't know when, but it's a certainty. If you don't help me, I won't help you."

He muttered something under his breath I couldn't quite make out. "What do you have to offer? You can't override Pellin's order of imprisonment, and even if you could, you can't soften Toria's heart." He chuckled again, but there were hints of hopelessness in the sound.

I'd heard that same self-mocking laughter from men about to be sent to the gallows.

"The central problem in measuring my cell," he went on, "is that I have no way of calibrating my instruments. Is my foot actually a foot? I can't remember."

"She's dead," I said. Self-accusation shot across my chest as I said it. I knew the conclusion Volsk would jump to, counted on it.

His laughter cut off. "You lie."

"I do not lie," I shot back. "Do I have your attention, Peret Volsk? The Vigil has been brought under the direct authority of the four orders of the church."

I heard a sharp intake of breath. "Fools. Don't they know the Vigil's task is impossible without autonomy? The four orders will descend into squabbling, maybe even warfare."

I ignored the invitation to rail against the shortsightedness of the church. "Pellin and the rest are gone. I don't know where, and I have no means of contacting them." I took a breath. "We believe Jorgen is corrupted and he killed a girl. I need to know if I'm right about the reason."

I waited for Volsk to respond, half expecting him to hypothesize about the length of his toes and whether or not those five wiggling members could be trusted to help him measure his cell.

"Who?" he asked softly.

"Viona Ness."

I heard him cursing, and as much as I hated the confirmation of just how bad circumstances had gotten, my heart lifted at the sound. His anger told me Volsk still held at least some hint of conviction and purpose within him. "How did she die?"

I told him everything, backtracking to tell him about Bas-solas and the dwimor attacks and even my conversation with Gael that led me to believe Viona had killed herself to keep from being taken.

"I knew Elwin," Volsk said. "He would never have taken part in creating monsters like the dwimor."

"Pellin said he did," I said. "But it hardly matters."

"It matters to me," Volsk said. "Elwin was like a father."

"Fine," I said. "But you knew him at the end of his life, a very long life. What old man have you ever known who didn't carry his share of some regret? Tell me about Viona."

"It's bad, Dura. She was the newest apprentice to help keep and train the sentinels here in Collum."

I hated being right. Once, just once, I wanted to be right about something that worked in my favor. "Why didn't Bolt tell me? Why would he lie?"

"I don't particularly favor your guard, but lying is constitutionally impossible for him. He probably didn't know. Pellin called him out of retirement to guard you, after Faran had chosen Viona to succeed him. It was a detail Pellin probably didn't communicate." He paused for a pair of heartbeats before he went on. "Viona knew what the dwimor was after. She died to keep the assassin from finding out where Pellin had moved the sentinel camp. Without the hounds, access to the Darkwater is unguarded. Anyone could blunder in there and back out again the next day."

"They don't have a reason," I said.

Volsk laughed. "Whatever has gotten free of the forest has been a step ahead of the Vigil all along. Even defeating it at Bas-solas did little more than slow it down for a time. There will be a reason. They'll make one."

"How can I find the sentinel camp?" I asked.

I hadn't bothered to lower my voice, but for a while I wasn't sure Volsk had heard me.

"I know where it is," Volsk said. Then he fell silent again.

Ah. "You can't imagine I have enough power or influence to free you," I said. "In case you hadn't noticed, I seem to be in the same predicament."

"No. You're not. You're being safeguarded, not guarded."

I laughed. "It looks the same to me, or maybe I'm just letting the fact that we're talking to each other through prison bars in total darkness unduly influence me."

"You said yourself that the Chief of Servants would be sending for you," Volsk said. "You don't have much time, Dura. You may not have any."

"How so?"

Volsk chuckled. "Why was Viona in Bunard?"

"She wanted to see her brother," I said.

"Granted," Volsk agreed. "But that's not the reason she was in Bunard. My guess is Faran sent her to get their winter supplies. Sooner or later he will deduce something happened and will have to send his other apprentice, Afyred."

And the dwimor was still out there in Bunard somewhere. "How old is Afyred?" I asked.

"A couple years shy of forty."

Afyred would never see the dwimor following him. The assassin would probably just hitch a ride on the back of the supply wagon and let Faran's apprentice take him back.

"You have to help me," I said.

Volsk grunted some noncommittal sound. "Actually, I don't."

"If the Darkwater wins, you'll die here."

He laughed at me. "Even if you win, I'll die here. I really would like to avoid that. I find that being imprisoned has revealed to me a whole host of priorities that I'd previously taken for granted."

"You can't imagine that she still loves you," I said.

His staccato laughter could have peeled bark off a tree. "You'd be surprised what a man imprisoned in the dark can imagine. I've discovered that I had many loves in addition to the one I bore for Toria—sunshine on my face, wind against my skin, a varied diet. I may have lost the most important one, but freedom would restore a whole host of others."

"I don't care for the idea of freeing a man who might conspire for my death," I said. "Again."

"Our cares are beside the point," Volsk said. "You have no way of communicating with the rest of the Vigil, and your time is limited—if you even have any. I can guide you to the sentinel training ground and then we can be rid of each other. I have something you need—you have something I need. Mutual desires have been the basis of satisfactory trade for thousands of years."

In the distance I heard the swing of a door and the pad of booted feet, a lot of booted feet. A moment later, I could see soft lighting in the hallway growing as it came closer.

"That's my offer, Dura."

I could have been watching a familiar play, the actors major and minor all rehearsed in their predictable parts, right down to the guard unlocking the door and the semicircle of sword points trained on me while I blinked against the light. "Him too." I pointed.

The captain of the guard, a short, brusque fellow with dark hair and pale skin, shook his head. "Our orders are to bring you to the Chief of Servants. Just you."

The windowless cells of the Merum prison kept me from being able to gauge the time with any accuracy, but it had to be past midnight. "I don't imagine the Chief of Servants is in a charitable mood at this hour," I said. To make my point I sat on the floor. "And before you get any ideas about using force on me, you might want to consider that I might be free shortly."

The captain didn't appear to be in the mood to negotiate. He pulled his dagger and shifted his grip, a prelude to hitting me in the head with the heavy pommel.

"She's going to want to hear what he has to say." I held my hands up. "You can always bring him back here if she orders it, but if you knock me out, she's going to have to wait that much longer to talk to me."

141

The captain looked at me for a moment with an expression that said he'd like to hit me anyway before he turned to the guard with the keys and jerked his head toward Volsk's cell. "Bring him."

I wouldn't have recognized the man they pulled from the shadows as friend or enemy. Volsk's beard, dark like his hair, had grown during his imprisonment, until it covered the upper part of his chest like a tattered carpet, and his eyes held the wide, unblinking aspect of a man kept in darkness for too long.

The fact that this same man had ordered the Chief of Servants around like a menial a few months before would add another layer of irony to the interview. If I hadn't felt so desperate, I would have laughed.

The Merum guards escorted us into the offices of the local Merum bishop, but there were no red-robed priests or functionaries in attendance. Even the local bishop had been excused from the proceedings. The Chief of Servants sat in a gilded chair at the head of a burnished rosewood table that could have seated a whole platoon of soldiers.

Peret Volsk and I stared across the expanse of polished wood at the shriveled old woman who held our fates in her hands. The guards withdrew, closing the door firmly behind them.

"Come, gentlemen." The Chief beckoned with one blue-veined hand. "We can hardly speak intelligibly across such a distance."

Volsk and I separated and approached from opposite sides of the table, coming within arm's reach to remain standing.

"I must confess," the Chief said to Volsk, her eyes glittering like agates, "that I find your presence here unexpected." She didn't bother to use his name.

He bowed from the waist while a smile wreathed his face. "It's good to see you as well, Brid Teorian."

She stiffened at the use of her name, continued to lock gazes with him. "Most people refer to me as Chief of Servants. I'm sure your time in the Merum cells didn't relieve you of that fact."

"Most people don't know that you're Elanian."

She looked away first. "I'm the Chief of Servants. Nationality is an accident of birth, and consideration of it is an impediment to judgment."

Volsk nodded. "I merely meant to convey my respects, Chief, by showing that you are important in and of yourself and not just for the title you carry."

She frowned. "Glib as always." With hardly a twitch, she dismissed him from her attention and skewered me with a look sharper than the point of a dagger. "You seem to be operating under a number of erroneous assumptions, Lord Dura."

I took a moment to consider how best to respond. Then I realized Volsk had already shown me—he had gone out of his way to speak first and show strength when he had none in order to communicate my position.

"I usually am. What would those false assumptions be this time?" I asked.

She stiffened at my tone but held up a single finger anyway. "First, you seem to think that obedience to the church is optional. If your position has not been communicated to you before now, allow me to do so. The Vigil serves the church." Volsk opened his mouth to speak, but the Chief silenced him with a glare. "Their autonomy has rested on ultimate obedience to the same core of ideals that the four orders share."

"I am rendering service, Chief," I said. "Unfortunately the nature of that service has required me to set aside more recent, less important strictures, a not uncommon occurrence in the annals of the church."

Her brows lifted while Volsk laughed. "He was a postulate in the Merum order. It appears that he knows a bit of church history as well. You might want to move on to your next point."

"Second," she said, holding up a second finger, her voice brittle, "you have treated your gift in a cavalier manner with wanton disregard for your place in history."

I waved my hand in dismissal. "Not so. I have used the gift according to the dictates of the situation and in accordance with the liturgy. Or do you expect me to light a candle and place it under a bucket?"

Volsk pulled out a chair and plopped into it. "May I be seated, honored Chief? My stay in prison has weakened me somewhat, and it appears that you're going to need some time to answer Lord Dura's rebuttals."

The Chief curled her two upraised fingers back into her hand before she leaned forward. "The duties of authority sometimes compel me to use levers of influence that I would normally disdain, Lord Dura." She leaned back in her richly upholstered chair, her eyes glittering bits of polished stone. "You have a friend, the chief reeve."

My stomach clenched. I gave one sharp nod.

"Though I have no doubt the ultimate responsibility rests with you," the Chief said, "I must point out that he does bear some burden for your escape." She paused to let me stew. "I understand he's just taken in an orphan. I'm not sure the company of a violent man is the best environment for a little girl."

I didn't want to hear any more. I didn't believe the Chief would follow through on the implied threat to take Jeb's little girl away, but I couldn't be certain. "It might help things move along if you could just tell me what you want, instead of threatening my friends."

Brid Teorian smiled. "I already have what I want. You, under guard, where your gift can be safeguarded and the threat that lies in your mind can be contained."

I shrugged. "Then why bother to bring me here?"

The smile stayed in place, but now it looked forced. "Because you've yet to fulfill your duties to the church, Lord Dura. As head of one of the four orders, I can hardly be expected to make informed decisions without complete information, information that you hold. Thus, your incarceration."

"And what of Queen Cailin?" I asked. "It doesn't worry you that you've taken her reeve and put him in prison?"

She shrugged her thin shoulders. "Queen Cailin is regent, not ruler. Her position is precarious enough without bringing a dispute with all four orders into the picture. I'm sure you understand why."

I nodded. The circumstances of Cailin's regency were still fostering rumors. I'd worked hard in the aftermath of Bas-solas to ensure that they remained just that. "You're asking me to provide you with information without the approval of the Eldest," I said. "That doesn't concern you?"

She shook her head. "That title is now more a matter of respect than of function. Authority over the Vigil rests with the church."

And we were back to the same impasse. Once I began taking orders from the Chief of Servants, the precedent would be established and then strengthened until the Vigil's autonomy was nothing more than an unwritten historical footnote. But I had nothing else to bargain with, and though the shriveled old lady in front of me didn't know it, circumstances had put me right in her lap.

"Very well," I said nodding. "I'm prepared to provide you some information without Pellin's approval. As an opening gesture," I added.

She smiled. "I am prepared to offer recompense in exchange for information, of course."

"I'm not interested in money, you understand."

The Chief of Servants sniffed. "Perfectly. We're speaking of more intangible rewards."

I nodded, concentrating on keeping an expression on my face as if I'd been forced to this moment. I'd discovered that sometimes you could get what you wanted in a forced negotiation by giving the other party more than they asked for.

More than they were prepared to handle.

"A pair of weeks ago, the daughter of a minor noble was killed in the lower merchants' section. She'd been missing from her household for two years." I shrugged. "At the time I was a guest under your guard, and though I knew something had happened, I didn't know the exact nature."

The Chief smiled at me. "If you're referring to your night walks, Lord Dura, you needn't be so circumspect. We've been apprised of them."

Perfect. She believed herself to be in absolute control.

I nodded. "What you may not know is the exact nature of the man who killed her."

An hour later, I finished my description of the events. The Chief of Servants looked at me, her face pale as parchment and her lips bloodless. I had to give her credit for maintaining her composure, but when she lifted an age-spotted hand to point at Peret Volsk, it shook.

"You've already told him this. His lack of reaction cannot otherwise be explained."

I nodded. "That brings us to those 'intangible rewards' you spoke of, honored Chief. I find myself in a similar position with respect to Peret Volsk. I need to find the camp where the sentinels are trained." I pointed at her chest. "And since the rest of the Vigil cannot be contacted quickly, he is the one person who can take me there."

Her mouth compressed to a thin line. "I hear accusations in your words, Lord Dura."

I shook my head. "Far from it, honored Chief. You hear responsibility. You and the other heads of the four orders took it upon yourselves to shoulder the burden for controlling the Vigil. Did you believe all such decisions would be to your liking and advantage?"

Her eyes narrowed. She would bluster and bluff, but in the end I would get exactly what I wanted, and she would be left to put the best face on it with the other heads of the church.

"Tell me what you require for your trip, Lord Dura," she said after a moment.

I bowed my respect from where I sat. Evidently, the Chief of Servants had no interest in pointless negotiation. "I need fast horses and supplies for four men, and only four men. I won't be taking Servants or Merum guards with me."

"He"—she nodded to Volsk—"of course, is one of the four, and you'll take your guard. Who else?"

"Bolt's apprentice."

"Ah." She blinked. "The young thief." She eyed me for a moment in which she appeared indecisive. "I'll give you five. I think you'll want to take your friend, the librarian."

"Why?"

"The fire in Aille that destroyed the library may not have been an accident. There were deaths involved that had nothing to do with flames or smoke."

I took a moment to consider that and what it might mean. "Who told you about Custos?"

"Lady Bronwyn. She indicated that he has some ability that the Vigil might find useful. I've spoken to the Merum bishop, and he's placed a guard on the library and alerted the Archbishop in Cynestol, but in light of your revelations, I thought you might want to take him with you."

I nodded my thanks, though I doubted Custos would feel the same. The books and scrolls of the library and the sanctum were his home. "I'm in your debt."

"I expect a full report when you return."

"Agreed," I said. If Pellin didn't like the terms I'd struck, he shouldn't have dropped me into the Chief of Servants' lap when he left. "One other thing," I said.

Her eyes widened, a signal that I'd crossed a boundary and was really pushing my luck. "What?"

"The girl Jeb has taken in, Aellyn," I said. "Her mind is broken, but I think healing is possible. I want your best healer to work with her every day. Whoever it is needs to understand that her drawings and Jeb are the keys to binding her fractured memories together. And they need to start tomorrow."

The Chief tilted her head before she nodded. "Very well, Lord Dura. It will be done."

The next morning, I cinched up my supplies for the ride north while Bolt, Custos, Rory, and Peret Volsk looked on. Rory sat his horse as if he'd been caught thieving and been forced to ride as penance. Custos peered at him from his perch atop a placid roan, his brows furrowed beneath the shining dome of his bald head. "There are quite a few treatises on riding," he said. "If you like, I can retrieve them for you."

"I don't think we'll have much time for reading, old friend. Rory will have to refine his horsemanship on the way."

The librarian nodded. "I could recite them for him, but it's said experience is the best teacher. I wouldn't really know." Then he smiled, shifting his weight in the saddle, testing its feel.

"How goes the search Lady Bronwyn requested?"

He shook his head. "Not well. I've exhausted the libraries here in Bunard of every scrap of information on children's rhymes and cross-referenced them with every proverb in the liturgy. As you might expect, there are numerous threads of commonality, but nothing that points to understanding the nature of the Darkwater, much less fighting it."

The Chief of Servants approached us from across the yard, thumping her cane against the ground with every other step as if the earth had offended her. "Why are you still here?"

I held up a finger, adopting a pose as though instructing a student. "'A wise man sharpens his axe before felling the tree,'" I quoted. I didn't usually make it a habit to toss pieces of the liturgy about, but something in the Chief of Servants brought out the worst in me.

"Well said," Bolt quipped.

She held my gaze for a moment longer before shifting to move away, but not before her expression became wary. I couldn't understand why she was so afraid of me. I followed her until I was sure we were out of earshot of everyone else. "Whenever you look at me, I see something in your eyes, Chief. What is it you see that makes you so afraid?"

A smile warred with the haunted look in her eyes and lost. "You hold the gift of domere and no one knows why you survived the forest, Lord Dura. Is that not enough?"

I shook my head. "No, and your answer tells me it isn't. I keep saying the same thing. If you won't tell me what I need to know, I can't succeed."

"I'm old, Lord Dura, but that doesn't make me immune to fear." She turned away. "You're asking me to put a sword in your hand."

I walked around her, forcing her to face me. "I'm asking you to help me." I waved my arm at the yard. "In case you hadn't noticed, there's no one else here. Everyone with the experience to know what to do has gone into hiding. There's only me."

"Very well." She nodded to Custos. "There are things written in the private libraries of the church, shared by the heads of each order that never make it to the great libraries of the world, of something old, much like destroying a vault," she said. "The Vigil didn't always move in the shadows, Lord Dura. There was a time, before the church split, when the Vigil held the rulers of the earth to account." She licked her lips before her mouth settled into a contemplative moue. "They held themselves up as judges of kings and queens."

"Why did they stop?"

She looked away, suddenly unwilling to look me in the eye. "One can only speculate. Even the oldest in the Vigil have no memory of the 'why.' The split was hundreds of years before Pellin's time in the Vigil began." Her gaze drifted until it settled on Custos again. "What's the child's rhyme about power, Lord Dura?"

I didn't have Custos's ability or share his passion for all knowledge, but some of the verses the children chanted in the streets while they played their games of lost-and-found or one-spot-less held universal truth for adults as well. "'Power seeps and soaks and rots and even the watchers become the watched.'"

She gave me a smile. "I've held my position long enough to work with most of the Vigil, Lord Dura. I find that I prefer Lady Bronwyn's company. She's told me that rhyme has hardly changed in all the centuries she's spent with the Vigil. Children chant it now, much as they have for hundreds of years." She tilted her head, seeming to listen to music no one else could hear. "I know this, Lord Dura, the children's rhymes that accompany their nonsense games of circles of six and nine and four are as old as the liturgy."

The Chief of Servants shrugged, stepping back to allow me to mount Dest. "It *may* be the wisdom of the children's rhymes amounts to nothing more than instructional parables. We will see." She cut her eyes to Peret Volsk. In the morning light he looked almost normal—bathed, shaved, and clothed mostly in black, according to his custom. Yet his eyes retained something of the look I'd seen by torchlight in the prison, a haunting. Volsk carried his own prison.

"Be careful of that one," the Chief said.

Bolt spent half his time scanning the Merum yard for threats and the other half looking at Volsk as if he couldn't decide which of his legs to break. Rory had a knife in hand, ready for throwing. "It's not me Volsk needs to worry about," I said. She was gone before I realized she'd never answered my question as to why the Vigil stopped holding the rulers to account.

CHAPTER 18

Pellin, Eldest of the Vigil, stood in the fenced-in barnyard of a small farmstead tucked in the hills outside the Owmead village of Docga. Allta had dismounted, sword in one hand, dagger in the other, and the guard stood on the balls of his feet ready to spring at the slightest threat or movement. He stayed close to Pellin's mount, ready to hit the horse with the flat of his blade to send him galloping away—though nothing in the yard stirred. Nothing.

Beside him, still in his saddle, Mark stared at the carnage, his light blue eyes, normally filled with mischief, wide in shock above an open-mouthed gape.

A figure lay sprawled on the hard-packed earth of the yard, the blistered skin on his face and arms the only indication Pellin had of when he'd died. Even without seeing his gap-toothed mouth he knew it to be Gelaeran, but where was his apprentice, Byre? He dismounted, waving away Allta's growl of disapproval. "He's dead and has been for at least three days. It's doubtful his killer would remain behind so long."

"Mark, dismount and draw your knives," Allta ordered. Their apprentice dropped to the ground on catlike feet, the shine of steel appearing in each hand while he was still in the air.

The silence filling the hollow—utter stillness so deep it defied even the wind to violate it—set the hair on Pellin's arms on end as he walked toward the barn. After three days, he would have expected low howls or even whimpers from within, but the hush didn't end at the barn. It started there.

"Let me go first, Eldest," Allta said. "Mark, guard behind him. Yell if you see or hear *anything*."

Pellin's guard, the thirty-sixth man to hold that position in his long tenure within the Vigil, stepped in front and without waiting for permission entered the gloom. Even from where he stood, ten paces from the entrance, Pellin caught the metallic smell of blood. But the silence was the worst, a noiselessness that spoke of death, a battlefield bereft of any evidence of life.

Allta emerged a moment later, his face filled with promises of violence he couldn't keep.

"Are any of the cages empty?"

His guard nodded. "Yes, but you need to see this."

The fact that some of the cages were unoccupied should have been good news. It meant that at least some of the sentinels might have lived to kill whoever had murdered their trainers. But when Pellin entered the gloom, the first thing he noticed was Byre, Gelaeran's apprentice—dead but still clutching a sword. Inside six cages lay the furred bodies of six sentinel pups, many of them still small enough to be picked up and held like an ordinary dog. In front of each cage, full-grown sentinels lay dead, each taken by a single slash across the throat.

Mark came up from behind, made a sound in his throat that might have meant anything.

Pellin stopped, reached out to grab Allta by the sleeve, not in shock but in warding. "Have you disturbed anything?"

"No, Eldest."

Pellin stifled his customary dislike of the title, only nodding in response. "Open all the doors. I want to see what happened." When Mark moved to follow, Pellin caught him by the sleeve. "Just Allta. Too many sets of footprints will confuse me.

Mark nodded, though he still looked at the pups as if he wanted to hold them. "Yes, Eldest."

Light flooded the barn, each shaft of brilliance illuminating motes of dust that hung in the air. Pellin inched forward, past the bodies of the full-grown sentinels, searching the packed earth for details of the struggle. He couldn't find any.

"Six adults and their pups," Pellin murmured. "And the earthen floor of the barn is bare of clues." Pellin stood and turned to address his guard, but Allta's face had gone pale.

"Almost, Eldest. There was only one killer," Allta said, turning from the dead sentinels to face him. "Eldest, we have to leave. I can't guarantee your safety here." He nodded to Mark. "Only he can, and he's not ready yet."

Pellin stared at the bodies of the sentinels, their jaws were unstained, empty. Not one of them had managed to wound their killer. Allta wasn't exaggerating their danger. Not even a man with the talent for space and a pure physical gift could kill six sentinels without taking a wound. If they met the killer, Pellin's guard, the best swordsman the Vigil could find and train on the entire continent, would be overmatched.

"I want to look at the body of Gelaeran again," Pellin said. He pulled a breath full of the stench of death into his lungs, pushed out a long exhale that did nothing to restore his sense of calm, and stepped back out into the yard.

He stood over Gelaeran's still form, but his attention was focused on the boy at his side. All of perhaps thirteen years of age, Mark looked younger than he had just a few weeks ago, his pale cheeks fuller, almost cherubic, beneath ash-blond hair. But his hands were older, already corded and strong from countless hours of practice with the throwing daggers that were the urchins' means of self-defense.

Pellin sighed. He wasn't good with people. How was he supposed to mentor a boy? Inside, anger flared at the evil that necessitated what he was about to do. The boy at his side should have been learning a trade or the responsibilities of the nobility. At the very least he should be back in the city practicing his larceny with a joyful air, the way other youths played games. Doubtless Bolt would say that when no other weapon was available, one that was untried would have to do.

"Before we touch him," Pellin said, "tell me what you see."

Mark nodded, his face devoid of emotion. But instead of replying right away, as expected, the boy knelt to peer at the body, moving ever closer until his eyes were a mere handsbreadth away, despite the smell. He moved, hovering over Gelaeran, searching from head to foot without touching until he'd absorbed every detail. Then Mark stood, walked ten paces away, and turned back to take in the scene as a whole.

If Pellin hadn't known better, he would have sworn the boy had been trained as a reeve. Grief at the circumstances that forced Mark to surrender his childhood lodged in Pellin's throat. More than anything, he wanted to see the mischievous light in the boy's eyes again.

"I think Gelaeran died after Byre," Mark said.

"Interesting." Pellin said this in a noncommittal way, even though the boy's conclusion matched his own. "Explain, please."

Mark pointed at the dead man. "Gelaeran's body is pointed as if he were trying to flee, his feet toward the barn and his head toward the house. I think he heard the commotion and found Byre engaging with and losing to a killer he couldn't see."

Mark shook his head as if unsure of himself. "He tried to run from someone he couldn't see, and the killer caught him from behind—there's a cut across his throat." He paused before turning to face him. "It won't work, Eldest. I can't really protect you."

"Why not?"

Mark's eyebrows, so light they were difficult to see, lowered as he frowned in concentration. "Because we're taking too long. Staying out ahead of any assassin that's trying to kill you, even staying on the move, won't work indefinitely. How long does it take to make a dwimor?"

"If the person making them is who I think, maybe twenty days."

Mark held his arms straight out from his sides, palms up. "Who knows how long he's been making them. We've killed a couple, but we have no way of knowing how many have been made and loosed. Say there are a dozen. If they keep coming at you individually, I . . . we have a chance, but if they come at us in groups . . ."

Pellin's apprentice opened up the fine cloak Pellin had bought him to show the daggers at his waist. "Even if I'm perfect with each throw, if too many come at us at once, I will run out of weapons before I've killed them all."

Allta, standing behind Mark, nodded. "That was well reasoned."

"If you don't stop the one making the dwimor—soon—you can't win," Mark said.

In spite of Bronwyn's concerns about Owmead's king, he had no better choice. "Then we burn the bodies and ride for Andred." His back and legs twinged in anticipation of the torturous journey they were about to endure. "I need to use King Rymark's scrying stone."

"Is that wise, Eldest?" Allta asked. "He hates you." He cleared his throat. "And the Grace of the Absold is there as well."

Pellin shrugged. In his search for the support of the kings and queens, he was now headed to the seat of the very king he had determined to avoid. "He has reason. And after he sees me, he'll have more. As for the Grace, it can't be helped. At this point my message is more important than my freedom."

CHAPTER 19

Eight days after leaving the sentinel camp, Pellin dismounted from his horse in front of the ostentatious gates to the royal compound in Andred and groaned. Innumerable horse changes had allowed a pace that had turned his backside and thighs into mush. Only nibbles from Allta's store of chiccor root and regular doses of averin had kept him in the saddle. The combination of pain, weariness, and stimulant worked together to put his emotions on the outermost layer of his skin.

"I'm going to need a few moments," he said, detouring away from the gates toward the cathedral that filled the space to the right. His voice came out in a groan. "We will need an introduction at any rate."

Allta shook his head. "King Rymark already knows who you are."

Pellin nodded without changing course. "True, but his functionaries do not, and despite the fact that our presence has been noted in Bunard, the rest of the continent is still thankfully ignorant of us. Hopefully, we can keep it that way." He pulled a breath into his lungs and gasped as the muscles in his back spasmed with the effort.

"Walking will help to ease some of the soreness, Eldest," Allta said.

Pellin smiled in thanks, but even that seemed a trial. "The fact that you felt the need to say so, coupled with the look on your face, tells me just how bad I must look."

Mark didn't look much better, but Pellin felt sure the resilience of youth would work wonders on the boy after some rest. His apprentice caught Pellin's eye and started. "You're as gray as a corpse."

His guard stiffened. "He is the Eldest."

155

Mark nodded. "My apologies. You're as gray as a corpse, *Eldest*. What good does it do to escape the assassins if you kill yourself doing it?"

Allta looked on the verge of offering Mark some sort of physical remonstrance, but Pellin stopped him. "I feel like a dead man, so it's no surprise that I look like one as well."

His guard shook his head, his hair shifting with the violence of the motion. "By no means, Eldest. It's just . . . "

Pellin tried smiling again. This time it only worked on half his face. "I'll remind you that we are still technically part of the church and that lying is frowned upon."

Allta stiffened, and Pellin watched as that directive and his guard's natural inclinations warred with each other. "You look terrible, Eldest. Your face is as pale as a sheet, and it's obvious you can't stand up straight. You hobble across the ground like a crone and your joints creak like—"

Pellin held up a hand, halting both his guard's tally and Mark's weak laughter. "Yes, I know. Let us see if the head of the Absold can be imposed upon to offer some remedy for my appearance."

He looked at the Absold cathedral without trying to hide the twist to his expression. Forty years ago, it had been confiscated from the Merum and given to the Absold by decree of Queen Arezia, Rymark's mother. In all the kingdoms of the northern continent, only in Owmead did the Merum lack the closest cathedral to the throne. Still, he was probably on better terms with the head of the Absold than any other order. That surprised him. Perhaps his own training as a Merum priest somehow served to create tension between himself and the Archbishop.

Three functionaries and ten minutes later they sat in the presence of the head of the Absold, a woman of forty-something years with lustrous hair that at turns appeared to be either burnished red or brown above deep-set green eyes and a strong nose. Her blue attire, a shade of sky at sunset that carried hints of violet, clashed with her olive skin tone, but the Grace, as the head of the Absold was called, had chosen a black stole to bring the color of her order and her personal appearance into harmony.

"Please sit, gentlemen." Hyldu motioned toward the chairs, her brows knitted with concern. Pellin did not so much sit as fall into the proffered chair, and Mark did likewise at his side. Allta maintained his vigil at the door, hand on his sword. Without asking for preference or permission, Hyldu turned aside toward the cabinet on the wall opposite the east-facing window and poured a glass two-thirds full from an ornate decanter. The smell of peaches and spirits filled the room.

Pellin breathed a sigh that carried almost enough voice to be a moan and took a generous swallow. The cramps in his legs and back eased somewhat, and if the flush in his face came from the drink rather than youth, he was in no position to complain. "Thank you."

Mark looked at Pellin's drink and cleared his throat twice.

The head of the Absold smiled. "I'm afraid I have to confess my ignorance, Eldest. I can only assume this is your traveling companion."

He nodded and took another pull from the glass. The pain from the cramps in his legs and back eased a bit more. "This is Mark, my new apprentice."

The boy shook his blond head in disgust, then shambled bowlegged over to the same decanter to pour himself a drink.

Hyldu's left eyebrow arched in question. "He's, ah, a bit young for the job."

Out of the corner of his eye—he was too tired to turn his head—Pellin saw Mark smile, then wince as he retook his seat. "She means I'm a bit young to be pilfering the contents of her decanter." He paused to take a sip. "That's good, quite good, but I've stolen better."

"Eldest?" the Grace asked.

"Mark's previous experience included stealing and swindling merchants in Bunard as a member of the urchins. It's a bit difficult to explain, but he's temporarily the most qualified apprentice we can find. He can accept my gift or his." He jerked his head back toward Allta, and the room took a moment to stabilize.

"Winters are cold in Bunard," Mark said. "The urchins were always grateful for a dram of spirits to help ward away the chill in the poor quarter." He downed the rest of the glass and sat, blinking contentedly.

"Ah, yes." The Grace turned again to Pellin. "I confess that I am surprised to see you here in Owmead and in such a state, Eldest." Unspoken questions filled her voice.

Pellin smiled. "You mean the last you heard, I was fighting monsters from the Darkwater and that I currently look like a league of bad road."

Hyldu smiled, bringing her face for a moment into harmony. "Yes, Eldest, but the subsequent messages from the Chief of Servants have been brief, and rumors claim the Darkwater evil has engulfed the whole of Collum." Hyldu leaned forward. "I confess to more than a little surprise that you would come here, Pellin. Brid Teorian is livid that you and the rest of the Vigil managed to sneak off before she could speak with you." She gave a small laugh at that but stopped when Pellin didn't join in.

"What you mean," Pellin said, "is that the Chief of Servants is upset that we fled before the church could take us all into custody and divvy us up like prized hogs."

Hyldu laughed and nodded. "Yes, I mean that." She favored him with a speculative look. "You've placed me in an enviable quandary, Eldest. I naturally assumed that Archbishop Vyne and the Merum would be the recipient of your company and services, leaving the three younger orders to squabble over Lady Bronwyn."

When she gestured at his empty glass and he nodded, she rose to refill it. The perfume of peaches filled the room once more, and he inhaled deeply through his nose and sipped. "What of Lord Dura?"

Grace Hyldu pursed her lips. "If you ask after his status, I can assure you that the Chief of Servants took him under her protection when she discovered the rest of the Vigil left Bunard."

Pellin smiled. "You mean fled."

Hyldu's smile matched his. "If you wish. However, if you are asking my opinion on which of us would or should receive the benefit of his services, I would say he sounds most suited for Collen." She waved a hand. "It seems he has an inexhaustible ardor for fighting evils large and small, real or imagined."

Pellin shook his head. "Collen would never allow the Vanguard to work with Lord Dura."

"Because of his vault?" Hyldu asked. "Don't be too sure. Collen is as zealous as any Captain of the Vanguard has ever been, but he shows a remarkable, and quite surprising, tendency toward grace for those who strike him as sincere in their repentance." She leaned forward, her eyes bright. "It makes me wonder what the Captain has in his past that should incline him to such a belief."

He didn't respond. Fatigue and peach spirits leached his ability and desire to engage in any unnecessary conversation. The silence stretched until the relatively lighthearted mood of their banter faded.

"What's really happening out there, Pellin?" Hyldu asked. "You and I have always extended the grace to be honest with each other, even when our positions forced us to keep our own counsel."

Though the drink made the muscles of his face sluggish to respond, Pellin mustered a smile. For a moment, he considered sending Mark from the room. Knowledge carried burdens, and he'd been sincere in his desire to have the boy as a temporary apprentice only. Mark regarded him and Hyldu with focused attention, no doubt a necessary trait for practicing his larceny. Yet it was a characteristic that might find use in service of the Vigil. Perhaps Mark's insights would prove beneficial.

"The truth is, Hyldu, I don't know. The tenor of the forest has changed and something of its evil walks among us now. Laewan fell to it, but I thought we had it beaten after Bas-solas."

"Rough business," Hyldu said. "You would have lost the entire kingdom if you'd failed."

Against his better judgment he took another long sip from his glass, let the peach brandy spread warmth over his tongue before he swallowed. "We were outmaneuvered. Badly outmaneuvered. While we had to win in Bunard or face total defeat, the enemy didn't. Then we spent weeks mopping up the aftereffects, not realizing someone has been cutting us in pieces from behind."

He focused on her gaze with an effort. If any argument would persuade her to let him retain his freedom, it would be this one. "Months ago, when communication from Laewan and Jorgen ceased, I sent messages to every sentinel trainer in the six kingdoms to move to completely new locations." His throat tightened. "Someone found the location here in Owmead. They're all dead, right down to the last pup. Now I know what Jorgen was doing while Laewan kept us busy."

Hyldu paled until her eyebrows stood out stark and livid against her skin. "Where was Jorgen stationed?"

"Frayel," Pellin spat. "If he's the one behind this, he's worked his way south and west around the Darkwater Forest."

"But that would mean the sentinels in Collum might still be alive," she said softly, like a prayer.

"Possibly," Pellin said. "Or he might have found them and killed them already. It took us over a week to get here."

"Can you make more?"

Pellin wanted nothing more than to let himself fall asleep in the Grace's chair, to let unconsciousness claim him so that, at least for a while, he could be free of the burden of authority. "We can—so long as a male and female remain. But even then we'll need to find someone gifted and with just the right blend of talent and temperament to train them. We found one in Bunard not so long—"

"You misunderstand me. I don't mean to ask whether you can breed more. If they have all been killed, can you *make* more?"

It was getting harder to focus on her face, even though his peripheral vision seemed to be narrowing. He went to take another sip, but when he upended his glass, nothing came from it except a drop or two that teased his tongue with hints of warmth.

"No. Aer help me, I wouldn't even know where to begin." He saw her draw breath and closed his eyes as he held up a hand. "You don't need to say it. Bronwyn and I have chewed over the possibility until it's been minced to syrup. If we lose the sentinels, the forest becomes indefensible." He nodded. "And that is exactly what the enemy wants."

He needed sleep with a desperation that made him want to curl up on the Grace's floor, but time weighed against them. Even the necessary diversion to the Absold cathedral made him want to clench his teeth. "My guard and I will need a change of clothes and an immediate introduction to King Rymark."

To emphasize his haste, he pushed himself from the comfort of the chair. "And we'll need someone to watch over Mark while we wait." At a look of protest from the boy, Pellin held up his hand. "There will be no discussion. The king of Owmead is not noted for his sense of humor. One wrong look or comment could spoil everything."

Grace Hyldu stood. "I'll have water heated for your bath immediately."

Pellin shook his head, wobbling on his feet with the effort. "No. Have the tub filled with cold. Time is more important than comfort, and I need to be awake and aware." He nodded toward the decanter. "Thank you for the brandy."

CHAPTER 20

Pellin came into the presence of the king of Owmead with a sigh from within his hooded cloak. His relationship with Rymark suffered by virtue of his kinship with Cesla and Elwin. His brothers had detested the diminutive king's lust for power and hadn't hesitated to assert their authority. Rymark, in return, had mastered the finer nuances of passive disobedience to the point he could have written the definitive work on the subject.

The Eldest of the Vigil surveyed the room from within the shadows of his cloak. Rymark had filled the relatively small audience room with functionaries, courtiers, and—judging by the aggressive plunge of her neckline that left a lot of flesh exposed—at least one courtesan.

Hyldu stared at the expanse of the woman's cleavage with an expression on her face that settled somewhere between disapproval and amusement. "Cover up, dear. If you catch cold your nose will drip all over your assets. That's the sort of thing that adversely impacts your profitability."

"What?" the woman asked, her forehead creased in incomprehension. Then a rose-colored tinge blossomed on her face and she jerked a thin shawl into place that did little to hide what was beneath.

"Oh well," Hyldu said, "it's better than nothing."

"I've always favored your sense of humor, Grace," Pellin whispered so that only she could hear him. "We'll need the room cleared of everyone except King Rymark."

Hyldu stepped forward until she stood at the focal point of the arc of courtiers surrounding the king. "Your Majesty." She bowed. "Much as it pains us to be separated from the brilliant lights of wisdom embodied within the fleshly vessels of your advisors"—she shot a look at the courtesan—"I bring tidings that are of a sensitive nature. I suggest you hear them in private before deciding how best to rule regarding them."

Although couched in far more colorful language than Pellin would have used, the tone of dismissal was readily apparent. Rymark flushed and pushed himself backward into the cushions of his elevated throne like a cornered animal, appearing on the verge of refusing.

Pellin stepped forward and raised his hand toward the dais. "Please."

King Rymark's eyes widened, and he pointed toward the door. "Everyone out, now."

The courtiers spilled off the dais, splitting into two columns to file past Pellin and the Grace. More than one tried to peer into the shadows of his hood, but he ducked his head, fixing his gaze upon the ornate marble inlay of the floor until he heard the sound of the door closing. Only then did he lower his hood.

With the room emptied, Rymark slid from the elevated throne and descended the dais to meet them. "All right, Pellin. They're all gone. The Vigil has proven again that they can pull my strings. What do you want?"

Pellin sighed. Rymark's tone left little doubt that he would have to wrestle obedience from the king, just as his brothers always had. "I take no pleasure in clearing your court, Your Majesty. We sent word ahead of our approach."

Rymark's mouth twisted to the side. "I received no word you were coming, Pellin, only the Grace. Admit it—you and your brothers have always hated me."

Pellin sighed. "If you received no word of my coming, Your Majesty, then I would look to your circle. It wouldn't be the first time advisors have tried to stir up dissension to create advantage for themselves."

He took a breath to calm himself. Rymark had always been ambitious, desiring the kingdom to the north and its seaports to cement his power over the western portion of the continent. But he'd never been accused of being stupid. As soon as Pellin made his request, the king of Owmead would be able to piece together much of what had happened. Pellin would have to surrender the truth one way or another. "You hold the gift of kings, Your Majesty. According to the liturgy of the church, the gift has come to you by the will of Aer, Iosa, and Gaoithe."

"Ha," Rymark spat. "According to the liturgy—which is a nice way of saying 'you inherited your throne and we have to deal with you.' You know our history better than anyone, Pellin. You don't believe the liturgy any more than I do."

He had no intention of getting drawn into such an argument with the king. "My brothers objected to your ambition, not to you."

Rymark waved Pellin's explanation away. "Sophistry. A man and his ambition are one and the same. Issue your orders and be done with it."

Pellin shrugged. "As you wish, Your Majesty. On the ride west I noted troops on the move. I know you must have heard some measure of what happened in Bunard on Bas-solas. The gift of kings passed from Laidir to his son, Brod."

For the first time, Rymark showed a measure of emotion other than offense. "Laidir was a worthy opponent. If he could have matched me in men and arms, he might have taken the throne of Owmead for himself. I doubt that Queen Cailin is his equal."

Pellin shook his head. "He never wanted your throne."

"Yes." He frowned. "It is totally incomprehensible."

"And you might be surprised about Cailin," Pellin went on. "Though she does not hold the gift of kings, her talents are considerable, but be that as it may, I *forbid* you to attack Collum. Both kingdoms have plenty of food."

Rymark's expression twisted. "I hated it when Cesla and Elwin used that word with me, Eldest. I don't like it any better coming from you." Yet, after a moment, he dipped his head in acquiescence and walked past Pellin to a side cupboard. "It pleases me to inform you that your assumption is in error. The troops you saw are headed north *and* east, to patrol the Darkwater." He pulled a drawer and removed a plain leather purse, tossing it with a backhanded motion so that it struck Pellin in the chest. "Look inside, Eldest, and thank me. I'm doing your job for you."

Pellin dumped the contents of the purse into his hand. Nuggets of gold bearing a faint bluish tint spilled across his palm, the metal unexpectedly heavy.

The king of Owmead pointed to the soft lumps. "A fight broke out in the village of Hord. It sits on one of the tributaries that flows out of the Darkwater, about ten leagues downstream. The locals were ready to hang the constable for confiscating their treasure for himself."

"I don't understand."

Rymark smiled, only the tightness around his eyes betraying the expression. "I didn't either at first, not until I spoke with Lieutenant Maere. Those nuggets were panned from the river, within sight of the twisted trees."

Hyldu peered at the nuggets. "But that's not possible. With that bluish tint, these had to have come from Frayel."

Rymark's smile wilted at the edges before it disappeared completely. "And how many people in my kingdom, *any* kingdom, know enough to make that distinction, Grace Hyldu?"

Pellin shook his head. The Grace had failed to see to the real issue. "How did the people come to believe there would be gold in the stream?"

"That, Eldest, is a very good question," Rymark said. "I've sent several men and women to Hord with enough coin to find an answer—people I trust to be discreet."

"Spies," Pellin said.

Rymark nodded. "They've found nothing except rumors that run in circles."

Despite his authority, protocol required Pellin to wait for Rymark's invitation to be seated. But he needed to sit. Turning to a large polished table of light-colored wood, Pellin gestured to the closest chair, inviting Rymark and the Grace to join him. After momentarily staring at Pellin with a lift of his brows, the king pulled a chair for himself, for once concerned enough to ignore the difference in height between himself and Pellin. Pellin and the Grace followed suit.

Then, with a deep breath, Pellin continued. "My apologies, Your Majesty, for presuming your intentions." He hefted the gold nuggets in his hand. "How many people know about this?"

Rymark shook his head. "More and more every day. We locked down the village, and I posted the garrison commander as close to the Darkwater as I dared, but word had already started to spread to the neighboring villages. But why, Eldest? Someone went to a lot of trouble to seed those streams with gold."

Pellin exhaled as he replaced the nuggets into the purse, handing it back to Rymark. "How many soldiers from your garrison have deserted to pan the river for themselves?"

Rymark sat back. "You see clearly, Eldest. At least a score so far, and some have been caught running south with gold in their pockets."

Pellin nodded. "And they have to venture closer and closer to the forest to get it, yes?"

"Yes. At first the fear of the sentinels kept them at bay, but they haven't seen one in—"

"The sentinels in Owmead are all dead," Pellin said. "And their replacements and the men we used to train them as well. Someone is trying to lure your people into the Darkwater Forest, Your Majesty, and they've done an excellent job of enticing them."

"But why?"

Pellin's heart and mouth closed around a fear he couldn't explain, like a child who wakes up in the night believing a threat lurks in the darkness but without the ability to put a name to it. "Reinforcements. The evil in the Darkwater is loose. It's what we fought in Bas-solas."

King Rymark blanched, his skin growing white behind the deep chestnut of his beard. "If you didn't know of the gold, Eldest, why did you come?"

"To use your scrying stone, Your Majesty. I need to speak with the kings and queens of the northern continent. Queen Cailin, in particular. We must safeguard the sentinels in Collum." Pellin caught Rymark's gaze and held it. "If they are still alive."

The king's gaze grew cunning, and his eyes darted to Grace Hyldu. "Rumors have come to me, Eldest, that your relationship with the heads of the church has become, shall we say, somewhat strained. I would be more than willing to offer you the protection of the crown."

"You've placed spies in my organization?" Hyldu spluttered.

The king turned his hands palm up. "And have you no spies here in the palace, Grace?"

Pellin put a smile on his face and cocked his head to one side as if considering. Odd that what he had desired with the other rulers was exactly what he'd hoped to avoid with Rymark. He suppressed a sigh. There was no help for it. Rymark and the other monarchs certainly had spies among the leaders of the orders. Even if those spies didn't know the exact nature of the Vigil, Rymark would be able to piece together what had happened from the hints and warrants issued for the capture of each Vigil member. "What would you desire in return, King Rymark?"

"Nothing very great," the king said. "Just bits of information that you've gleaned over the years from your contact with other monarchs and, possibly, their generals."

"No," Hyldu said as she stood. "I forbid it."

Rymark looked up at the taller woman, and slowly stood as well, his grin feral. "For some reason, when you use that word with me, I find that it doesn't bother me so much." He shrugged. "Perhaps it's because you have no power to enforce it."

Hyldu stepped closer to the king, accentuating their difference in height. "No? In this the four orders are united, King Rymark. Every city, town, and village in your kingdom boasts people faithful to one order or another. Within your palace and army are those who place a higher value on their faith than any other facet of their life."

Rymark laughed. "You speak of a different time, Grace. The faith people wear now is like a tunic, easily replaced with one of a different color, or have you not noticed how many of your 'faithful' find their way to a different order if they hear something in yours that offends them?"

Hyldu stiffened. "Do you wish to put it to the test?"

Pellin forced himself up on his aching legs and stepped between them. "There is no need."

He turned to Rymark. "I will never use my gift to help you further your dreams of conquest, and you should be glad I wouldn't—else I might come to favor some other ruler who has taken a liking to your throne."

"Well said," Hyldu nodded.

Pellin shuffled around to face her. "But I will not allow myself to be taken captive when the Darkwater threatens to engulf the entire continent. Nothing you've heard about what happened in Bunard can convey the reality, Grace." He pointed to the lumps of gold with their bluish tinge. "Imagine this. . . . Driven by the lust for gold, swarms of your people do what is forbidden and enter the forest to mine the earth. After a night in the Darkwater, they go insane, killing everyone around them"—he caught the eye of Rymark—"moving like the gifted."

"That's not possible," Hyldu and Rymark said at the same time.

He stabbed them with his gaze. "Do not speak to me of what is possible when I have seen it with my own eyes! Do you think your soldiers can withstand a charge of gifted, King Rymark? Do you think your homilies will keep the faithful from the Darkwater when gold calls to them, Grace?" He held up his clenched fists. "Are you fools that you know so little of human nature?"

Rymark was the first to turn away. "What do you need, Eldest?"

Pellin didn't hesitate—the gold in Rymark's possession precluded every other option. "Access to your scrying stones. I must speak with the kings and queens of the northern continent." He turned to Hyldu. "And the heads of each order now as well, and all of them at the same time."

CHAPTER 21

"I told you to watch him," Pellin snapped.

Allta nodded, looking as chastised as the block of granite he resembled, which was to say, not at all. "Yes, Eldest, but I cannot watch the Mark and fulfill my principal duty to keep you safe at the same time." He shrugged and his massive shoulders swelled beneath his tunic like lungs inflating. "I believe the Mark is aware of this and is using that truth to gain his freedom from your oversight."

The fact that Allta was correct on all counts only irritated Pellin further. "Stop calling him that. His name is just Mark, if it's not something else I decide to give him. Acquiescing to that larcenous affectation only serves to cement the little thief's notion that he can continue swindling people."

"Yes, Eldest."

He eyed his silent guard with frustration. At least Bolt would have offered up some disgustingly trite piece of soldierly wisdom that would have afforded Pellin an outlet for his annoyance.

"He usually returns fairly quickly, Eldest. I doubt he can get into too much trouble in such a short time. He doesn't need to steal anymore now that he's under your protection."

Pellin seized on the opening, gaping at his guard in disbelief. "Are you mad? I delved him! That cherubic-looking little urchin has the soul of a thief. He steals because he enjoys the challenge of it, and the bigger the risk, the greater the pleasure. It's a game to him." Pellin threw up his hands. "And the little rat knows that since he's attached to me, I

168

have no choice but to use my influence to bail him out of trouble or let my own authority and reputation suffer. By all that's holy, I'm being held hostage by a boy!"

Pellin's back was to his guard at that moment, so he didn't recognize the unfamiliar sound. He spun in amazement to see Allta laughing, actually laughing, at the Eldest of the Vigil and his predicament. Surprise at the evidence that his guard possessed a sense of humor washed away any anger he might have felt.

"I see Bolt didn't completely beat the humanity out of you after all," Pellin said. "I'll have to have a word with him next time we meet. He's getting soft in his old age."

Allta swallowed his mirth, clearing his throat and having the decency to look abashed. "Begging your pardon, Eldest, but there was a boy in my village—the son of the mayor—who wasn't quite right in the head, if you take my meaning. He refused to look anyone in the eye. It made people feel uneasy and a bit distrustful. No one would take him for an apprentice. Whenever he went to market, he couldn't seem to keep his hands off the melons. He'd go up and down the street, touching each one, almost caressing them and muttering to himself. It made the women of the village nervous."

Pellin would have interrupted, but amazement glued his jaws shut. Allta had probably spoken more in the last two minutes than in the entire previous month.

"One of the merchants took pity on the lad," Allta went on. "Instead of shooing him away like all the others had done, he just let him touch the melons, following him closely to make sure he didn't damage or steal anything. After a while the merchant noticed the boy was saying how many days it would be until each melon would be perfectly ripe. And the lad was never wrong." Allta's smile held Pellin where he stood. "The merchant couldn't apprentice him quickly enough. The last I heard, the merchant was one of the most profitable in Aille and the boy his chief factor. He even looks people in the eye every now and then."

Pellin nodded. "So if I can't change our little thief's character, I need to use it."

Allta nodded. "If he has to steal, make it information instead."

"That's the sort of thing a man gets killed for, Allta."

The guard nodded. "If he's caught stealing by someone who doesn't know of his connection to you, Eldest, he'll be killed anyway."

The next day, Pellin sat in Rymark's study staring at a pair of scrying stones on the table, one tinged pink, the other with the faintest hint of green. Pellin's own yellow-hued diamond was nestled in his cloak, wrapped in layers of cloth to prevent it from inadvertently sending their words across the distance to whoever held its like. This time, Mark sat at his side. For once, circumstances seemed to have attained enough weight and scale to cow the boy into respectful silence, and Pellin wanted his apprentice's impressions of the meeting, no matter how it went.

"Remember," he whispered to the boy. "Say nothing. See everything."

Mark nodded, playing the part of the intimidated apprentice to perfection. Only the barest glint of mischief in those blue eyes hinted at anything else.

While he waited for the monarchs and church leaders to assemble, he took a moment to survey the room. Despite the long years of his service, he had never before seen the private study Rymark called his own. Every ruler holding the gift of kings had one, a place that reflected their personality and often revealed their deepest desire. Laidir's had been more of a library, filled with collections of stories. Ulrezia of Frayel possessed a hall filled with every musical instrument imaginable arrayed around a harp, with tapestries on the walls to deaden the sound.

Rymark's chamber resembled a war room, despite the relative peace that had ruled the kingdoms for the last century. Maps covered the walls, and books on military strategy filled the shelves. For a moment, Pellin almost pitied the diminutive king. He would have been happier if he'd been born into a time that could have let him exercise his talents.

A faint sound, like a whisper, came from one of the stones, and Rymark leaned forward to speak to the greenish diamond in front of him. "Are we all assembled?"

"Aye," a melodic voice came from the stone that Pellin recognized as Ulrezia of Frayel.

"I'm here," Ellias of Moorclaire announced in an annoyed tone, with a hint of rolling his *R*. "What is this about?"

"In good time, my fellow king," Rymark said.

"I'm here as well," said another woman, Queen Chora of Aille.

Pellin sighed. Of all the monarchs, her struggles with the church had been the most pronounced by virtue of sharing her capital city, Cynestol, with the Archbishop of the Merum.

King Boclar of Caisel and Queen Phidias of Elania voiced their attendance before Rymark offered a perfunctory greeting.

"I am here as well," Cailin said, "as regent for my son."

"Well met, daughter," Ellias said. The king of Moorclaire's voice was deeply formal.

"Father." She replied in respectful tones, but Pellin thought he detected a hint of frost there.

Grace Hyldu leaned forward to direct her voice to the stones in front of her. "Within the charisms of Aer, the talents of man—".

"I think we can dispense with the coda to the exordium, Grace," Pellin said. "Are you here and alone, Archbishop, Captain, and Chief?"

"I am," came three voices from the stone.

"What is this about, Pellin?" the Archbishop demanded. "Where are you? And where is the rest of the Vigil?"

A cacophony of voices poured from the stones as the leaders of the church and the seven kingdoms each attempted to ask their question over the others. Pellin sat back and waited until the sound faltered and died under its own weight before speaking again.

"If you will all be patient," he said, "I will endeavor to answer your questions." He took a deep breath. "Let me begin by telling you that I am here in Andred in the company of King Rymark and the Grace of the Absold." He looked across the table at the man and the woman who sat with him, still wearing wide-eyed expressions of shock. Perhaps he could use that to his advantage. "I also feel obligated to inform you, Archbishop, Chief, and Captain, that I am not under the 'protection' of the Absold, nor will I allow myself to be."

"Why have you not taken him, Grace?" Collen, Captain of the Vanguard, asked. "If he should die without an apprentice, the northern continent will fall."

Hyldu leaned toward the stone. "The Eldest has convinced me that his freedom is essential to preventing just such a fall. Please hear him."

"Thank you," Pellin said. While he had their collective attention, Pellin explained the occurrences at Bunard, his suspicion that Jorgen had been corrupted by the same evil from the Darkwater that had taken Laewan, and his discovery that the sentinel base in Owmead had been destroyed, as well as Rymark's revelation of their enemy's attempts to lure people to the Darkwater with seeded gold. He made no attempt to couch his words to lessen the shock. Rather, he painted the disaster that had befallen the sentinels in the most stark language he could contrive.

"What do we do?"

Pellin wasn't sure who asked the question, but it didn't matter. He accepted the opening and leaned forward until his mouth was inches from the pair of scrying stones. "Our armies must cordon off the Darkwater until the Vigil can find the source of this infection and eradicate it. If you need to manufacture a reason for the excuse of war, then do it, but find a way to put your best soldiers around the forest with orders to kill anyone coming out of it or panning for gold."

Across from him, Rymark shook his head in disagreement, but didn't speak. Pellin breathed a prayer of thanks. Rymark knew already what the other kings and queens would soon discover. All the threats in the world wouldn't keep a man from seeking out gold.

"If we do this, Eldest, the world will know the sentinels have died," Ulrezia said.

"They will know it soon enough. The mystery of the forest has always drawn the curious and the foolhardy."

"And if we should find any sentinels alive?" Boclar asked.

Pellin stifled a sigh. He couldn't afford to show weakness now. Not here. "I pray that it will be so. I will give you the locations of the sentinel base in each kingdom. Dispatch men to investigate. If you have someone with the gift of devotion and a strong talent for nature, send them as well. Their affinity for animals will offer them some protection. Get word to one of the Vigil if any of the adults or pups are found alive. If there is any chance of rebuilding the pack, we must take it.

"Chief of Servants, I must ask you to release Willet Dura from your protection so that he and his guard may seek out the sentinel camp in Collum. If Jorgen is responsible for the death of the sentinels, he would get to it last. It stands the most likely chance of surviving."

Brid Teorian's voice came from the scrying stone. "Lord Dura is gone."

Pellin stared at the crystal in disbelief.

"You can't count on the church to do anything right." Rymark shook his head. "They shouldn't have taken him captive, but when they did they couldn't keep him. Somehow, I'm not encouraged."

"That comment is beneath you," Hyldu said.

"Is it?" Rymark asked. "I was under the impression that you and the rest of the heads of the church thought very little was beneath me. Aer help us, if you can't even be relied upon to imprison a man, how are we going to win a war?"

"This isn't a war," Hyldu said.

"If you think that," Rymark spat, "you're a fool. Or did you believe that we were going to just put a few hundred thousand men in the field for our personal amusement?"

"You misunderstand me," the Chief of Servants' voice came from the stone. "Lord Dura has already left for the sentinel camp."

"Impossible," Pellin said. "He doesn't know the way."

"But Peret Volsk does."

"Are you mad?"

Pellin heard the accusation, but in the clash of voices he couldn't be sure who'd made it.

When a cacophony erupted either in support or against the Chief, Pellin leaned closer to the stones. "Stop! We have no time for such squabbles. We must trust that Dura's guard will safeguard him against any treachery Volsk might attempt. Rymark is correct. We must be prepared for war, but for the moment we have to focus on cutting off our enemy's lines of supply." He caught Rymark's and Hyldu's gaze, held it. "If we can prevent anyone else from entering the infection of the Darkwater, then the enemy will soon have no one to fight for him."

"And if the infection is reaching out from the forest itself?" the Captain of the Vanguard asked.

Across from Pellin, Hyldu shivered and made the sign of the arcs on her forehead. "Then the Vigil will deal with it," he said. "But to that end we will need scrying stones."

"What of yours?" Queen Chora asked.

"Jorgen still retains one of the stones, and even if he did not, they are not all accounted for. I sent to the southern continent for replacements, but they never arrived."

"What do you suggest?" Hyldu asked.

"I must be able to communicate at need with Lady Bronwyn and Lady Deel. I am asking the heads of the orders to loan us the use of their stones until replacements can be found."

Hyldu opened her mouth to speak, then thought better of it.

"Since the heads of the church reside in Cynestol, Andred, Bunard, and Loklallin, they can use the stones of the monarchs, if needed."

Pellin sat back and waited for the wave of objections he knew must come. In the entire world, nothing held more value than scrying stones, and only aurium, a metal more rare then gold, came close. How many wars had been won or lost because one side could communicate more effectively than the other? Nearly a minute passed without comment, but by the tightness that came and went in her expression, Pellin could see the struggle his request had created in the Grace of the Absold.

"If you lose my stone," she whispered, "you owe me a replacement."

Pellin nodded, suppressing a smile. Any replacement he bought would come from church funds Hyldu and the rest commanded.

"I will surrender my stone to the Eldest," Hyldu announced.

A heartbeat later the Archbishop of the Merum and the Captain of the Vanguard agreed to surrender their stones to Bronwyn and Toria Deel.

"You will have to find them first," Pellin said. "Look in the towns and villages close to the forest."

"And what of Willet Dura?" the Chief of Servants asked.

For a moment Pellin hesitated. As forthcoming as he'd been in their previous conversation, he'd avoided sharing his deepest suspicions and fears regarding Dura and his vault. Little would be served by giving voice to it now. "Keep your stone, Chief. We will try to find other ways to communicate with Lord Dura." He tried to ignore the twinge of guilt that flashed through him and failed. "Now I must return to the forest myself. Jorgen is out there." He didn't bother to say that he didn't have the slightest idea of how to find him.

"We should do something about that one," the Chief of Servants said.

Pellin shook his head as if the Chief of Servants could see him. "If you try to take him, you'll just lose your men. He's not human anymore."

After a pause, Hyldu spoke. "Circulate his likeness among the kingdoms with a hefty price on his head. We might not kill him, but it may curtail his movements."

"Agreed," Pellin said.

"A moment." The Archbishop's voice came from the pink diamond. "Eldest, you have won a reprieve because you have convinced us of the need, but if another of the Vigil should fall and your strength be reduced to three, then you must understand we must safeguard what remains."

Queen Chora spoke almost before the Archbishop had finished. "Even if that means the kingdoms must unite to take you captive."

Pellin waited for dissent and argument, but no one spoke. It seemed the others had broken off communication without further discussion. Rymark nodded, then reached forward to take the green shard of diamond from its stand and wrap it in cloth.

Hyldu nodded toward the pink-tinged stone still on the table. "It's yours, as agreed. But tell me, Eldest, why you made no request for the fourth member of the Vigil. Doubtless, the Chief of Servants could have given him her stone. Brid Teorian is nothing if not accommodating."

Pellin bit his lip, considered not answering, especially in the presence of Rymark, who might very well try to use the information for personal advantage. But the question was enough for that purpose. Perhaps if he answered well, he could convince the king of Owmead that Dura carried more risk than reward.

"Dura's vault presents a dilemma, Grace. While he seems to be immune to its usual effect, it cannot be denied that it has its origin in the Darkwater. We don't know if the enemy can use it to spy on us or not."

Rymark smiled. "Then feed him misinformation and see if the enemy bites."

Pellin nodded. The same idea had occurred to him. "That is a strategy I would have been more than willing to try had we not already deceived the enemy by using it with the scrying stones."

"Bas-solas," Rymark and Hyldu said at the same time.

"Exactly. I doubt whether it would work again, and I'm unwilling to lose another member of the Vigil, even a flawed one, in the attempt."

CHAPTER 22

After leaving Bunard, we rode north and east along the banks of the Rinwash for almost a week, moving backward in the season from late to early summer, the farms growing more and more scarce, the men or women living there unwilling to fight the protracted winter to wrest subsistence from the earth.

I'd never been to the village of Hund—had barely heard of it, in fact—but we followed Volsk, who with Bolt's dour encouragement rode his horse at a numbing trot designed to eat up the leagues of distance, his direction as unerring as a compass.

The sixth day out we camped by the banks of the river close to a copse of fir trees mixed with cedar. With the sun no more than a circle of crimson above the hills to the west, we slipped from our saddles. Bolt alone managed to walk without the bowlegged stagger the rest of us had worn for days.

Rory slipped to the ground with a cry of pain, clutching the inside of each thigh. "This is what I get for taking up with a growler," he whimpered. "No self-respecting thief would choose to work for a reeve."

I tried to bend over and touch my toes as Dest looked on. My fingertips made it halfway between my kneecaps and my feet before I gave up. I couldn't be sure without delving him, but I thought my horse's face held a hint of justified amusement at my suffering.

I turned to see Custos watching us from his saddle. As he pulled his left foot from his stirrup and lowered himself gently to the ground, I moved toward him, ready to offer a hand in case he needed it. But he stepped away from his mount with an expression made of equal parts discomfort and pride. After a couple of faltering steps, he managed an almost normal walk.

I couldn't help but shake my head in disbelief. "Is there some secret stable in the library I don't know about, old friend? I wouldn't think being the Merum librarian would offer you much time for riding."

"It doesn't, but I've read every text on the subject." A small wince ran across his features as he paused to stretch. "Quite a few of them deal with minimizing discomfort." He tried to squat, then thought better of it, shaking his head. "I'm going to have to amend some of them." He smiled. "I think some of the authors overestimated their expertise."

Volsk grunted as he moved about the clearing, duck-walking to ease the cramps from his legs. Rory tried to stand and fell back to the ground with a groan. "I'm never moving from this spot."

Bolt spared a glance for Volsk, but the erstwhile prisoner had busied himself with stripping the tack from his horse and seemed to constitute little threat. He walked toward his apprentice, his gaze flat. "Get up. It's time to continue your training."

Rory gaped. "Are you mad, growler? It'll be days before I can walk normally again, yah?" He pointed at Bolt's chest. "You're pushing the pace on purpose just to keep me from being able to steal. If I hit the rooftops like this I'm going to fall and break my neck."

Bolt turned away to grab a pair of wooden practice swords from the pack behind his saddle. "You're not injured, yet—you're just sore," he said. "And soreness can be endured or ignored. I don't much care which of those you choose, so long as you choose. Now get up or I'm going to beat you until you do."

Bolt waited perhaps half a heartbeat and then started whacking Rory on the legs. At first the thief tried to roll away, but Bolt followed, his strikes coming harder and faster. Rory shifted and dodged on the ground, working to get his legs beneath him, but Bolt pursued, pinning him there. I gaped as their gifts and talents manifested, each slash and dodge coming so quickly that I could hardly see them.

Rory feinted left, and when Bolt's practice sword came whistling, pivoted on the ground with his hands tucked next to his head and flipped backward to a crouch. "All right! I'm up, you crazy growler."

Bolt relaxed for a second, the point of his sword dipping toward the ground before he flexed his wrist to send the wooden stave streaking toward Rory's side.

Whack.

Rory doubled over. "*Kreppa,*" he snarled. "What did you do that for?"

Bolt stepped back. "Two reasons. First, your job is to protect him." Bolt gestured toward me with his free hand. "Never, ever, let your guard down—not for a moment, not for anyone." He paused. "Not even for me."

"Second, until you take my place at his side, you will do what I say the first time I say it."

I stepped between the pair to face Bolt and lowered my voice to a whisper. "Go easy. He's not a soldier. The military chain of command is unfamiliar to him. The streets are all he's ever known, and the urchins question authority as naturally as breathing."

My guard nodded. "I know and that's one of the reasons I picked him, but until he shoulders the idea of unceasing vigilance, this is the way it will have to be. Stay out of this." Bolt stepped around me and tossed the practice sword toward Rory.

"Have you ever fought with a sword before?"

Rory, his face still closed as a thundercloud, shook his head. Bolt sighed. "I hope I can live long enough to complete his training."

"How long does it take?"

Bolt twitched his shoulders. "It varies, and the decision is made by the master—that's me. When I have nothing left to teach him, he'll be ready, but it's going to take years."

I looked at Rory with his musician's hands and his acrobat's build. The boy was already more deadly than most anyone in Bunard. "I would have thought the boy's physical gift would shorten the time."

Bolt barked a laugh. "Oh, he'll be deadly enough after a month to beat anyone without a gift." His gaze slid to me. "But that's not what we need, is it?" He turned to face Rory. "You have to be the best. I'm not talking about the best in Bunard or Collum. I'm talking about the entire world."

Rory shook his head. "What's the point?"

Bolt lunged forward and grabbed Rory's tunic, hauling him close. "The point is that there are people out there like Lord Baine—physically gifted but hiding it from the church so that they can sell their sword to the highest bidder. And the world has changed. That used to be all we had to worry about."

He thrust Rory away. "Hold your sword like this."

I turned from their practice session as Bolt ran Rory through the five parries, a lecture I'd heard myself when I was conscripted into Laidir's army and again when I'd become a reeve. I squatted next to the tree where Custos sat watching Bolt's instruction as if a book had come to life.

"Interesting," he said, glancing up at me. "I've read all the books on sword training and technique, of course, but it's quite a different thing to see them put into practice." He pointed to my guard. "Your friend Bolt is not only a master swordsman, he's a master teacher. Half a dozen times now, he's corrected flaws in young Rory's approach, building a flawless foundation, explaining why to a depth that puts most of the books on the subject to shame."

"Custos, I need your help," I said.

His head swiveled toward me like a bird's and he gave me an owlish blink of his large brown eyes. For a moment he almost grinned. "I don't suppose you have any almond-crusted figs for my price?"

"Not this time, my friend."

He shrugged. "All those sweets are probably bad for me."

I rubbed the bald dome of his head in affection. What had I ever done to deserve a friend such as him? "What do you know about children's rhymes?"

He shook his head. "Nothing really." Custos saw the look on my face and went on. "Oh, I know all of them, of course, but I don't know anything about them."

I laughed. "Forgive me if I'm being dense, old friend, but that makes absolutely no sense whatsoever."

His head waved like a dandelion on the end of a stalk. "It does. In this case there is a difference between knowing a subject and in knowing about a subject. Bolt not only knows how to fight, I'll warrant he knows where each technique originated, its history, and the advantages and disadvantages of it. I can recite every child's rhyme to you in perfect detail, but I don't know much beyond that because nobody has ever bothered to write *about* them."

I nodded. "Lady Bronwyn and the Chief of Servants said something back in Bunard that seemed important. They said the rhymes and non-sense games children play are much like they have been for countless centuries and that they're at least as old as the liturgy."

Custos nodded. "That would explain Lady Bronwyn's penchant for reciting them."

"You know all of them?" I asked.

"Of course."

"Would you write them down?"

Custos laughed. "I don't think we have time."

I shook my head. "I only want the very oldest and in the oldest form you can recall. If there's something there that can help us, you're better equipped to find it than anyone else."

He nodded. "The language will be a problem, Willet."

"How so? You taught me to understand it, remember?"

He nodded. "But I couldn't give you knowledge I didn't have. You'll be interpreting it as I would, which is only as good as the books I've read."

I sighed. Nothing was ever easy. "Let's try anyway."

He pointed toward Bolt and Rory. "It will be a better use of my time than watching them practice. At my age, mastery of the sword is unlikely. How about 'The spirit is willing but the flesh is weak, since the proud became the meek.'"

He grinned at me. "I'll write the original form of that one first." He busied himself with his ink and parchment, and I turned toward the final member of our party, who reclined a few paces away under a tree.

I touched the door I'd built in my mind after I'd delved Volsk before Bas-solas. Just thinking about it brought an awareness of the construct I'd built to handle the memories of everyone I'd delved, a round room modeled after the sanctum in the Merum library with doors leading to each remembered life. Even now they fought to get loose, and occasionally a memory would slip free and visions of people I'd never known would come to me.

Then I would relive acts of violence and depravity I'd never committed.

Knowing I was innocent didn't help. I always felt as if I'd fallen into the gutter, the filth clinging to me like a second skin. I wandered over to the man who had tried to kill me, stopping three paces short.

Volsk opened one eye, glancing at me before he sighed and sat up. "Custos is trying to unravel the mystery behind the Darkwater."

"He'll need a healthy dose of luck," Volsk said.

"Bronwyn thought he might be able to do it."

He pursed his lips. "I doubt it. More accurately, she probably thought he had a chance, however small, of uncovering some facet of the cursed forest that might help."

I didn't care for his tone and said so.

His head swiveled toward me. "Try to understand this. The Vigil and their counterparts on the southern continent have been trying to understand the evil that lies within the forest here and the desert there for uncounted centuries. We're talking about people who live for almost a thousand years, with a lot of time to fill. Don't you think that if the key was hidden within a book they would have found it by now?"

"None of them can do what Custos can," I said. "His memory is perfect, and he only needs to read it once."

He nodded. "So you've said, but the Vigil as a whole, along with the people who work for them, can approximate his skill as a group."

I smiled. No matter how much I tried to explain, Peret Volsk had no idea what the man in front of us, intently scribbling on parchment, was capable of.

Half an hour later the sun dipped below the horizon, leaving us with the purple light of dusk. Rory sat on the ground with his head down, sweat dripping down his nose as his lungs worked like a bellows.

I stood, tried to stretch three days' worth of soreness out of my legs, and made for the trees. "I'll see if I can find some dry wood."

Bolt's voice stopped me before I took a second step. "No fire," he said. "Not tonight or any other night." Bolt looked north toward the mountains of the cut, his mouth tight. "Let's move the horses beneath the trees. We'll sleep a bit warmer if we're out of the breeze."

A thought occurred to me as I fell in beside Volsk. "Why are you still here?" I asked. "You could have run."

He broke from the glassy stare he must have mastered in prison to consider the question. "It's as good as any other place," he said. "For the moment."

"You could have left as soon as we were free of the city," I pressed. "You could have slipped away the first night."

Volsk nodded toward Bolt. "That's what he wants. Even when it looks like he's not watching me, he is."

Bolt nodded. "'Keep your friends close . . .'" He turned to Volsk. "A part of me hoped you would try to leave. That would have given me all the excuse I needed to hunt you down and kill you."

Volsk almost smiled. "That same thought occurred to me. Sorry to disappoint you." He looked at me. "My allegiances never changed. I've hated the Darkwater since I was a boy, and I've wanted to fight it for as long as I can remember wanting anything."

"When did that turn into working to get me killed?" I asked.

To his credit he didn't try to deny the accusation or make excuses for it. "From the moment the priests at the House of Passing described Elwin's death. His gift was meant for me."

"Answer this . . . " Bolt said, his voice flat and hard as an anvil.

Volsk turned away and shrugged, as Bolt continued. "You were Elwin's apprentice. How is it that you were absent at his death?"

"Apprentices are not guards," Volsk said without looking at anyone. "It's not our duty to watch over our masters without ceasing."

"Glib," Bolt said, "but pointless. Where were you? What were you doing while Elwin was dying?"

Volsk's eyebrows drew up over his smirk. "You accuse me of Elwin's death?"

But Bolt shook his head. "If by that you ask, do I think you held the sword, by no means. That was Robin's doing. Yet I can't help but notice you haven't answered."

My guard took a step toward Volsk, his hands empty, but that meant little to someone in possession of a gift as pure as his. "Where were you, Peret Volsk, when Elwin was attacked? Were you watching, waiting for him to die, hoping for his gift?"

Volsk's skin flushed, and he refused to answer. But he held his ground as well, planted like a tree, accepting Bolt's questioning without protest or defense. My guard made the most of the opportunity.

"This is beneath you," I said to Bolt. "He's agreed to help us find Faran, and you yourself told me the rest of the Vigil delved him before they put him in prison. If he had been complicit in Elwin's death, they would have killed him then and there."

"Perhaps." Bolt nodded. "But they never said where he was, and our former apprentice, the man who was going to be the strongest holder of the gift in a thousand years, hasn't answered my question. Well, Volsk?"

I threw up my hands. "Oh, for the love of Aer, have mercy."

Bolt turned his attention to me. "That you would say such a thing shows how little you comprehend the nature of the Vigil. Mercy is for those who can afford it. You hold the gift of domere. You judge. You don't grant mercy. Not ever."

I shook my head. "No. I won't sacrifice the rest of my humanity. I've already lost enough of it, and I refuse to believe it's necessary." I nodded toward Volsk. "And neither is this conversation. I touched him—remember?" Searching through the construct of the Merum sanctuary I'd built in my mind, I found the door that held Volsk's memories.

"That was when you were drugged," Bolt said. "What could you remember?"

I opened the door. "I don't think the gift cares." Memory flooded into me, most of it centered on Toria Deel in uncomfortable intensity.

I drifted back—still unused to experiencing memories as both owner and watcher—until I came to Volsk's memory of riding to the House of Passing, fear so desperate that it nearly robbed me of the ability to breathe. Then, just a bit further back in time, seeing Robin's body by the stone wall next to the Rinwash River, overhearing the guards speaking of Elwin.

I followed the strand of memory backward until I came to a darkened room, saw the flare and dancing flame of a lamp and two other men that I knew to be Elwin and Robin. Within the part of me that was the Eldest's apprentice, I knew the hour to be well past midnight, yet both Elwin and Robin were dressed.

"Peret," Elwin said, "Robin and I must run an errand. We'll return shortly."

I rubbed sleep from my eyes as I rolled from my bed. "It will only take me a moment to dress, Eldest. I'll come with you."

Elwin held out his hand, palm forward, and shook his head. "No need." His unblinking gaze flicked toward Robin at his side, and he cleared his throat. "No need. This will take but a moment."

But when I looked at Robin, he wore the expression of a man attempting to hide the evidence of an argument.

"Let me come with you, Eldest," I said.

But Elwin shook his head. "No. You're young. There's no need for you—" he paused—"for you to lose sleep as well."

He lifted his hand and put it on my head, and for a moment I wondered if he would release his gift to me.

"Soon, Peret, you will hold the gift," Elwin sighed. Then resolution filled his expression. "Soon. But I have a task to complete first, a promise made."

Elwin turned to leave the room, his back to both Robin and me, and for an instant by the fading light of the Eldest's lantern I could see Robin's face.

"Follow," he mouthed without a sound. Then he left to accompany Elwin on his errand.

I waited until I could hear the sound of their footsteps descending the stairs, decision warring within my chest. As Elwin's apprentice for the last four years I had sworn to obey him. What was the word of his guard against that? Guards did not hold the gift, could not imagine the depth of insight their masters held. I shook my head and put the boots I held in one hand to the side and stretched out on the bed, trying to find sleep. Two hours later I rose to check my master's room.

I closed the door to Volsk's memories. Blinking, I saw my companions gazing at me by the last light of dusk, the sense of dislocation I always felt fading as my real identity reasserted control.

"I'm having a hard time trying to figure out who I want to hit most," I said. I looked at Bolt. "If the rest of the Vigil were here I'd tell them just how incredibly stupid they've been." I turned to Volsk. "Aer in heaven, how could you be so dense? The man knew he was going into danger. It was written all over him."

Volsk shook his head. "I wouldn't expect a rogue like you to understand the obedience the Eldest of the Vigil commands."

This was more familiar, this rationalization. I'd seen it all too often in those left alive at the end of the fighting, witnessed it in those who'd held back while others charged. "Let me say this in a way you can understand." I swept Bolt and Volsk into my gaze. "You are all idiots," I said enunciating each word singly.

I saw them both stiffen, but I stabbed a finger at Bolt. "That Pellin, Bronwyn, and Toria Deel all delved him and knew of this but didn't tell me is past believing. I can't begin to describe how utterly stupid it was."

"Why should they tell you?" Volsk challenged. "Who are you compared to them?"

I saw Bolt shake his head. At least he understood.

"Who am I?" I asked. "I'm the one member of the Vigil who's been a reeve. They have hundreds of years of experience, but they don't deal with people." I pointed at Bolt. "He's already told me what life in the Vigil is like. Years of inactivity and solitude with the occasional hunt for someone who has brought their insanity back from the Darkwater."

Volsk looked at me, his expression completely uncomprehending.

"You really don't understand, do you. Look at your last memory of Elwin," I snarled. "Look at him! Did you notice how often he said there was no need for you to accompany him, how he stared at you without blinking, how he stumbled over his words? How many ways does a man have to scream 'I'm lying!' before you figure out he's lying?"

"Well said," Bolt nodded.

I rounded on him. "Shut it! You've helped them keep me ignorant of the very memories that might have helped me find Elwin's killer."

Volsk chose that moment to interrupt me. "You said Robin killed him, Reeve."

"Whatever turned Laewan and Jorgen came for Elwin too." I shivered, remembering a thousand dark strands that came for me from the depths of Barl's mind. "Robin didn't kill him—he saved him."

I shook my head in disgust. "Pellin promised to let me delve him, but he stayed away. He knew I wouldn't be able to hold him to his word while we were . . . " I stopped, not wanting to use the word that came closest to describing what I'd done. I clenched my jaws. If I had to deny mercy to others, as Bolt said, then I would have to deny it to myself as well. "While we were *killing* those tainted by the Darkwater." I took off my glove. "He's not here," I said to Bolt, "but you are. Enough. I need to know everything I can."

"'Be careful what you wish for,'" Bolt said.

"That one could be from Bronwyn or Toria." I chewed my words as though they offended me. "Something more military would suit you better."

I walked over to my guard. "I can't solve this unless I know what I need to know."

Bolt nodded and held out his arm, the skin thinned with age but tight over thick cords of muscle that could put a sword through a man within the blink of an eye.

"You cannot," Volsk said. "You were ordered not to allow it."

Bolt's brows lifted a fraction. "And you still don't see what unquestioning obedience has done to us? Even now, after the price of your inaction has been laid bare? You're a fool."

Red tinged the dark skin of Volsk's cheeks. "I admit I should have followed as Robin told me to. There, I've said it. But this is different, and you know it. He has a vault in his mind. Would you hand the enemy the means to destroy us?"

I stopped, my hand within inches of Bolt's arm. "Explain."

Volsk laughed. "You say you read people? Well and good, but the Vigil knows more about the possible implications of the Darkwater than you can begin to fathom. They've spent centuries trying to understand it, using each survivor to test their theories, refine them."

"Word games," I said. "They have no idea what it is."

"Think, Reeve," Volsk said. "Use your own experiences and teach yourself why you shouldn't touch any of us. I would never have let you touch me if I'd known you were going to survive. What happened during Bas-solas? What made Laewan so dangerous, so deadly?"

My hand was still within inches of Bolt's skin, but now I was afraid. I pulled my arm back. "He knew," I said, my voice barely loud enough to reach my own ears. "Laewan knew what each of his servants from the Darkwater saw."

"Exactly," Volsk said. "And when you touched the butcher, Barl, while his vault was open, you confirmed something the Vigil feared but had suspected only in their worst nightmares."

I lowered my arm. "The vaults are a window for the evil within the Darkwater." I shook my head in denial. "I'm not them."

Volsk almost laughed at me, even after cutting his gaze toward Bolt. "So you say. You might even be right. Do you blame Pellin and the rest for not taking the chance? Anything you know could be used against the Vigil."

I stepped backward until Bolt's naked arm was out of my reach. It should be easy enough to verify. What had the Vigil told me that had been used against us, some stratagem that could have only failed because it had been intercepted by the enemy directly from my mind?

Casting back through my memories, I couldn't recall any, but that didn't mean Volsk was wrong. It only meant it hadn't happened yet. Of course, Pellin and the rest had kept their own counsel, so there wasn't much for me to reveal.

Bolt still held his arm out like an offering. "And it's also possible that you represent the greatest threat to our enemy. You're a man who knows the Darkwater like no other and also holds the gift. 'The best weapons have more than one edge.'"

As much as I appreciated Bolt's gesture of confidence, I didn't move. "What can you tell me that can't be used against us?" I asked both of them.

Despite the enmity that existed between them, they shook their heads in unison. "Impossible to know," Volsk said.

"Perfect," I said. "I might as well return to Bunard and let the Chief of Servants throw me back in prison."

We found a dry spot beneath the trees, and each of us rolled into our cloaks, using our saddles and provisions as pillows. After a few moments I heard the regular breathing from Rory that signaled sleep. Volsk hadn't stirred from his original position. From Bolt's spot, I heard nothing except the occasional breath of his horse. I rose and backtracked the way we'd entered the stand of trees. If someone followed us, they'd come to this point. Bolt stood in the shadows of a large evergreen ahead of me, watching the river. The barest hint of light reflected off the water from a new moon.

He acknowledged my presence with a nod.

"What are we riding into?"

He shrugged. "I don't know. Even if we find Faran and his other apprentice hale and whole, we've had enough bad news to fill our plates for a long time."

I shrugged. "How can it be any worse than losing one of the Vigil and having an entire city go crazy?"

Bolt might have shaken his head. "That's just the problem. It wasn't an entire city, just a portion of it. If we've lost the sentinels, the next time will be worse, but that's the wrong question. You've got to know what the sentinels are to understand."

I laughed. "Everyone knows what the sentinels are. Mothers scare their children with tales of them, and every now and then some idiot gets drunk enough to attempt the forest and ends up as a meal. They're waist high at the shoulder, and they can tear a man apart in seconds."

Bolt didn't reply. He just stood watching the river. His silence and the hollowed-out feeling in my stomach confirmed my suspicions. "They've kept the whole truth from me again—am I correct?" I asked.

I might have imagined his nod in the darkness. "The Vigil is having a hard time committing to trust. They've spent centuries hunting down individuals with a vault in their mind, and now they find themselves having to work with one." He brooded over the river for a while before he went on. "There's more to the sentinels than just breeding and train-ing, Willet, but even if that were all, it would be enough. I don't have the words to tell you how hard it is to kill one." His voice grew louder in the stillness by a fraction. That was the only way I knew he'd turned toward me. "There's a reason we use them instead of human guards to patrol the boundaries of the Darkwater."

Tendrils of fear, like a child's terror at being alone in a dark room at night, worked their way down my back. "A dwimor?" Inside I prayed, but I didn't know for what.

"Aer have mercy," Bolt breathed. "I sure hope so. I'd much rather fight something that could kill half a dozen sentinels by stealth than something that could take them in a straight-up fight. Overmatched doesn't begin to describe it."

I shook my head. "You're telling me you think a dwimor could sneak up on a sentinel?"

"You have to see one to understand," Bolt said, as if that would satisfy me.

Nothing stirred on the stretch of grass that separated us from the river, the sound of frogs and crickets incongruously loud in comparison to the sounds of Bunard at night. "I don't remember the Darkwater being this loud," I said. It was more an attempt to fill the silence between us than anything else, but Bolt latched onto it.

"It wouldn't have been," my guard spat. "Nothing with any sense lives in that forest. The sentinels hunt the plains around it for food, or their trainers bring it to them if game is scarce."

In the darkness, with the noise filling my ears, I never heard the footsteps.

CHAPTER 23

"Wha-mmmph."

A skinny hand covered my mouth, and I turned to see its twin over Bolt's.

"Shh." The sibilant whisper fell on my ears, and I forced my tongue to silence. The pounding in my chest had a harder time obeying orders.

"Something's coming."

Rory's voice drifted across to me like a tendril of fog, and I waited for my heart rate to slow until I could almost count the beats. He pointed back among the trees.

I searched the shafts of silver moonlight that hit the forest floor between branches, following Rory's point and squinting until my eyes hurt with the effort. Once or twice, I thought I saw a shadow move, a shift of black on black beneath the trees.

"I see hints of movement," I whispered, "but that's all."

Next to me Bolt peered into the darkness, his gaze filled with deadly intent and his hand on his sword. "Nothing," he whispered. "Absolutely nothing."

Rory shook his head. "He's only twenty paces away now. How can you not see him?"

"Dwimor," Bolt and I whispered at the same time.

"He's gone still," Rory said. "Say something, anything." Then he melted away, merging with the shadows.

I shook my head, but Bolt was quicker. He turned back to his contemplation of the river as if nothing untoward had occurred. "The only thing that lives in the Darkwater is the forest, trees with gnarled roots and black leaves that create a canopy so thick you can hardly see the ground, even in the daytime." Sweat beaded on his brow, and I tried not to stare behind me, but my back muscles clenched against the sword or dagger thrust that had to be coming my way.

"How many times have you been there?" I asked. My voice came out half an octave higher than normal, but my effort served to cover the sound of Bolt pulling his sword. I shifted, trying to shield him from the direction Rory had pointed.

"More times than I care to recount, but at least once for every year I was part of the Vigil."

Then it came, the softest break of pine needles beneath a foot not more than three paces away. I put my hands on my daggers, one gripped for throwing and the second for parrying, though I had no idea how to defend against something I could barely see in a well-lit tavern, much less in darkness.

I whirled to the sound of impact—of a dagger finding its mark—and swung, finding only air. A split second later I heard the rush of displaced air and the *chunk* of another blade finding its mark, then the crunch of twigs as a body hit the forest floor.

Bolt leapt forward, his gaze and sword focused on the back of a man I could now see clearly by moonlight.

Rory stepped into a shaft of moonlight. "He's dead. I put the second one in his heart."

I rolled him over, my heart somehow stopping altogether as I looked on the face from Aellyn's drawing. If I hadn't been terrified enough to throw up, I would have been able to appreciate that little girl's mastery of parchment and pencil.

"Dwimor!" Bolt growled the word. "What direction was he coming from when you first saw him?"

I waited, hoping, but deep in my chest I already knew the answer.

"Northeast," Rory said.

I nodded. Bolt and I would have been dead if the assassin had come from behind us, tailing us from Bunard.

Bolt growled a curse. "He wasn't following us. Faran's dead."

My heart missed a pair of beats, and I fought for breath. "Custos!"

"The librarian's fine," Rory said. "The assassin never came closer than twenty paces of where we slept."

"You were awake?" Bolt asked.

Rory nodded in the moonlight. "I've never really been outside the city before. Everything is different, noisy in a strange way. I got up to take a look around. I heard the two of you talking and saw him change course, sneaking this way."

"Rory," Bolt said. "Wake Custos and Volsk and get the horses saddled. We'll ride the rest of the night. According to Volsk, that should put us at Faran's by midmorning."

The thief melted away in the darkness, but Bolt caught my arm as I moved to follow. "We have a problem."

"A problem?" I asked. "As in just one? That's a relief, because the way things were going, I thought we had a whole squad of them. The sentinels are being killed, leaving the Darkwater unguarded. Pellin can't find the missing gifts." I paused and my throat tightened. I would have held in what I said next if I could have. "And Gael wants me to find a way for us to be together when I'm not even sure I can find a way to stay alive."

"Are you done?" Bolt asked, his tone neutral, as though he really just wanted to know whether or not I'd finished.

"Yes," I sighed. "I'm done."

"It's Rory."

For a moment I didn't understand, but then I caught a glimpse of our dead assassin in the moonlight. "If he's the only one who can see them . . . he's the only one who can kill them."

Bolt nodded. "True enough. 'When the battle's going against you, use the weapon that works,'" he quoted. "There are requirements to being a Vigil guard that go beyond having the combination of giftedness and talents to make the best swordsman. Despite all the strings the Vigil pulls to make the rest of the world dance, they're all priests at heart. I didn't choose Rory just because his hands were quick."

I sighed. "It was because he took care of the urchins."

"Yes," Bolt said. "Despite all the training, most Vigil guards have killed less than a handful of men. Hah, even as an errant I did more threatening than killing. He's too young to shoulder the burden that comes with taking a life over and over again."

How long before Rory's heart turned into something hard and piti-less? "But we don't have a choice."

"True, but we have to find a way to keep his heart soft." Bolt shifted to move past me.

I thought about all the grudges I carried from court and how many times I'd dreamt of evening the score with all the nobles who made it a point to put me in my place. "I haven't exactly done a great job with myself."

I waited for a response, but I'd spoken to the air. I didn't know if Bolt had heard me or if it mattered.

We rode our horses at a walk with Rory in the lead, the night vision of a trained thief better than anything the rest of us could muster. When the sky lightened enough to hide the stars and the landscape became a blend of predawn grays, Bolt and Volsk moved to the front, Custos and I followed closely, and Rory took up the rear. We turned west and cantered toward a line of forested hills with barren tops.

Volsk cast a look at Bolt, who rode close enough to reach out and touch him if need be. He shifted his horse and Bolt followed, closing the distance to just within sword reach. The Vigil's former apprentice gestured at the empty landscape with a smirk. "Is there some threat here you feel compelled to safeguard me from?" When Bolt didn't answer, he went on. "Do you sense some danger from me that I've yet to reveal?"

Bolt's gaze went flat. "I don't trust you. I've never trusted you."

Volsk's mouth pulled to one side, but the expression fought with the tightness around his eyes. "Then allow me to be the first to congratulate you on your keen perception, master guard. Much heartache could have been avoided if the Eldest had taken your council." Volsk made a point of twisting in his saddle to look around. "But since there seems to be no threat imminent in the dawn, perhaps you could deign to give me space to reflect on the crimes of my wasted life."

"This," Bolt said, pointing at Volsk, "this is why I never trusted you. Your glib answers never revealed what was in your heart."

A door opened in my mind—not far, and not much, but enough to allow a memory to slide through that could have been my own except it had a different face attached to it. "Go easy," I told Bolt. I would have said more, but for an instant the mask of mocking and self-deprecation fell from Volsk to show something wounded beneath.

With a gesture he called Rory forward and pointed. "Come, gentle-man thief, I have something to tell you." When Rory came forward, he pointed. "You are in the presence of men whose mortality weighs heavily upon them. From what Pellin told me, Faran's place should be about a half mile ahead."

Rory blinked and squinted against the morning glare. "This place doesn't have much to recommend it. I like cities better."

Volsk nodded. "Understandable, but you may change your mind about that someday."

"Doubtful, considering what we're about to find," Bolt said.

We rode the rest of the way in silence, and soon turned to enter a thick stand of woods. For as far as I could see, the trees stretched away from us, not the black twisted oaks of the Darkwater, but old nonetheless—ancient towers whose trunks supported a handful of thick limbs stood close to young saplings no bigger around than my arm. Animals scurried away from us in the underbrush, and the trill and lilt of birds filled the air.

"Is this the Everwood?" Custos asked, looking around, his eyes bright and curious.

Bolt nodded. "The southern tip, anyway. It extends north and west from here for ten or twenty leagues before the trees all turn to softwoods."

The librarian peered into the shade beneath the canopy, his head jerking to catch each movement of a rabbit or squirrel that darted away from us.

"Are you hoping to catch sight of the Fayit, old friend?" I asked.

He turned to peer at me, chewing on his lower lip in false indigna-tion. "Have you ever wondered, my boy, why those legends never die? As far back as the history of man on the northern continent goes, the legends of the Fayit go as well." He tilted his head to sing.

> *"By the lakes and forests old,*
> *The Fayit guard their eldritch gold.*
> *Walking the wood and water there,*
> *Call the Fayit, if you dare."*

He stopped. I'd heard the song any number of times and had sung it myself when I was a boy in Bunard and we would play the circle game.

"And if you catch one—" I laughed, feigning a grimace to match his indignation—"will you force him to surrender his wealth?"

"Humph. First you ask me to tell you what I know about children's rhymes, and then you dismiss them. You're inconsistent, Willet." He stared through me for a moment the way he did whenever he pulled his focus inward to the vast library he kept in his head. "That one hasn't changed much, but the language is odd."

"How so?"

He shrugged. "It's like many of them, actually. The words are so old, it's almost impossible to ferret out the original intent. Too many of them could have multiple meanings."

Rory laughed the clean, joyful sound of a boy, and for a moment my heart lifted. "All you have to do is catch one and ask him."

Volsk stopped, turning his horse to check directions or landmarks before he caught Bolt's gaze. "We're close."

Bolt shook his head the way people do when they're commanding silence. The sound his sword made as he drew it drained the joy from our conversation like water running out the hole of a bucket. "Draw your knives, Rory. If you see anyone, *anyone*, you tell us. Don't assume that we can see them as well."

Another two hundred paces farther into the wood we entered a clearing and the smell of blood. Bolt growled an unceasing stream of curses under his breath at the sight. Volsk echoed him on the other side of me. Mounds of fur matted with blood were scattered across the clearing between a small cabin and a barn. Dead sentinels lay everywhere. So still.

And two human bodies.

I hadn't realized I'd dismounted and walked to the first of the dead sentinels until I'd already knelt to place one hand on the thick, coarse ruff of fur around the neck. I peered into the empty blue-eyed stare of the oversized hound, caught by the same spell that had kept me in thrall since my days in the Darkwater. "What do you see, boy?" I asked. "What's out there beyond the sky and stars that draws you so?"

"Willet?" a small voice called behind me. "It's dead."

I turned to see Rory looking at me, his expression uncertain and a little afraid. Of course. He wasn't aware of the malady that afflicted me in the company of the dead. Volsk stared at me with an expression that left me feeling naked and exposed. My mutterings might have been justification or confirmation for his betrayal. I couldn't tell.

Bolt just looked at me, waiting, his sword out, but in the deep wrinkles that tracked across his forehead I thought I detected an emotion I hadn't seen before. Resignation. Whatever had killed an entire pack of sentinels was more than a match for a Vigil guard.

With a start, I stepped back from the sentinel. *Aer, have mercy.* It was just an oversized dog. When had I ever been drawn to the stare of a dead animal? The farmyard pitched in my vision, tilting back and forth like the ocean seen from the deck of a ship. First Ealdor and now this. What was happening in my mind?

I dropped to my knees and squeezed my eyes shut, digging my hands into the dirt of the clearing, trying to prove its reality. But Ealdor had been real. I remembered his touch, warm and welcoming on my shoulder, recalled him standing next to me while I officiated behind the altar. Oh yes, Ealdor had been real right up until Bronwyn had proved he wasn't.

"What's wrong with him?" Rory asked.

Hands that felt strong enough to gouge stone hauled me to my feet, and Bolt's thumbs pried my lids open. Bolt gazed at me, his face close, peering from one eye to another.

"Is it real?" I asked. He couldn't possibly understand my question. I didn't know myself.

"It's real," he nodded. "Willet, you need to be a reeve now. We need to know as much as we can about who did this and why."

I stepped away and pulled my shoulders back. Yes. I could do that. I looked at Rory, tried to give him a comforting smile that must have failed, and then nodded to Custos and Volsk. "Don't touch anything."

I backed away from the dead sentinel and searched the ground for the impressions that might tell me what had happened. I didn't have Gareth's knack for it, but I hoped I wouldn't need it. "Volsk, how many people lived here?"

"Three," he said. "Faran." He pointed to the crumpled body of an old man within a couple of paces of the cabin's door. "That's him there. The other one is his apprentice, Afyred. Viona you know about already."

I tried to keep the contents of my stomach where they belonged.

"Viona killed herself to keep this place secret, and it didn't matter. They found them anyway."

Volsk nodded, his eyes dark. "They had to have supplies. Faran and Afyred had no way of knowing what happened to her."

A thought struck me. "Why two apprentices?"

"Faran was almost done. When we stumbled across Viona a couple of years ago, we recruited her." His voice hitched. "They were all different, like your friend Myle."

That caught my attention. I knew the answer to the next question but asked it anyway, testing to see if I could trust Volsk's answers. "Were they all gifted?"

He shook his head. "No, only Faran held the gift of devotion, but they all had surprisingly strong talents for nature."

I stored that away in case I needed it again and moved to each of the bodies, checking their boots, memorizing the shape of each heel in the hopes of finding something I could use. But when I surveyed the ground around the sentinels, I had to swallow my disappointment. The hard-packed earth denied impressions that might have aided me. A smaller mound of fur near each of the sentinels caught my attention.

Whoever had killed them had struck down the pups as well. That only made sense, but it still heated coals within my chest. Back in Bunard, I'd never had much use for men or women who made it a practice to abuse animals.

I stopped. "Custos, count the sentinels. Rory, you count the pups."

They moved off to circle the clearing while I pondered the strange assortment of bodies. Faran and his apprentice had been done in by sword strokes, as had the sentinels and the pups. Many of the small furred bodies had been cut almost in two, killed instantly by sword strokes from various angles, scattered around the clearing as if they'd been killed while they were in chaotic motion. I shook my head. But not the adults. In fact, every wound on the adults had been placed with surgical precision. Vast pools of blood surrounded each of them. It appeared as though it was as Bolt had expected and hoped for—they'd been killed by a dwimor, presumably the one Rory had killed the night before.

A scattering of arrows lay in random positions close to the center of the clearing near one of the sentinels, and a bit farther away a couple of daggers littered the ground as well. I picked up one of the arrows.

The broadhead dangled from the rest of the shaft, held on by a few threads of wood. "Somebody saw the dwimor coming," I said to Bolt. "Volsk told me Afyred was nearly forty."

"Yes, he'd apprenticed under Faran for almost twenty years."

"That doesn't fit. Afyred had ten years on me, and I could barely catch a hint of the dwimors I saw. Unless there's something about the way Myle's type of mind works that allows them to see someone no other adult can, I don't think Afyred ever saw the dwimor. He probably fired his bow the same way you aimed your sword strokes in Braben's."

I sighed and handed the ruined arrow to Bolt. "The dwimor knocked at least one of Afyred's arrow down with his sword in midfight." I caught Bolt's gaze. "Could you do as much?"

He gave me a tight gaze and nodded. "It's not as hard as it appears. Killing the sentinels would be more difficult."

I shook my head. "Obviously not. Look. Each of them was taken in the throat with a single stroke."

Bolt nodded. "The adults couldn't have seen him coming. Not even Robin could have killed a pack of sentinels. You'd have to see one fight to understand."

My mind conjured the ferocity that could take down the most gifted trained swordsmen in the world. "I'd rather not."

I kept coming back to it, though. I'd witnessed Bolt in a fight. He didn't flaunt his gift the way I'd seen others do, with acrobatic jumps and leaps that defied imagination, but even advanced in years, he could move so fast the eye had a hard time keeping up. How could a single oversized dog hope to defeat such a man?

"Twelve." Custos broke me from my abstraction.

I looked to Bolt and he nodded. "The trainer here in Collum kept more sentinels in reserve since the border with the Darkwater is longer."

"Ten," Rory said, walking up, his gaze filled with threats. "Who kills a bunch of pups?"

Bolt's eyebrows lifted.

Volsk's gaze sharpened, turning outward from whatever hell he'd been reliving within his memories. "It's not impossible, but highly unlikely. Half the sentinels are females, and they always give birth to a pair. Always."

Custos's eyes widened. "Fascinating, but dogs will often lose a few of their litter, yes?"

Bolt shook his head. "Sentinels aren't dogs. They're hardier. I'm not saying it's impossible, but it's more likely that there are a couple of pups hidden beneath the adults." He looked at me. "We have to be sure."

The four of us moved to the nearest sentinel and worked together to roll the body, a female, over. I grabbed the legs and lifted, overwhelmed with shame at the indignity of the animal's death and the necessity of moving it like an oversized piece of furniture. "I'm sorry, girl," I said. "We're trying to find your puppy."

Rory's face twisted as he tried to keep from crying. "I'd like to put a dagger through the eye of whoever did this."

The earth beneath the sentinel was bare. We moved to the next, a male, and repeated the process with the same result. When we put our hands on the sixth one, another female, sound came from the forest behind us and we stilled, listening. I put my hands on the sentinel again and heard a faint growl that ended in a whimper.

I straightened. "That's one," I said. I looked at Bolt. "What do we do now?"

"We need that pup," he said.

"No question."

"It's hurt," Rory said.

"Is there some greeting or training you use to distinguish friend from foe?" I asked Bolt.

Volsk shook his head. "We never needed one. Each trainer has at least half a dozen sentinels to protect him. It would take scores of men to get through such a defense." He waved at the trees. "And almost no one knew he was here."

"I'll get it," Rory said.

"Boy," Bolt said, "that is about the stupidest thing I've ever heard. It may sound small and hurt, but that sentinel pup is already fifty pounds of teeth, with fur so dense you'd be hard-pressed to cut through. If it goes for your throat, I won't be quick enough to help you."

Rory's eyes hardened in defiance. "I know what it means to be an orphan."

Bolt opened his mouth to respond, but a moment later he nodded. "That you do. Be careful."

Rory walked to the edge of the brush bordering the clearing, and a growl rumbled from the foliage. Then he sat on the ground and spread his arms. Leaning forward he made kissing noises. "It's okay. I'm here."

The growl scaled upward in pitch, as if the pup questioned him. Rory continued to beckon, and a few minutes later a black nose poked its way between the leaves where two bushes grew together.

"C'mon, boy," Rory crooned to the nose. A moment later the rest of a black-and-gray muzzle emerged. Then, dropping its head as it came limping from the bushes, the sentinel pup emerged, watching Rory.

Bolt tensed, but his posture held conflict, as if he didn't know who to save.

The pup put its nose into Rory's cupped hand and then moved to lie down, exposing a long, open cut along its flank. The rest of us, even Volsk, all breathed silent curses. I'd seen hunting dogs with less severe injuries put down to save them from a slow death by infection.

"Rory," I called softly, "we can't save him. He's half dead already."

Rory's head jerked. The pup started, then whimpered in pain. For a moment, no one else spoke, neither condemning nor supporting my suggestion.

Then Bolt stepped forward. "Yes, we can."

"Look at that wound," I pointed. "You can't be serious."

"We have to at least try. Do you think this is the only camp that got attacked?" Bolt asked. "That pup may be our only chance at restoring the sentinels."

I turned on Bolt with a mix of anger churning in my gut—that the pup would suffer needlessly, that Rory would have to watch it die slowly, that I alone had been put in the role of executioner. "It's a pup. We'll never be able to get it to stay still enough to heal."

I gestured at the oozing trench that ran down the side of the sentinel. "How many feet of thread do you think it will take to close that wound? How is that going to happen?"

Bolt's face hardened, going from stone to iron. "We'll take him to a healer."

I looked skyward, but Aer didn't seem of a mind to help me make Bolt understand. I pulled a deep breath and let it out in a long sigh. "Fine. We need to be about it then."

Bolt shook his head. "Not yet. We have to find the other one."

"We don't even know if there is another one," I said.

"There's always the same number of pups as there are adults," Bolt said. "Always. Help me with the others."

I shrugged, resigning myself to Bolt's strange sense of duty. "Custos, search the cabin, and, Volsk, the barn. Let's get Fluffy over there fed and watered before we ride out of here. The little fella's going to need all his strength for the ride."

Bolt and I searched beneath the rest of the bodies for the missing pup. The stench of blood and death couldn't dispel the strange attraction I felt every time I met the gaze of the dead animals. Bolt preceded me to each one, closing their eyes before we checked beneath them.

"We'll need to drag the bodies into the barn and fire it," Bolt said. "It's not perfect, but there will be fewer questions that way."

I pointed at the sky. "A plume of smoke isn't exactly subtle."

"There's no one in the area to see it."

Custos came out of the cabin laden with supplies and stood a few paces away from the pup, watching it the way a city-bred man would eye a snake, wondering whether or not its bite would be poisonous. Volsk exited the barn soon after.

"Volsk," Bolt called. "Where is the closest healer worth anything?"

The former apprentice to the Vigil pulled his attention from the pup nuzzling Rory's hands. He pointed off to the northwest. "Gylden, but we'll have to cut through the southern portion of the Everwood."

Bolt nodded. "Three days. Maybe more, if we have to slow our trip for the pup."

"Gylden? Are you crazy?" I closed my mouth around what I'd been about to say and tried not to gape. "You want me to voluntarily walk into the seat of Duke Orlan's power?" I didn't bother giving Volsk and Rory context for my outburst. They knew. Everyone in Bunard and most of the people of Collum who possessed a working pair of ears knew I'd exposed and killed the duke's brother for gift stealing. The fact that he'd intended to set himself up as king hadn't earned me the duke's favor. He viewed his brother's actions as a stain on the family honor, a very public smudge that my death would help to clean.

"If I'm recognized, someone is going to try very hard to put a knife in my ribs." I stepped closer to Bolt. "The pup can't survive. You know this. A man might allow a healer to put ten feet of thread in his skin and remain still enough through the following days to recover, if he didn't bleed to death first—but not a dog, a pup." I shook my head. "No. I will not walk into Orlan's stronghold and give him the opportunity to kill me."

Bolt looked at me, and I wondered how eyes so clear could hide so much. "You're doing it again." I ran through Jeb's vocabulary in my head, but none of his words seemed like the right fit. "Out with it. Give me a reason to put my life in jeopardy for an animal that can't survive."

Bolt glanced down at my hands, then over at the pup cradled in Rory's arms. "You'll need to take your gloves off."

Someone must have cut the strings holding my heart in place, because I felt it drop into my stomach. I pulled the glove from my right hand and walked over to the pup, its light-blue eyes eerily similar to Bolt's. The thick fur on the hound's head ran from pitch black at the neck and ears to a light gray around the muzzle. At the top of the head, a ghost-white patch in the shape of a rough circle only served to accent the deep hue of the rest of the fur. The effect gave the pup a perpetual frown. I tried to ignore the open wound and the blood that matted the fur as I reached out to put my hand on its head.

My experience delving my horse, Dest, hadn't prepared me. With a lurch I fell through the pup's eyes and into memories that carried hints of reasoning and intelligence, an awareness no animal should have possessed.

Pain flooded through the bond, and I sucked air and flinched against the wound in my side. Thousands upon thousands of smells cascaded into my awareness—blood, plants, woodland animals, birds, horses, men, and steel all painted the clearing and woods around me in a tapestry I could almost touch and see through my nose. Thought colored each odor, evaluated and catalogued it, separating each into classifications of friend, food, or foe.

I fell back through time, saw figures on horses that I recognized as myself and my comrades entering the clearing, bearing the smell of men, but not knowing if they were enemies or allies. Further back I saw the eyes of my dam, one paw on my head as she breathed her last, awareness stifling the pain that danced along my side like tongues of fire. Mourning cut through me like a second sword stroke, the loss of the pack.

One last memory came across the link. Three men, one carrying a sentinel pup away—my sister, Modrie—as I crawled into the brush to hide my fear and mourning, waiting to die.

I fell back, breaking contact with the sentinel pup, and the texture of a thousand different smells faded from my awareness. I looked at Bolt in disbelief. "What has the Vigil done?"

CHAPTER 24

Bolt glanced at Rory before giving me a slight shake of his head. "We don't have time."

"Take time," I snapped, biting off my words as I jerked my glove back onto my hand. "Here. Now. Explain to me why delving this oversized dog is so much like delving a man."

Rory, who had no religious training or context to understand all the implications, stared at me in disbelief.

I waved a hand at the sentinel pup, who had managed to shift just enough in Rory's lap to watch me with almost human comprehension. Could it understand speech? I didn't know. Nothing in its head suggested it, but those humanlike memories started from the moment its mother placed her paw on its head. Aer have mercy, a sentinel had invoked the rite of blessing.

"As the king's reeve, I'm supposed to haul you and the rest of the Vigil before the magistrate. Aer help the Vigil—if they've gifted these animals, they should be executed."

"No one gifted them," Bolt and Volsk said at the same time.

"Don't give me that," I snapped. Spinning on one heel, I walked among the dead, checking the adults and pups to confirm my intuition. I hadn't noticed before, but every adult and most of the pups bore the same mark. "Look," I pointed. "Every sentinel has the imprint of a paw on its head." I found a pup that didn't. "Except this one. What happens when a sentinel's gift goes free? Curse you, I killed a man for a crime like this. According to the church, putting a gift into an animal is an abomination. We're supposed to kill it, not find a healer for it."

I walked back over to Rory and the pup, knelt down to survey the wound again. It seeped blood and didn't look any less horrific no matter how often I checked it. "It's going to die anyway."

"Not if you tell him to stay still," Bolt said.

"Do you think it's going to listen to me?"

He sighed. "That's not what I meant. Use your gift to put a picture of riding still in his mind."

"I can do that?"

He nodded. "How do you think the dwimor were made?"

I didn't want to think about how far I could push the power of domere. "How did they get the gift?" Despite my protests, it hurt to see the shape the pup was in. There was always something about animals in pain, the powerlessness to understand their suffering and the immediacy of it that wrung my heart. In my days as Laidir's reeve, if I suspected someone of serious crimes, the kind I didn't tell Gael about, I watched them with their animals, looking for casual cruelty.

"The originals were ennobled," Volsk said. I turned to face him but he seemed disinclined to add anything more. Bolt didn't bother to contradict him.

I couldn't help it, I laughed. "Ennobled? The hand of Aer's son, Iosa, touched them and made them sentient?"

Even to my ears, my laughter sounded harsh, abrasive, but it flowed around and away from Bolt, like water diverting around a boulder in a stream. "I'm not saying Iosa was the one who ennobled them, but why do you think we call them *sentinels*?" he asked.

"Myths and legends," I said. "Ooh, there's the Everwood." I pointed to the forest stretching away to the northwest. "As long as we're at it, why don't we go find one of the Fayit and get him to tell us where his gold is?"

Something warm and wet glided along my hand. I looked down to see the sentinel pup, its eyes filled with intelligence, looking back at me, and the strange draw I'd felt in the presence of its dead parents made sense.

"Actually," Volsk said, "according to legend it was the first man, Cuman, who held the power to ennoble beasts, in the act of granting them their name. When men first came across the strait to settle the northern continent, the Vigil brought the sentinels with them."

Custos nodded, as if confirming his explanation.

"What did you see when you delved it?" Bolt asked.

I shrugged. Somehow my hand had ended up on the sentinel's head, stroking it, and the longing to use my gift rose in me again. "A world defined by scents and three men leaving the clearing. One of them had the other surviving pup in his arms."

"Did you see their faces?"

"No," I sighed. "I assume one of them was the dwimor we encountered last night, but the others could have been anyone. The question is, how do we find them?"

"Easy," Rory said. "Wag can track him."

"Wag?"

Rory smiled. "He needs a name, and I like the way his tail moves even when the rest of him is really still."

"'A righteous man is kind to his animals,'" Bolt said.

I grunted. "A quote from the liturgy? You're branching out."

Bolt cocked his head to one side. "I've always considered myself an ecumenical sort of fellow."

I took off my glove. "All right, if we're going to do this, let's be about it. Rory, give him to me. I need to figure out how to get an idea into Wag's head about what needs to happen—otherwise he's not going to make it to Gylden, intelligent or not."

Rory bent to murmur into the sentinel pup's ear. "Go to Willet, Wag. He's your master and he needs to talk to you."

I didn't know if it was Rory's shift in weight or if the dog really understood him, but Wag rose, shaking, to his feet and stood before me.

"Rory, Volsk," Bolt called. "Help me bring the bodies into the barn."

I took off my glove and held my hand above Wag's head, unsure of just what I intended. I needed to plant an image in his head, a picture of Wag riding on horseback, calm and unmoving, but when I placed my hand on the wiry fur a tidal wave of impression overwhelmed me.

Master! Master! Master!

I pulled my hand away. Wag's tongue lolled out of his mouth in what must have been the equivalent of a dog smile. "Great," I muttered. "How am I supposed to get you to understand me if I can't get you to be quiet?"

Wag pulled his tongue in and dropped his head, looking up at me from beneath his brows. "All right, you understood that, which is a little scary."

I put my hand back on his head and focused on a picture of Wag riding still and quiet on horseback, repeating the image over and again. Then I took my hand away for a moment and put it back to see if the image remained. It hadn't. Wag looked up at me, tail thumping despite the wound in his side. "I can't get this silly dog to remember anything."

Bolt stopped and looked at me in the midst of carrying one of the dead pups into the barn. For a moment I suspected him of mirroring Wag's amusement. "You've never had children, Willet. It's a puppy. Its attention span is going to last just until the next distraction. It was the same with Robin when he was a child."

I shook my head. "The way you talk about him, I thought Robin sprang into being like some mythical god come to life." As soon as the words left my mouth I gasped, trying to pull them back in. The recent death of Bolt's son would surely still be an emotional wound no less grievous than Wag's, and I'd just jabbed a thumb into it with my unthinking jest.

Bolt stared at me for a moment in shock, and then he laughed—not the cynical chuckle that he usually assayed when someone around him had decided to be spectacularly stupid, but an honest laugh. His eyes, however, showed the ripping grief the loss of his son carried, and tears wet his face. He made no move to hide them or wipe them away but just continued to laugh and cry at the same time, until his mirth and pain ran their course. By the time he called my name, I'd long since dropped my gaze out of embarrassment.

"Willet, thank you," he said. "Robin was a child and a boy and a man like any other, with virtues and faults. I do him a disservice if I present him as something other than what he was. Lying in the name of the dead is a foolish custom. Truth be told, from the time he could totter around on his chubby little legs, Robin could be incredibly stubborn, even to his own detriment." He nodded to the dog in my lap. "Be patient and persistent."

I put my hand back on the pup, grateful for a chance to move on from the subject of Bolt's dead son. I concentrated on implanting the idea of riding quietly in Wag's head until half an hour later it remained.

Bolt stood in front of the barn holding a flaming torch, flanked by Volsk, Custos, and Rory. The urchin's expression filled with speculation before his gaze flicked over the barn and away, and back again, both drawn and desperate to be elsewhere.

Bolt cocked his arm to throw.

"Stop," I said.

"We're kind of in a hurry here."

Rory had finally settled on a single point of focus, a spot of the Everwood, waiting. "It won't take that long to teach Rory the antidon. Aer knows he'll probably need it again."

Rory turned to me his brows arched in disbelief. "It's not enough that you're turning me into a growler, you want to make me wear a robe, yah?"

I nodded. "If you're going to be part of this, you'll have to be both." I pointed to Bolt. "He's a guard, but he works for the church, so, yes, he's a growler in a robe, if you want to put it that way. But this is about respect. Even in the urchins, you honored your dead."

Rory took a moment, but he nodded all the same. He still didn't look thrilled about reciting part of the liturgy, but he didn't try to assault me with his fake accent either.

I nodded to Bolt, who threw the torch onto the hay and wood piled around the bodies of the men and sentinels. "Repeat as much of this as you can. We'll work on this, and the rest of it as well."

"Forasmuch as it pleases Aer to receive the souls of the departed we therefore commit their ashes to the earth, time without end, knowing . . ."

Surprisingly, Rory hung in and recited the entire thing, watching while the flames licked their way across the wood piled within and then jumped to the boards of the barn itself, the ends blackening before puffs of fire burst forth from the smoke.

"Wag will have to ride with you," Bolt said to me as we finished. We'd put food and water into Wag until he seemed satisfied and packed the rest onto my horse.

Rory's hand found the dog's head, and Wag leaned into it weakly as he scratched behind his ears. "Why can't he ride with me?"

Bolt shook his head. "You're a Vigil guard. You have a job to do."

Rory shrugged. "You keep telling me I'm just an apprentice. 'Try not to cut yourself with your sword, boy.' You say it all the time."

"And I'm right," Bolt said, "but you're the only one of us who can see a dwimor clearly."

"Oh," Rory said, "I forgot."

"You can't afford to forget, not ever," Bolt said. "Don't let the last few days give you the wrong impression. We're called the Vigil because we keep watch. Very little of our lives are spent fighting. 'Soldiering is nine parts boredom and one part terror,'" he quoted.

"That's the truth of it," I added. "Even during wartime."

Rory's mouth pulled to one side. "I can't believe I signed up for this."

"You were tricked," Bolt said. "I told you about the interesting parts first and never got around to mentioning the rest." He shrugged. "Or perhaps I forgot. I'm getting old, and my memory isn't what it used to be."

I pointed to Volsk. "What about him?"

Bolt shook his head.

"His part in this is done," I said.

"You want to set him loose?" Bolt asked. "Do you not remember what happened the last time he was left to his own devices? We almost got killed."

I looked around the clearing and at the forest. "I don't see any threats here."

"I'd still rather have him where I can keep an eye on him."

Volsk nodded. "I would rather stay in your company."

Bolt didn't look pleased to have the former Vigil apprentice agree with him.

"If I am found alone," Volsk said, "I will certainly be thrown back in prison."

"That's inevitable," Bolt growled, "and well-deserved."

Volsk shrugged. "All the more reason to delay it as long as possible."

"I have an alternative that might keep you out of prison, at least for a while," I said. "Do you have pen and parchment?"

He nodded.

"Perfect. I'm going to draft a letter to the orders that might just keep you free." He cocked his head at me. "You're going to take Custos to

Aille. Show him the Vigil library." I glanced at my librarian friend, and his eyes widened with apparent joy.

Volsk nodded, his dark eyes filled with suspicion. "Why?"

"Why what?"

"Why are you offering me my freedom?"

"Because Custos can't get there on his own, and no one else is available. But understand this. . . . " I leaned forward to point at his chest. "I'm making his safety your responsibility. If anything happens to him, you'll wish one of the sentinels had gotten hold of you instead of me."

It sounded good, but I could tell my threat didn't really impress him. Bolt must have seen it to. He stepped up to Volsk until their noses were less than a hand apart. "I like the librarian. I consider him to be a friend." Then he turned away.

I wrote my letter, addressed it to the order heads—including the kings and queens, for good measure—and explained Custos, the task Lady Bronwyn had laid upon him, and the necessity of Volsk's protection.

After a solemn good-bye and my promises that we would see him soon, Custos mounted and turned his horse to leave. Volsk reined his horse next to me, without a word took the letter, and rode away, never looking back.

"He might just abandon Custos and disappear, you know," Bolt said.

"I don't think so. It's more likely he'll work himself to death trying to earn his redemption. I just hope he doesn't take Custos or anybody else down with him."

I mounted Dest and Bolt handed Wag to me. I settled him in front and he straddled my horse, his legs hanging down each side. The wound in his side still bled, staining the cloth we'd wrapped around it. It was a simple proposition, really—could we get him to a healer before he died of blood loss?

The trees that loomed over us as we entered the Everwood had nothing in common with the twisted oak and ash trees that comprised the Darkwater, the verdant green of these leaves as different from the forbidden forest's oily black as day was from night. That knowledge did nothing to suppress the chill that crept over me as we passed from sun to shadow.

"Are you all right?" Bolt asked me.

"I'm not a fan of forests. Bad things happen to me in them."

Rory laughed. "Bad things happen to you everywhere, Willet, yah?"

I nodded. "I thought war had taught me just how bad things could get. That was before I spent a night in the Darkwater."

"Well, there's nothing in the Everwood," Bolt said, "except an abandoned village about halfway to Gylden." We left the burning farmstead behind us and rode deeper into the gloom.

CHAPTER 25

After a day and a half of riding through the forest along game tracks up and down the folds of the rolling hills, we came to the deserted village of Idel. Wag rode in front of me, and though he remained quiet and slept most of the time, he still took food and water.

But I worried. I regularly found myself bending over the pup to sniff the air above the boiled linen we'd used to bandage his wound, waiting for the sickly-sweet smell that meant the injury had fouled. I tried not to think of how Rory would react or the look in Wag's eyes when we put him to the sword.

Bolt slowed, eyeing a wall of ivy before he dismounted to wade through thigh-high grass to chop at the vines with his sword. The verdant green fell away to reveal gray stones and crumbling mortar of an abandoned building.

"This is it," he said. "We can stop here for the night. Gylden is almost a full day's ride west, but that's just as well." He gave me a brief nod. "Duke Orlan's holding is probably not the best place to be seen during the day, for several reasons."

The only saving grace was that I was quite sure the Duke was still in Bunard with the rest of the noble court.

He sighed, and on any other person I would have said his gaze grew wistful. "I didn't think the forest would take it back so quickly."

"What happened?" Rory asked.

Bolt's mouth pulled to one side. "Nothing unusual. It was a prospecting town, and after the river panned out, most of the people left. The

212

few who remained tried farming, but it's too far north and the soil was too rocky. Throw in conscription for one of the wars with Owmead and a fever and, there you have it, the perfect mix of circumstances to kill a village." He cast a glance overhead. "No rain tonight, but I'd still rather have a roof, such as it is, over my head." He pointed to a broad expanse of high grass. "There's a church at the end of the lane."

The sanctuary stood open to the sky, but one of the small outbuildings still held its covering, the roof somehow still in place despite the ravages of time, inattention, and weather

As we set up camp, a strange abstraction came over me, a division within my mind that spoke of equal parts fear and wonder. It had been ten years since I'd let nightfall come upon me in any woods. Since that fateful time in the Darkwater, I'd avoided forests and even gave the wooded gardens within the city a wide berth after sunset.

Long, nearly horizontal shadows interrupted by beams of yellow made it plain I would have to swallow my fear and endure a night in the Everwood. I held out my hands, surprised that they didn't tremble. At the same time, something about the village whispered to me, speaking some sense of peace in its abandonment, as though the people who'd built it had served their purpose and were rightfully gone.

I shook my head at the strange notion, eyeing the short, thick stone buttresses along the walls of the sanctuary. I counted back and realized I hadn't celebrated mass—or imagined I had—since just before Bassolas back in Bunard.

"I'm going for a walk," I announced.

Surprisingly, Bolt didn't protest or order Rory to follow me. Instead he looked to the sentinel pup. "Wag?" The hound lifted his head and stared into the forest while he sniffed, his nose making a small twitching motion and his ears up, but after a moment he laid his head back down and closed his eyes.

Bolt gave me a small, confident nod. "It's safe."

I didn't bother to try to disguise the doubt on my face.

He nodded to say Wag's nose settled the matter and put another stick into the crude pyramid for a fire. "After Wag's healed, I'll show you. The king of Moorclaire's best hunting dogs can't begin to approach what a sentinel is capable of. If Wag's not worried about anything in the forest, there's nothing to worry about."

Moorclaire, with its long stretches of rolling plains, boasted the finest hunting dogs in the world, and the best of those belonged to the king. The nobles there bred and trained dogs the way other monarchs lavished their time and attention on horses.

I pointed at Wag. "Just how much of the forest can he smell?"

Bolt straightened. "The wind is swirling here between the hills. There's nothing anywhere close."

The hills surrounding us were miles away. At first I thought he'd made a joke, but the craggy lines of his face remained in their unamused position.

The inside of the church reminded me of Ealdor's parish. Perhaps abandonment had conspired to reduce both edifices—one in the city, the other in the forest—to their essence.

Saplings had pried the stones apart on the main aisle leading to the altar. I threaded my way between them, noting the stone pews on the way. I paused to survey the interior of the sanctuary a bit more closely. Except for the roof, which had rotted away, everything in the church had been sculpted or fashioned from stone. The roof had been mostly thatch resting on a lattice-work of wood strips laid across a few beams.

I stepped over the crumbling remains of one of them that had fallen from its lofty perch to shatter against the altar, knocking one of the stones loose from the corner. On a flat smoothed stone in the center of the altar the intersecting arcs of Iosa—the symbol of faith, regardless of order—had been carved. I traced it with my fingertips, then stared out over the benches, but the expected longing didn't wash over me.

I stood there pretending to address the shades and shadows that constituted my congregation and raised my hands in benediction or warding. "The world is more than just priests and altars and celebrating haeling."

I heard the soft tread of a footstep an instant before the voice.

"You mean you don't want to officiate anymore, Willet?" Ealdor asked me. He walked out from behind a crumbling stone buttress to one side of the dais where I stood, draping his worn linen stole across his shoulders. I stared at the phantom as it approached. Aer help me, I could hear his footsteps.

"You're not real," I breathed.

His eyes narrowed as he smiled. I couldn't help but search the dust for footprints. Mine were easy enough to see even in the fading light. I walked past Ealdor, or the image of Ealdor, or the latest piece of insanity my mind had conjured, and searched the path he'd walked for proof.

There wasn't any.

I looked up at the trees that served as the roof of the abandoned church, mocking me with their ordinary healthy green. "It's the forest," I muttered. "Nothing good happens in the woods, Darkwater or no."

Ealdor shook his head. "These woods have nothing in common with the Darkwater, Willet. You know that."

He looked so solid. "You're a phantom," I said to it. "I conjured you from my pain and loss and turned you into a friend I thought I'd known since childhood." I stopped to sift through the memories of my life before war and fighting and the Darkwater twisted it from Aer's intention. "And I don't have a single memory of you with anyone else around."

He smiled. "And do your senses and memories determine what is real?"

I almost laughed but stopped just short. The more I fed my mind's notion that Ealdor was real, the harder it would be to dispel. I needed to leave. Arguing with it only gave it more of a hold over me. "Yes, what better?"

"You've never been to the southern continent, Willet," Ealdor said amiably, "or Aille, or Caisel, or Moorclaire, or—"

"I get your point," I said. "But I have verification that those places and the people in them are real."

He nodded as if I'd just offered up my bishop or queen in a useless gambit on the ficheall board. "So only the things that can be independently verified are real. Is that what you're saying?"

I knew this trap from my days as a Merum acolyte, knew that as soon as I answered Ealdor would have me. If I said *yes* he would pose the question of faith and how men could have faith in Aer without material proof of His existence. If I answered *no*, then I'd refuted my own argument.

But either answer only played into a larger trap, that of conversing with Ealdor at all. By engaging in a theological argument with him, I gave this figment of my wounded imagination all the force and authority of reality. "I'm not talking to you anymore. You're not real."

"It doesn't matter if I'm real," Ealdor said softly.

I didn't answer, but I didn't leave either. The figment my mind had conjured and named Ealdor had been one of the few friends I could boast after the Darkwater. Between him and Custos, and to a lesser extent, Gareth, I'd forged enough companionship to keep me from slipping into the downward spiral that had consumed so many of my brothers-in-arms. I'd managed to avoid the deaths—quick or slow, drink or drug—that came to so many of us by our own hand after war.

Ealdor had been my closest friend, a priest who'd heard my confessions of night-walking, of entering the Darkwater and coming out alive the next day, of wanting Gael and knowing I couldn't have her.

I sat on the moss-covered steps of the dais. "I should have seen it. No one was ever in your church. The building kept getting more and more decrepit. What kind of priest turns down offerings to help rebuild his parish?" I thought through our conversations. "And you never told me anything I didn't already know. Nothing new, just advice I would have given myself in my better moments."

He laughed and sat down next to me, but the dust didn't stir with the motion. "That's all any priest with sense does. Wisdom has to be earned."

I gave a weak little laugh, resolving not to tell Bolt or Rory or anyone how I'd been outwitted and outargued by a phantom of my own imagination. "I don't even know what we're fighting. Laewan's dead, but now somebody with the power and knowledge of the Vigil has sent dwimor to kill us. I didn't even know what they were until a few days ago. That puts another tally mark on the list of things Pellin hid from me. I wonder how many other secrets the Vigil holds."

I turned my head just enough to see if I'd taken Ealdor by surprise. He sat there staring into the empty gloom, my phantom pretending to be a man with his own memories. Of course not. "And we're still no closer to the real enemy." I swallowed against a surge of fear and bile that tried to close my throat. "What is the Darkwater? Why is it evil?" I shook my head. "Pellin and the rest of the Vigil, for all their age and wisdom and experience, are no closer to the knowledge than I am. There are a thousand questions, and they don't have any answers. Pellin looks to his gift, Bronwyn searches children's rhymes, and Toria Deel quotes proverbs, all of them covering their ignorance with their favorite trick. They don't know the truth of what we're fighting. They only know who the current captain is."

He reached out to pat me on the shoulder, and I jerked away, standing.

Ealdor shrugged. "You're a bright fellow, Willet, and the queen's reeve. I'm sure you can find a solution if you put your mind to it."

I laughed. "That's real helpful. Why don't you tell me something I don't know, something I can use?"

"You said I couldn't," he replied with an arch of his brows. "Focus on what's happened here. Your enemy is going to a lot of trouble to eliminate all of the sentinels."

I nodded and tried not to think too hard about the fact that I stood in a crumbling, abandoned church talking to myself. "Thanks, but I know that with both parts of my brain. The enemy still has the same end in mind—get as many people into the Darkwater as he can and then use them to fight." I shook my head. "But that just brings us back to the same questions the Vigil can't answer. To what end? What does he want?"

Ealdor's pale blue gaze locked onto mine. "You know the questions you can't answer—at least you can't answer them yet. You're missing something, something small and important." He gave a small laugh.

I stared at him. "What's the joke?" I shook my head. "Something small and . . . ah, the pup." I knew Ealdor to be nothing more than an externalized part of my mind, a ghost I'd conjured so that I would have someone to talk to, but I answered him as if he were real anyway. "The pup's not going to make it," I said. "I've seen wounds like that before. We're too far from a healer to keep it from fouling."

Ealdor pointed at the saplings growing in the sanctuary, small trees with soft leaves that were half a shade lighter than those of a full-grown maple. "You know most medicines come from the forest. Those are young bation trees."

I turned to look at them, the hint of a memory lurking just below the surface of my mind. It seemed I had heard something about them once upon a time. I shrugged. Born and raised in the city of Bunard, I had no woodcraft to speak of, but if we dressed the sentinel pup's wound with bation leaves, it might help. Without some intervention the animal was going to die anyway. It certainly wasn't going to hurt.

I stripped the two closest saplings of all the leaves I could reach.

Behind me Ealdor lifted his hands as if he were officiating over haeling instead of watching me stuff my pockets. "'And the leaves of its tree will be for the healing of my people,'" he quoted.

I laughed and turned to see him smiling at his own jest and had to remind myself he wasn't real, just a created apparition that didn't bother to leave footprints. "If all the enemy wanted was to let people into the Darkwater, he would have killed all the sentinels, but he took one." I paced the aisle, ducking under the branches of the saplings that were the little church's only adherents to the faith. "He doesn't need it for protection. What can the pup do that he can't?" A memory of Wag came to me, his nose lifted, searching the smells of the forest for danger and not finding any. I still wasn't sure if Bolt had exaggerated the pup's abilities, but knowing the paranoia with which he viewed his responsibility, he at least *believed* Wag could smell danger from that far off.

I spun back to Ealdor, saw him watching me, his brows framing eyes the color of a cloudless sky at noon. "Who is he tracking?"

Ealdor shrugged. "Anyone who represents a threat."

"The Vigil. They're on the move and they're impossible to find because they're hiding from the heads of the orders." I took a deep breath and let it out in a long whispering sigh. "I remember when the only people that wanted to kill me were the nobles in Laidir's court. I didn't know how good I had it." Ealdor sat, placid as any priest, and watched me work through my logic. "If the men I saw in Wag's memory double back for any reason, we'll die. Bolt and Rory can't defeat them, and against that kind of giftedness my sword is as useless as Custos's books."

I couldn't answer the deeper questions of the Darkwater, but I knew the question that needed answering next. Walking back to the dais with its ancient altar I extended my hand, felt Ealdor's grip and the warmth of his smile. "I know you're not real, but it was good to see you again." I turned, looked around at the crumbling ruins around me. Friends who cared for you without the prospect of gain were hard to find and harder to leave behind once you'd found them. Even the imaginary ones. "Do you only appear in abandoned churches?"

But when I looked back Ealdor was gone, the dirt and debris where he'd walked and sat, perfectly undisturbed.

CHAPTER 26

Bolt and Rory sat by a small fire that punctuated their intermittent conversation with pops and cracks and occasionally offered commentary with understated hisses. Rory fed Wag from the provisions we'd taken from Faran's cabin, the pup careful to lick his hand clean after each bite.

I knelt next to Rory and pulled the bation leaves from my pockets. The linen binding we'd put around the pup's wound was still wet. "Here, I found some bation leaves in an abandoned church. They'll help keep his wound from fouling." Rory blinked at me. "He seems to like you best," I said. "Put these on the cut and rewrap it."

I accepted Bolt's offer of a wedge of cheese. "We have a problem," I said.

Bolt's eyebrows lifted. "Only one? Things are looking up."

I shook my head, letting Bolt's invitation to banter slide by. "I've been ta . . . thinking," I said, ignoring my guard's frown of disapproval. "The only reason our enemy would want a sentinel pup is so he can track down and kill what remains of the Vigil. But I don't think he knows that Wag survived." I stepped over and rubbed the pup's ears through the thin leather of my glove, smiling as his tongue came lolling out. He didn't move, just gave a weak thump of his tail.

I looked at Bolt. "Do you think Wag can track the other pup and the men who took it?"

He nodded. "You know I won't be able to protect you from him in a straight-up fight."

"You have a habit of assuming the worst."

He nodded. "I tend to stay alive that way."

That last might have come from me. "When we get to Gylden, we'll find an alchemist and buy some solas powder," I said.

Bolt shook his head. "If he comes on us by surprise, we'll be dead by the time we get it lit."

"If Wag smells danger, we'll light torches against the darkness, but that brings us to the other problem. We need a way to throw the other sentinel off the track. Is there any way to confuse their sense of smell?"

Bolt gave me a level look. "The things people try don't actually work, even on regular dogs."

I pulled a breath filled with the scents of growing things into my lungs. "All right, it was worth a try—anything that could buy us time."

"'Dying later is better than dying earlier,'" Bolt quoted in agreement.

Memory sent pinpricks running up and down my arms. I'd heard that saying before—from the commander of the southern mercenaries just before we escaped into the Darkwater.

Across the fire, Rory pointed down at the sentinel pup dozing on his lap. "Why don't you ask Wag?"

I shook my head. "How would he know? His conscious memories are all of three days old."

Bolt nodded. "His are, but that spot on his head means something more."

Intrigued, I pulled the glove from my right hand and reached out to put it on Wag's head. He saw the movement through half-slitted eyes and his tail twitched in anticipation. "It's not a scratch behind the ears," I told him.

I fell through the crystalline gray-blue eyes and into Wag's consciousness. Pain still clouded everything and I could feel the weakness of his injury as if it were my own, an aching line of unquenchable fire that ran the length of my ribs and kept me from breath. In his vision I saw myself and all the rest of our company sitting around the fire, seen in oddly muted colors where yellow and blue predominated and everything else showed in shades of gray.

But our scents filled my nose with wondrous detail, as if the world had suddenly been transformed from a child's crude sketch to the depth and breadth of a master painter's reality. Bolt smelled strong and resolute, even obstinate in his commitment to die rather than let harm come to his packmates. Rory's smell carried the strong, almost acrid, scents within his sweat that presaged his body's transformation into adulthood. But already those odors were associated with the companionship I had used to identify my littermates within the pack.

Volsk had departed, but his lingering scent carried bitter tastes, undercurrents that colored his movements, leaving taints of despair upon the wind wherever he went. In the part of my mind that I kept as myself, I considered that. Not just one, but several different odors of anguish followed and flowed from the former Vigil apprentice. Within Wag's mind, I couldn't help but note the similarity between Volsk's smell and the one I had carried during my wounded time alone.

The scent memory of Custos was light and of barely any consequence, yet it carried a sense of kindness and friend. Strangely, within my mind, it smelled somewhat like the almond-crusted figs he so adored.

I turned my attention to the man who rested his bare hand on my head. His smell came closest to Bolt's, but it carried doubt and fear mixed within the resolution, and deeper, far beneath those, lay an essence of corruption that raised the hackles on my neck and brought a growl to my throat.

I gathered a sense of myself, Willet, and searched for and found the memory of Wag's littermate being taken away. I followed the receding scent in his mind until it faded beyond reckoning to the south. My throat tightened around the terror and fear that permeated the doggy smell of my friend. The smell coming from the men would have been laughable it was so ordinary. They'd made no attempt to disguise it at all. None. I followed the memory back in time until I could smell them coming, entering the clearing with their swords drawn, but the pack leaders raised no alarm. They must be friends. Then the swords fell. I tried to understand, wanted to run, but my dam and sire weren't moving. Strokes of steel fell from the direction of the sky and the hot smell of blood came from everywhere. At the last second I gathered my legs beneath me where I lay by my mother, but too late. Fire raced along my side as the edge of the man's blade parted fur and skin and muscle. Then my mother's paw found my head, imparting awareness as she died. I lay on the ground, breathing as shallowly as I could manage, knowing that to whimper was to die.

I returned to myself, lifted my head and blinked, wavering where I sat as the world shifted, receding from one defined by the nuances of smell to be replaced with the brilliant colors and myriad shades that defined human perception.

I shook my head. "We could probably all use a bath—especially you, Rory," I said, "but I doubt if there's a way we can confuse a sentinel's sense of smell." I shook my head again, trying to find the words to describe the complexity with which Wag perceived the world. "He knows what everything smells like. They pass down their ability and their knowledge. Try to imagine playing seeker and lost except all the lost are the ones wearing the blindfolds. He smelled the men coming to kill him."

"It all makes sense, except for one thing," Rory said and everyone else nodded. The problem stared us right in the face.

I sighed. "Yes. If it's impossible to fool their sense of smell, how did those men manage to sneak in and kill them? The sentinels should have smelled them coming for days."

"Alchemy?" Bolt asked.

I shook my head. "Not possible." I waved my arm at the forest around us. "Wag could tell you exactly what route Volsk took when he left, right down to each tree or bush he brushed against on the way."

"Maybe they bathed?" Rory asked.

"There's no bath that can take your smell off," Bolt said. "Hunters don't even try that. Instead they go out into the woods for a few days until they smell more like the natural surroundings, but that wouldn't work on a sentinel."

"Do the sentinels have a way to distinguish between the smells of friend and enemy?" I asked.

Bolt cocked his head to one side before giving a small nod. "The members of the Vigil are all friends." He must have seen my expression. "Even if one of the men who came here was Jorgen, that wouldn't explain how the dwimor managed to sneak up on them."

"That's it, then," Rory said as if that settled it.

"What?"

He lifted his shoulders and let them fall back into place. "The sentinels are smart like people, so when they get old enough they can be fooled like people. It's not like your eyes quit working, your vision just slides past the dwimor. They must be able to do the same thing to the adult sentinel's sense of smell."

Bolt growled under his breath. "That would also give them another reason to kill the pups. They can't hide from them."

I put my glove back on and turned to look Wag in the face. He gazed back. Now that I knew it was there, I could spot awareness, the telltale sign of almost human intelligence in his gaze. "We're going to get you to Gylden," I told him. "We're going to get you a healer and you're going to help us hunt these men down." His tale thumped on the ground.

I looked at Bolt. "They made a mistake."

He nodded. "They left us a weapon."

CHAPTER 27

We came within sight of the towers of Gylden and its steep-roofed houses just before sunset of the next day, slowing our horses to a casual walk to time our arrival after sunset. The smell of people and forge fires drifted to us on a breeze blowing from the northwest. Even in the fading light we could see the mountains immediately to the north of the city, mountains that held the secret to Duke Orlan's wealth.

Gylden boasted more of the gifted than any city in Collum except Bunard, the king's hold. Those within Orlan's domain bent their gifts and talents toward finding precious metals, devising ever-more-efficient means for extracting wealth from the streambeds of the countless flows that came gushing from the mountains each spring.

But there were rumors—old even when I was a boy—that the rivers within Orlan's duchy had panned out long ago and that the duke had done what was forbidden. He'd used the gifts and talents of his people to mine the deep places of the earth, searching for silver and gold.

And whatever traces of aurium he could find.

Laidir had never pursued those rumors. The constant threat of war with Owmead had kept him from it. His widow, in an even more precarious position, would likewise have to turn a blind eye and deaf ear to the duke's supposed criminal activity.

And so the house of Orlan was enriched.

Rory looked down at Wag, who slept draped across the back of my horse, his breathing shallow. "How are we going to get him through the gates?"

I exhaled a long slow breath. In Bunard I'd built up enough goodwill with the guards to have them look the other way or pretend selective blindness when I needed it. Entering Gylden with a wounded sentinel pup was the type of thing the guards would likely report.

"Cover him," Bolt said. "Tell the guards it's a wolf that attacked us in the Everwood and we're going to have it stuffed."

It might have been coincidence, but Wag opened an eye and blinked at that.

"And if they pull the blanket back and see he's still alive?"

Bolt held up his hand and made a wiggling gesture with his fingers. "Tell him to keep his eyes closed and play dead."

I took off my glove and put my hand on Wag's head, the fur thick and coarse to the touch. Every scent I'd noted on our approach to the city intensified a thousandfold, imbued with nuances and flavors I'd never suspected. I shunted aside odors of sweat, forge fires, and a thousand different foods and concentrated on planting an idea in Wag's mind, a game quite nearly as old as the custom of keeping dogs itself. I told Wag to play dead, reinforcing the necessity of the idea with the smells he'd already come to associate with danger.

Behind his happy acceptance of my instruction lurked two impressions I tried to ignore but couldn't. The first was something I had noticed before—the scent of evil, a slight tang of corruption that Wag associated with my touch. I didn't spend much time wondering what that might be.

The second was a growing weariness that came through our connection, a fatigue born of continuing blood loss. Even Wag's memories carried a diffused cast to them, a dark penumbra that reminded me of Kera. We needed a healer, and we needed haste.

I pulled my hand away from his head. "Now, boy," I said, "and don't stop until I tell you." He went limp across the back of my horse and closed his eyes. I covered his form with a blanket and, with a sigh and a prayer, twitched the reins.

We passed by the outer gatehouse without comment, then through a wide arch in the heavy walls. I turned in my saddle to inspect the dark, heavy stones as we went, their surfaces worn smooth by weather and water, moss clinging to the shaded crevices. "Old," I said. "Not so old as Bunard, but nearly so."

Bolt nodded. "Even if there'd been no silver here, Gylden would have remained for the quarries and the trappers." We stopped on the other side of the deep entry arch and paused to survey the towers of Orlan's stronghold lit by torchlight. "Though it wouldn't have been nearly as big," he added.

At the other end of the entrance tunnel a guard met us, his pike loose in one hand and his beard-shadowed face bored. I didn't want to be the interesting part of his day. "Your business in Gylden?"

I coughed. "We're looking for a healer."

The guard jerked back and drew his sword. "No one enters the city carrying the fever."

I shook my head. "Touch me if you like. The healer is for stitches." I pointed at the blanket. "There's why."

The guard twitched the blanket aside to reveal Wag's head, eyes closed and tongue hanging out. By the torchlight I couldn't detect breathing or any other motion. I hoped the guard couldn't either.

He put the blanket back, nodding. "But why bring it here?"

I opened my eyes, pretending surprise. "I've never killed a wolf before. It's a trophy."

He shook his head and swung his arm toward the crossroads ahead of us. "Stupid custom, stuffing dead animals."

We stopped a few paces on, where traffic, noise, and the charcoal light of dusk combined in a dizzying soup that overwhelmed the senses. "We need to get off the street," I said, keeping my voice low. "Or have you forgotten that I'm not exactly a favored son here?"

"I haven't been here in a long time," Bolt said, omitting my name, "and then only once. My memory is good, but not like yours." He turned to peer north, then east, then west. "Most cities are laid out the same. This way, I think."

"That makes sense," I said. "There are probably traders and money-lenders there as well, fairly close to the gate I'd imagine."

"Along with higher-priced night women," Rory said, shaking his head. "There's no point in letting a man's successful venture go to waste."

Ten minutes later we arrived at the noise and light that marked the Pick and Shovel, apparently a well-trafficked establishment, despite its name. We dismounted, and Rory and I led our horses to the large stable behind the inn while Bolt went inside to pay for rooms. I slipped the hands a bit more than required to take care of our horses and lifted Wag as gently as I could from Dest's back, coughing to cover his soft whimper.

We climbed the back stairs to the second of three floors and waited. Bolt came around the corner a few moments later and motioned toward the third floor. We took a large room by the stairwell that led to the stables. I put Wag, blanket and all, on the bed.

"I'll find us a healer in the morning," Bolt said.

I shook my head. "No. He needs one now." I held up my hand, the one I used when I delved.

"That's the kind of thing that gets noticed," Bolt said.

I couldn't disagree. "It can't be helped. His wound hasn't closed and there's a cast to his memories that I've seen before."

Rory levered himself up from the bed where he'd been sitting at Wag's head. "I'll find one." He untied the knot at his throat and tossed his cloak over a chair.

Bolt shook his head. "No. You can't leave him," he said, pointing at me. "Not ever."

Rory looked at me, then back to Bolt. "You need a healer who works at night without asking questions or talking about what they've seen."

"How do you know Gylden even has such a healer?"

Rory barked a laugh. "Every city has thieves, and sometimes thieves need medical attention. The healers willing to treat them cost more, but they keep their silence."

"Tell me where to find one," Bolt said.

The young thief shook his head. "That's just it, I can't." He patted his chest, hips, and the small of his back, checking his knives. "I'm going to have to go into the city and find a thief." He held out his hand. "And I'm going to need money."

The lines of Bolt's face hardened as he prepared to argue, but a heartbeat later he pulled his purse and tossed it to Rory. His apprentice withdrew three full silver crowns and wrapped them in a piece of cloth, keeping them separate. Then he tossed Bolt's purse back to him and tucked the wad of cloth holding the coins into his tunic.

"Is that going to be enough?" I asked.

Rory shook his head. "Probably not, but it will get him here. After

227

that we'll have to slip him enough to buy his silence." He cut his eyes to Bolt. "And it might not be a bad idea to offer him the hospitality of our room for the night just to make sure he doesn't decide to sell information about us to the guards."

I thought Bolt might raise one last protest, but he stepped away from the door and Rory left without saying anything more, his footsteps all but soundless as he went. I settled myself next to Wag to wait.

Two hours later we were still sitting that way when a soft rap at the door brought us to a standing position. Farthest from the door, I reached for my throwing daggers, noting that Bolt already had his sword in his right hand. He nodded to me and opened the door, blocking it with his body.

A short figure holding a large bag peered at us from the shadows of his hood, making placating gestures, but his feet were pointed resolutely into the room. Then a delicate hand rose to sweep back the hood and a cascade of chestnut hair framed a face I knew from my more normal nightmares.

"You're Orlan," I said.

She stiffened, straightening as though someone had replaced the natural curve of her spine with a rod of iron. "My father has never bothered to admit his paternity. My name is Fynn."

"Come in," Bolt said, but he made no move to sheath his weapons, even as Rory followed her into the room.

"Perhaps I should go," she said.

I shook my head. "So that you can alert your father's men? No, I don't think I'd like that."

When she frowned at me, I could see the stamp of her father's arrogance in her features. "Did you not hear me, friend?" She nodded at the blade in my hand. "Or do you think with your steel like every other man around here?"

Bolt stifled his laughter and moved aside. Fynn edged into the room, attempting to keep as much distance from his weapons as she could.

"Do you know who I am?" I asked.

She cocked her head, her green eyes tight with challenge. "You don't know me or of me, so you can't be from Gylden, and the only other place the duke visits is the king's city. You're probably someone from Bunard who's managed to draw my father's unwelcome attention." She shrugged. "That doesn't narrow it down overly much, but then 'Da' does manage to get around."

The thought of delving her crossed my mind more than once, but I couldn't see any advantage to it. I wasn't prepared to kill her and we weren't going to let her leave until we were headed out of town. "You understand that we must have your discretion?" I said.

Fynn blinked and gave me a slow nod that focused the light on her hair. "Yes. Your thief has told me of your unusual requirements." She cut her gaze to the bed.

"What happened to you?" Bolt asked Rory. "I thought I'd trained you better than this."

Rory gingerly touched the swelling around his left eye. "Thieves have their own way of doing business. I had to pay for the information that led me to Fynn and prove I was desperate enough to be willing to take a couple of blows for it. Ducking the leader's fist and putting him down would have been fun, but we needed a healer."

Bolt nodded his approval. "It usually takes years for me to beat that kind of discretion into a guard. You did well," he said to Rory. "Did anyone follow you?"

Rory shook his head. "Not unless they're better than I am." He slipped out of his shoes. "I'll go up to the roof to have a look around anyway. I'll knock twice, then three times."

Fynn moved over to the bed where Wag lay, watching each of us in turn, probably waiting for one of us to finish so that we could scratch him behind the ears. "I don't treat animals," Fynn said. "They bite and it's hard to get the dosages right."

I pulled my glove and moved to stand by Wag's head. "He won't move, just give him half of whatever you think he'll need."

Fynn shook her head. "He's just going to chew the stitches right out of his wound."

"No," Bolt said. "He won't."

The shrug Fynn answered with conveyed surrender, not agreement. "Light all the candles"—she pointed around the room—"and keep him still. The binding you've put on the wound will probably stick despite my efforts." She opened the bag, searching, before she pulled forth a bottle of clear liquid and a pair of clean, bright shears.

"What's in the bottle?" I asked. "A healer named Galen used spirits on me once. He almost had to scrape me off the ceiling."

Fynn smiled, and I saw what Orlan would have looked like if he'd been young, female, and kind. "It's just purified water. I'm going to wet the bandage to make it easier to remove."

The healer poured the water slowly across the bandaged wound, waiting for each trickle to be absorbed before adding any more, her fingers deft as a musician's. After nearly a quarter hour she took her shears in her left hand.

I gestured toward them. "I imagine those cost you quite a bit."

She looked toward me and nodded. "Between my wrong-handedness and my face, not too many people believe Duke Orlan when he says he's not my father, but it hardly matters. His silver and gold have managed to buy the semblance of belief, if not the reality."

She squinted at Wag. "Exposing the wound to the air will be painful. If he makes a move to bite me I'm leaving, and that will be *after* I scream loud enough to draw the city guard."

I nodded. "He won't. Give me a moment." Fynn didn't look convinced. I put my bare hand on Wag's head and wobbled a bit on my feet as the room shifted in my senses. Fynn wore nervousness and lilac, but he found the odors of her art more interesting. Through our connection, I put the image in Wag's head of lying still as the bandages were removed. It kept sliding away, dispelled by the strange smells coming from the healer's bag, but each time I put it back until it achieved some measure of permanence. For the healer's sake I crooned encouragement to Wag at intervals.

"You're safe now," I told Fynn.

She slipped the shears beneath the linen, muttering as she squeezed the blades together in minute snips. "I'll have to pour numbing liquid on the wound and cut away whatever flesh has fouled before I stitch him up. That goes for the muscle as well. If the sword stroke got to his organs, I'll stitch those as well, but even if you keep him still, it will be a dozen rolls of two if he survives."

I nodded. In the game of bones, rolls of two and eight were the least common and two was seen as a sign of bad luck as well. "He'll be fine," I said. "He has to be."

After the last cut, Fynn straightened and took a step back. "Now, very gently pull the binding away from the wound."

When I looked at her, Fynn shook her head. "This requires no particular skill and he obviously trusts you. Just don't yank it."

I nodded and sent the image of Wag lying still once more before I lifted the cloth away from the wound. The smell of blood and serous fluid washed over me, but not, thank Aer, the smell of corruption.

Fynn leaned forward to peer at the leaves we used to cover the flesh of the wound, her bottle of water in hand. "What is that?"

"We were in the woods," I said. "We didn't have any salve or ointment with us, but there were bation saplings there."

She looked at me in disbelief, then bent to wash the leaves away. "It's clean." She shook her head. "I've never seen the like. The wound is as fresh as if it were made no more than an hour ago. Where did you learn this?"

A tingle, like the warning of danger, danced on the back of my neck. "I just knew. It's common knowledge, isn't it?"

Fynn arched her eyebrows, squinting at me, but for a moment the diffidence that covered her like a cloak was absent, replaced by earnest curiosity. "No, it's not. I've used haelroot ground with common mint, burnwood bark boiled with lamb's ear leaves, and even finely ground silver in fern paste for large wounds, but I've never heard of anyone using leaves from a bation sapling."

"I must have heard of it somewhere." I shrugged, but a suspicion grew in my mind that all my internal conversations couldn't dismiss. "I would imagine the medicines used depend on what's available. Different plants grow in different areas."

Fynn didn't look convinced—disagreement hardened her features. "I haven't spent my entire life in Gylden." She blinked. "I've studied every text I could find in Collum on healing. I don't remember anyone using bation leaves for anything."

"My apologies if I gave offense," I said without paying attention to my words. "I'm just a reeve."

She nodded. "Amazing," she murmured to herself. "He has lost a lot of blood, and there's a nick in one of his arteries, but I don't think your pet is in any danger of dying from infection."

Wag gave a soft growl at that.

"He's more of a companion than a pet," I said.

Fynn gave no sign that she'd heard me as she continued. "I'm going

231

to pour easeroot balm across the wound before I do anything more."
She washed the wound with a faintly yellow liquid that carried a soft
scent of lemons. Even to my human nose it smelled soothing, and Wag
blinked slowly, drowsing. Fynn pulled a needle and a spool of strange-
looking thread from her bag and poured more of the balm over them.
"Your friend there is about to get some very expensive stitches. These
are made from cleansed animal intestine. They'll bind the artery and
the muscle long enough to heal before they dissolve." She gave me a
direct look. "Your thief hasn't covered the price."

"We'll pay it," Bolt said.

"How can you leave the stitches in without the wound fouling?" I
asked.

Fynn looked at me and shook her head. "You know about bation
leaves and not this?" She looked away from me to finger one of the leaves.
"Hold his head. Even with easeroot, he'll probably feel this. Remember
what I said. If he tries to bite me . . ." She didn't bother to finish.

"Fair enough," I said and concentrated on putting an image of remaining still in Wag's mind while the smells of the room intensified at
the touch of my hand on his head.

Half an hour of wax burned off the candles before she finished,
but Wag never moved—though I could feel each stitch going into his
side as if I'd been pierced myself. "Amazing," she said as she tied off
the last knot. "If you can keep him still I can seal the wound so that
it heals faster."

When I nodded, she covered the wound with a thick brown paste
that filled the air with an odor of concentrated pine. Wag jerked each
time she put it on, the sting coming through the delve strong enough
to pull small gasps from my lungs.

"Interesting," Fynn said. She gave her head a bemused shake. "I
wouldn't have thought I could use that on an animal. Most people
can't manage to sit still for it."

"It smells like pine tar," I said.

Fynn smiled, blinking. "It is, partly. Old medicine, but it still
works." She packed the implements of her craft back into her bag,
pocketing some of the withered bation leaves as she did so. "My
thanks," she said.

I pulled my purse to pay the rest of the promised fee, but Fynn stopped me with a gesture. "That's not my price." She glanced at Bolt before she shifted to bow in my direction. "Lord Dura."

Bolt muttered a few words under his breath that didn't sound like soldierly wisdom. I heard my name a few times.

Fynn smiled at our reaction as if we'd given her a gift. "I told you I'd read every book I could find in Collum. And I have recently returned from Bunard. The streets were abuzz with your exploits, Lord Dura." She turned to Bolt. "And yours as well." She cocked her head to one side. "I expected you to be bigger."

Bolt smiled with half his face. "Most people do."

"My price, Lord Dura, is quite simple," Fynn said.

On anyone else the sound that came out of Bolt's mouth would have been a groan. From him it sounded more like a threat. "*Simple*," he muttered, "rarely means the same thing as *easy*."

Fynn smiled. "When you return to Bunard, force my father to admit his paternity."

"How about if we just tie you up and leave you here?" Bolt said, but Fynn never looked his way.

"You're asking me for something I may not be able to deliver," I said. "Why not take the money and go to a different city? Most people enjoy thinking about revenge more than actually getting it."

She laughed. "I'm not after revenge, Lord Dura. I'm after access."

I shook my head. "I don't understand."

A bit of humor slid from her expression. "Who's the greatest healer on the continent?"

Bolt shifted on his feet. "She wants to go to Elania to study under Crato." He shrugged. "He's kind of eccentric."

Fynn nodded. "He won't apprentice commons."

I understood, but I still had to say no. Orlan despised me, and I didn't have time for diversions. Then I felt something warm against my hand. When I looked down, Wag had managed to turn his head enough to give me a few feeble licks.

"All right," I said. "I'll try. If I fail, I'll send the rest of the money north to you."

"Someday," Bolt said, "we're going to have to have a serious conversation about these impulses of yours to help everyone. That's a serious character flaw you have there."

I nodded. "It's a good thing I have such steadfast friends to help me shoulder the burdens."

He looked at me in disgust before turning to Fynn. "We're kind of pressed for time, girl, and now that we have a new commitment, I'd rather not wait for dawn. Can you get us out of the city?"

She smiled. "Of course. Follow me."

CHAPTER 28

A day out of Andred, Mark asked, "Aren't you worried about King Rymark or Grace Hyldu changing their minds?"

Pellin shook his head. "Not at the moment. The death of the sentinels has frightened the church and the rulers into allowing us our freedom."

Mark nodded, gave one last longing look toward the south before settling deeper into his saddle. "It won't last."

Pellin nodded his agreement. At best, fear was a temporary motivation, but what made Mark think so? "Why do you say that?"

"Living with the urchins, you get scared a lot—scared of not getting enough to eat, scared of not being able to stay warm when the wind comes out of the Cut during the winter, scared of getting caught thieving." He shook his head. "When something really bad happens, it seems like the world is coming to an end, and it might be, but when it doesn't happen right away, the fear isn't as strong." Mark turned in his saddle to look behind them. "They might change their mind about locking you up to keep you safe."

"That was well reasoned," Pellin said. "But for the moment, I no longer need to pit the ambitions of the rulers and the church against each other. Lady Bronwyn is patrolling the border of the forest, and Toria Deel is searching out the truth behind the Clast. Doubtless, they could use our help." After several days spent recuperating in Andred, he felt more prepared for the task.

"I hope not," Mark said.

Pellin smiled. "Agreed. Tell me, Mark, what did you think of our meeting with the powers of the north?"

"You're right—they are scared," Mark said. "Terrified even—though they did a fair job of keeping it hidden." A smirk crept up his left cheek. "It's too bad we don't have time to remain in Andred for a few weeks. With a bit of preparation I'd be able to use that fear to separate King Rymark and Grace Hyldu from a substantial portion of their treasury."

Pellin ignored that last remark, finding it easier to do since he'd delved the seemingly playful boy at his side. What drove the Mark in his larcenous endeavors was a rage at the suffering life brought. That passion filling the boy's mind was so vast that Pellin had emerged from the delve with an entirely new perspective. He'd yet to share his findings with Bronwyn, but the potential within the boy and the failure of the Vigil to keep corruption at bay—losing first Laewan and then Jorgen—left Pellin musing.

The selection criteria for apprentices to the Vigil had always centered around empathy, but most of those they'd chosen had experienced little in the way of personal hardship. Had the Vigil taken the wrong approach all these centuries?

"What will they do?" Pellin asked when it appeared as though Mark took the prolonged silence as an invitation to doze once more.

"For now, exactly as they have said," Mark answered. Again, he failed to use the honorific of *Eldest* that everyone else applied to him. Pellin found it refreshing not to be reminded of his responsibility at the end of every sentence.

"And later?" he prompted.

"Whatever insanity pops into their heads," Mark said. "You should let me show them how to run a con. That would teach them the importance of creating a detailed plan and sticking to it." He shook his head. "I doubt most of the rulers could even attempt a decent bluff."

"They're not criminals," Pellin said.

"No." Mark shook his head more vigorously. "They most certainly are not. They are kings and queens and heads of religious orders reacting to each new circumstance just as expected."

Pellin stared at his young companion. "You're suggesting someone is running a con on us?"

Mark laughed. "We have a saying in the urchins—'If it looks as though someone's not conning you, you're not paying attention.'"

"That's a very cynical view of life, boy."

Mark only laughed harder. "Just because I'm cynical doesn't mean I'm wrong."

"There is good in the world also," Pellin said, "and not everyone is trying to get something from someone else."

Mark sobered enough to nod in agreement. "The urchins don't get much of a chance to meet those types, but I've met some." His gaze became direct. "A few. But I don't think the people who are planting gold in the streams of the Darkwater have your best interests at heart."

"So why call it a con?"

Mark nodded. "A con, at its heart, is quite simple—it's getting something from someone by trickery that they would never give you on their own. Most of the urchins I trained always started out making it more complicated than it needs to be. The basis of a good con is to know your target well enough so that when you get the plan started, he or she will react exactly how you expect."

Pellin felt a weight settle into his stomach. "That's what happened at Bas-solas. If we'd lost, then the enemy would have proceeded in one way, but when we won and killed Laewan, the enemy already had plans for that in place."

He pulled morning air that still held a hint of mist into his lungs. "Aer help me," he prayed. "We have to do something unexpected."

Mark smiled. "You're not really used to doing that sort of thing, are you, Eldest?"

Pellin shook his head ruefully. How, in the name of all that was holy, had he ended up needing counsel from a boy thief? "No."

They rode in silence for a few moments before Pellin braved the question on his heart. "Mark, let's put aside the rulers and heads of the orders for now. What can you tell me of our enemy?"

Mark's face grew solemn as they rode, and when that silence stretched beyond a few moments into over a quarter of an hour, Pellin became convinced his apprentice had forgotten about the question.

Then, out of his peripheral vision, he saw Mark shake his head.

"I can't tell you anything you don't already know. His servants can't abide light, he needs a supply of people to come to the Darkwater to create them, and he doesn't want to just destroy your power, Eldest, he wants to use it."

A dangerous idea began to form in Pellin's head. It frightened him, because it would put him at risk, and it was so unlike what he would normally do that no one—not even Bronwyn or his own brothers— would ever suspect such a possibility, but it would take planning. And supplies. Lots of supplies. Aer have mercy, where and when had he learned to contemplate such risks?

Something unexpected indeed.

He looked up to the heavens. "Where are we, Allta?"

His guard peered at the landscape around them. A series of rolling hills stretched away to the north and the east, while plains stretched to the west and south. "We're heading north, but we're still some distance from the Havilah River. If we continue in this direction, we should hit it in two more days, if we ride hard."

Pellin inhaled, committing his will and courage to an idea even Lord Dura would call foolish. Something unexpected. "I want to avoid the river and the traffic on it," he said. "More, I want to avoid the armies of King Rymark and the gold hunters that will be panning the Havilah and its streams. Let us turn east instead."

Allta must have sensed something in his manner, some hint of recklessness that showed in his expression or tone of voice. "Eldest?"

"We'll make for the Sundered Hills," Pellin announced. "It's the closest portal to the Darkwater Forest. Perhaps we can pick up Bronwyn's trail." Something unexpected.

CHAPTER 29

Toria Deel rode east with Lelwin and Elory at her sides. Somewhere in the next day or two, they would leave Owmead behind and enter the low rolling plains of Caisel. For weeks they'd followed rumors of the Clast, riding from village to village, stopping to delve every crier or agitator they could find. She sniffed at the memory. Their minds had been as empty as their rhetoric, nothing more than collections of mostly imagined injustices fueling resentment at any whose lot in life seemed a little better than their own.

Once, she encountered a memory of the leader, but her initial exhilaration at the discovery had faded. The memory consisted of nothing more than a brief glimpse, masked and hooded, standing next to a full-throated speaker who demanded unquestioning obedience.

"What happened here?"

Lelwin's voice broke her reverie, and Toria looked up to see they'd crested a line of hills overlooking a broad valley, burnt and blasted. "This is the boundary between Owmead and Caisel. It has a lot of names: Valley of Blood, Vale of Salt, Widow's Dell. There are other, less proper titles, epithets that widows and orphans cry in their grief when husbands and fathers don't come home."

They rode down the slope past earthworks, defenses that time and weather had managed to diminish somewhat. "Sowed as it is with blood and curses, it's a wonder anything grows here, but even with all that, the land yields its fruit in season."

To each side of the road, farmers worked to wrestle another year's worth of produce from the land, at peace with their counterparts who mirrored their labors across the boundary—a river at the bottom of the valley that flowed south, meandering until it emptied into the southern sea.

"Aer willing, the drought won't come again in our lifetime." She breathed it like a prayer, hadn't realized she'd spoken until Lelwin looked up from the book Toria had given her.

"The drought always comes," Lelwin said with the feeling and finality of an executioner, and then returned to her reading. With several weeks of decent food, her narrow face had filled out enough to reveal a heart-shaped contour and her collarbones no longer held such prominence against her clothing. Though she would never be considered a great beauty by court standards, more than one man would find the intensity of Lelwin's gaze beneath her dark eyebrows compelling enough to want to discover what thoughts lay within her mind.

Elory lifted an eyebrow at the girl's pronouncement but, other than that, made no comment. The youngest of the Vigil guards, he had yet to temper the stoicism that Etgar, her previous guard, had taken pains to instill in him. She'd been grateful for that stoicism after Peret had revealed himself, but in the days since, she'd had cause to wonder if Elory had desired to give her some warning about her burgeoning affection for Peret Volsk.

"I wouldn't have listened," she admitted out loud, surprising herself with the noise. She started and turned her thoughts inward, checking the doors within her mind that led to the memories of others. They were all secure, the model of the Merum library in her head as peaceful and calm as she could wish. There was no need to worry yet. It took hundreds of years for the accumulated memories to break down the personality of those who held the gift. Carefully, she unlocked one of the doors and stepped into the memories of Lona, queen of Aille, dead for over ninety years.

"You still love me," she asked in surprise to the man, "even after time has ravaged and wrecked my appearance?"

The man on the ornate bed beside her, as consumed by the years as she, smiled before answering. "I do, and if the fire for you has dissipated from my loins, it burns ever hotter in my heart. You, body and mind, are the one I love and desire."

She laughed. "You always were a flatterer. There are thousands of women in Aille with their smooth olive skin and unlined faces that define beauty, but I thank you for your words."

"Silly girl," he chided softly. "There were a thousand upon a thousand women that others would have considered beautiful in our youth, but none of them sufficed. When the priest corded us together with his seven strands and pronounced us wed, you became the standard, gazed upon and made new each day, by which others were measured, and they were all found wanting. Silly girl," he mouthed, his breath coming too shallow here at the end to push the words against the cords in his throat with enough force to make himself heard. "There was never anyone else."

Toria Deel came out of the link, shaking her head at her own memories now. Queen Lona had never quite believed her husband could have married her for herself instead of the power she wielded. Toria, barely five years into the Vigil, had allowed herself to be persuaded to use her gift to confirm once and for all the husband's love. He had spoken true.

In that moment, Toria had sworn she would never make Lona's mistake, that if real love came her way she wouldn't doubt, not for a moment. And in that decision, she, Toria Deel of the Vigil, had laid the foundation for her heartbreak. Peret Volsk had indeed loved her as deeply as any man had ever loved a woman, so much so that he had become willing to sacrifice himself and the lives of others to keep it. She shook her head. The paradox would have been funny if it hadn't bored a hole through the center of her heart.

"Lady Deel?"

Toria turned in her saddle to Lelwin's curious expression, casting back for the last words to leave her lips. "I . . . wouldn't have listened to those who might have cautioned me against the man I loved. Some lessons must be learned firsthand."

Lelwin's lips compressed into a line, and her gaze went flat. "I have little to worry about on that account, Lady Deel. I have no interest in the thing men name love."

Toria had yet to delve the earnest thief, but Lelwin's presence in the urchins—pretending to be a boy of thirteen instead of a young woman of eighteen—provided probable insights to her past. The young thief spoke of men with the jaded finality of a woman two or three times her age.

"Even you might find yourself lonely someday, Lelwin."

The girl surprised Toria by turning that earnest heart-shaped face toward her with amusement. "I've heard the others talk around it often enough, Lady Deel. Just how old are you?"

Toria covered her surprise with an approving nod. "Good, you can make sense of circumspect conversations. Considering your previous profession, you should understand why some women would be uncomfortable discussing their age."

"Silly custom," Lelwin said. "As if painting their cheeks with rouge and their eyes with shadow could fool anyone who wasn't too drunk to walk a straight line. I hid my age because the people I marked on the street needed to believe the picture I put before them. I've seen men look at you, Lady Deel, the way they look at a woman in the flower of her youth, as something to be taken, the look a cat gives to the unsuspecting mouse before it strikes."

Toria sighed. "I stopped counting quite some time ago, but I am over one hundred years old, and I believe every one of us, man or woman, whatever their age, desires love and companionship."

Lelwin shook her head. "The poor quarter is a warren of thieves and night women. What all men and many women name companionship is nothing more than an appetite, quickly and easily satisfied. Some men trade coin for it. Husbands, pretending love and affection, will offer gifts or service to their wives for it if they are patient." She grew quiet for a moment. "If not, the threat of violence usually suffices to pry a goodwife from the bonds of her clothing."

There at the last, Toria Deel heard a hint of the past that jaundiced Lelwin's view of the bond between a man and a woman, but some instinct kept her from following that thread. Instead she kept to a strategy she'd learned from Pellin long ago. She asked a question.

"And is there no man for whom you might hold a different opinion?"

The girl's slight pause, almost too brief to be noticed, provided her with some hope.

"No, no one who is not already claimed by another," Lelwin said.

"And if they were not claimed?" she asked.

Lelwin pushed through her reticence, but her gaze found someplace else to land besides Toria's face. "Willet Dura is one whose touch might be borne or even enjoyed. What other noble ever sacrificed himself for the urchins?"

Toria nodded, but within her chest too many opposing emotions clashed for her to speak: Dura held a vault within his mind. He had revealed Peret's treachery. He alone of the Vigil had faced Laewan in Criers' Square. He was betrothed to Lady Gael. He was a rogue.

"I understand your reticence, but I will hold out some small hope for myself. I have been alone for quite some time."

Lelwin tucked the book in her saddlebag and turned her attention on the road ahead of them. "Alone," she sighed. "It sounds like balm for the soul."

If only, Toria thought. She considered the door that held Queen Lona's memories along with those of her consort, but she left it closed, for now.

CHAPTER 30

Five days after their departure from Andred, Pellin and his guards came into Broga, a village nestled on the western side of the Sundered Hills. Somewhere in his approximately seven hundred years of memory, a recollection of the village surfaced. How long had it been? Three hundred years? He didn't know for certain. Regardless, there was nothing about the village now that resembled its earlier condition, except its location against the series of foothills that climbed upward until the landscape fell away into the broad bowl that defined the cursed forest.

Most of the buildings—simple plank-and-post affairs with thatched roofs—huddled together in a hollow between the two westernmost hills. At his side, Mark looked up from his latest slumber and regarded the village with the expression of someone who'd encountered a scene he found slightly nauseating.

"This is stupid. Why is there a village here?" he asked.

"Even they don't know," Pellin answered. "The reason for the village is doubtless recorded in some dusty tome that no one has read for hundreds of years, but the people remain. Their lives carry a certain momentum. They won't change unless they're given a pressing reason to do so."

"Sometimes not even then," Allta said.

Pellin nodded as he nudged his horse forward. "Let us see if we can secure lodging for the night."

Mark shook his head. "You think there's an inn here?"

The boy's expression was laughable. "Not in the usual sense, but wherever you have people, you have a tavern, if not an inn. We should be able to find something that will suit our needs."

Dust swirled and trailed behind them as they rode past one building after another. The sameness grated on Pellin's nerves, and though there were children present, their play and calls in the street lacked some quality of joy or mirth he couldn't pinpoint.

The desultory blows of a hammer rang out from beneath a shed where a blacksmith worked without the benefit of a sign to advertise his trade. A farmer sold barley and turnips from the back of his cart, his eyes barely registering Pellin's passing. Across the street a woman traded a pair of mended shoes for a few copper coins. Her house at least held a faded sign with the cobbler's symbol on it.

In the center of the village, they found a larger building with a broad porch where a few men and women had gathered to nurse ale from battered tankards. The sense of displacement, that some circumstance had skewed the village and its inhabitants, grew within his mind. "Mark," he said loudly enough for the villagers on the porch to hear, "see if you can locate the provisions we need." He checked the porch. Other than a glance or two, the villagers paid him no mind. "Be careful," he muttered under his breath, "but find out what you can about this village. Allta and I will meet you here."

Mark dismounted to tie his horse to the rail in front of the tavern. Pellin followed his lead, Allta a half step behind him with his hands close to his weapons. The undersized room of the tavern held only four tables, three of them unoccupied. At the other one, a lean man with reddish hair leaned forward on his elbows, one hand raised as he spoke to the other man at the table, but his gesture seemed tenuous, unsure. His gaze swept over Pellin and Allta in mild surprise, and he blinked as if trying to conjure some memory of purpose.

"We're traveling," Pellin said, "and hoping to rent a room where we can bed down for the night."

The man blinked, his brows drawing together in obvious concentration. "A room," he muttered. Pellin watched as his head went slowly from side to side. Something in the man's mind must have cleared. "Yes. Just the one." He squinted with the effort of thinking. "It's around the back by the stable, but it's yours if you want it."

Pellin moved in random directions, edging closer to their table, surveying the interior of the inn. The air smelled of must, the open door and windows insufficient to dispel the odor of disuse. He pointed to one of the tankards. "I see you have ale. Do you have anything to eat?"

Again the man's face showed discomfort with the question before he managed to give another vague response. "Nothing cooked," he said. "There's some cheese and bread."

"That will do nicely," Pellin said, moving closer and tucking his gloves into his broad belt. "My companions and I appreciate your hospitality." He stuck out his hand. The man he assumed to be the innkeeper stared at the unfamiliar gesture for a moment before taking it into his own.

Pellin fell into the delve, burrowing through the innkeeper's abstracted gaze and into his thoughts and memories. Streamers of memory flowed past him like a river, but instead of the brightly colored strands of thought and emotion he expected, these were muted, nearly colorless. He found it far easier than he should have to maintain his own sense of self and identity. Nothing within the innkeeper's immediate past possessed enough emotional importance to capture him.

With a mental surge, he pushed, moving backward against the tide of time and experience, and as he did so a curious thing happened. Slowly, almost imperceptibly, the innkeeper's memories began to show a bit of vitality, hints of color revealing some joy or sadness that had touched him. The further Pellin went, the brighter they became, until, four or five months in the past, they appeared almost normal. Nowhere did he see evidence of Bronwyn or Toria Deel passing through.

Then he saw the vault, there at the bottom of the innkeeper's mind, as a black scroll with indecipherable writing. He pushed back further, searching for the source, but found nothing. What had possessed a man living on the edge of the Darkwater to brave sentinels and insanity alike to venture in?

He broke the delve, straightening and smiling into the vacuous stare of the innkeeper before turning to the other man at the table and offering his hand. "Perhaps you'll allow me to join your conversation over a tankard later this evening."

The other man, shorter and with dark unkempt hair, peered at the customary greeting just as the innkeeper had before he took Pellin's hand.

Again the interior of the inn disappeared as his gift asserted itself, but this time the presence of memories without color or vitality held no surprise for him and he allowed them to flow by. Racing backward into the past, he noted the flashes of light and darkness within the man's mind that evidenced day and night, and he counted them until he saw the vault within the man's mind.

He made a cursory search of this man's memories, just as he had with the innkeeper but didn't linger. Frustrated but unsurprised by the absence of the memory he sought, he broke the delve and released the man's hand, digging into his purse to place a silver half crown on the table.

"Thank you for your room. If you'll be so good as to draw three tankards for us, my companions and I will join you shortly, after we take care of our horses." He turned to Allta, concentrated on keeping his voice calm. "Let's not keep these gentlemen from their discussion any longer."

Outside, three-quarters of the sun shone above the horizon, bathing the town in crimson light, like an omen of blood. "How much time do we have until full dark?" he asked.

Allta spared a glance west before answering. "This far north we have a bit less than a quarter of an hour until sunset and then another quarter of an hour of dusk."

"That's what I thought." Pellin walked toward the far end of town, toward the weathered church he'd seen on their way in.

"Eldest?"

"Keep an eye out for Mark. If you see him, call him to us. We have about half an hour to find someplace defensible for the night."

CHAPTER 31

Pellin checked over his shoulder. The nearest villager stood in front of the smithy some twenty paces away. From his stance it was impossible to determine if he was a customer or a member of the man's household. He gazed at and through Pellin and his guard in the same absent-minded manner as the two men in the tavern. He didn't bother trying to attempt a delve with the man, but if there was a priest of any order remaining in the village, that would help confirm his suspicions.

"Both of those men in the tavern have a vault," Pellin said under his breath. He put a hand on Allta's shoulder, felt the dense muscle beneath the cloak. "But I don't think they've been to the forest."

Allta shook his head. "How is that possible?"

"I don't know, but I'm hoping a conversation with the priest will provide a clue." He stopped in front of the weathered door of the church, more of a chapel, really. It might have had room for fifty people, but certainly no more.

"Let us see if anyone remains."

Allta took the lever of the door in one hand, his other holding a dagger hidden in the folds of his cloak. They entered into the gloom of unlit spaces at sunset, and Pellin noted the dust first, then the same smell of disuse that had filled the tavern. "These people are barely alive."

With Allta leading, they passed through the small narthex and into the sanctuary, where they proceeded up the narrow aisle in single file. Dust covered the backless benches and the penitent's rail. The inter-secting arcs, the universal symbol of the faith, hung suspended over the altar next to a wooden carving of an oversized sword, the emblem of the Vanguard, but dust covered even these, and of the priest, there was no sign.

Or almost none.

"There," Allta pointed. Footprints marred the dust, leading to and from the back of the altar, heading toward a small door in the back.

They entered a small rectory, hardly more than a single room added on to the church, constructed of posts and planks and smelling of old wood. They found her there, sitting in a chair that had been placed so that as much light as possible from the single window would find her. Her white robe held a single stripe on the sleeve, marking her as a sublieutenant in the Vanguard, which was no surprise. A village this small barely rated a priest. Its proximity to the Darkwater, not its population, would have been the deciding factor for the church to place a parish here.

At first Pellin thought her dead, her stare unfocused and unblinking. Then she shifted slightly, turning her face from her mute consideration of sunset, and it was only then that Pellin noticed that the skin of her face stretched over her skull, leaving her cheekbones protruding like the blunted edge of an axe. Her lids fluttered in a blink that took far longer than it should have.

"What's your name?" Pellin asked. *Fool.* The emaciated woman probably couldn't speak.

"See if you can find some water," he told Allta as he stripped his gloves off. His guard's footsteps sounded loud against the ancient floor-boards, but sight and sound faded as he reached out for her hand.

He fell through the vacant, brown-eyed gaze into another stream of colorless memories. Again he raced backward in time, searching for the memory when the priest beneath his touch had left her parish to enter the forest and stay as night fell. Just as before, he found the vault in her mind, but no memory of entering the Darkwater to go with it.

Realization and awareness came to him at the same moment Allta entered holding a dusty pitcher scavenged from inside the church or rectory. He forced his old man's legs into a run. "Follow," he rasped. The sound of weapons being drawn followed him as he ran back through the church.

And almost bowled over Mark come to find him.

"Eldest . . . " His apprentice clutched at his sleeve, but Pellin didn't slow. *Please, Aer, give us enough light to get away.*

"There's some kind of plague here," Mark breathed. "All the animals are dead."

He ran back through the entrance of the church without bothering to explain, Allta and Mark trailing in his wake. Horses. They had to get to the horses.

A semicircle of red fire still showed above the horizon to the west, bathing the dead village in blood. Pellin cudgeled his old man's legs to go faster, back toward the horses they'd left at the small tavern.

Without pause for breath or explanation, he untied the reins from the rail and threw himself into the saddle.

"Chase the sun!" he screamed. "We have to get away from the village before nightfall."

He dug in his heels hard enough to make his horse rear before it thundered down the road into the sunset. Holding the reins in one hand, he slapped his horse's hindquarters with the other hard enough to sting, and for an instant he fell into its mind and smelled his own fear.

"Eldest," Allta yelled at him as he pulled even, "how do we fight?"

He shook his head, screaming over the rush of wind. "We can't fight this! The Darkwater has claimed the village. Don't stop riding until the light is gone. Only distance can save us." The sun slipped lower, the horizon to the west eating the light.

Two miles out from the village his horse dropped out of its gallop. Allta's and Mark's faltered a split second later, but the dim light obscured his vision, frustrating his efforts. He didn't see any signs, but there hadn't been any in the village either. He raised his hand, prepared to force his mount back to a gallop.

Allta caught it on the way down in a grip that could have doubled as a carpenter's vise. "Eldest, I can't protect you if I don't know what we're running from."

Didn't he understand? "The boundaries of the forest have spread. It encompasses the village now."

Allta's eyes widened in the lurid sunset, but no sign of fear touched him. "If we don't know where the boundary is, we run the risk of not reaching it if the horses drop beneath us," Allta said.

Panic filled his mind and chest, screaming at him to run the horse until it died if necessary. "We have to get away."

"Eldest, those people in the village have vaults. It will be dark soon and there is no moon tonight."

Pellin dropped his hand as a different fear fought the first, and he gulped for air.

"What do we do?"

"Alternate between a fast trot and a gallop until dusk fades, Eldest. We'll get more distance from them."

Pellin nodded, pushed back against the unreasoning terror that filled him. He dug his heels into his horse, following Allta and Mark as they set out westward once more. He watched the sun sink beneath the horizon, the sliver of crimson visibly shrinking until the barest hint of fire remained.

Questions chased each other around his head, queries that centuries of service in the Vigil had failed to answer. When did the poison of the Darkwater overtake those who entered it? Did it claim you if you were within its boundaries any time after dark, or did it require more time to infect you?

He searched through his mind like a man fumbling in the dark, feeling his way with the gift of domere. Would he feel it when he went insane? Would he even know? The doors within his mind, so many after centuries of exercising his gift, remained secure. No strands of black, as Lord Dura described them, came from the darkness to ensnare him. His own thoughts, even filled as they were with panic, seemed to be his. Nothing within gave any hint they were under attack.

The sun vanished.

A chill breeze swept across them, but Allta kept their horses trained like an arrow toward the west. They rode as before, but while they rode, Allta searched the graying landscape ahead, seeking. "Eldest, we must choose."

Choose? What choice was there to make? They had to make sure they were outside the Darkwater's boundary. "What can we do but ride?"

Allta shook his head. Already, details in the distance were lost to sight. "The boundary of the Darkwater is undetermined, but you have delved some of the villagers. We have to assume they are all infected, and night is falling. Will they remember our passing?"

Pellin nodded. "Those with vaults in Bunard acted based upon the knowledge their daylight experiences provided, though it does not work in reverse."

His guard nodded. "Then they will surely come for us."

"I don't see how," Mark said. "None of them seem able to hold a hand aloft for more than a moment."

Allta shook his head even as he pointed to an outcropping of rock in the distance to the south. "Ordinarily, you would be correct, but those who have a vault defy the normal physical boundaries of their existence, able to push their bodies past pain and fatigue until they are almost gifted. We must assume they will come for us."

Pellin reluctantly nodded. "Agreed."

"Then we must find a place to hide and, if we are discovered, make a defense." He gestured to the rocky hillside a few hundred yards away. "We have just enough time to gather firewood. They cannot abide light."

"From a distance that very light will draw them to us," Pellin said. "No, we must hide."

Allta shook his head. "Eldest, they will track our horses. There is no hiding from them in the dark."

"It's a shame we have no solas powder," Mark said. The young thief dug into his saddlebag as they rode, rummaging until he found a wide strip of cloth. "I would have liked a bit of moon better." He draped it around his neck.

Pellin shook his head. "I appreciate your efforts," he said to Mark, "but you've spent all day in the light. Putting your thief's cloth around your eyes after the sun has set seems a bit like locking the barn door after all the horses escaped."

Mark nodded. "We're ten miles from the village. Even if they move like gifted, they have no horses to ride and they'll have to track us. That will give us enough time to build a fire and allow my eyesight to adjust—some anyway. If I can lure them close enough to the flames, I can take care of some of them."

The grim smile that wreathed his face should have looked ridiculous on those downy cheeks. A chasm split and opened in Pellin's heart as he envisioned his apprentice killing one villager after another. "If they come at us in strength, you'll never be able to get them all."

Mark's smile never wavered. "I won't have to. I'll just take care of the ones he can't," he said, nodding toward Allta. "By the time they get close enough to the fire to attack me, he should be able to put an arrow into them."

His guard nodded. "It's not a bad plan, but I'll need enough light to use my bow." He reined in as they reached the base of the rocky foothills. "We'll want to keep them on the plain in front of us."

Pellin clamped his mouth shut around his next objection. All of their planning and preparation wouldn't save them if they were still inside the boundary of the Darkwater Forest. Evil would take them and put a vault within each of their minds. They might not even realize they'd been corrupted.

They dismounted, and Allta and Mark foraged for twigs and old deadfalls that they could use for fire. Pellin offered a quick prayer of thanks. While there were a limited number of trees on the rocky hillside, there were plenty of dry sticks and thicker branches they could scavenge. Allta and Mark would have no trouble getting their fires to light.

"Mark, place the pile about two hundred yards out," Alta said. "That's the farthest I can shoot with any reliability." He watched for a moment as Mark ran. "Make the pile as big as possible."

He then pointed to a large boulder that had tumbled from higher up the hillside. "Eldest, hide behind that rock."

"They see better in the dark than owls," Pellin said. "Where can I hide that they cannot find me?"

"No amount of night vision will let them see through rock," Allta said. "If the Mark and I can keep them distracted, they may not know you're there."

"Perhaps," he said, "but I think hiding will avail me little. They've seen all of us, and they will hunt all of us."

Allta shook his head. "Laewan is not here. There is no one to guide these villagers in their attack. If you can stay hidden, they will have no reason to search for you."

"I hope you're right, but we are in uncharted waters," Pellin said. He swallowed against a new fear. "The forest has leapt its boundaries."

As the sky faded from charcoal to black and a few stars peeked through the clouds, Mark returned, his right eye covered by thick swaths of cloth. Sound drifted to them on the night air, grunts and groans of exertion. Allta leaned forward, listening, as he knelt down and repositioned the pile of sticks at his feet. "They are still some distance away. The ground is hard. Perhaps they are having difficulty tracking us."

"Well and good," Pellin said. "Mark, what can you see?"

A sensation of movement came to him out of the night air that might have been nothing more than Mark shaking his head. "Little more than you," the boy said. "My eyes haven't had enough time to adjust." His soft laughter whispered in the night. "All in all, I think I would prefer it if the ground prevented them from finding us."

Pellin nodded, knowing the gesture to be pointless. "Agreed, but it's foolish to rely on that hope."

Allta heard his unspoken question. "The hills behind us will offer us the advantage of height, and the fire will distract them, but 'if battles were fought on the strength of plans . . .'"

"'Then men wouldn't need to die,'" Pellin finished.

"With luck," Mark said, "Allta will be able to see the villagers by the light of the fire and pick his targets at leisure." His dry tone said plainly what his thoughts were on their having such luck.

"The church teaches that there is more to the universe than blind circumstance or luck," Pellin said. He'd run into doubters countless times over the centuries, but Mark's casual disbelief, as if the existence of Aer couldn't have the slightest bearing on him personally, grieved him.

"Urchins have no need for the three-fold god," Mark said. "Religion is for those with full bellies and warm hearths and time to indulge it."

A knot of desperation clenched in Pellin's chest, tight with the need to convince his apprentice of the truth. "And do you not acknowledge the necessity of a creator? Look up." Despite the darkness, Pellin pointed at the sky. "Even in the night, the stars and moon proclaim him."

"Oh, I see them all right," Mark said in a tone that was the verbal equivalent of a shrug. "I've heard all the arguments. I've seen the carpenter craft his chair"—his tone turned amused, but it carried harsh undercurrents—"and I've seen that same carpenter sit on his chair, but I've also seen chairs that didn't turn out well thrown into the fire for kindling. That's what life did with the urchins."

After a moment, the boy's sigh just made it to Pellin's hearing across the stillness. "They're nice to look at—the stars, I mean—but they really don't have much to do with me."

Pellin withdrew into himself, stymied by Mark's simple and eloquent denial. Seven hundred years of reading and thinking offered him nothing in the way of evidence for the existence of Aer's love and goodwill. In this Mark argued from a position of greater strength. By acknowledging the possibility of a creator, but denying his personal involvement, the urchin could immediately point to his own experiences as a foil to any theological argument Pellin could offer.

"Perhaps in time, you will see things differently," Pellin said.

"I'd like that," Mark responded, and for a moment Pellin's heart leapt within his chest, "but if the exordium of the liturgy and all the rest that followed were true . . . why did no one bother to help the urchins until they were forced to?"

It was a small opening, and Pellin could see the flaw in what he was about to say, anyone could, but he grasped for it like a man swept downstream reaching for a branch he knew would break. "But someone did," he said. "From what I'm told, Willet helped the urchins and the night women of the poor quarter almost every day."

"Willet wasn't part of the church," Mark said. "He was one of us."

"That's what the church says about the three-fold one," Pellin said, "that while we were lost, Aer sent himself to be one of us. The currency of the church is sacrifice."

"Currency? That's the silliest—"

Screams rent the darkness with jagged edges of sound across the distance. Pellin could make out different voices, cries of terror and hatred tearing loose from the throats of men, women, and children. And they were closer now.

"They must have found our tracks," Allta said. He paused, listening. "If they spread out on the plain, they'll come upon us from a dozen different directions. We need to draw them in. Mark, light the fire now."

"They may be too close," Pellin said. "Build a fire here instead."

Allta turned from him, his face and expression lost in shadow. "Mark, you will ignore any order from the Eldest that conflicts with mine. That fire must be lit."

Pellin could sense the boy's uncertainty as he weighed the conflicting commands, but in the blink of an eye he was gone.

"Mark," he hissed, "get back here." Nothing. "Mark!"

"He's gone," Allta said. It was impossible not to hear approval in his voice.

"He's not supposed to go!" Pellin snarled. "He's supposed to be my apprentice."

"But he's mine as well, Eldest," Allta said. "And he understands that."

Tears Pellin never expected turned the moon and stars into smudges of light. "He's just a boy. Does he even understand he just refuted his own argument? Running off into the darkness to save us?"

Allta nocked an arrow and waited, unblinking. "Some see more clearly with their heart than their mind, Eldest."

CHAPTER 32

"Get him back here!" Pellin ordered. "Now!"

Allta stood unmoving and unanswering in the darkness, nothing more than a shadow against the black of night.

"If you will not retrieve him, I will." Pellin set his eyes on the first hint of fire in the distance and managed to lift one foot to move in that direction before Allta's hand clamped on his arm.

"Eldest, consider." Allta spoke in a reasonable tone of voice at odds with the grip that threatened to render his flesh into mush. "The Mark can see better in the dark than either of us. Doubtless he can hear better as well. You and I are not equipped to aid him. Plus, he is in no danger as of yet. Listen."

The screams—obviously human but with an animal quality that raised the hair on Pellin's neck—sounded once more, drifting across the distance.

"There's nothing out here to absorb or block the sound, Eldest, and the weather is clear. The villagers are still some way distant. They have not encountered the Mark yet." He bent and struck flint and steel to light the small pile of wood and brush by his feet. "Hopefully, the Mark's bonfire will blind them to this one. Regardless, I need enough light to aim by."

In the distance the glow of light flared and danced until it strengthened into a steady flame that licked at the darkness. Pellin peered into the night waiting for some sight or sound that Mark lived. Time dragged as if he'd dropped into a delve.

Then a scream—a man's, thank Aer, and not Mark's—pierced the silence with a thorn of pain, and Allta drew the bow and loosed. Out by the fire, Pellin saw a hint of movement just before Mark stepped into the ruddy circle of light, a knife in each hand, crouched, his head jerking from side to side.

No more screams sounded. "You missed," Pellin said.

By the light of the tiny fire he used to aim, Allta nodded. "A shot in the dark. Poor odds."

Out in the night, hints of movement taunted Pellin's eyesight, as if playing a childish game of keep away. Mark jerked in the dancing firelight, shifting back and forth like a crazed marionette, his gaze intent on the darkness.

Pellin pointed. "What is he doing?"

Allta's gaze narrowed. "He's trying to keep the fire between himself and his attackers." He shook his head. "But he's doomed to fail. Already his fire is dying."

Bands of fear constricted Pellin's chest. "Why doesn't he come back to us?"

His guard considered for a moment before answering. "Doubtless, he has reasoned that if he departs the circle of light, they will be able to attack him. For the moment, he is safe and playing for time."

With a sudden jerk, Mark turned his back to the night and the villagers who filled it and then spun back again, his arm sweeping out in a backhanded throw that he concealed until the last instant. A cry sounded in the darkness, abbreviated. Mark resumed his odd dance around the fire.

"That was well done," Allta nodded. "Your apprentice is a fine marksman with those knives."

Pellin looked at the dimming light of the fire, the flames reaching toward the stars a little less with each guttering flare. Within his chest, hope for Mark's survival died. As the fire dimmed, shadowed figures moved to surround the boy, those behind him closing in whenever he turned his back. The glow from the fire barely kept them at bay. In moments, they would have him. "Aer have mercy," he breathed. "He's dead."

"Don't borrow trouble from the future, Eldest."

"He needs help now," Pellin rasped. "Shoot them!"

Allta shook his head. "They're moving with him. Any arrow I loose will find nothing but air and dirt. If the boy is going to live, he's got to save himself."

Out in the night, Mark continued to circle the fire, but his movements were more frantic now. Without warning, he dropped and rolled, practically on top of the coals of the fire, and Pellin saw a glint of reflected firelight from a thrown dagger.

Another followed the first, and Mark's scream of pain and anger tore through the darkness.

"They have him now," Allta said. "Come, Eldest. You must hide. I will hold them off as long as fire and light allow."

Pellin tried to pull his arm from Allta's grip, knowing it was useless. "A man should have at least one friend with him when he dies."

Two more daggers flew in the darkness, and they watched as Mark threw himself aside, landing on his back on top of the fire. Flames danced on the edges of his cloak, and he continued his roll, leaving the thick cloth behind.

Light blazed like a beacon, swallowing the darkness around Mark and capturing the villagers in its glare. Over a dozen howls of pain and surprise cut the air as the villagers curled to protect their eyes against the sudden flare.

"Now!" Pellin screamed. "While they're stunned!"

But Allta was faster. Already three shafts were in the air, whistling toward their immobile targets. Pellin blinked against the spots in his vision, but by the time his vision cleared the fire, the Mark, and the villagers were gone.

Pellin searched the darkness, but the distant embers were too dim and too few. He clutched Allta's arm as his guard lowered his bow. "Where is he?"

Howls of rage filled the air.

CHAPTER 33

Pellin listened in the dark, his ears straining for some sound that might indicate Mark's approach, but the sounds of his own labored breathing and the cries of the dying villagers mixed with the howls of those who remained alive frustrated his efforts.

"Eldest," Allta said at his side, "we have to abandon our fire. It draws them to us like moths to a flame."

"We cannot abandon Mark to them."

Allta shook his head. "We can and will, if necessary. If you fall here, the northern Vigil is all but dead." He stooped to gather the rest of the branches they'd gathered, placing them on the fire so that they created a cone. Instantly, the blaze intensified and the circle of light grew. "Come," he said as he pulled on Pellin's arm.

They led all three horses higher up the hillside by the light of the flaring fire.

Screams punctuated the darkness, fewer than before, and none of them carried the timbre of Mark's voice. Pellin stumbled over a rock, so fixed was he on listening. His heart labored in his chest with the exertion, its rhythm broken and unsteady. He shouldn't have been surprised. He'd grown old. Even with centuries to live, decrepitude had taken him unaware. With a sigh, he stopped. "How many arrows do you have?"

"Two, Eldest."

"Then do what you must to save Mark," Pellin ordered. "I can't go on."

Pellin's head rocked back as Allta bent and lifted him from his feet, throwing him over one shoulder as he led the horses with his free hand. "The protection of the Mark is not my duty. Here, the ground is not so steep." He deposited Pellin on one of the horses and gripped all three sets of reins in his fist. "I will put as much distance between us and the villagers as I can, but beyond the light of the fire, I will have to feel my way." He steered toward a scraggly, weathered tree, its branches bare.

Handing all the reins to Pellin, he paused to grip a branch as thick around as his forearm and as long as he was tall. "We may find some use for this," he said, but he made no move to break it loose from the tree.

"Why do you wait?" Pellin whispered in the silence.

"I'm listening," Allta said. An instant later a chorus of screams, the cry of insanity thirsting for blood, rent the night air, and in that moment Allta snapped the limb loose, the wood splintering free with the sound of bones breaking.

Each time a cry split the air, Allta broke wood. Finally, he handed pieces a bit more than half a pace long up to Pellin along with his cloak while he retained the longest branch for himself. "If you can fashion these into torches, it may give us some protection." He sighed in the gloom, but Pellin couldn't read his expression. They were too far from the fire. "Though there is much remaining of the night."

Allta turned and led them into the darkness, feeling his way forward with the longest branch. Howls shattered the silence again, but they seemed no closer. Perhaps it was just imagination, but the cries seemed to carry as much frustration as bloodlust this time. He hoped so. Perhaps Mark still evaded them.

An eternity later his horse crested the hill and started down the far side. Allta probed with his branch, stopping whenever the slope became too steep for the horses to hazard forward in the darkness, turning to search out a safer path. Pellin held onto the unlit makeshift torches he'd fashioned, but sleeplessness and fatigue left him dozing in his saddle.

Allta stopped, jerking as he drew back with an oath, and Pellin heard the clatter of rocks tumbling a great distance directly in front of them, then all around them.

"Call my name softly, Eldest."

"I'm here, Allta," Pellin said.

He sensed the presence of his guard in the darkness, then felt strong hands feeling their way up his right leg.

"I'm going to light one of the torches, Eldest," his guard said. "Dismount on your right. Stay very close to your horse."

The tenor of his guard's voice held a subtle shift, less resonant. Pellin set himself on the ground and felt Allta groping for his arm before the reins of all three horses were placed in his hand. There was a scrabble at his feet before Allta gave him a final admonition.

"If the horses bolt when I light this torch, Eldest, let them go. Do not try to hold them if you value your life."

A moment later sparks jumped from flint and steel onto the tattered strips of Allta's cloak, the miniature flares of light bright in the darkness. The horses jerked their heads but made no effort to run.

When the torch caught fire, Allta stood, raising the flame overhead, and Pellin's breath fled from him. They stood on the tip of a promontory—a splinter of rock that seemed to hang in the air—overlooking a sheer drop on all three sides. Pellin turned, careful to keep his feet directly beneath him, and saw the path they'd taken to their extremity. A handful of steps left or right and they would have plunged to their death in the darkness.

Howls split the air from the top of the hill behind them—no more than a handful but shocking in their proximity and focused on their light. They sounded again, closer, no longer frustrated but gleeful. The sound of dislodged scree accompanied them out of the darkness.

Pellin took a step toward the sound, halted when he saw Allta unmoving, staring into the darkness. Bile filled his throat when his guard turned to hand him the torch with a terse command. "Keep another close to you as well, but keep the light hidden until the opportune moment. Then hold it as high as you can."

The earth spun in a swirl of vertigo as he turned to look into the pitch black of the abyss surrounding them on three sides, open and yawning, beckoning him to flight and death. "You can't mean to fight them here," he breathed.

"Better here than anywhere else," Allta said, his voice flat. He drew his sword and advanced to put space between himself and Pellin. "Be clever with your light, Eldest," he reminded.

Pellin used the nearest horse to shield the light, but the glare kept him from making out any detail farther away than a handful of paces. The sound of footsteps flying over gravel reached his ears a fraction of a heartbeat ahead of Allta's cry.

"Now!"

Pellin thrust the torch into the air, its hiss matched by those of the villagers. By flickering light, he could see Allta bounding forward, striking with steel and wood to knock a pair of men off the side of the promontory. Wailing cries came up from the darkness to be cut off a few seconds later. The rest of the villagers retreated beyond reach of the light.

He strained his ears for some hint of attack, but nothing beyond the roar of blood in his ears and his own labored breathing came to him. "Have they given up?"

Allta shook his head before answering. "Does the madness of the Darkwater allow surrender?"

Out of the darkness, with a crunch of impact that brought gorge to Pellin's throat, a rock the size of both hands together crashed into the foreleg of his horse. The scream of the wounded animal sliced through him like a dagger against his ears. Without transition, Allta spun, his sword whistling through the air to cut through the arteries of the horse's neck. The animal's scream faded to a gurgle as it lurched from side to side before falling to the ground.

The two remaining horses reared, shifting Pellin's foothold, and for a moment the chasm yawned at him as he teetered. His knees buckled as the horses started to rear again, but their efforts were ill-timed and they dragged him across the thin splinter of rocky earth to the edge.

Instinct greater than their fear of blood stopped them at the last moment from pitching into the darkness, but Pellin's feet slipped from beneath him as he tried to rise and only the reins wrapped around one wrist kept him from falling. His vision narrowed to a flickering point.

"Allta!"

His guard appeared, kneeling to grip him by the shoulders, and Pellin felt himself not so much lifted as thrown to his feet. In the flickering light of the fallen torch, his guard appeared to shift without transition. Even in the midst of terror, Pellin marveled at his gift.

He heard rumbling. "They're trying to knock us from the cliff. What do we do?"

Allta darted to his side to grab the torch. Then he tucked Pellin under one arm and deposited him behind the dead horse. "Stay here. Keep the other horses from falling off the cliff, if you can."

Allta moved forward until he stood no more than five paces from the point where the promontory joined the side of the hill. Pellin gripped the reins of the other horses and tried to light the remaining torch, but the horses whinnied and shied, keeping him from striking his flint.

The rumbling increased in intensity, and boulders came rolling out of the darkness like phantasms from a child's nightmare. Pellin watched as Allta met the avalanche of stone and scree. Twisting and dodging, he attacked the boulders, timing kicks that Pellin could barely follow to send the threats off the edge of the cliff to either side. The retort of his boots striking stone might have been the breaking of his bones, but he rebounded each time, leaping toward his next target.

Pellin stared openmouthed as Allta bounced in the dim light of the torch like an acrobat. But for all his gifted prowess, stones piled up against the other side of the horse, creating a shallow ramp that would allow larger stones with greater momentum to roll up and over.

The sound of Allta's labored breathing fell against Pellin's ears, threads of desperation in the darkness. His guard's kicks no longer carried their previous force, and his efforts were barely enough to shunt the larger boulders off to the side.

Twin behemoths of rock came at them out of the night, one behind the other. Time slowed as he saw Allta launch himself through the air, spinning and twisting to land with his feet against the side of the first rolling boulder.

The rock twitched as if shrugging off his feeble attack, but the change was enough. It struck other stones that guided it off the cliff three paces to Pellin's left. But the second boulder came at him undeterred. Allta's struggle had taken him out of its path, and he lay within a span of the edge of the cliff.

Pellin watch the boulder come, trapping him. It hit the scree on the other side of the horse with the crunch and crack of breaking stone, slowing. When it hit the dead horse, the sound of breaking ribs filled his ears and . . .

It stopped. Pellin hung his head, filled his lungs with dust-laden air and tried to talk his heart into resuming its duties within his chest.

Perhaps the scree beneath the massive boulder shifted, or possibly, the horse's body compressed beneath the pressure of the stone, and slowly, inexorably, the boulder started rolling toward him again.

"Push, Eldest!" Allta cried from the other side. "To your left."

Groans of exertion poured from them as they fought to move the massive rock from its intended course. Allta appeared beside him, his feet set against the debris of the hillside, the vessels in his forehead bulging as he strained.

With a last crying shove, they shifted the stone just enough to send it crashing down the hillside, grazing one of the horse's shoulders as it went past.

Pellin dropped to his knees, heedless of the dirt and blood that matted his trousers. Allta lay prone on a bed of shattered rocks next to him. At first he heard nothing past the sound of his own desperate gasps and those of his guard, but after minutes passed, he became conscious of his surroundings again, and he clutched Allta's shoulder, a move that brought a gasp of pain from his guard.

"Listen," he whispered. "The rocks have stopped."

Allta mustered enough energy for a weak nod. "Look to the east."

"Dawn." Pellin breathed the word as a prayer. "Thank Aer."

His guard made no move to rise. Placing a hand on the dead horse, Pellin levered himself to his feet, his motions as steady as a drunkard's. In the dim morning light the precipitous fall to either side of the promontory beckoned to him and he reeled. Ten paces away the spit of earth they rested upon joined with the rocky hillside, promising security. Fishing through one of the packs on the horses, he found a bit of bread and a waterskin. There was no wine.

Without ceremony, he tore the bread in half and handed it down to Allta, who took a bite where he lay. Pellin knelt and placed the bread and water on the rocks in front of him, his hands shaking with fatigue. Looking east, he closed his eyes and breathed in the air of morning as he lifted his arms into a wan beam of light.

"The six charisms of Aer are these: for the body, beauty and craft; for the soul, sum and parts; for the spirit, helps and devotion. The nine talents of man are these: language, logic, space, rhythm, motion, nature, self, others, and all. The four temperaments of creation are these: impulse, passion, observation, and thought. Within the charisms of

Aer, the talents of man, and the temperaments imbued in creation are found understanding and wisdom. Know and learn."

He paused, breathing with the effort of keeping his hands aloft.

"For the justice and protection of the people, we thank you for your gift of domere."

He let his hands fall before reciting the liturgy that went with the rest of the haeling and then added a prayer for Mark. He would speak to Allta about searching for his body before they continued.

After they'd consumed the bread and emptied the waterskin, Allta rolled to his knees and pushed himself to his feet, the motions of a man who carried a mountain on his back. They led the horses back to safety, picking their way with high steps across the rocks.

"We need food, water, and rest," Allta said.

"No argument there," Pellin said. "South. There are a couple of villages close to the Sundered Hills where we can find provisions."

Allta stopped, staring up the hillside. "We will need enough for three, it seems—and another horse."

Pellin lifted his eyes to see a thin figure running down the hillside toward them, his strides quick, but with the gangly movements of adolescence.

Mark.

Pellin stood, his smile breaking the layers of dust caked to his face, waiting until Mark joined them, dusty and dirty, but not nearly so much as they were.

"I imagine there's a story here." Pellin smiled as he pulled the boy into his embrace. Subtly, he delved his apprentice, searching for signs of a vault within him and breathing a word of thanksgiving when he found none.

Mark gave him a knowing smile. "I don't think my story can match yours. In the urchins, the second thing you learn is how to throw a knife. The first is how to hide. I found a hole and a rock, and I stayed there until I saw sunlight. You should have heard them howling when they couldn't find me."

"We did," Pellin said. "Come, we can share our tales as we ride. I want to be away from this accursed place."

CHAPTER 34

A week after leaving Gylden, I could tell Wag had grown stronger, but that presented a different problem. "We're out of food," I said. I looked down at our new companion. "How can you eat so much?"

"There's a sizable village five leagues south of here," Bolt said. "Isenore, a mining town that's seen better years."

I nodded. "I've heard of it. It's older than Gylden."

Bolt sighed. "It's been around for a bit over a thousand years. Gylden has surpassed it, of course, but it still does a decent business in mining equipment for prospectors who aren't too concerned about the prohibition against delving the earth."

"Sounds like my kind of place," Rory said with a grin.

Bolt didn't smile. "Normally, I'd agree with you, but Isenore is a rough place filled with unsatisfied greed and villagers who don't like each other." He barked a laugh. "They like outsiders even less." He looked at Wag. "I'd suggest skirting it if we could, but a quick stop should be safe enough, so long as we don't spend the night."

Four hours later we rode through a cut between two hills and saw the village of Isenore beneath us. Temporary, dilapidated wooden buildings, many of them obviously abandoned, surrounded a far older central core of stone edifices. Soot covered everything, and as we rode closer, I could see ancient streaks of rust running down the granite blocks from ironwork that had long since been scavenged.

"Not a very inviting place," I said.

Bolt nodded his agreement. "That's by design. Keep your voice down. The second-most profitable industry here is robbery."

Rory's eyebrows lifted in a look of professional interest. "There's three of us and we're armed from teeth to toenail. Would they really consider us a target?"

Bolt shook his head. "Weren't you listening? They don't like outsiders. We stay together and we get out of here as quickly as possible."

I pointed along the sorry excuse for a road toward the south end of town. "If it were a normal town, the butcher and the tanner would be on the south end. The wind comes out of the north for most of the year," I said. "This current breeze notwithstanding. It keeps the smell from the rest of the village."

Behind me, Wag gave a soft yip, then whimpered and growled. I reached back with one gloved hand and scratched him behind the ears and he settled.

"I think the sooner we leave here the better," Rory said under his breath. "I've seen a dozen villagers give us the once-over already."

Without looking, I became acutely aware of men and women, all of them armed with very functional-looking weapons, busying themselves with inconsequential tasks that allowed them to observe us as we passed. Most of them found some other spot for their gaze when Bolt sent a casual glance in their direction.

Most, but not all.

Somewhere in the back of my head there was a door waiting to be opened, the portal to whatever lived inside of my skull and woke me whenever someone was murdered while I slept. I hadn't had a night walk since we'd picked up Wag, but there was something within me that put the sentinel on his guard. Injured as he was, I still didn't want to chance having him see me as an enemy. I looked at Bolt. "I can't spend the night here."

His mouth pulled to one side. "I don't think any of us are willing to argue that. I've seen friendlier faces on the gallows."

We found the butcher at the end of the main street, his business close to the tanner's. The smell of blood and meat that drifted from his shop and the building out back brought Wag's head up from his position on the back of my horse, and I saw him tense.

"Not now, boy," I said. "We don't want attention."

He didn't bark, but I saw him crouch with his legs beneath him, ready to spring from Dest's back.

Bolt nodded to Rory. "Get at least fifty pounds—a hundred, if possible. It won't hurt to let people see a couple of those daggers."

I kept one hand on the hilt of my sword and the other on Wag, who had started shaking the moment Rory had disappeared into the butcher's.

"I don't understand why King Laidir tolerated a place like this," Bolt said.

"Much of the land north of the Rinwash falls under the domain of the Orlan family," I said. "I'm sure you can imagine why they allow it." While I waited, I surveyed the village again, searching for a reason for my discomfort beyond the fact that we were surrounded by ruffians who would gut us for our purses the moment our backs were turned. Isenore filled a cut in the land that ran north to south, with most of the old stone buildings bordering the river that came down out of the mountains.

Hints of stone still showed where there might have been a cobblestone street, but they had long since been scavenged, and residents and visitors alike had to negotiate the mud for their business. We'd have to wash and brush the horses tonight. A few honest businesses—at least they appeared honest—populated the street: a smithy, a cobbler, and a dry-goods store were visible in addition to the butcher's and tanner's place.

Then it hit me. "There's no church here."

Bolt looked at me, then performed his own assessment of the town, catching the eye of a rough-looking woman standing outside a boisterous tavern. She stood in a tight blouse that revealed an alarming expanse of bosom, regarding him with a look of challenge I'd seen the night women in Bunard wear, but the scar running down the right side of her forehead and into her cheek gave it a different interpretation. He nodded and patted his sword and the woman smiled and lifted her drink as if he'd paid her a compliment. "I don't say this often," he muttered, "but some of these people are more than a little scary. Do you wonder that there's no church, Willet? Have you seen anyone here who looks like they want to be saved?"

He went on. "I wonder when the church surrendered and withdrew."

That struck too close to home, and I didn't want to think about how quickly it might have happened. My own experiences as reeve and soldier had shown me just how thin the patina of civilization on mankind was. Beneath it, we were all raving.

Rory stomped out of the butcher's with his hands filled with wrapped meat, his shoulders bunching with the strain. "I don't see why I had to carry it."

Bolt smiled. "The life of a guard is service, boy, and service means work."

Rory gave him a sour look as he wiped blood off his hands. "Funny how every time there's an unsavory task to be done it's suddenly time for me to render service."

"And you're perceptive," Bolt said. "That's another reason I chose you as my apprentice."

Rory tied the meat into place on the back of his horse. "Your purse is substantially lighter than you might expect. Everything in this town costs twice as much as it should, and everybody looks at you strange." He jerked his head toward the shop. "Especially the butcher."

Wag's nose twitched, and he extended his head as far toward Rory's horse as he could without falling. "Shhh. You'll eat as soon as we get clear of the town," I said.

We turned our horses south and rode away. A small crowd of villagers, each of them sporting scars and weapons, watched us leave. Bolt reined up and paused long enough to meet their collective gaze. Then he drew his sword and executed a series of sword cuts that were impossible to follow, but the hiss of the blade cutting the air was all too easy to hear. When he stopped, his sword appeared as if it had materialized in his hand, the point trained on the heart of the nearest villager.

"Do you all understand?" he called.

The man on the receiving end of Bolt's display was the first to nod and turn away, but the others followed soon after.

We rode out of Isenore and put the horses to a gallop for a league, then alternated between a canter and a trot. We didn't stop until we couldn't see the road. Then we made a cold camp in the woods, eating while we listened for signs of pursuit.

I watched Wag tear through a small mountain of raw meat, ripping and swallowing chunks whole, nabbing bits in midair with the skill and speed of a gifted acrobat. His muzzle blurred, and he bore no resemblance to the oversized dog that had ridden quietly with me for the last week.

In the midst of feeding he stiffened, and I heard low rumbles in his throat that made me want to be somewhere else. I could see his nose twitching, and a chorus of whines, growls, and yips created a tapestry of sound in the air. Bolt pulled his sword and motioned to Rory. The boy's hands blurred, and the next time I could see them clearly he held a knife in each one, the blades grasped almost delicately between his fingers, ready for throwing.

"Stay with him," Bolt said to Rory. "I'll check to see what's out there."

"Let's get next to the trees," I said to Rory. "If the villagers come at us with arrows we'll want to put something between us and them."

The two of us waited, our backs against the boles, ears straining for some sound that might presage an attack, while Wag stood at attention over his half-eaten meat. I couldn't hear anything out of the ordinary. Or so I thought. The trouble was I'd been sired and raised in the city. I couldn't distinguish between the footfall of a deer and the step of a man. Rory's gaze darted at each sound, his daggers dancing in his hands as if he were playing an instrument only he could hear.

Thirty minutes later, with the last muted light of day fading, Bolt entered the small clearing shaking his head. "There's nothing out there that I could find, but a sentinel's sense of smell is never wrong." He pointed to Wag and his brows furrowed. "I don't think it's the villagers he smells."

It took me a moment to understand, then I saw it. "He's facing south." I peeled off my glove and put my hand on Wag's head. All sight and sound fell away as my perception tunneled through Wag's eyes and into his mind. The lure of meat just in front of my paws made me drool with the desire to taste the flesh still salty with traces of blood, but beneath that aroma lay odors I knew, eddies on the wind that evoked memories of loss and pain. There could be no doubt. As I smelled those unique scents, earthy and human, I saw again the vision of a man carrying a sentinel pup out of the clearing of Faran's farm.

Within Wag's mind I followed the trail of the memory backward and cursed myself for a fool.

"They've been here," I said as I lifted my hand from Wag's head and the world became dominated by sights once more, "and in Isenore before that. Two of the men who killed the sentinels and the other pup. Three scents."

"When?" Bolt asked.

"About a week ago, I think." I looked at Rory. "You said the butcher looked at you strangely. That was probably the second time he'd gotten a request for that much meat."

"It's too bad we missed them," Rory said. He flipped both daggers into the air and caught them at the same time by their handles. "I'd like to show him what I think of men who kill defenseless animals."

Bolt shook his head. "Sentinels are hardly defenseless, not even the pups. I'm just as happy they have a week on us. It's likely that one of the men is gifted like Laewan and the other is a dwimor. I don't want any part of that here in the forest.

"If we can track the man who stole the pup to a city or even a good-sized town, we have a far better chance of taking and killing him there. He's looking for someone and he's going to be using that sentinel to find them." He shot a look at me. "It's not too hard to guess where he's headed and who he's hunting."

CHAPTER 35

"That's not right," Fess said, pointing across the dell of rich green that separated them from the village. Without waiting for a reply, he shook his head in rebuttal. "No. No. No."

Bronwyn shifted in her saddle, keeping her face neutral. She was a woman who loved her silences, but expressions she'd employed over the years to quiet commons, merchants, and nobles alike seemed to have no impact on Fess. Neither did the tone of voice she'd cultivated to communicate displeasure. Glance and glare alike were absorbed by Fess's enthusiastic equanimity, as if they simply didn't exist. Even when maintaining one of his brief and infrequent silences, he still managed to convey a sense of noise.

"Aer, help me," Bronwyn muttered to herself. "I've apprenticed an enthusiast."

"Your pardon, Lady Bronwyn?" Fess said, turning to her.

She gestured toward the village. "Tell me what you see." The town of Havenwold lay before them, situated at the northern tip of Caisel, where it bordered the forest. A low stone wall, no higher than ten feet, circled the town with gates facing east, west, and south.

"Look at the traffic, Lady Bronwyn." He pointed.

Unlike the villages that bordered the Darkwater farther north, traffic here appeared brisk out of each entrance, but heaviest from the east and west gates, those closest to the Darkwater Forest. Most of the comings and goings appeared to be people on foot or with a single pack-horse or mule.

Fess dismounted and moved to the pack at the rear of his horse. "If what I've read is true, that's strange. Not many carts going in or out."

This was another facet of Fess's personality that Bronwyn hadn't anticipated. The boy read constantly, an unintended benefit of his church-based swindles, and he often displayed a depth of knowledge that surprised her. Yet even at that, he managed to undermine the peaceful solitude people were meant to experience while reading. Instead, he laughed out loud, argued, and generally kept a running commentary on his source material via a series of grunts that she found unnerving.

"Doubtless you're more accustomed to the bustle of Bunard," she said. "Havenwold is a town, hardly more than a village. Its traffic is proportional to its needs."

Her apprentice frowned. "Perhaps, but I think it would be wise to gather a little more information. Which is the dominant order in Havenwold?"

"Aer forgive me," Bronwyn whispered as she squeezed her eyes shut. "Normally it would be Vanguard this close to the forest," she said more loudly, "but Havenwold boasts a large presence of the Absold."

The perpetual grin that ran across the boy's face turned positively feral as he rummaged through his pack. After a moment he pulled a robe dyed in royal blue, the color preferred by the Absold order of the church, and pulled it over his head.

Bronwyn sighed. Newfound experience from the three previous towns they'd passed through told her what would surely follow.

Fess must have caught her expression. "It's not as if I'm lying, Lady Bronwyn." He smiled, the picture of innocent joy. "You yourself said that we serve all orders of the church. So, in a sense, I really am an acolyte of the Absold."

"Humph," Bronwyn said. "Just as yesterday you were a postulant of the Vanguard and the day before that the Servants."

As usual her remonstration slid off of him like water off hot iron. "You can ask any one of the urchins, Lady Bronwyn—I've always had difficulty making up my mind."

Balean covered his mouth with one hand and coughed. "The information he's brought to us has proven helpful," he said. Bronwyn suspected Fess, in some way unknown to her, had managed to suborn her guard's unyielding stoic obedience.

She stiffened in her saddle, powerless to keep her mouth from tightening into a rictus of disapproval Fess would merely ignore. "I can't gainsay it." Truth to tell, the information *had* been useful, if somewhat less than urgent. The Clast had established small but well-attended associations in each of the towns they'd passed through. Once the threat from the Darkwater had been neutralized, the Vigil would have to step back and let the orders settle how they intended to deal with this latest incarnation of that ancient heresy.

With an effort, Bronwyn forced the muscles in her face to relax as she favored Fess with an approving nod. "As Balean has said, the information has been valuable. You have a way with people that encourages them to talk to and sometimes even unburden themselves to you. I suspect that you have a talent for others. What I cannot abide are the tales that follow whenever you return from these little fact-finding expeditions of "gifts" the brothers and sisters have bestowed upon you. I won't demean either of us by having Balean search your bags or your person for evidence of your profiteering." She paused to take a breath. "Once again, I forbid you to con these poor churchmen out of their provisions."

Fess's smile slipped. "The con isn't really my specialty, Lady Bronwyn. That's always been more in keeping with the Mark. He's tried to teach me a bit about it, but I've never had the patience for it, if you see what I'm saying. What I'm doing is called a bluff. It's quick and mostly for small sums, usually forgotten in a fortnight. A con is something else entirely."

He patted his robe, nodding amiably, then placed his foot into the stirrup and mounted once more. "Where will I find you, Lady Bronwyn?"

She mused for a moment. She'd been through the village of Havenwold several times over the years, but none of the inns had made a particular impression upon her memory. "Find the inn closest to the south gate," she said. "We'll be there this evening."

Fess rode off at a canter, the wind ruffling his blond hair in a way that could only be interpreted as mirthful. She shook her head. Her past and circumstances had contrived to forge her into a person of serious character, or so she'd always thought, but when had she become so resolutely dour? Her apprentice, by all accounts, had encountered his own share of suffering—losing his parents to a fire, then his aunt to fever, which put him on the streets and then into service to the urchins.

Once, and only once, Balean had caught sight of Fess bathing in one of the simple wooden tubs the inn had set aside for such use. He told her he had seen grizzled veterans with less adornment. All the remonstration she had to offer couldn't shame Fess as completely as an unobstructed view of the scars that laced his torso. No amount of sympathy could pry their tale from the boy's lips.

She shook herself out of the memory. "Let us see what information we can glean in the taverns." She shook her purse. "I'll look a little out of place, but I think with enough lubrication, anyone will talk."

"Shouldn't we stay out of sight, Lady Bronwyn? If someone recognizes you . . ."

She held up a hand. "Then you will have to rescue me from whatever prison the local head of the Absold can devise."

Every trace of expression dropped away, until only the implacable purpose of a Vigil guard remained. Even for a Vigil guard, Balean was considered cold.

Hours later Bronwyn sat at her table in the shabby inn nearest Havenwold's southern gate. She fingered the glass of wine from the arid region surrounding the city of Elbas. The innkeeper had surprised her by having it. And she wondered how he'd come to possess it. The dark red vintage danced on her tongue and left hints of orange and tamarind on her palate.

She replayed the weeks that comprised the previous months within her mind. Every step she and the rest of the Vigil had taken to combat the threat coming from the Darkwater had carried merciless necessity. Not one could have been delayed or omitted, right down to Toria's investigation of the Clast or her own patrol of the forest

That—she thought as she took another ungracious gulp of the wine—scared her more than anything. Every step and response of the Vigil might as well have been nothing more than the movements of a gifted dancer. She shook her head. No. That comparison held too much imprecision to be useful. It implied a certain amount of cooperation and independence. No. An analogy with a master puppeteer and his marionette would have been more apt.

Even their victory over Laewan at Bas-solas had been turned back upon them. She leaned back in her chair, thinking uncharacteristic thoughts. How many of those poisoned by the Darkwater had the Vigil managed to save after the slaughter of the festival? None, of course. The poison of the Darkwater was perfectly virulent, or nearly so.

And what had they learned from breaking the vaults of those poor damned souls? Nothing.

Black thoughts combined with desperate memories to create accusations that struck her like flails. Cesla and Elwin had known the cost and requirements of leading the Vigil. With the additional centuries of experience after the Gift Wars, they would have simply ordered those corrupted by the Darkwater to be put to the sword. Unlike Pellin. If the Vigil had done that, instead of staying in the Merum cathedral in Bunard for weeks to break each vault in the hopes of more information, they would have departed the city earlier. Perhaps they would have left before the leaders of the four orders took it in their heads to take them all prisoner. Perhaps they would have escaped before the first dwimor had come for Lord Dura.

Balean turned from where he stood at the window facing the street, and she pushed herself up in her chair, trying to ignore the way her bones protested the effort. He crossed quickly over to her table and sat next to her.

"He's coming," he said.

"Is anyone chasing him?"

Her guard shook his head. "Not this time, Lady Bronwyn." He paused to chew on his lower lip. "But he looks serious, very serious."

That alone might have been enough to give her alarm, but Fess appeared in the doorway at that moment, his visage confirming her guard's appraisal.

"Aer help us," she said. "He's swindled someone with a temper, and now we have to run for it."

Fess caught sight of her and moved to take the seat across from the pair of them, unmindful of the instinct that drove other members of the Vigil to sit facing the door. He still didn't smile.

He nodded. "Lady Bronwyn."

She pointed to his traveling clothes. "Where's your robe? Did the Absold here realize you weren't part of their order?"

He gave one quick dismissive shake of his head. "No. There's something wrong in this town."

Her heart fluttered in her chest like a bird trying to escape. "What did you find?"

"I'm not sure. . . ." He made a vague discarding motion with his hand. "Nothing of substance." For once, his thoughts seemed to run close enough to his words to create those pauses in conversation others took for granted.

"Explain, please."

He nodded. "In the other villages and cities we've passed through, I've impersonated whichever order has held ascendancy."

"Yes, I know," Bronwyn said, a hint of frost creeping into her voice.

Fess raised his brows and pointed to her mouth. "Did you know that your lips get tight whenever you disapprove of something I've said or done?"

She inhaled to show him just how cold and sharp she could be, but he held up a hand to forestall her. "I do not mean to mock you, Lady Bronwyn." He looked over his shoulder, gauging the distance to the closest patron before speaking again. "On the streets, we learned to read people the way priests learn to read the liturgy. I'm not as good as the Mark, but I'm close. You can't bluff or con someone if you can't read them well enough to see what they're thinking."

"So you've said before. And as I've pointed out, it indicates that you and Mark have strong talents for others."

Fess leaned forward, his voice dipping almost to a murmur. "In all the villages and towns we've visited there are two orders that inspire trust and two that don't—I've yet to see a farmer, merchant, or tradesman display the slightest caution or hesitation in their speech in the presence of someone wearing the brown of a Servant or the blue of the Absold."

She nodded. Her own far-more-vast experience encompassing centuries had shown her this as well, but did he see the causes the same as she? "And why do you think this is, young Fess?"

He smiled as always at the appellation. "Because it's not in the nature of the Servants or the Absold to judge the actions of others. The browns are too busy healing and feeding, while the blues believe grace covers every action. They see the sins of men and women as an opportunity to draw them closer to Aer." His expression hardened. "Of course that was for regular people, those who lived north of the poor quarter. Those worth saving. The only reason I know as much as I do about the church is because I've made it a habit to steal from them."

She stiffened at his rebuke, felt it like a dagger in her chest, a personal attack she couldn't deny. "I understand your feelings, Fess, but the church, for all its flaws, performs a vital service."

He laughed and the dagger twisted at his dismissal. "Service to others, those *worth* saving, those who can put something in the offering box." He held up a finger. "Here's something you'll never hear in the poor quarter." His head tilted and he donned a vacuous smile. "'It is not the judgment of Aer that draws us to Him, it is His mercy,'" he quoted.

Before she could stop herself, she reached out and slapped him. "You will not mock the church. Not when we have done so much."

"What have *you* done?" he snarled.

"Given you a home," she shot back.

"Because you were forced to," Fess said. "Because you needed our skills. Because you needed children to fight for you during Bas-solas."

"I'm not talking about them," Bronwyn said. "I'm talking about you, about me. I'm giving you a home, because that's what Aer and love tell me I should do."

His eyes widened in shock for a split second before the expression in his eyes became hollow, his emotion swallowed. Shame she hadn't felt for centuries overwhelmed her, and she blinked away sudden tears.

"I'm sorry, Fess." She struggled to keep from sobbing. "I should never have hit you."

He rubbed the cheek, shaking his head. The skin remained unbroken and unbruised—she no longer possessed the strength to do more than sting.

"Why did you?" he asked.

She swallowed against her regret. "Because however much you may believe what you say to be true, however much it *is* true, you should never hold anyone or their beliefs up for ridicule. How will you ever reach them if you've mocked them?"

She forced her back to straighten, and in her mind she imagined her pride and arrogance as a man she could fight and take hold of by the throat. "What I did just now, Fess, was more wrong than I can express. Will you forgive me and tell me how I can make it right?" She waited with her head bowed, unwilling to coerce his forgiveness with more words or by staring him down, allowing him time to deny her or state the conditions of atonement.

"Nobody has ever apologized for hitting me," he said, his voice far older than the decade and six he carried. "'You are forgiven,'" he quoted, "'and absolved from this moment forward.'"

She looked up, saw him rub his cheek, his gaze focused in a way that scared her. "When we are done with our conversation, Lady Bronwyn, you will need to delve me."

"That is not necessary," she said. "Pellin has already done so."

He shook his head in denial. "Pellin looked within each of us to see if there existed any immediate threat to the Vigil. Our apprenticeship is intended to be temporary."

She jerked. "How did you know that?"

He assayed a smile, but it faded, swallowed perhaps by remembered pain. "We're urchins—we eavesdrop as a matter of course." He leaned forward. "I want to be your apprentice in truth. That is my price."

She didn't have the authority to do as he asked. He had to know that. So why had he asked? Was he testing her, pushing to find the depth of her repentance? If the situation hadn't been so immediate and serious, she would have laughed at herself. How could it be possible to live for centuries and be so completely caught off guard by the actions and motivations of a sixteen-year-old boy?

"I will delve you, Fess, if that's what you wish. And if I find within you what I believe is needed to be a member of the Vigil, I will ask Pellin to appoint you as my apprentice." She saw his mouth tighten in disappointment, and she almost smiled, remembering how their conversation had started. "More," she went on, "I will grant you this. If death takes me before I can meet with Pellin, I will pass my gift to you instead of letting it go free. If I am able."

When he nodded his agreement, she lifted a hand to prompt him. "You were telling me about how people react to the different orders."

"Yes, in the towns we've visited, those held by the Vanguard or the Merum, the only information I've been able to gather has come from the members of those two orders. Most people prefer not to speak overly much in their presence. They have a reputation for judgment that the Absold and the Servants do not." He shrugged. "I'm only saying what I believe to be true, Lady Bronwyn. I have no gift for seeing into the minds of others."

"Yet you've said nothing with which I would disagree, Fess. What does this have to do with Havenwold?"

He checked over his shoulder again. "I'm talented at pretending to be what I'm not, Lady Bronwyn. I have an ability to create trust quickly with people I've just met." His serious mien vanished between one blink and the next, and he smiled at her, white teeth showing beneath his thatch of blond hair and warm blue-eyed gaze.

She smiled in return, and he pointed at her mouth.

"You see," he said. "I'm not boasting. I do this very well. But I met merchants who never looked beyond the robe to see my face, Lady Bronwyn, and they never spoke an unguarded word in my presence."

"Tell me about these merchants, Fess. What were their trades?"

He nodded. "One was a farrier, the other a journeyman to a black-smith."

"Only two?" Bronwyn asked.

Fess shook his head. "No, there was one other. Dressed in common, well-used clothing, but I couldn't discern a trade, and his manners didn't fit his clothes."

"How so?"

"In the smithy he moved among the implements with an eye toward them as if he was afraid of soiling his garments, watching his sleeves as he passed close to the anvil." Fess shook his head. "I followed him, at a distance, to an inn on the other side of Havenwold, toward the north. He's not native to this town."

She sat back to regard her apprentice, finding the sensation of being surprised, so seldom felt the past couple of centuries, to be quite pleasant. "As my apprentice, what would you suggest?"

"Delve them, Lady Bronwyn," Fess said. "It should be a simple matter to approach one of the three and arrange some circumstance that will allow a casual touch. I would suggest the one who is not a merchant, as he seems to be the leader, but if he's not native to Havenwold, it may be harder to get close enough to him without rousing suspicion."

She smiled. "That, you can leave to me, Fess. Over the years we have mastered the art of inconsequential contact." She nodded toward his arm as she pulled her glove loose from her fingers and removed it. "Now, give me your hand."

CHAPTER 36

The sun shone to the west, an oversized red ball resting on the horizon that cast weak shadows on the streets of Havenwold. Bronwyn, dressed in nondescript browns and grays for traveling, made her way with Fess to the inn where he'd spotted the suspicious merchant. At the northern end of the town they came to the small single-story building set on a back alley.

She flexed her hands inside of her gloves, anticipating the moment when an accidental brush, carefully contrived, would reveal the merchant's mind to her. She slowed as she approached the steps to the inn, allowing the weight of years to stoop her back and shorten her stride until she wore the fragile shuffle of an old woman.

Three steps up, with her hand clutching the rail, she stood upon the covered porch of the inn. Two, only two, sat at a table, playing some variation of bones and taking pulls from their tankards, their voices filled with the tenor of those with manageable hopes and fears.

Balean and Fess came behind her, her guard doing his best to leave enough distance between them to appear unattached, her apprentice walking upright and smiling as though the dying day offered nothing but joy and opportunity.

Inside the inn a man moved from table to table, wiping them with a filthy rag. No other servants were visible. She spied a table in the corner, situated away from the fire that might reveal them but close enough to the door to allow her to see the entirety of the room and its exits. She sat and Fess joined her while Balean took a position at a table to one side to wait.

"What do we do if he's not here?" Fess asked.

She pulled a deep breath that held old aromas of meat, ale, and people, each holding a faint hint of something beneath—as though the meat were slightly rancid, the ale turning to vinegar. "What can be done?" she asked in return. "We either find him or approach one of his compatriots."

"Let me go into the city, Lady Bronwyn," Fess said. He looked around the interior of the tavern, his gaze landing on bits of food that littered the floor.

She shook her head. "If you are my apprentice, you must learn patience. To be in the Vigil means to hold vigil. In my experience everything can be brought to light if one simply has the patience to wait for the opportune moment. Use the time wisely and read what I've given you."

He squinted in the gloom. "It's too dark, and this isn't the place for us to wait," Fess said. "We're too noticeable."

Bronwyn looked around the interior of the ramshackle room. Despite the impending sunset, no one had bothered to light the candles or bank the fire, and deep shadows covered everything, doubtless an attempt to keep patrons from inspecting the food too closely. The three of them sat removed from the ruddy glow of the fire upon the hearth. Anyone entering would have to search for them.

"We can hardly be seen, my boy," Bronwyn said with soft laughter. She glanced outside. The pair of men on the porch must have surrendered their game.

Fess shook his head, irritated. "Lady Bronwyn, you don't think like a criminal."

"I should hope not."

"Look around the room," Fess said. "You're the only woman here. Despite the lack of customers, no one has come to offer drink or food." He pointed to a group of three men on the far side of the room, also situated as far from the light as possible. They sat hunched over their tankards in a posture of defense and warding, their faces shielded. "Men sit like that when they expect violence. Lady Bronwyn"—Fess's voice held urgency—"we need to leave."

She looked out the window. The tiniest sliver of sun showed above the hills to the west, and just enough light remained for her to see the tables were empty. "I've been a fool."

Just as the sliver of sun disappeared, she rose from her table—Balean moving to stand by her, and Fess digging frantically in his travel pack.

At the far table the men stiffened and rose to face them, their eyes wide. Their collective gaze swept across Balean and Fess to her, and they jerked in recognition, one of them pointing as he muttered, "Block the door." The tavern keeper moved out from behind the bar to join them.

Fess growled a pair of words that he couldn't have possibly gotten from the manuscript she'd given him and darted away from her side, a throwing knife in one hand and sheets of parchment clutched in the other.

Balean's hand flew to his belt, and his blade jumped into his hand.

Footsteps pounded along the hallway that led back toward the rooms, and three more men entered. They locked onto her with identical unblinking gazes. "Don't kill the woman," they said in unison.

The room erupted in chaos.

Moving like gifted, the men at the table came for her, two of the men darting between tables while the other man and the owner leapt like grasshoppers. With his free hand Balean threw a chair that hit one and jumped up to meet the other in midair. Sparks accompanied a clash of swords, and a splash of hot blood hit her in the face.

Fess turned, his cloak billowing to hide his throwing hand, then flicked a dagger toward the other three men. Swords swept the knife from the air and coarse laughter mocked her apprentice. The three men shifted to cut off his escape from the room, moving to block him from the kitchen and the front.

But Fess was already moving away, rolling across a table to throw the sheets of parchment he held.

Balean's blade swept in an arc that she heard rather than saw, a cry of displaced air. The ring and echo of steel sounded in the room as he engaged a pair of swords. His free hand crashed into the top of her shoulder, knocking her to the floor, away from the outstretched hand of the third man.

The man rolled, darting toward her, his fingers reaching for her bare skin. Above her Balean parried the strikes of the other two and lunged, drawing blood.

284

But he couldn't disengage.

She cried out as the bones of her wrist ground together. Fingers pried their way beneath the leather of her glove and ripped it free. Desperate to avoid his open vault, she tried to make a fist, screaming with the effort to close her hand.

A throwing knife flew from across the room to take the man in the shoulder. He growled in pain, shrugging off the impact. Knuckles smashed into the tendons on the back of her hand and the man pressed her fingertips to his.

Time slowed and lengthened as she fell into the delve. The edges of her vision faded, but she could see the room in lurid detail despite the lack of light. Above her a rope of blood hung in the air, suspended in time as Balean's sword found its mark, cutting through the throat of one of the attackers.

To the side Fess stood in the path of a sweeping blow that couldn't help but find its mark in his side. Her apprentice would never see the blow that killed him. He faced her instead of his attackers, his attention on the path of the dagger that he'd thrown toward the man who held her.

The room narrowed and time slowed even more. Balean's sword hardly moved, his muscles flexed for a return strike. Fess's dagger floated through the air, tumbling on a path that would miss its mark.

The last thing she saw was shadows.

Memories filled her and she became Rhue, a laborer without gift or discernible talent, a man who made a meager living with his back. Bitterness filled her, black as tar, scorching as bile at every memory that carried the image of those who held gifts or talents, those who lorded their worth over him.

Someday he, Rhue the porter, would find a way to put those with their gifts and talents in their place. If they would not acknowledge him, they would die.

A shock jolted Rhue's memories, blurring them, and for an instant she knew herself. Outside the delve, someone must have struck true against her attacker.

Praise Aer.

From out of the acid memories, black tendrils and laughter reached for her. She recoiled, fleeing along the strand of Rhue's resentments, trying to hide, but the scorn followed and a thread of midnight coiled around her, anchoring her in place.

No. Focusing, she concentrated on her gift, her Aer-given ability to break the vaults within other minds. Reaching out, she snapped the black thread that held her and continued her flight. Other threads came for her, but she slashed them all with a thought, bright and razor sharp, and they fell away.

Another shock sent her mind tumbling, and the colored threads that constituted Rhue's life dimmed, their light pulsing. From out of the inky black behind her a myriad of threads shot forward, flying toward her like the sticky ribbons of a spider's web. She slashed at them, and the pieces fell, disappearing into nothingness.

But she couldn't open her hand. Rhue's memories dimmed, and several of them blinked like the last flicker of an ember and died.

Fess! Balean! Pry him loose.

But they couldn't hear her. Outside the delve she would appear perfectly calm, utterly tranquil right up to the moment Rhue died and her mind died with him.

Light fled from his memory and she fell into nothingness.

She hurtled downward, pressure building, scaling upward until she felt the cords that bound her soul to her mind stretch, a preface to shattering. Dissociated past feeling, she imagined herself lifting her fingers from Rhue's skin.

And raced away from the delve. Sobs of relief that would never touch her face wracked her mind and soul. But just before she blinked and became aware of her surroundings once more, threads of blackness came for her.

With a contemptuous swipe of her gift, she cut them all away, watched them fall into dissolution.

All but one, a fragment that lodged in her mind, a splinter of purest black.

She opened her eyes to firelight and blood.

Fess had his hand pressed against his side. Trickles of blood filled the cracks between his fingers, flowed in crimson rivulets. A steady patter of drops hit the floor, oddly loud in the silence, but he held a throwing knife in the other hand in a shaky grip. A bit of broken furniture burned on the fire.

Balean held her head in his lap, scanning the interior of the inn. The fire made it impossible to see beyond the shadows it cast. Inside its radiance they were safe, but the streets of Havenwold were dark.

"It's inside me," Bronwyn whispered.

Her guard laid her head gently on the floor and searched her for wounds, his hands professional as a healer's and as thorough. She hardly cared. Inside the organized memories of her mind, she could feel the splinter, a shard of the purest black.

"I can't find any injury, my lady," Balean said. "If you can walk, we must go. We can't stay here."

She shook her head. "You don't understand." Aer help her, she could feel it in her thoughts. "It's here." She tapped her forehead with one finger. "The two of you aren't safe."

"No argument there." Fess kicked a piece of broken chair toward the hearth, his face white with the effort. "But you're not the problem, Lady Bronwyn." He nodded toward the windows. "It's still the early part of night. If they were going to attack us, wouldn't it be happening now?"

"I don't know." She had to force the words past the constriction of her throat.

"Either way, we need a healer," Fess said. "I'm starting to feel . . ."

His knees buckled and he fell forward. Balean gathered his legs and launched himself across the space separating them in time to catch Fess before his head could hit the floor.

"He's right," her guard said.

Bronwyn levered herself up, her body communicating in distinct terms the exact location of every bruise and scratch she'd gathered during the brief fight. She blinked in the growing light of the fire, searching for her bag, then found it beside an overturned table. "Pull his shirt up," she ordered. "I'll tend to him."

"You?" Balean asked.

She nodded. "You've been my guard for fifteen years, and you've been a friend to an old lady as well, Balean, but I'm over six hundred years old. It shouldn't be a surprise that sometime during my long sojourn I thought it would be a good idea to study the art of healing. Now pull up his shirt. He doesn't need someone gifted—he needs someone now."

She positioned herself by the fire and managed to spear the eye of a needle with fine dark thread. The color reminded her of the splinter lodged in her mind, and she fought to control her stomach.

Fess, pale and unconscious, lay in the light of the fire.

"How are you going to stitch the wound without touching him?"

She sighed. "Very carefully, and with your help."

"No, Lady Bronwyn, I can't guard you and help you at the same time. We need to leave this inn. Of the six that attacked us, three escaped. We cannot remain."

She reached out and grabbed his sleeve, knowing he could have avoided her with childish ease if he had wished, but his respect for her kept him rooted to the floor. "You will do as I say." She stopped, took hold of herself. Anger wouldn't help her. "Balean, there is a splinter in my mind, a shard of blackness that comes straight from the evil of the Darkwater. I have no idea what it will do to me, but evil grows. He's my apprentice." She paused for a moment. "I may have to pass my gift to him far sooner than any of us wish."

He checked the room one last time, then knelt beside her with his sword on the floor in easy reach, but his eyes held something she'd never seen before.

"Check the wound to see if it's clean," she ordered.

"If it's not?" he asked.

"Then we'll have to flush it," she said.

He looked around the interior of the inn, his nose wrinkling in distaste. "In here? Anything you use will probably foul the cut."

"Rough men like rough drink. There's probably a bottle of spirits stashed somewhere."

Balean lifted Fess's shirt, the blood thick between the cloth and his skin. A network of thick scars originating on his back wrapped around his side and then tapered away. Balean pointed to one that crossed the wound. "I don't know about the rest of those scars, Lady Bronwyn, but he should wear this one with pride."

"We will let him decide that," she said, pulling a clean cloth from her bag. "Open the wound so that I can clean it."

Balean followed her instructions, and fresh blood pulsed from the center of the cut to soak her rag. "I'm going to have to stitch his artery first." She pulled a pair of medical grips from her bag.

"Hold him steady," she said, her voice tight. "If he flinches while I'm doing this, we're going to lose him to blood loss." She pulled a deep breath. "Aer," she prayed, "keep this boy still."

Fess moaned at the first bite of the needle, but Balean's hand on his chest kept him from rolling against the pain. Bronwyn moved as close to the wound as light and space would allow, overstitching the cut along the artery until the bleeding stopped. Twice she had to go back and add sutures.

She dabbed at the wound, searching for the telltale pulses that would signal any other cut arteries.

"I think you got it," Balean said.

She nodded. "Agreed." She pulled the rest of the thread from the needle and resupplied it from the spool in her purse. "Squeeze the wound together. Try to line up the edges. There's no reason to make the scar any worse than it has to be, and it will heal faster."

Bronwyn measured time unconsciously with the beats of her heart rushing through her ears. As she leaned over to begin stitching again, she slipped, and reflexively she caught herself with her other hand on his bare chest.

Unbidden, she fell through sight and sound and into his mind, but this time the delve was hers to control. Only a few days had passed since she'd last looked into his memories, and the few he'd garnered since then were shared with her and Balean. They carried no weight, but as she made a conscious effort to break the contact she'd made with his skin, she sifted through them.

And gasped. Every memory of her since she'd slapped him and apologized for it carried a different tenor. Though Fess nodded his respect and called her Lady Bronwyn, within the depths of his mind he called her something else. Mother.

She blinked, her guard's face coming back into focus. "No," she sighed. "I can't bear it."

"My lady?" Balean asked.

Perhaps it was the fatigue or possibly the stress that made her tongue unguarded, but she answered even as she reached out, almost brushing the hair back from Fess's forehead. "He thinks of me as Mother." She caught Balean's gaze. "Laewan was like a son to me, and despite all the love and encouragement I could give, he fell into the corruption of the Darkwater. Somewhere I failed him."

"That burden doesn't belong to you." Her guard's voice was flat with denial. "The Darkwater has changed. Its evil must be fought, no matter the cost."

"You're loyal," she said, "even to my feelings, but Laewan was my responsibility, not Pellin's, or Jorgen's, or even Elwin's. My inexperience cost us one of the Vigil. I find myself filled with wishes and regrets, but mostly I would like to know exactly how I failed him."

"In battle, men fall," Balean said. "Sometimes they are new to the sword, and sometimes they are the best on the line—betrayed by poor footing or a chance arrow that finds a weakness in their armor. Their brothers-in-arms grieve and keep fighting. They do not waste time accusing themselves."

He was right. Questions of failure and blame were unanswerable, but she still couldn't help wondering. She forced the needle through skin on each side of the cut that had laid Fess open and pulled, the thread cinching the flesh back together. By the time she finished stitching and binding the wound, nearly an hour had passed.

"One would think that the commotion of our fight would have brought the town watch," she said.

Balean shook his head. "Fights in taverns such as this are a common thing. No watchman with sense will intervene until he's sure it's safe. As long as it's dark, Lady Bronwyn, we're in danger here. We've barely started the night." He shook his head. "I don't understand it. If those three men had wanted us dead, a few arrows through the front window would have done the trick."

"No. This is what we discovered in Bunard. Those corrupted by the Darkwater cannot abide light. To aim well, they would have to look into the light, which they cannot do. Their very strength becomes their weakness. We need only attract the attention of the watch somehow and they can escort us to safety."

On the floor, Fess stirred, and his eyelids fluttered but without achieving consciousness.

CHAPTER 37

Bronwyn's eyes snapped open, brought to wakefulness by a host of aches and pains that combined to make even the slightest movements a trial. Her gaze found Balean by the door, standing with his weapons ready, the same position he'd adopted after the watch guards had escorted them to their room at the inn near the southern gate the previous night. Outside, the palest suggestion of gray heralded sunrise, but no hint of yellow or orange showed in the sky yet.

Fess slept on the other bed, coaxed to sleep by the draught of mint and paperin the healer had given him. A bit of color had returned to his cheeks. She didn't want to remember how he'd looked lying on the floor. Already pale complexioned, blood loss had contrived to make him spectral, and only the rise and fall of his lungs told her he lived.

He would probably sleep for a week, which was fine with her. Yet when she rose from her bed, her body mimicking the creaks and groans of the furniture, her apprentice blinked and, after a misguided effort at rising, tucked his arms against his side and rolled off the bed to his feet.

He grunted from his bent position. "Are they all dead?" The expressions that chased each other across his face as he tried to straighten would have been comedic had she not known their cause.

Balean answered for her. "Half, thanks in large measure to your daggers." He stepped from the door and put a pair of knives on the bed. "I sharpened and oiled them for you." He gave her half a shrug. "It gave me something to do last night."

"What of the three who came in after?"

"They fled as soon as the parchment you threw onto the coals of the fire flared into light." He nodded his approval. "Quick thinking. If you had a physical gift, I'd be willing to take you as my apprentice."

"Those were the men from the marketplace. We have to find them," Fess said.

"No." She pointed to his wounded side. "You need at least two weeks to heal and get your strength back." A growl from his stomach punctuated her refusal. "You see. You require food and rest."

He set his jaw and stood, trying not to show any discomfort and failing. "Lady Bronwyn, I'll be happy to rest so long as those men are in Havenwold, but we interrupted some plan last night. If they're still here, nothing has changed. You need to delve them."

A tremor started in her right hand, the one she used for delving, and she clenched a fist. It was inside of her. "We can talk about that later." She looked away.

"Lady Bronwyn?"

"Go easy, lad," Balean said. "You weren't the only one injured last night."

"No, the boy's right. There's been no outcry here in Havenwold. No constables searching for killers after last night's fight. Doesn't that strike you as strange? Something is amiss, and we need to trace it to its root." Her stomach chose that moment to growl. "We'll eat, then see what we can find." A memory, unbidden, came from behind one of the myriad doors within her mind—innocuous, of porridge and dark bread.

She'd never eaten dark bread for breakfast. With a mental thrust, she put the memory away. Perhaps she just needed to rest. Yes, that was it. A few days here at this inn would do both her and Fess well. "They may have left the city already."

Balean shook his head. "Possibly, but don't forget the guards we saw when we entered the town. Those men would have to find a way to sneak out the gates or bribe the watch. They're here."

"I'll find them," Fess said. He turned toward the door, too quickly, and gasped with the effort. His face lost what little color it held, and he tottered.

"You're not going anywhere," Bronwyn said, pointing to the bed for him to sit. "The first thing you're going to do this morning is eat."

She sniffed. "I can't believe you would even suggest such a thing. Those men have seen you twice now. You'll be recognized."

Fess cocked his head to one side, then nodded, but he moved to his pack and proceeded to unroll the blue robe he used to impersonate an acolyte of the Absold. "Actually, Lady Bronwyn, if what you've told me is correct, they've only seen me once. It's daylight. What they've seen in the night while their vaults were open is inaccessible to them."

She stood. "Very well, don your robe, but my command remains. We will eat first. I won't have my apprentice dropping dead of blood loss in the street. Pellin frowns on that sort of thing."

Another memory, her own this time, came forward with such force that the room and her companions instantly faded from awareness.

"What do you think of our newest apprentice?" Pellin asked.

She nodded. "He's brilliant. If I didn't know it to be impossible, I would suspect that Peret Volsk holds the gift of kings, so quickly does he learn and understand everything he's taught."

Pellin nodded. "His ability to synthesize and extrapolate is impressive, and . . ." He stopped, catching her expression. "Something's troubling you."

"I've noticed him watching Toria Deel. It's not the way an apprentice usually looks at one of his mentors."

Pellin chuckled. "She's still young by the way we count such things, Bronwyn. Physically she is probably still in her twenties, and she's beautiful. Don't fault Peret for noticing what any other man would."

She caught Pellin's gaze. "She returns those looks, Pellin. I think one of us should tell the Eldest."

A mask, old and familiar, dropped over Pellin's expression at the mention of his brother, the way it had for hundreds of years. "Doubtless he knows already," he said. "Cesla knows everything."

The room, her guard, and Fess came back into focus. Neither of the men commented or appeared to have noticed her slip, but inside her mind she searched for the splinter.

An hour later Fess left to find the men he'd first seen in the marketplace, and Bronwyn surveyed the carnage he'd left behind. She waved at the pile of dishes. "I'm almost tempted to recite the antidon for the dead, Balean. Look at it all. I know I told him to eat . . . " Words failed her. "But *look* at it."

Balean nodded. "He lost a lot of blood, Lady Bronwyn, and he's a growing young man." He glanced down at the mound of plates and scattered morsels of food that had somehow escaped Fess's rapacious appetite. "And don't forget he spent years on the streets as an urchin. Hunger became a way of life for him. For the first time in his life, he knows what it is to be filled. Being with you probably seems a bit like heaven to him." He looked down at the table and grunted. "But I have to admit, it *is* a little alarming."

There was no gentle way to broach the topic, and she had never believed in mincing words anyway. People who did spent far too much time dancing around a subject only to end up having to confront it head on later. "My mind is slipping," she said. "Is your knife sharp?"

Balean stared at her, stillness falling over him until he became a statue, the product of the temperament of observation that all the Vigil guards possessed. "You're not even as old as Pellin."

She shook her head. "Age is only part of it. You know this. Elwin was of an age with Pellin, but he was mere weeks from passing, used up by his gift and his search for Cesla's killer."

"You're not him," he said flatly. "You use your gift even more sparingly than Pellin."

A whisper of a sigh escaped from her. "Look at me, Balean." She lifted her hands to trace the withered skin of her face and neck. "Did you think I would outlive you?"

When he didn't answer, she went on, oddly nervous in front of the man who lived to safeguard her every breath. "After I woke from the delve last night, there remained a splinter in my mind, less than a vault, but more than a memory. Balean, I can't lock it away."

She'd had hundreds of years to prepare for this moment, to ready herself for the day when she would have to surrender the gift to another. But in all her imaginings in which she'd envisioned that necessary rite of blessing, she'd seen herself enfeebled physically by age, her mind still intact. In her nightmares she remembered Cronin, old nearly past reckoning when she'd first come to the Vigil, succumbing to the weight of memories, his decline into crippling senility made faster by the gift he carried.

In the end, he'd lost all sense of himself, his mind too broken to carry out the simple requirements of keeping his body fed. The periods of lucidity made his condition worse because it was in those moments he knew the horror of what had happened to him.

It had been a blessing when he finally deteriorated to the point that his guard, Nikola, delivered the mercy stroke, opening an artery in the old man's left hand, Cronin's right upon his apprentice, Jorgen. In that moment, she'd learned how cruel their gift could be, what *used up* really meant, and how deep the loyalty of their guards ran. Nikola, himself wearing only ten years of service, left the Vigil the next day, undone by Cronin's death.

Every other member of the Vigil who had passed since she'd joined had gone quietly, their bodies no longer able to serve them, but their minds and the myriad walls within it unbroken. She'd spent hundreds of years denying the possibility that Cronin's end might be hers as well.

"The walls within my mind are failing." She swallowed and met Balean's gaze, her back straight, pretending a courage she would never feel. "When the man in the tavern forced me into the delve, his vault was open. Threads of darkness, like a spider's web made of tar, tried to anchor me to his mind even while he lay dying."

"Like Dura said."

She nodded. "Lord Dura still has much to learn about his gift. I was able to cut those threads each time they came for me, but a splinter remained after I escaped, like an arrowhead lodged in my mind."

Balean bowed. "When we rejoin the others, I will inform Allta of my resignation. There is no place in the Vigil for a guard who fails in his duty."

She waved his self-recrimination away. "Don't be ridiculous. The decision to go to that inn was mine. Even when you voiced your objection, I overruled you. Besides, I'm not sure how long I have." She leaned forward, driven by the need to ensure his obedience even after she died. "Once my mind is gone, you will need to administer the mercy stroke. It must be done in such a way that the gift does not instantly go free but instead will give me an opportunity to give it to Fess."

Balean, stoic as all the guards were trained to be, couldn't hide his surprise. "He is at the beginning of his apprenticeship, Lady Bronwyn. I know you promised him your gift, but that was under the assumption you would live to train him how to use it first."

"There's no time, and there's no one else." She took a deep breath, ignoring the temptation to check the walls in her mind for the hundredth time that morning. Instead, she brought forth a memory, one of her own. "Listen, here is how it must be done."

Balean shook his head. "I already know, Lady Bronwyn. All the guards know."

She nodded. "Yes. I suppose they do. If needed, I want you to slow the bleeding so that Fess has every chance of receiving my gift. Then stay with him. He will need all the experience you can give him and more. I forbid you to surrender your place in the Vigil out of some misguided sense of blame."

After the serving staff cleared away the remnants of her apprentice's carnage, they waited, sipping tea, until Fess returned two hours later wearing his blue robe.

Bronwyn pointed at the robe. "Is that wise?"

He shrugged, his gaze roving over the table as if searching for any food that might have been inadvertently left behind. "I considered trying to find them without the benefit of disguise, but if they recognized me as the acolyte they saw yesterday and I wasn't wearing the robe, it would have been as much as telling them I was spying on them."

Bronwyn nodded. "And if they recognized you from the fight last night?"

A grin snuck up one side of his face, making him appear younger than he was. "I considered it," he said, one hand rubbing the wound in his side, "but it's daylight. You've said their vaults would be closed to them."

"Don't place too much trust in what I've said." She sighed. "I've been wrong too often lately for you to risk your life on my words."

"There's little else to use, my lady," Fess said. "And we're risking our lives at any rate." His smile grew. "Be that as it may, I found them making preparations to leave the city, and though they saw me, their eyes held nothing more than the slight familiarity you'd expect from yesterday's first encounter."

She shook her head in disbelief. Of all the things she'd forgotten about being young—impetuous decisions, the feeling of immortality, the hunger for experiences—it was this that always surprised her, the unquenchable enthusiasm. Fess sat across from her with half a foot of stitches in his side and his face pale from last night's attack, and not only had he insisted on jumping back into the fire this morning, he wanted to make sure it was lit.

"In the daylight they are no match for you," she said to Balean. "Follow them from the city and execute them for their crimes."

"You cannot order me from your side, my lady," Balean said.

"Nonsense." She sniffed. "Fess is here, and thanks to you his knives are razor sharp."

"His wound prevents him from throwing with any certainty, my lady. You know this."

"True," Fess smiled. "It will be a few days before I can find the mark. We need to stay together under his protection." He nodded at Balean. "As you said . . . Lady Bronwyn, it's daylight. Those men have seen me, but not you. You can touch one or all of them at the next village."

The thought of delving anyone—even a newborn with only its memories of warmth and water—made her cringe. She wanted nothing more than to find Pellin, have him delve her and take away the splinter of darkness infecting her mind.

But that would be foolish, perhaps the worst decision she could make. If the splinter affected Pellin, managed to infect him the way it had her, then the Vigil would be down to two. She shuddered at the thought of Toria Deel and Lord Dura fighting the Darkwater, leading with their emotions and leaving their logic to catch up later.

"Very well," she said without meeting her apprentice's gaze. "We will follow them, but let us see what we can discover without delving them."

"Lady Bronwyn?" Fess asked.

She did her best to look decisive. "We have depended on our gift for uncounted centuries, believing that our ability to judge a person's innocence or guilt made us impervious to error. Now we know differently. Let us see what insight and intellect can tell us of what's happening in the forest."

Chapter 38

Toria Deel stepped onto the gangplank of the boat they'd taken down the Soul's Ease, the river that flowed from the southern tip of the Darkwater to the western edge of the city of Treflow in Aille. There, the river split into three parts: the Mournwater, flowing east into Moorclaire; the Dirgewater, flowing southwest toward Vadras, the seat of Caisel; and the Sorrow, which meandered south through the plains until it came to the largest city in the northern continent, Cynestol.

Toria pressed a full silver crown into the palm of the ship's master and took possession of her horse from the gap-toothed deckhand. For a moment she allowed herself a glance south across the uncounted leagues. Born and raised Elanian, with the dark hair, dark skin, and blue eyes typical of those whose blood carried traits from the people of both continents, she still considered Cynestol her home. Since joining the Vigil a little less than a century ago, she'd managed to spend twenty years in the city, a time she'd marked with Peret Volsk's courtship.

Her time in the Vigil had forced her to segregate her memories. She sighed. A mere five years before, living as though she were a separate person, Toria Deel had basked in the warmth of Cynestol's evenings while the Vigil's newest apprentice wooed her with ardor and honesty. She would have to put those memories away. They were useless now.

Lelwin and Elory awaited her, mounted and expectant, though her guard eyed her uncovered head more than once with disapproval. As she drew near, Elory murmured, "The drawback of being beautiful, Lady Toria Deel, is that people will remember you long after the blush should have faded from your bloom."

She waved a hand. "I haven't been in Treflow for thirty years. I'm unlikely to be recognized here, Elory."

He shook his head. "My village lies a scant twenty leagues to the southeast, my lady. This is not Collum or Elania. The people of the region follow the floodwaters of the three rivers, and are almost as fluid in their choice of homeland."

Strange that after joining the Vigil her chief complaint had not been the isolation or the requirement that she move every ten years or so in order to keep people from realizing she hadn't aged. No, she hated having to cover her head if she revisited a region before enough time had passed to ensure anyone who could recognize her had died. And she'd only worked within the Vigil for a hundred years. How did Pellin and Bronwyn stand it?

She raised the hood on her cloak, the breeze blowing from the north just cool enough to warrant the behavior. She added her sigh to the wind and nodded toward the city.

"Will it work?" Lelwin asked.

Toria felt reasonably confident she knew the reference behind the girl's question, but Lelwin's habit of starting her conversations in the middle required correction. Often, her apprentice would pick up the thread of a discussion hours or even days afterward. There was too much possibility for misunderstanding in that habit, and the duties of the Vigil required clarity.

"Will what work, Lelwin? Be clear."

Her apprentice shrugged. "Pellin's plan to pit the interests of the nobility against those of the church. It seems a risky venture, considering both sides must be evenly matched for it to succeed. In negotiations between merchants, one side always desires the goods more than the other. It's the basis of trade."

Toria nodded. "You're right, of course, but access to the Vigil is more complex than bidding for melons or wool. The dynamics of power between countries and orders of the church are larger and therefore take a longer period of time to resolve. Pellin knows this and uses it to his advantage. By making the kings and queens of the north aware of the intentions of the church, he counters them and buys us time in which to move freely. Hopefully, he started with King Ellias in Moorclaire."

Lelwin nodded. The girl was a remarkably quick study, even though she tended to see everything, even close relationships between men and women, through the lens of buyer and seller. According to the exordium, she probably held a talent for all, the ability to see and grasp complex relationships in the world. Those who held the talent were often the most successful merchants and kings.

"Why him?" she asked.

Toria had pondered this question herself each day they'd ridden or floated toward their destiny. Pellin had been stingy with the specifics of his plan. He might have tried his luck with the kingdom of Caisel first. "The king of Moorclaire is different."

Lelwin shrugged. "Everyone is different."

Toria nodded. "Yes, but the monarchs are usually different in the same way. The gift of kings rests on Ellias of Moorclaire more heavily than his peers. The portion of his inheritance, the gift of parts, which affords him the ability to understand crafts of all types, dominates his personality." She shrugged. "That kingdom has ever held the mathematicum in high esteem, and he has always displayed a strong talent for logic. I sometimes wonder if he came to the throne completely whole."

Lelwin cocked her head the way she did whenever she needed additional explanation. "Is there something wrong with the king of Moorclaire?"

"No," Toria said. "I'm not sure I can make you understand unless you've met his like. In your time in the urchins did you ever meet one of your fellows whose mind seemed different?"

Lelwin grew still as her thoughts and memories turned inward. "Lady Deel, children who have been orphaned by design or circumstance are always broken in some way. The question should be, when did I not?"

Toria nodded, playing for time. Lelwin's response offered another opportunity for her to question the girl about her past, to uncover those circumstances that led her to regard love—and more particularly, men—with such a jaundiced eye. Only those discussions would allow Lelwin to begin healing. She pushed that impulse away. She'd tried too often of late to bring the conversation about, and Lelwin's natural reticence had grown in proportion.

With a small sigh, she picked up the thread of their discussion. "I'm not referring to the brokenness that comes from extreme circumstances. Ellias of Moorclaire holds no such memories. Rather, I speak of someone whose gaze seems to slide past you as if in discomfort, and when they engage you in speech, their thoughts appear to run in a predetermined path that compels them."

"As if they must speak of it and nothing else," Lelwin said. "Yes, I've seen such, but not just in the urchins."

Toria nodded her approval. "That is the way with King Ellias of Moorclaire and the mathematicum. He is a brilliant man and a decent king, but most of the responsibilities of the kingdom have been delegated away while he works in his laborium."

They rode through the gates of Treflow and into a market square a hundred paces on a side, amidst the din and noise of the town at harvest. Carts and wagons jockeyed for position, their riders yelling curses native to their kingdom as they strove to move their goods to the appointed place.

Elory pointed to a street running south, away from the market. "If memory serves, the criers congregate that way, closer to the docks on the Mournwater."

They edged to the outskirts of the market until they came upon the main thoroughfare leading to the south part of the town. After a few hundred paces the houses grew larger and came farther apart, evidence that they had left the homes of more common tradesmen behind and ventured upon the houses of more prosperous merchants.

They followed the turn of the road and came to a square with blocky, stone-built edifices on each corner guarded by heavily armed men. Toria pointed, answering Lelwin's unspoken question. "Moneylenders. Sitting at the head of the three rivers, Treflow occupies a unique position. Boats travelling though this place have access to nearly half the continent's population. The guards you see outside are but a sample of the precautions the settlement houses take against thievery."

Turning to follow the sun, they entered a square a couple of hundred paces farther on that put Toria in mind of Criers' Square in Bunard, complete with the stands where each order's designee enjoined the crowd or read from the daily office.

"That's a surprise," Lelwin said. "I thought the square was particular to Bunard."

Toria shook her head. "The Order Wars brought a new kind of horror to our continent."

Lelwin shrugged her shoulders. "War is war."

"No, this was different." Toria pointed at each of the four stands. "The Gift Wars and the Wars for the Gift of Kings had cemented the idea that men fought for power and that those men were nobles intent on expanding their reach. When the Merum church split, then split again, and again after that, it set a new type of conflict into motion."

Lelwin's gaze became fixed on a point somewhere over the top of her horse's head, as it always did whenever Toria spoke of the church, an unmistakable sign of boredom. Toria reined her horse closer and reached out to take the younger woman's arm. "You need to understand this."

"Why?"

The blunt forthrightness of the question took her off guard for a moment. "Because I've yet to see mankind make a mistake that it was unwilling to repeat." She let go. "If you become one of the Vigil in my place, it may fall to you to stop the Order Wars from coming again."

Lelwin cocked her head, thinking, before she nodded.

Toria pointed at the criers. "Before, common men fought because their lord or king told them to or because they needed to defend themselves from some other noble who wanted to amass enough gifts to walk a little closer to Aer. Now they fought because they believed they were right. By the time the war had flowered completely, every order of the church had managed to decree that each of the other orders was apostate and their corruption of the faith had to be extinguished."

Lelwin's eyes widened at that. "Even the Servants?"

Toria nodded. "The war that came was unparalleled in savagery and casualties. Concepts of strategy and tactics were secondary to extermination."

Her apprentice frowned. "I would have thought that even after the split, the Merum church would have commanded enough resources to subdue the others."

"Men are opportunistic," Toria said. "Alliances during the war were as ephemeral as mist and about as long lasting. The kings saw the war as a way to come out from beneath the rule of the Merum, and when one order was threatened with total defeat, other orders would restore the balance of power."

"How did it end?"

"Everyone started to run out of men." If she hadn't been looking at her apprentice, Toria would have missed what she said next, so softly was it spoken.

"Good."

Anger brought a flush of heat to Toria's skin, and she rubbed one cheek, biting back the first and second response that came to her, replies that would inevitably push Lelwin back into her protective shell. "No, there's never anything good about a lot of men dying."

"What about Bas-solas?" Lelwin asked, her tone sharp.

Toria nodded to herself. Better. The girl could think instead of just react. "That was necessary . . . but hardly good. *Good* is a term we reserve in the church for those circumstances that align with the will of Aer. Death doesn't qualify, no matter how crucial it may be." She pointed at each of the stands in the square. "This is far better than swords and halberds."

Whatever she was about to say next was lost as a figure at the far end of the square mounted a makeshift platform, the people around him more attentive, more animated than the rest of those attending, the crowd far larger. Dressed in plain clothes befitting a common merchant, he lifted his hands as the other priests had, but even that similar gesture held violence instead of blessing. And though he had yet to speak, his face held the ruddy cast of one who'd been screaming. Even the other criers turned to hear him.

"I speak for the Clast!"

Toria beckoned Elory closer, her conversation with Lelwin forgotten. "At last, we can take a closer look at this heresy." Casually, so that only he would notice, she pulled her gloves free and tucked them into the wide belt that circled her waist.

"Lady Deel, I cannot safeguard you in such circumstances."

She pointed to the crowd. "Look at them. As rapt as children at a puppet show. Why? What is he offering them?"

Elory's head swiveled as he searched for threats. "Can we not wait until the crowd has begun to disperse before you delve the speaker?" he whispered.

After a moment, she nodded. "Yes, there is time. Let us hear what the Clast has to say."

CHAPTER 39

Toria Deel waited at the edge of the crowd gathered around the crimson-faced speaker—screamer was more like it—with her hands bared but safely tucked into her cloak.

"Fools!" the man screamed as the color of his face deepened until it took on a purplish cast. "You are all fools playing a game that only the church and the nobles can win. They line their pockets with the sweat of your brow, and you can think of no response except to hope that a free gift will come and elevate you to the very nobility you despise. Yes," he sneered, "you are all fools."

"And who are you to be calling us fools?" A bearded man with dark eyes held up a fist, and Toria could see fresh soot and old burns on the skin. "Are your clothes so fine?"

The man on the platform laughed. "Like you, I was a fool once. I worked for my noble, plying my trade, rising before the sun and working long after it had set. Most of my work went to line my lord's pockets, but like every good man or woman, I took a portion of what was left to me in poverty and gave it to the church to help those whose straits were worse than mine.

"Until I discovered that the poor they were supposedly helping never got any less poor unless they joined the ranks of the Merum, the Servants, the Absold, or the Vanguard. No, the rich got richer and the poor stayed poor. Yes, I was a fool like you."

The speaker held out his arm, pointing, and swept his arm and his lurid gaze across the crowd in silence. Toria felt it slide across her like the chill from a cloud blocking the sun. The mass of people fell silent, waiting.

"What can be done?" the speaker said softly. And hundreds of people leaned forward, straining to hear. "What can ungifted cobblers and smiths and weavers do with their sorry lot in life? Only this . . . " He held up a finger. "Stop listening to the lies that come from those who say you're powerless and stupid." He shook his head. "Perhaps I ask too much of you. Perhaps your belief in the lies of the nobility and the church is too ingrained. Perhaps"—his voice rose—"you do not have the strength and the courage to challenge your most basic assumptions."

The smith, the man who'd questioned him earlier, shouldered his way through the crowd. "My name is Angis, and I will gainsay any man who says so." He held up a horseshoe, took an end in each hand, and pulled until it had flattened into a broad arc.

"Well and good, Angis," the man said. "You have the strength, but are you courageous as well? Can you fight your fear in the hope of a greater good for yourself and your family?"

Angis raised a fist the size of a melon. "Try me and see."

"Then I tell you all this," the speaker said. "The oldest lies have the most power. For generations we've been told the Darkwater Forest is evil. 'Don't go into it,'" he said in a mocking falsetto. "Ask yourselves this: What is it they don't want you to know?" He reached into his pocket. "I have been to the forest. Do I look crazed?" He pulled his hand out and held up a yellow lump of metal with a faint bluish tinge between his thumb and forefinger. It was no larger than Toria's thumbnail, but the crowd gasped at the sight of it, and everyone took an involuntary step toward the speaker. "If you wish to know whether the rumors of gold in the forest are true, here's your answer. The nobles and the church have the gifts and the gold. What do you have?"

He took a step back toward the stairs leading up to the podium. "I have nothing more to say except this—the Clast opened my eyes. When you tire of living someone else's lie, we are here to help you see the truth."

Toria watched as the speaker descended the rude ladder back to the ground, his guards enforcing space around him, keeping everyone who'd witnessed his speech and display at bay. More than ever she needed to touch him, to use her gift to delve into the speaker's mind to discover his true intentions.

"He's well-spoken for a rouser," Lelwin said.

Toria started. She'd forgotten the presence of her apprentice, so intent she'd been on the speaker for the Clast. "A what?"

Lelwin chuckled softly and smiled, enhancing the heart shape of her face. "A rouser is what we call someone who works a crowd. We don't have any in the urchins—people don't really respond to calls for action from a child—but we've hired a few from the thieves' guild from time to time to create a distraction when we needed to steal during daylight." She shook her head. "None were so skilled as this one, though. The gold nugget was a perfect touch. A few dozen speeches like that one and the Clast could field its own army."

Toria nodded. "And that may be exactly what he intends." She flexed her hands, checking over her shoulder for Elory. "Lelwin, stay close. Elory, follow at a distance."

Her guard's face went flat. "No. I cannot protect you. Let us wait until he separates himself from his guards."

She put her hand on his chest, avoiding any contact with his bare skin. "Even then there is no guarantee you could keep me safe." She nodded toward Lelwin. "A pair of women will hardly be seen as a threat. A brief touch of greeting coupled with a few inane questions about the Clast and we will retreat." She tightened her hand into a fist. "Then, if we find what I suspect, we will send word to the kings and they can stamp out this heresy once and for all."

Lelwin shook her head. "Heresies, especially the attractive ones, die hard."

"No," Elory repeated. "I cannot allow it, Toria Deel. The survival of the Vigil is in our keeping. This is foolish."

He actually meant to defy her. "You are sworn to protect and obey me. In this instance you cannot do both the way you would wish." The speaker for the Clast had negotiated the end of the crowd and was moving away, toward the inner part of the city. "Do both as well as you are able. I am going to follow and delve him now. If you are by my side, our danger increases."

Without waiting for his next argument, she turned and hurried after the man she intended to touch with Lelwin by her side. Elory, shaking his head and his face filled with lightning and thunder, dropped back until ten paces separated them and moved out to the side, walking parallel to her in a meandering path so that no one would suspect they were together.

The speaker for the Clast rounded a corner into a street that ran perpendicular to the river, his strides eating up the ground. Toria debated calling out to the speaker but was saved the trouble when another man, the smith, Angis, also following after the speaker, hailed him.

"Speaker! Speaker!"

The red-faced man turned, his gaze imperious, and watched as the man approached. Toria fell in just behind him, hoping the speaker would assume they were together.

"What do you want?" the speaker asked.

"I want the truth," Angis said.

The speaker's gaze took in the smith from head to toe and back again, then slipped to Toria and Lelwin, his face filling with disdain. "Few have the stomach for the truth. Besides, I've already given it to you." He turned, nodding to his guards and walked away.

For a moment, Toria quailed, her opportunity slipping away, but Angis was undeterred. He hustled after the speaker, calling for attention, and Toria followed.

But the speaker ignored them, moving farther from the docks and the boats, heading deeper into the city.

Angis, his face florid, lost patience just as the speaker stopped at the juncture of a narrow alley and the street, and Toria nearly ran into him at the sudden stop. "I am Angis, the smith." He held up one huge fist. "You will answer me."

In the back of Toria's mind an alarm sounded. The smith's threat of violence was stiff and clumsy, the gesture of a player who had lost his lines and was left with no choice but to improvise.

Lelwin must have divined the truth as well. Her mouth opened to call the watch even as her hands darted to her belt for the knives she kept there, but the smith's first blow took her in the temple.

Toria saw the second fist coming, knew she would be unable to duck it. She lurched back and flung up one naked hand before the blow brushed aside her fingers and crashed into her skull.

Everything went black.

She woke inside a room that smelled of old wood and dust. Pain lanced up her fingers and wrists like bolts of lightning, and her elbows twitched in response. The room glowed faintly by the light of a pair of candles resting on a crude trestle table to her left—the only piece of furniture other than the chair that bound her.

She corrected that. On her right, Lelwin sagged in a chair against the ropes that kept her prisoner. A trickle of blood ran down one cheek from a split on her temple, emphasizing the pallor of her skin.

The speaker stood in front of her along with a single guard from the group that had surrounded him during his speech. Of the smith and the rest of the guards there was no sign. The speaker waited for her to take in her surroundings, his face no longer red from the exertions of his speech. For a moment she considered bluffing her position, but a glance at Lelwin persuaded her otherwise. Much of the blood on the side of her face had already dried. So, they'd been more than just momentarily unconscious from the smith's blows. Elory wouldn't be coming for them. She swallowed against her guilt.

"Do you always treat postulants this way or just the women?"

His pale eyebrows lifted and she noted the green of his eyes in the candlelight. "So I'm to believe you followed me to join the Clast?"

"Why else would I follow you?"

"You're better clothed than most who wish to join our order," the man said. "Soft, well-made boots, a skirt of fine wool, an expensively dyed linen shirt and vest. These all speak of some wealth, if not nobility."

"And have you never had anyone come to you as a refugee from their own house?" she asked. Elory had to be seeking her. She refused to believe he might be dead. The Clast could not possibly own men gifted enough to kill her guard, and the sun had still been up when she and Lelwin had been taken.

"A few, but none so calculating in their approach."

Her stomach tried to fall through her lap to the floor. Somehow she'd been spotted and taken, but how had they escaped Elory? "I only wished to learn more of the Clast."

He nodded, his head bobbing up and down. "Oh, of that I have no doubt, but you were guarded by one of the gifted." The speaker smiled at her, the expression of a man who'd just won a great prize. "And a pure gift at that. Even I was surprised at how long he fought to regain your side. But as the church likes to say, all men die." He reached into his cloak and withdrew a piece of folded parchment. "Allow me to answer your deepest question."

Moving to the table, he slid it across the floor until it and the candles it held were in front of her. By the light, she could see thin wisps of blond beard on his cheeks. With careful, almost reverent motions, he unfolded the parchment one crease at a time. Open, it faced him and he regarded it, his gaze roving across it as if to reassure himself of its contents. Then he turned it to face her, tilting it so that the light of the twin candles fell upon it.

She had no physical gift or talent that would have made her an artist or sculptor of renown, but she enjoyed drawing, and portraiture most of all. She recognized a similar talent, not gifting, in the lines that flowed across the parchment. Lines that showed her face in accurate detail.

The speaker nodded and refolded the parchment. "I was surprised to see you, yet I will be rewarded for my vigilance in taking you captive."

She tried to breathe, but the air in the room had become thick and close, and her lungs worked against the constriction of her throat.

"Wiggle your fingers," the speaker commanded.

Spellbound by the realization that she'd been the one being hunted, she moved her wrists against the bonds, straining to bring blood and feeling back to her hands. When burning pain came an instant later, she reached with her fingers and found cloth covering her hands.

"You are fortunate beyond expectation, Toria Deel." The man smiled. "You will have what you've desired. You will meet the leader of the Clast. I am commanded to take you to the Darkwater, where you will meet the Icon."

Her throat opened at last and she drew breath to scream, but the speaker stood in front of her. Laughing, he stuffed a bit of dirty rag into her mouth. Then he pulled a stoppered bottle from his cloak and sprinkled the cloth with a thick, yellowish liquid.

CHAPTER 40

For three days we had ridden toward Bunard as hard as our horses would allow, starting each morning when the sky lightened to charcoal from black and continuing past sunset each evening, using Rory's night vision to guide us until it failed before setting up camp. On the afternoon of the third day we came in sight of the tor, rising up from the foothills and overlooking the broad flow of the Rinwash River.

"I don't see smoke," Bolt said. "That's a good thing. It doesn't seem to matter what goes wrong in a city, you can always count on some fool starting a fire."

"Perhaps they skirted Bunard," I said as I dismounted, but I didn't really believe it. I pulled my glove to put my bare hand on Wag's head. The wound in his side was still visible, but new pink tissue showed beneath the covering of tar, and after the first day out of Isenore, he'd jumped lightly from Dest's back to run alongside the horses for long stretches.

A thousand scents of the city I'd never known existed jumped into my awareness, but mingled with those were "sister" and two that Wag knew as "killers."

"The men we're following and the sentinel are both here," I said. "Or were as of five days ago. Their scents are a bit fresher, but we've only picked up a day or two."

We came at the city from the northwest and boarded the ferry that would take us into Bunard proper. I motioned Bolt to join me at the rail, where I tried to keep Wag shielded from the farmers and villagers who'd boarded the ferry with us. I hoped they would just assume he was a big dog, but there was no mistaking the unnerving sense of intelligence in his clear gray eyes. Normal dogs might show a quizzical tilt of the head, but Wag's glances held too much comprehension.

"We need a plan that doesn't involve us walking into a trap."

Bolt looked at me. "You might not be a target."

I nodded. "I certainly hope not, but the wind shifted this morning. It's coming out of the north now and there's little chance the other sentinel hasn't smelled her brother. The only question is whether or not the man managing her is aware of it."

Bolt grew still, and the crags of age and weather that lined his face grew deeper. "It would be like Bas-solas all over again, both of us hunting the other, one with the advantage at night, the other with it during the day."

I nodded. "I'd really like some way to weight the bones so that the odds are in our favor."

Bolt looked out across the rail to the city, his eyes narrowed in thought. "The first thing you should do is check to see if he's in the city. Find out where he's been and you'll get a good idea of who he's hunting. Just don't do it anywhere you will be noticed," Bolt said, shaking his head. "You have this issue with Brid Teorian, if you recall. If the Chief of Servants sees you out and about in Bunard, she might drop you into the deepest prison she can find and leave you there. She let you go once. Don't take that to mean you have your freedom permanently."

"What will she do once she discovers the sentinels have been all but wiped out and someone is hunting the Vigil? What kind of woman is the Chief?"

Bolt's thick shoulders shifted beneath his cloak. "A few months ago you could have told the Chief not only what you were going to do, but what she was going to do as well and she would have done it. Her respect for the Vigil went that deep, and Brid took it personally that Elwin was killed in her city." He shook his head. "But things have changed.

"I like Pellin, but he's not as good with people as Elwin was, and nobody commanded respect and obedience like Cesla. The heads of the church don't snap to and nod for Pellin. Worse, they're scared—and rightly so. The Vigil is on the edge of extinction on the northern continent." He gave me a very direct look. "The fact that you came to the Vigil through unorthodox means, along with your personal circumstances, makes it even less likely Brid Teorian will allow you to keep your freedom."

I shook my head. "Stop talking around it. I have a vault."

Bolt nodded. "All right, you have a vault." His head jerked. "I make it a point to be adaptable, but even I can't say that without the feeling I've got rats in my gut. We've spent too long hunting people like you. Nobody knows the truth of you, Willet. Not the Eldest. Not the heads of the church. Not even you."

"And hopefully not whatever has gotten free of the Darkwater," I added.

"'Don't borrow tomorrow's trouble,'" Bolt quoted.

"I like that one," I said, "but I don't have to borrow it. I wake up with it every day and too many nights." We stared out over the rail as the other shoreline drifted closer. By the time the ferry nestled into its dock and bumped the pier, I knew the first thing I had to do was to keep a promise. It wasn't wise or smart or planned, but it felt right. "Let's go see the queen."

We came around to the main entrance on the south side. I didn't see the point in trying to hide from the church soldiers just yet, and by the time word got back to the Chief of Servants that I'd returned I would already be in the queen's presence.

I hoped.

I tried not to tally up all the times in the past few months I'd started with a perfectly good plan and then had to improvise my way.

"Lord Dura," the guard at the left of the entrance called in a voice that could probably be heard in the poor quarter. "You're alive."

"Indeed I am, Sevin—though you seem surprised. Did you doubt?"

He shook his head. "Not for a moment, but the odds were tempting when they shifted after the first few days you were gone."

I gaped. "You wagered on whether I was still alive? You bet against me?"

Sevin held up his hands. "Not me, Lord Dura. I've seen you survive too many times to put stock in rumors of your death, but some of the newer lads are going to be disappointed to see you in a vertical posture."

He shrugged, pulling his shoulders all the way up to his ears before letting them fall. "And as for wagering, well, it gets a mite boring playing bones all the time." A huge gap-toothed smile split his face. "Putting money down on people is a lot more fun."

I shook my head, but I envied him and his cohorts their simple existence and pleasures. "I need to see the queen, Sevin. Can you send word ahead and take us up?"

"You don't need my permission, Lord Dura. They'll be seating for the evening meal and you've still got your title."

"I intend to go. I just don't want to surprise her. I imagine she'll want to speak with me alone, after I present myself, and sending word will give her a chance to set any other appointments aside."

"You're really going into court?" Sevin asked.

Nodding got me a laugh, and Sevin shifted to speak with one of the other guards. "I'll be taking Lord Dura up to the throne room—send word to the queen." He pointed at Wag and turned to me. "But I'll wager you'll want to leave the dog behind."

Wag gave a low growl that pushed Sevin back a half step.

"Queen Cailin will want to see him," I said.

He shook his head. "I doubt it, but that's a decision for her and her personal guards. You know how Carrick and the rest are. They see threats in thin air."

We began the ascent, and by the time we arrived at the entrance to the throne room, strains of music floated on the air, mixing with the smells of food. Wag's tongue came out and flopped over the top of his snout before running down each side of his mouth. We shifted away from the door where Sevin waited to escort us in.

"We can't take him in there," I said. "We'll have to split up."

Bolt looked at me for a moment before he shook his head. "Not a good idea. If you go without Rory, he can't protect you from any dwimor that might be in the tor."

Rory smiled, but I couldn't help noting the sardonic tilt to his head and cynical squint around his eyes.

Bolt was right. I needed Rory there with me. "As long as he doesn't let his mouth get ahead of his brain, he'll be fine. And he's dressed better than he used to be."

"Ha," Rory barked. "You should take your own advice about think-ing before you speak, yah?"

Bolt looked from Rory to me. "He has a point. And I need to be in there in case Duke Orlan decides to take offense to you again, or do you believe a man like that is going to take his time replacing a killer like Lord Baine?"

"I wish I could have seen you fight him," Rory said. "I heard your swords had barely crossed before you put him down in front of the court, the king, and Aer."

I shook my head. "We're going to have to do something about that bloodthirsty streak of yours."

Bolt looked at Wag and let out a long exhale. "Bribe the guards at the door and once we're inside tell Wag to wait for us in a dark corner." He paused to chew his lower lip. "It wouldn't hurt to have one of the servers bring enough food to keep him distracted for a while."

I could feel the muscles in my neck starting to tense. I hated going into court. "Well enough. I'm thinking I should have just emptied my purse into Fynn's hand and begged her to take the money instead."

"You're just now thinking that?" Bolt asked.

I walked over to Sevin. "We're going in. Can you get Wag through the guards at the door?"

He looked at us in our travel-stained clothes, armed from our temples to our toes, and smiled. If there was anything Sevin enjoyed more than watching chaos erupt around me in the throne room, I didn't know what it was. Idiot.

"I'll, ah, need something to motivate them, Lord Dura." Sevin held out his hand.

I nodded to Bolt, who pulled his shrunken purse of silver out of his cloak and counted a pair of coins, before he grudgingly put the whole thing in Sevin's meaty palm. "Give the guards whatever they need. The rest is for you to stay with Wag and keep him fed and quiet until we're done."

Sevin's eyes goggled before he nodded and walked up to the guards at the door. Bolt had just paid him a month's wages.

"All right," I said. "Let's see if we can persuade Duke Orlan to recognize his daughter."

We passed by the guards, who all conveniently orchestrated coughing fits that kept them from seeing over fifty pounds of fur and teeth pass by. I knelt and put my bare hands on Wag's ruff. "Stay with Sevin," I said aloud, but in my mind I pictured the guard and a dark corner filled with meat and bones.

Wag led Sevin over to a corner to the left, where he could keep an eye on the hall without being seen, and I led Bolt and Rory into the chaos of light and sound that typified court in Bunard.

For once I didn't have to endure the barrage of insults from other nobles as I made my way toward the front of the throne room. I didn't know whether that was due to rumors of the events surrounding Bassolas or the fact that Bolt stood at my shoulder. I didn't really care.

Even so, most of them managed to convey an almost palpable distaste for my presence among them by the way they studiously avoided even incidental contact. For some odd reason, that pleased me.

"There he is." I nodded toward a large cluster of people milling about just to the right and in front of the throne where Cailin held regency.

"You sure you want to do this?" Bolt asked. "He's surrounded by at least thirty people. I've found having an audience makes a man a lot less willing to compromise." He shot me a look out of the corner of his eye. "Are you going to tell me your plan before we get there?"

I didn't say anything.

He stopped and threw out an arm that felt like I'd walked into an oak branch. "You do have a plan, don't you?"

I nodded. "You won't like it."

He barked a laugh. "I never expected to like it. I just want to know what it is before I have to draw steel."

Rory laughed. "I've never been to court before. Is it always this exciting?"

"Unfortunately, yes," Bolt and I said in unison.

I gave Bolt a meaningful look as I held up my bare hands and flexed my fingers.

"What makes you think you're going to get close enough to touch him?" he grumbled. Two nobles near us turned our way. "The man despises you."

"Do you not know how to whisper?" I asked. "I'm going to be subtle." I tried to ignore Rory's laughter.

The gaggle of sycophants around Orlan saw us coming from ten paces and parted to grant us access. It seemed everyone, even the duke's allies, appreciated theater. Orlan's gaze registered my presence and then Bolt's—and the fact that I wasn't going out of my way to avoid him. I stopped and bowed, offering the precise obeisance his rank required of me, certainly no more, but not a dagger's width less either.

"May I approach, Your Grace?" I asked.

Murmurs erupted around us, and even nobles who had no part or stake in the house of Orlan were beginning to take notice.

"Subtle," Bolt grunted.

Orlan's wife, attired as always in a red dress, with her jet-black hair flowing across her shoulders, leaned in to whisper in his ear, darting glances at me I couldn't decipher. I couldn't hear a word and thought about sending Bolt to her for lessons.

He straightened and nodded, his expression a mixture of curiosity and distrust. "Approach," he said, my title obvious in its absence.

I stopped again, two paces away, a distance that seemed respectful but would allow me to speak without being overheard by everyone. "Your Grace," I bowed again. "I have recently been to Gylden." I stopped to give Orlan a chance to search his memories and conscience. The duke was, like most of the nobles, a schemer to one degree or another, and I hoped to work his fear of discovery to my advantage.

I wasn't disappointed. Orlan and his wife stilled until they might have been nothing more than sculptures placed to adorn the court. Bolt looked bored, and Rory appeared to busy himself searching the crowd for dwimor.

"I am uninterested in your travels, Dura."

I gestured to the throng of Orlan's hangers-on. "Perhaps I can interest you in an agreement, Duke Orlan. I desire to repay a debt, and to that end I seek a boon that only you can provide in exchange for my discretion."

Now I had his attention. "Might we go apart a little way and discuss this as nobles?" I asked.

He gave me a slow look that drifted down to my feet and back up again, his gaze catching each spot and smudge on my travel-stained clothing. "It seems we're at least one short."

I smiled. "At least one," I agreed and waited for the insult to strike home. I spoke as soon as I saw his eyes widen. "If we cannot discuss the matter as nobles, perhaps we can discuss it as men."

His mouth opened to toss some rejoinder before he thought better of it. The problem with Orlan was he surrounded himself with sycophants who would never allow themselves to respond to his barbs. As a result, the duke thought himself to be more clever than he actually was. As a member of the Vigil, I shouldered the weighty responsibility of disabusing him of that notion.

At the last, I thought he might refuse, but I stepped past him, gesturing toward an empty spot some fifteen paces away. He muttered something I couldn't make out to the duchess and swept past me.

The moment I'd been waiting for.

I turned and let my right hand swing out from my body just enough for my fingers to brush the back of Orlan's hand.

The throne room disappeared as I raced down a long tunnel into the stream of the duke's memories. I had to hurry. Orlan would never accept a gesture of familiarity from anyone outside his family, but fortunately our conversation had brought his guiltiest memories to the forefront of his mind. They were the first I touched, bright gossamer threads that represented his most joyful moments.

The delve ended and I blinked to see Orlan two paces past me. It might have been a shift of the light or shadows, but he appeared different.

He stopped and faced me, wringing every fraction of height from his posture and boots in order to look down on me. "I find your presence distasteful, Dura. I pray you, be brief."

"Very well," I said. "In truth, Your Grace, I never intended to go to Gylden. My business was to the east, on the border of the Everwood, but one of my companions was in need of medical attention."

"And Gylden is the closest city with a healer," Orlan said.

"Just so."

"But what you didn't say is that you required a healer of significant skill, perhaps even gifted. Otherwise you could have simply stopped at the nearest village to see a midwife or herbalist." He shrugged to show his disdain. "And you managed to avoid mentioning the nature of your friend's need. Why do I doubt it was illness, Dura?"

I nodded my admission. "You are correct, Your Grace. My companion was wounded and we needed a surgeon. Yet when we journeyed to Gylden, we faced another problem."

Orlan smirked at me. "You were afraid of being recognized. Your fears are well-founded, of course. Let me guess, your companion died and your peasant sense of honor demands recompense from me, the man you blame for their death."

"No," I shook my head. "We found a healer. She's quite good, though not gifted, and while she's a member of your family, oddly enough she bears *me* no ill will."

"Fynn." He ground it out as a curse, but I'd delved him and knew his reaction to be a lie.

"She favors you, Your Grace," I said with a little bow. "Unfortunately, when she recognized me she elected to change her fee."

His eyelids dipped. "The girl seems intent on my embarrassment. Let me guess, she asked you to force me to acknowledge her."

When I nodded, he laughed, but I knew this dismissal to be a lie as well. "It occurs to me, Your Grace, that there's a mystery here."

"Yes." He sighed. "And we all know how you love those."

"Why would you let her live?" I asked and inched closer. "You're the most powerful duke in the kingdom, and I know firsthand that you've got no problem with killing or having someone killed. If she's such an assault to your dignity, why not have her eliminated? She's in your home city, where you own everything and everyone." I shrugged. "A quick accident, a carriage in the street, and your problem goes away."

The duke glanced over my shoulder to the other nobles in the throne room. "I don't spill Orlan blood, Dura." He pulled a deep, shuddering breath. "I would have spared my brother if I could have, but you removed that option."

"I know you love your daughter, Your Grace. She just wants to study medicine."

He shook his head. "My wife will never allow me to acknowledge her, for obvious reasons."

I let my gaze sweep the throne room as I searched for a solution. At the far end of the hall I saw Sevin looking my way, his expression faintly disappointed. That was it. I turned back to the duke. "What if Queen Cailin forced you to acknowledge her, but did so privately?"

Orlan shook his head. "Pointless. Fynn's presence in Gylden would still be a thorn my wife would try to remove. She'd have her killed."

"Your Grace, Fynn doesn't want to remain in Gylden. She desires to study with Crato in Elania, but he won't apprentice commons."

He shook his head, but more slowly this time. "Why would the queen force me to acknowledge her?"

I kept myself from smiling, just. If Orlan agreed to my plan I was going to have to make a show of losing my temper. "Someone slaughtered all of the sentinels. Your daughter saved the last one in Collum."

The barest touch of a smile ghosted across his expression. "Fynn?" Then he nodded as understanding lit his eyes. "That's why the queen is pulling the garrisons east."

I nodded. "Your daughter has given us some hope that the sentinels can be restored. A great service to the crown, wouldn't you say, Your Grace?"

"But the duchess . . . "

"Can you be angry with me, Your Grace?" I asked.

"Easily enough."

I took a step back just in case he considered trying to strike me, and I saw his eyes blaze. Then he delivered an insult so vile it made my skin crawl and he said it in a voice they might have heard in the poor quarter. But when he put his hand on his sword, Bolt and Rory materialized at my side. Bolt hadn't drawn, but Rory was rolling a dagger across the back of each hand so that the steel caught the light.

"Then we will let the crown decide," I yelled back.

Orlan pushed his way past me and preceded me to the dais, where Queen Cailin sat regarding us with an expression that signaled she'd been half a drummer's beat from intervening anyway. The duke played his part enthusiastically, using the opportunity to speak to me and about me with a deft combination of condescension, bile, and revulsion. I suspected the duke possessed a measure of talent for language.

Or maybe he'd just been saving up for the occasion.

We were commanded to the north part of the tor, which held the queen's private audience chamber. I whispered a command to Bolt to bring Wag as well, but when we arrived, Ronit, one of the guards who'd watched over Laidir before Cailin, barred our way. He gave Bolt an inscrutable look that probably had something to do with the knowledge my guard could tie him up like a bow despite his age and smaller stature. "She's on her way and asks that you wait for a moment so that she can receive you."

"She's already in there," I said.

"Peasant," Orlan muttered. "Do you still not understand the ways of the nobility? A short wait serves to gently remind visitors of the authority of the crown. Otherwise, peasants and nobles alike would begin to think of the queen as a peer."

Ronit looked more serious than usual, which was like saying that a piece of ice had somehow managed to look colder than before. "I've been away from the city, Ronit. What news?"

I didn't really expect an answer, so it surprised me more than a little when I got one.

"War."

The sound of footsteps beyond the door, the heavy tread of boots, cut off my next question. Ronit turned on one heel and motioned. "Follow me. You'll have to surrender your weapons, and the dog will have to remain without."

"She'll want to see him," I said. "And he's not a dog."

Ronit turned back, met the clear gray stare of Wag's stare and gaped, his mouth working to speak without his throat's cooperation. "Are you crazy, Lord Dura?"

"Probably," I quipped. "At least that's what most people keep telling me."

As usual, humor had no effect on the queen's guard. They surrendered it when they accepted the job. "He goes where we go," I said. "No exceptions."

"The queen will decide," Ronit said. "It's smaller than I expected."

"He's just a pup," Bolt said. "By the time he's full grown, he will weigh as much as you and I together."

Ronit exchanged places with two guards from inside the chamber as we made a pile of weapons to the side, Rory drawing more than a couple of stares as he produced half a dozen throwing knives in addition to the sword Bolt made him wear. The guards shook their heads in disbelief and ran their hands over his clothing from head to heel before Adair disappeared inside to speak to the queen.

When he came out, he spoke to Carrick. "They may enter, but the queen requests all of us attend her. We'll bar the door."

Memories of the king filled the air around me. The library had been changed, but some of the king's personality remained: many of the books on the shelves were collections of tales, moralistic stories Laidir had referred to as books of wisdom, and odd bits and pieces of devices that had captured his interest.

But the clutter was gone and I grieved its passing. The organization of the king's private study had been an insight into the man himself and it had shown a wonderfully complicated individual with surprises everywhere. The queen's style, while neat, was too severe to reveal much about her personality except that she liked order. Despite the fact that I'd delved her twice, her officious demeanor left me with the impression that I hardly knew her. She'd resolutely refused to be shaped by her past and circumstances.

Cailin embodied a mystery I needed to solve for other reasons as well. She was the one person besides me who'd survived the Darkwater with mind and sanity intact. But she'd done it better. Not a trace of the forest remained in her mind. I knew. I'd broken her vault months before with the full expectation she'd come out of that delve like all the others—a drooling, mindless shell.

I still had no idea how she'd survived the process, nor did anyone else in the Vigil.

I entered the room along with my companions and Wag, pausing to descend to one knee at a respectful distance from the throne that had been Laidir's, Cailin's doting husband, the man she'd killed when her vault had opened during Bas-solas. Beside me, Duke Orlan bowed, giving the precise acknowledgment his title owed the ruling monarch. But while he flowed smoothly through the moves of his respect, I faltered on my way down, catching my balance with one hand on the rich carpet.

In retrospect I should have known Gael would be here, but her presence surprised and unbalanced me, as it always would. An ache in my chest made me aware of a hole I hardly knew was there until I looked at her.

"Rise," Queen Cailin said.

I came to my feet, my gaze still drinking in the sight of Gael.

"It's customary for supplicants to the throne to reserve their attention for their liege," the queen said. "Though you might be forgiven."

"Peasant," Orlan muttered, "will you never learn?"

"Probably not," I said.

Queen Cailin sighed audibly as she glanced over my shoulder at Ronit. "They did surrender their weapons, didn't they?"

At his nod, she allowed the merest hint of a smile to touch her lips. "Good. Your Grace," she prompted, "what is this about?"

Duke Orlan managed to fill his glance for me with the affection a man would feel for the weevils in his porridge before he answered. "Lord Dura—even that lowly title is unfitting—means you to force me to acknowledge the woman, Fynn, as my daughter." He took a deep breath.

Cailin nodded. "Ah, yes, the young girl who came to court some months back. I will ask you the same question now as I did then. Is she your daughter?"

Orlan just stared at her for a moment, and then said, "The question is pointless. I forbid it."

I may have underestimated the duke. With that one command, he'd removed any other option from the queen. Anything less than her forcing Orlan's acknowledgment of Fynn as his daughter would make her appear weak—and as regent, any sign of weakness would prove her undoing. The other nobles would throw off all restraint.

"You are dismissed, Your Grace," the queen said in a voice like ice breaking. "I will speak with Lord Dura alone."

Orlan gave a bow stiff enough to make me wonder why I didn't hear his spine cracking before he turned to lean in close to speak in tones only I could hear. "If she forces me to acknowledge Fynn, Lord Dura, you will no longer have anything to fear from me." A hint of amusement wove its way into his voice. "But my wife may be another matter. Best you keep your guard close."

After the door closed behind him, I turned to see Cailin and Gael eyeing me with surprise and amusement. "Skillfully done, Willet," Gael said.

The queen nodded her agreement. "I suspect the duchess will see through Duke Orlan's ruse, but it was well played." She smiled. "It seems both of you will have what you wish. I will force the duke to acknowledge his daughter."

I nodded, split in my satisfaction—thankful to have aided Fynn but not so pleased that in doing so I had also aided Orlan.

Now on to my business with the queen. "I have tidings, Your Majesty."

"Doubtless," Cailin said, "but I have to wonder why those tidings are being brought to me instead of the Chief of Servants."

Cailin did not hold the gift of kings. That had passed to her son, but Collum's blond-haired queen held talents in several areas that almost rose to the level of gifted.

"Doubtless you know of my imprisonment at the hands of the church," I said.

"Hardly imprisonment, Lord Dura," the queen said. "They merely wished to keep you and your gift safe."

"If I gild the iron bars with gold do they not still create a cell?" I asked. "However we wish to define it, I needed my freedom." I stepped to one side, allowing the queen to see the sentinel pup behind me.

I saw the queen take note of Wag's eyes, then fix on the long wound that ran down his side. She nodded. "Well done, Lord Dura. Are there others?"

"No." I stopped. "Yes," I said after a moment. I paused before correcting myself again. "No."

Cailin's delicate brows rose as she watched me fumble for an answer. Then I realized what her question meant. "You knew the sentinels were in danger?"

She gave me a single inclination of her head that monarchs use to appear wise and regal. "Hardly a week after you left, the Chief of Servants and I received tidings from the Eldest that the sentinels and their trainers were being killed." She nodded toward Wag, who sat in the middle of her rug regarding the proceedings with his own royal disdain. "We believe all the other sentinels are dead, Lord Dura. Please tell me you managed to save more than one."

"There are two sentinel pups alive, Your Majesty, but the female is in the hands of our enemy."

Already fair, the queen's face paled, and she regarded Wag with a kaleidoscope of emotions running behind her eyes I couldn't hope to understand. "Who is our enemy hunting?" she asked.

"Those who threaten him the most," I said.

She almost smiled. "Glib, but we both know it's you and the rest of the Vigil he's after."

A seed of doubt, no larger than a single grain of wheat, pulled the next words from me. "We've been surprised before."

"And what will you do to surprise him in turn, Willet Dura?" Gael said.

I paused to enjoy the way her resonant voice caressed me with my name before I answered. "We tracked him to Bunard, but the wind shifted just before we crossed the Rinwash. If he's delved the other pup since then, he knows another of the sentinels has survived. Regardless, our next step is clear. We use Wag to hunt him."

"Ah," Cailin nodded. "And you are here because you hope to convince me to aid you, knowing that the Chief of Servants would never agree to let you go free to pursue such a foolish plan."

She stood and descended the shallow steps of the low dais. Gael came with her until she stood close enough to touch.

"And it is foolish in the extreme, but I do agree, Lord Dura."

CHAPTER 41

I looked from the queen to Gael and back again. Behind me I heard Bolt mutter something ominous about a woman's agreement under his breath that sounded like a warning.

"Naturally, my aid will have a price, Lord Dura," the queen said. "You're asking me to let you go free in defiance of the church."

I held up one hand. "It's not defiance, exactly. I merely came to you first and you agreed to aid me when you saw the necessity of protecting the Vigil. The urgency of the situation kept you from consulting with the Chief of Servants before the decision was made." I smiled.

Cailin returned my expression. "That's a splendid plan, Lord Dura. If the Chief of Servants is an idiot—which she is not—or if I could deceive her into thinking I'm an idiot—which I can't." She turned and ascended the dais to resume her seat. "You needn't worry, my lord. The price I ask is an inconsequential thing. No more than a moment." She looked around the room. "But I think I prefer to tell you in a more private setting. Guards, please escort my guests and wait without. Only Lord Dura, Lady Gael, and I will remain."

When the door closed behind Adair, the queen inhaled deeply and let her breath out in a long sigh, her posture loosening until the chair embraced her like a cup holding water. She reached up with her right hand to remove the circlet of gold from her head. "How did Laidir stand it?" she breathed. "Having to appear kingly all the time?"

I tried not to dwell on the irony of Cailin's visible affection for her dead husband. "He took as many breaks from formal court as he could, Your Majesty," I said. My throat tightened. "And he kept friends, genuine friends, around him."

Cailin glanced at Gael and gave her a smile. "He was a wise man." She ran her hands through her blond hair, pulling it back away from her face. "You will take Lady Gael with you, Lord Dura. That is my price."

"No," I said before I could exert any semblance of control over my mouth.

The queen's eyes flashed at my defiance. "This is not a negotiation, Lord Dura."

I nodded, once, sharply. "As you say, my queen, it is not. I will not take Gael with me." I caught her in the stubborn gaze I gave the queen. For once, the fact that her eyes had turned from an agreeable blue to the slate of storm clouds failed to sway me. "Putting her in harm's way is needless and foolish."

"The same may be said of you, my lord," Gael said. She still stood close enough to touch. I tried not to remember what her skin felt like beneath my fingertips.

"That's different—I have to go."

"Hardly," the queen scoffed. "Your guard can manage the sentinel and use it to track your enemy."

"That's just it," I said. "He can't. In all of Bunard there is only one person who can, and that's me."

Cailin and Gael, both of them more intelligent than I, absorbed this information in stoic silence. Then I saw understanding dawn in their eyes.

"What does this have to do with your gift?" the queen demanded.

"The sentinels are more than just large dogs, Your Majesty. They're gifted. From the moment Wag's dying dam put her paw on his head, he became more." I shook my head. "His thoughts are much like what you would expect from a puppy, but his mind is growing. He's beginning to grasp language." I shook my head in amazement. "And his sense of smell is so keen it borders on magical. When I delve him, I smell everything he does."

Shock and fascination chased each other across the queen's face before Gael spoke, her voice tight. "Aer help us. He's hunting you, Willet."

"You know this?"

She nodded. "Five nights ago the guards at my uncle's estate were killed."

"That same evening, watch guards reported seeing a man with a large dog prowling the area around the tor," Gael continued, "never quite coming into the light, always slipping away as they approached."

I opened my mouth to argue, but my denials died on my lips. Gael's estate would be the easiest place to pick up my scent. Entering the Merum cathedral or the tor would have been too risky even without his aversion to light, and I never used my small estate in the nobles' quarter.

"Perhaps," Queen Cailin interrupted my thoughts. "But perhaps not only you. There were other incidences around the city as well, odd occurrences that might have been our enemy trying to pick up the trail of the rest of the Vigil."

I tried to digest that information, but it sat in my stomach like a rock. "The sentinels remember scents the way we remember faces, Your Majesty. There is nothing preventing him from having more than one target. Regardless of who he is hunting, I have no choice but to use Wag's gift and my own to run him to ground and, hopefully, kill him."

The queen and Gael nodded, Cailin in acceptance, Gael in fear, but she could see the grim necessity as well as I. "Your Majesty"—I bowed—"I need your aid."

Cailin's brows rose—she was unaccustomed to being surprised. "Haven't I already given it?"

"You have, but this goes deeper and is of a more personal nature." I looked up, meeting the gaze of green eyes like seawater under sunlight. "Of all those who have entered the Darkwater Forest only two people have emerged with a vault in their mind and survived." I swallowed. "And they are both in this room."

Cailin grew so still Bolt would have complimented her on it. "And we have survived in different ways, have we not?" she asked, her voice soft. When I nodded, she went on. "Pellin came to me in the days after Bas-solas."

"He wanted to delve you."

She nodded, then cocked her head at me. "But I refused. The reprieve you'd granted me was still too new, too tenuous, to grant another access. Pellin mustered every ounce of authority he could to persuade me to allow it. Later, he sent Bronwyn, and I almost relented, but I still couldn't quite bring myself to believe some part of the Darkwater didn't remain in my mind."

I saw grief gather at the corner of her eyes, but Cailin strengthened, putting steel in her frame, and the tears remained unshed. She stood, walking the breadth of the dais like a lioness. When she turned back to me, her eyes were dry.

"Finally, Pellin sent Toria Deel, and she swore oaths to preserve my life and the regency no matter what she found." The queen's eyes flared at the memory. "But I had nothing to gain by granting such a request. I already held my life and the regency under my own control. What could I possibly gain by risking that for her guarantees?"

"Nothing, Your Majesty," I said. There would be no point to making my request. The queen had made it plain I had nothing to offer her in exchange for the privilege of delving her. I cursed myself for my ignorance and inexperience. If I had been more focused on truly delving Cailin after Bas-solas instead of exacting revenge by breaking her vault I would have access to all of her memories instead of the trifling sample I now held.

"But I will allow you, Lord Dura, to do what no other member of the Vigil has been permitted to do," Cailin said. She held out her arm, slender and bare, as if she were offering a sacrifice.

I shook my head. "You have no reason to grant me this, Your Majesty." I glanced at Gael. "Unless there is something you want from me in return. Why is it so important for her to accompany me? There is nothing but the threat of death, and any oath I take to keep her from it would be a lie."

Cailin never blinked or shifted on her throne or gave any other sign that I had done anything other than offer my agreement to her terms. "Because she asked it of me, Lord Dura."

I almost laughed. "She asked it of you?" Gael stood in the light of the queen's library like a study in contrasts. Too tall for most of the men at court, I found her height and grace compelling. Far from the small-featured beauty currently in fashion, she owned a more aquiline nose, but the fullness of her lips and the sweep of her jawline brought her features into harmony, if not agreement, with the current standard of beauty.

Then I did laugh. "Granted, I find it difficult to refuse her anything, but I doubt if she exerts the same influence over you, my queen." When Cailin didn't answer, I went on. "And once I delve you, I will know the why of your request at any rate."

She nodded. "But before then I will have your oath that you will allow her to accompany you."

I tried to remember the last time I'd won an argument with a woman, any woman, and couldn't, but Gael accompanying me wasn't some trifle. She could die, or I could die trying to protect her, or both of us could die.

"Why?" I appealed to her directly. "You know all the reasons you shouldn't accompany me."

"A queen pays her debts, Lord Dura," Cailin said from her throne, straight-backed and imperious once more. "At the moment, that is all you need to know."

A mulish refusal curled my shoulders forward and I set my head as if I expected blows. "If you have a debt to her, this is a poor way to show your regard, Your Majesty."

"Lord Dura," the queen said, "I don't think you understand the lengths I'm prepared to go to secure your agreement. If you do not accept Lady Gael's company, I will summon the Chief of Servants and inform her of your plan to track your enemy. I'm sure you can predict her response as well as I."

I shook my head, but before I could speak, the queen leaned forward to spear me with her gaze. "Before you deny me again, Lord Dura, understand that if you refuse, one or possibly all of the Vigil will die."

"Why would you do this?" I pleaded with Gael.

"To keep you safe, husband," she said.

"I'm not your husband."

She gave me a smoldering look that at any other time would have transformed me into flames. "If you live you will be."

I stood unspeaking, and Cailin moved past me to the door. For a moment I considered laying hands on the queen without her permission, but the tiny part of my mind that could see past my anger restrained me. Barely. She put her hand on the latch. "You must believe me, Lord Dura. I will do as I've said."

"Very well, Your Majesty, I accept your terms." I turned to Gael, as angry as I'd ever been in my life. "You and I are going to discuss this at length, my lady."

She took an involuntary step back before setting her shoulders and chin in defiance.

The queen held out her arm, but I nodded toward a pair of chairs to one side of the throne. "We should be seated, Your Majesty. This may take some time."

I tried to clear my mind of the frustration and anger that seethed within it like a boiling stew. Somewhere within the queen's mind lay a clue to understanding the Darkwater's poison and perhaps to surviving it as well. For a moment, my concentrated abstraction broke and all the *what-if*s of our fight overwhelmed me. What if the enemy found a way to bring a vast number of the ignorant into the cursed forest? What if war then consumed the entire northern continent?

What if we lost? Would the entire world descend into darkness with every man, woman, and child consumed by bloodlust?

What if we won?

The last question frightened me enough to send my stomach roiling, and for a moment I saw myself, spending years breaking the vaults of those who'd gone to the forest, trying to understand an evil that defied comprehension. But that was silly. If we won, the kings and queens of the north would simply have the entire opposing army put to the sword.

We probably wouldn't have the manpower to dig all the graves we'd need.

I thrust all these thoughts away and put my hand on the queen's arm, the warmth of her flesh surprising me, as though I'd expected Cailin's skin to be as cool and detached as the woman herself. I lifted my head, and the green of her eyes leapt toward me as I fell into her thoughts.

I skimmed along her memories, marveling at the intensity of color attached to each of them, and in that moment I understood just how much energy the queen put into her show of reserve. The vibrancy of her thoughts and emotions had been suppressed in order for her to show the image she'd crafted for court life, aloof and unapproachable and completely in control of her surroundings and herself. But I knew the truth. I saw a memory flow past me in the stream and reached out with my mind to grasp it.

I, Cailin, queen regent of Collum, stood before the assembled court, my hands on my son, Prince Brod, staring down the families of Orlan, Faral, and Alainn, defying any of them to deny he'd received the gift of kings from his father.

I followed the memory back until I came to a blood-soaked image of the royal bedroom, my husband and king lying dead on the bed, his reeve standing before me.

I slowed the stream of time and memory, examining it, living and feeling it in such detail that it became painful, an occurrence of grief and horror that had become an eternity in and of itself.

What had I done?

Before me stood the king's reeve—Laidir's jackal, the royal assassin, Willet Dura. And he knew, just as the castellan knew, that it had been my hand that had put the knife in the king's heart, though I could find no memory of it within my mind.

I saw Dura put out his hand, expecting and demanding that I take it. Fear coursed through me until I became cold and bloodless. I knew that to take that hand was to die, though I could see no means immediately visible. No talent I possessed would save me from the sword cut or dagger stroke.

Why had I gone to the forest? The first contraction of muscle in my shoulder lifted the weight of one hand from my lap, a prelude to extending it to Lord Dura, a prelude to dying. I cursed myself for my foolishness and fear. I had been loved and had refused to love in turn, hiding my true self, protecting the core of who I was because of the hurts done to me in my childhood. That longing, that desire to be free from anyone's touch or control, had been the reason I'd covered myself with indifference for five years—every day I'd been Laidir's wife. The walls of ice and detachment I'd built had become too ingrained to surrender. Each time I tried, fear turned me aside from returning even the simplest gestures of affection.

But even through my practiced abstraction I could sense a stirring within the kingdom, and a few trips out of the tor had confirmed my suspicion. Some enemy contrived to send Laidir's subjects—my subjects—to the Darkwater.

So I followed, foolishly convincing myself that my purpose or strength of will or intelligence would somehow preserve me

And for a week after I entered the forest, I assumed it had. The terror of each approaching night faded until I came to believe the evil of the forest was nothing more than a myth, or its malice had somehow lost its vitality.

And then I'd killed my husband, the one man who had consistently loved me without ceasing, without surrender, without demand.

I reached out to take Lord Dura's hand, knowing death had come for me in the form of the kingdom's most minor noble. But it had been my hand. I was guilty. At the last, I could at least be honest with myself. I would not go into the long dark clothed in my pretense. I prayed. Not that Aer would forgive me, but that Aer would find a way to let my husband know I had loved him, that I had conquered my greatest fear at last.

I shifted within the queen's memories, living every moment that led to that fateful decision to investigate the forest, searching for some reason she'd been able to retain her identity after I'd broken every strand the vault had created, but I couldn't find one. For an instant, I thought I saw a figure by her side, but like a shadow it fled from me.

Defeated, I absorbed into myself the recollections of the queen's life since Bas-solas, paying extra attention to her interactions with Lady Gael. I came out of the delve in defeat and surprise, wanting nothing more than to rail at my betrothed for her foolishness. But what do you say against someone who has sacrificed everything for you?

"You said the guards were attacked." I accused her, but I kept my voice soft, out of respect.

She nodded and light flowed along the cascade of rich, dark hair. "They were."

I stopped the smile before my lips parted. "In the city watch we call that a lie of understatement, my lady. More than attacked, your entire household was killed. Every servant. Every guard. Even your uncle."

She nodded.

I took a deep breath. "And your gift returned to you."

She nodded again, more slowly this time. Her shoulders lifted and fell in a dismissive gesture. "You asked me for my help before and I was unable to give it. In the absence of my gift I found that I no longer desired to traffic in cloth and clothing. I wanted something different, something more, my husband."

I bowed. "Not your husband," I said, "but yours, Gael, always yours." I straightened. "Who did you trade with?"

"Her Majesty helped me." Gael looked to the queen, and I heard Cailin clear her throat.

"It was a simple enough matter to petition the Merum to open their records to us." She nodded toward the sealed door of her study. "Your friend keeps a well-ordered library."

"We found the purest physical gift within Collum and I petitioned them for the trade," Gael said. She smirked, an expression that made me want to cover those full expressive lips with kisses. "The queen's blessing and encouragement helped somewhat."

"I've lost my best musician, Lord Dura," Cailin said, "but you must know that Lady Gael traded more than just her gift."

My betrothed waved away the queen's assertion. "My uncle competed with the other nobles in Bunard, keeping score with his wealth. I find no need to measure myself against others in such a way."

"You bartered your estate?" I gaped.

She smiled as if I'd just paid her a precious compliment. "Yes, but you should see me play the mandolin."

She twitched aside her cloak and tapped the rapier at her side. Now I could see that it was more than just a decorative sword for a lady. Worn leather covered the grip, and instead of an ornamented cross guard, the sword had a full bell to protect the hand. "I will be able to help protect you, and I rather enjoy knowing how dangerous I am," she said.

I pulled in a deep breath. "You've always been deadly, my lady."

Her eyes smoldered. "I have another gift for you, Willet, down in the city."

CHAPTER 42

I lifted the heavy iron bar from the door of Cailin's private audience chamber, and we stepped into the hall where the queen's guards and my companions waited. When Gael nodded to Adair and Carrick, signaling them to resume their places at Cailin's side, Bolt's eyes narrowed in speculation.

"'Surprise is the bane of friend and foe alike,'" he quoted.

"I haven't heard that one before," I said. Gael shifted to take a position next to me as if there might be threats in the narrow hallway leading from the queen's study. "You have another apprentice."

Bolt nodded. "I thought as much. I've never trained a woman before. They're soft."

Gael stiffened. "Perhaps I'll give you reason to reassess your presumption, master guard."

"Keep that fire, girl, you're going to need it to take your mind off the bruises. First lesson about your gift—stop swaggering. It'll give you away." He glanced at me before giving her an impudent grin. "She moves differently. Not that there was anything wrong with the way she moved before. How did you manage to acquire the gift, milady? It's forbidden to carry more than one at a time, even for a few moments."

Gael nodded. "So the priests told us. We used intermediaries." She put one hand on my arm. "And paid a lot of money to keep the trade a secret. The church frowns upon what I've done, even though there's no proscription against it specifically."

"Clever," Bolt said. "Lady Gael, you will accompany Willet as his betrothed. Unless I give you permission, you will not draw your sword or throw a dagger, and you will refrain from any movements that will reveal your gift."

Gael's blue eyes darkened a shade, but Bolt cut her off before she could speak. "No woman has ever been a Vigil guard before, milady. Would you give away your best advantage?"

She nodded, her eyes returning to a more normal hue.

"You mentioned another gift," I said. I didn't want to think about Gael putting herself in the path of whatever decided to come for me. So far that had included crazed villagers from the Darkwater and assassins that were almost impossible to see.

Gael smiled, and I watched her full lips part to show her even, white teeth. It might have been my imagination, but even the way she smiled seemed to carry more grace than usual. I followed the track of that thought to the next, obvious conclusion only to realize that she'd already answered my question.

"What?" I asked.

Bolt snorted, then tried to cover it with a cough.

"Myle has something for us," she smiled. "I think you'll find it useful."

As much as I wanted to force Gael to remain behind, as if I could *force* her to do anything now that she had a physical gift, she'd just given me another reason why I couldn't. Myle, brilliant and broken-minded, had given Bolt and me the solas powder that had meant the difference between living and dying when we'd first confronted men unnaturally strengthened by the Darkwater. Gael was one of the few people Myle trusted enough to actually engage in conversation.

"Let's hurry, then," I said. "The trail is getting cold."

"You really mean to track him?" Bolt said.

I looked at the people gathered around me: Bolt, Gael, and Rory. I nodded, inexplicably confident. "Who else can boast three gifted to protect him?" I put my hand on Wag's head. "And a sentinel."

"You don't want to fight?" Gael asked Bolt in surprise.

My guard's face crumpled in disgust, the furrows across his brow deepening. "Of course not. Why would I want to do that?"

"But you've spent your whole life training for this very thing."

He nodded. "And any man or woman with sense would want to keep on spending their life training for this very thing. Training is predictable, neat, orderly, and without surprises. And no one dies, least of all me."

We left Myle's workshop with the sun a handsbreadth above the horizon and sinking fast. "We need a place to stay," I said to Bolt, "and the only place secure enough is one where they might want to throw me in prison. We should have stopped by to see the Chief of Servants first."

My guard shrugged at me. "Send her word if you think you should. You do outrank her."

"I doubt that."

"It's true," he said with a shrug. "It's the boring kind of thing Custos would want to read, like eating sand, but I've looked through some of the original writings from the earliest days of the church." He paused to laugh. "Bronwyn is very protective of those. The parchment is so old it's faded to deep amber and it smells a bit like mold."

"Custos loves that smell," I said. "He calls it the perfume of knowledge."

"The seven members of the Vigil were given authority commensurate with the Merum Archbishop," Bolt said.

"Ah." Now I understood. "And since the other orders came centuries later, the theologians would say the authority of the Vigil predates and supersedes them, but right now that doesn't really matter, does it? They have more guards and swords than we do."

Bolt nodded. "Good point." He held up a finger. "'Authority is weighed in steel.'"

I shrugged. "Not really your best, but where we spend the night isn't something we can leave to chance, not if Jorgen is still in the city." I turned north, back toward the tor and the cathedrals that bordered it. "When we get to the Merum cathedral, we'll send for the Chief. Perhaps if we contact her voluntarily she'll be more inclined to acknowledge my nominal authority, or at least my freedom."

"If you grovel politely, she might not throw you in prison," Gael said.

"Groveling is good." Bolt nodded. "Do that."

Darkness had just enveloped the city like a shroud when Brid Teorian, the Chief of Servants, stumping forward with the aid of a cane, entered the room where the Merum had served us dinner. At least a dozen red-clad guards surrounded her, not brown. For some reason I couldn't identify, it irked me that the servants refused, even now, to put aside their vow of nonviolence. Other people would have to bear the burden of the lives that had to be taken.

"Chief of Servants," I bowed as I rose from my chair. "We've returned."

Her eyes, birdlike with age, took in the details of the room, noting the presence of those who sat with me, her gaze pausing to linger on Gael. "Has your company grown then?"

"By one," I admitted.

The Chief of Servants gave me a tight-lipped smile. "The presence of friends is a balm and a *gift* to the soul."

I didn't bother trying to negotiate, hoping the Chief would prefer blunt honesty. "The sentinels, except for Wag here and one other, are dead."

She nodded. "I've just come from a meeting with the queen. Is there something you wish to tell me that you didn't tell Cailin?"

"No, but I need to know what's happening with the rest of the Vigil."

Brid Teorian crossed over to a chair and sat, thumping her cane on the floor in front of her seat as if she were calling us to order. "As do I, the Grace, the Archbishop, and the Captain," she said. Her voice scaled upward with each name and she spat her words as though she couldn't wait to get them out of her mouth.

"Pellin went to Owmead. There, he managed to convince the heads of the orders to surrender our scrying stones to the Vigil." She grimaced. "His logic was impeccable. I don't like encountering people older than me. If I'm going to bear the weight of all this age, at least I should be the best at it. Pellin's habit of winning almost every argument we have is very annoying."

"You gave them your scrying stones?" Gael blurted, then took a step back in embarrassment.

"Sounds insane now, doesn't it?" the Chief asked. "Well, that's not the half of it. Pellin has his stone—he picked it up from the Absold the very day he proposed the idea—but the men sent from the Vanguard and the Merum haven't been able to find any trace of Lady Bronwyn or Toria Deel. We've scoured the towns and villages bordering the

Darkwater in all six kingdoms." She shook her head, her mouth as pursed as a prune. "Nothing."

"The man we're following will lead us to them," I said.

A younger woman's eyes would have grown wide with the look the Chief gave me, but Brid Teorian's stare made me uncomfortable even so. "Don't play word games with me, Lord Dura."

I blinked. I didn't have a clue what she was talking about.

She lifted one hand from the pommel of her cane to point a bony finger at my chest. "You're not hunting a man. Get that through your head. It may walk on two legs and eat and drink, but *it* has killed the sentinels and corrupted members of the Vigil. The humanity of this killer is the last thing you need to worry about."

I braced myself for the argument that would surely come from her refusal to let us follow the trail. Instead, she sighed, slumping back in her chair. "How did we come to such desperate decisions so quickly?" Her chest rose and fell, and with each breath she appeared to shrink in on herself. "You must go after him, of course. Is there anything the church can give you?"

"The stone," I said and held out my hand.

For half an instant I watched her waver on the edge of indecision before she shook her head. "I'm sorry you asked. It would have been easier if you hadn't. Pellin has ordered me not to surrender it to you." Her birdlike stare fixed on mine. "I'm sure you can understand why."

Bolt nodded but managed to appear unhappy about it all the same, but Gael drew breath, and her eyes turned from blue to slate between one heartbeat and the next.

I reached out to put my hand on her arm. "Pellin might be right on this one," I said. "I'll explain later."

The Chief nodded. "You might have been disappointed at any rate. I've tried to contact Pellin any number of times already. He doesn't answer."

She stood, pushing down on her cane with both arms to lever herself to an upright position. "The Archbishop carries more influence with the southern continent. He's sent messengers to tell them of our plight."

I gaped at her as the pieces of what she'd just said fell into place. "Are you telling me I'm the last member of the Vigil?"

She stumped her way to the door as though I hadn't spoken before she turned to answer. "No, Lord Dura. I'm only telling you, you *might* be. If that is the case, be assured I will surrender to you your proper address when next we meet."

She kept leaving me behind in the conversation. "Proper address?"

Brid Teorian nodded. "Eldest."

"If we meet," I said.

She nodded. "Yes, it does seem more than a little likely that at least one of us will die soon." She stabbed a finger as skinny as a splinter toward my chest. "It may be in your power to save or doom us all, Lord Dura. Try to remember that."

After the Chief of Servants left with her contingent to make her way across the square back to the House of Servants, the sound echoed more and the room felt empty at their departure. We stood there, staring at each other as if none of us knew what to do next. The idea of a night spent in relative security without the sleepless vigilance we'd practiced in the forest seemed strange.

"To bed," Bolt said. "If we're going to attempt this insanity, we ought to be well rested for it."

CHAPTER 43

We walked the length of the Merum cathedral, but I let Bolt and Rory move ahead of me while I strode beside Gael, letting the distance between us grow until the space offered some semblance of privacy.

"The brothers here in the cathedral have some interesting traditions," Gael mused beside me as we made our way toward the guest quarters.

I nodded. "I'm familiar with almost all of them, though I spent much of my time as an acolyte down in the city." I knew her well enough to know that she never engaged in idle banter. Spirited banter? Yes. She and her sister had made a sport of it until they could wield words the way Vigil guards could swing swords, but speech without purpose was unknown to her. I wanted to reach out and take her hand, feel the warmth of it against my own, but I was unwilling to drop into a delve. "Did you have a specific tradition in mind?"

She had a way of nodding, a single slow dip of her head that I had always thought regal, and it displayed the graceful lines of her neck to good advantage. "In their chapel, the small sanctuary reserved for the use of the brothers and sisters who live here, they always have a priest available to take confession or administer the rite of haeling if any desire it."

I snuck a sidelong glance at her. "You wish to partake of the rite before bed, milady?"

Her lips turned up at the corners just enough to convey amusement before she answered. "No, Lord Dura." In the months I'd spent at court, no one had ever managed to imbue a single utterance of my title with so many hints and suggestions as Gael. I think she did it on purpose to see if she could make me stammer. Most of the time she succeeded.

My voice dipped. "Is there something you wish to confess?"

She laughed a deep, throaty sound at odds with the stern hallways we traversed. "No, Willet. If I ever feel the need to confess, I will tell you."

"I'm not a priest," I said.

"I'm just as happy about that," she quipped. "Merum celibacy would be such a waste." She sobered slightly. "But you were almost a priest, so you can tell me if my presumption is correct. Am I right in assuming that any brother or sister of the Merum order who has been ordained to officiate in the rite of haeling may also consecrate the bond of marriage?"

Everything stopped.

I stopped walking, blinking, breathing, thinking. It all came to a halt as I faced Gael and her intention became clear.

I stalled for time while I tried to find enough air to breathe. "You're serious, milady?"

She drew closer until she filled my sight, paused, then tilted her head and made the Merum cathedral and its halls disappear. I became dimly aware of her hands knotted in my hair as though I might pull away before she wished. In the back of my mind I became aware of unaccustomed strength in her embrace, and her kiss left me reeling.

She stepped back.

I hadn't delved her, knew I couldn't have since my gloves still covered my hands, but the hallway reeled anyway and I put out a hand against the nearest wall. Fire flowed across my skin.

"I am in earnest, Willet," she said, breathing deeply. "The ceremony need not be protracted with grand statements or stately walks, and I have no wish for a crowd of witnesses who will require pleasantries as they wish us a long and happy union." She shook her head. "I know that is not possible. My family is dead, the Vigil is shattered, and it is unlikely both of us—either of us—will survive." She moved close and again managed to pull the air from my lungs. "Twelve hours of darkness are not enough time for me to express my love for you." Her head dipped until her chin almost touched her chest, and she gave me an unblinking smolder through her lashes. "But it would be a start."

Conflicting sensations covered me, the cool air in the hallway and the fire flowing across my skin, the aching need for Gael that felt like a grand emptiness and the way she filled my arms, the spin of a million thoughts in my head and the focused white-hot desire of wanting union with her with every facet of who I was.

I stood on the edge of paradise, the promise of heaven every order recited or interpreted from the liturgy, and my eyes drank in the sight of its fulfillment: the raven hair, the rich blue eyes and full lips, and the lithe curves that her clothing couldn't hide. Refusal was impossible. Ecstasy had called me by name.

I took a step away—then another. The cool air washed a bit of the heat from my skin, enough for me to realize what I was about to do and regret it.

"If I marry, bond with you, I can't do this," I said. "This thing I need to do—finding the man who slaughtered your household, who wants to turn everyone into the raving animals we fought during Bas-solas—I can't do that. I might try to fool myself into thinking it would give me something more to fight for, but that would be a lie.

"If I marry you tonight, Lady Gael, and spend the next twelve hours in your arms, I'm undone."

She didn't cry, but I could hear her breath shudder as she inhaled. "Must it be so?"

I mustered enough control over my body to force my head down and back in a nod. "I've seen—a few times—how union consumes the newly married who earnestly and truly love and desire each other. What would it do to us, milady?"

Aer bless her, she took a moment to let disappointment and anger run loose behind her eyes, but no more than that. Then she stifled those emotions, throttled them until no hint of them showed in her gaze or posture, and gave me a smile that went with the coy inclination of her head.

"You're a wise man, Willet Dura, and you know me well. Once we are married and I take you to my bed, I will do everything to make sure you never wish to leave the room." She gave me an arch lift of her brows. "I'm given to understand those with a physical gift and the talents for space and motion are quite . . . dangerous," she said, finding the bantering tone I'd first heard over a year ago.

"My own gift, Lady Gael, will not be without benefit. With a touch, I will know what you think and feel . . . and desire." Her eyes widened, and a split second later, we laughed and resumed the journey to our separate quarters. I would have kissed her again on the threshold of her door but stopped just short. The tension between us allowed me to pick up my task and continue with what I had to do. Heaven would have to wait.

Her door closed, and I sagged against the wall for support. "Aer, help me find a way to keep us both alive." It wasn't elegant and I had no idea if He would choose to answer it.

I woke the next morning when a nearly horizontal beam of sunlight hit my eyes as it came through the window. A rasping sound rolled me over and through the door that led to the sitting room, where I saw Bolt in a chair, running his sword over a whetstone, first along one edge and then the other. He could have shaved with it.

"How long have you been here?"

"I stood in the hallway until you'd finished your conversation with Gael and then waited until I was reasonably sure you were asleep." He gave a soft chuckle. "I remember, dimly, being a young man who could sleep until noon. The onset of age puts so many different things we desire beyond our reach. I can't sleep past dawn anymore—haven't been able to for years."

I was still in my small clothes. That meant I hadn't night-walked and no one had died last night. The realization of that fact settled into my heart with a soft, delicate warmth, but it didn't last. "We're going hunting. How do we win?"

He shook his head. "I don't know. If I were a betting man, I'd put a lot of money on us to lose. We're outmatched here, Willet, and not just in physical terms. 'When your victories are short-lived and your defeats aren't, you're beaten.'"

I nodded approvingly. "Is that yours?"

He shook his head. "It's from one of the captains who chronicled his campaigns during the Gift Wars. I think his name was Lawton."

A bit of the Chief's conversation slipped through my mind. "If we fall, Custos may be the last hope of the north." I shook my head. "Even if we don't, the heads of the orders don't exactly hold me in high esteem." I shook my head. "It's like being back in court."

"Heh," Bolt laughed, "those people really don't like you."

"I'm glad I can offer you some amusement," I said. "I hope Custos can provide some insight into our enemy. You know what they say . . . "

"'Knowledge is sorrow, but wisdom is power.'"

Less than an hour later we were mounted and making for the east side of the city. Bunard stretched south in an arc from the east of the tor around to the southwest with the broad flow of the Rinwash bordering the city to the north and continuing toward the west. Wag, almost completely healed, rode behind Rory.

Gael snuck sidelong glances at the sentinel when she thought no one would notice. We were trying not to attract attention. The fifth time I saw her find an excuse to put her gaze on our hairy companion, I tugged her sleeve from the opposite side.

"Startling, isn't he?"

She shook her head and gave a nervous little laugh. "It's actually not that much bigger than a hunting dog, and I've seen plenty of those around court. I think what's bothering me is that I can see it's still just a puppy. How big is it going to get?"

The object of our discussion lifted his head from his vantage point atop Rory's horse and gave us a low growl. "His name is Wag," Rory said. "He doesn't like to be called *it*, and whatever you do don't refer to him as a dog."

I could see this startled her. "Isn't he?" she whispered.

Another growl, a bit louder, came from the back of Rory's horse. "You do know his hearing is better than ours, don't you?"

I took a breath, debating how to frame what I meant to say next. "The sentinels don't really see themselves as dogs. It's similar to the difference between someone who has a pure gift along with a lot of talent and someone else who has neither."

Gael's brows drew together and she shook her head at me. "*See* themselves? What do you mean by *similar*?" On her other side I saw Bolt smirking at me in obvious enjoyment.

I sighed. "I mean *exactly*."

"Don't be silly, Willet. That's not . . ." She stopped. I wasn't smiling.

"Wag is gifted. I don't know how much he can understand about what we're saying, but his mind is growing and along with it, his grasp of language. If we live long enough, I think you'll be able to talk to Wag the same as you would to me."

"And you'll probably get a more intelligent response," Bolt said.

We came to the easternmost part of the city, a jut of land up against the first of the branches of the Rinwash River that comprised Bunard's defense. I whistled to Wag, who jumped lightly from the back of Rory's horse and came padding over to me. I took off my gloves, unwilling to leave anything to chance misunderstanding.

"Why did we come here?" Gael asked.

"The wind is blowing west to east," Bolt said. "Wag knows the scent of our enemy, as well as his littermate. From here he'll be able to pick up the trail and location of every place they've been."

Gael laughed. "That's im—"

"Think about the impact a pure physical gift would have on a dog's sense of smell," Bolt said.

Whatever Gael said next was lost in the swirl of sensations that swept me away when I put my hands onto the thick fur covering Wag's head. As it had before, the world shifted, turning without transition from sight-dominated to scent-dominated. I sneezed as Gael's perfume overpowered me. I pulled my thoughts from Wag's long enough to motion her behind me.

Wag's tongue found my cheek. *Master. Master. Master. Do we hunt?*

I must have jerked in surprise because I came out of the delve long enough to find myself staring down into Wag's eyes for a heartbeat or two. "We do hunt," I said out loud. "The man-thing that stole your littermate has been here." I put my hands on him again.

Wag growled in agreement. Within his mind I shared a fierce anger, a rage that desired flesh to tear and bones to crack. The memory of his littermate came forward in my mind, a canine scent as unique to him as a person's face would be to me. With it came the scent of those who'd killed his family.

I could have tried putting my thoughts directly into his head but chose instead to speak. The others would need to know how much Wag understood. I straightened with my hands at my side. "Wag, can you find the most recent scents of your littermate and the men who took her?"

His tongue came out and for a moment I thought he would bark.

"He understands you?" Gael asked.

I nodded. "His language skills have grown since the last time I delved him. It's a little startling, actually."

"Good," Bolt said. "He can lead us right to them."

"Maybe not *right* to them," Rory said. "Wouldn't we want to stop a little short to give ourselves time to plan?"

I pictured what would happen if we blundered headlong into someone with Laewan's power without preparation and shuddered. We'd be slaughtered. "Wag, don't bring us any closer than a hundred paces of your littermate. Stop first."

He looked at me with his head cocked to one side.

"Hmmm. Evidently sentinels don't measure distance the way we do."

I put my hands back on his head and lost myself in the scents of the city wafting past us for a moment before I immersed myself in the memories he'd accumulated since his mother had awakened his mind.

Within his memories, I found and partook of his concept of space, discovering that sentinels held within their minds two different means of determining distance. I came out of the delve, turning to my companions, vaguely surprised to see my own two-legged form matched theirs. "Interesting," I said. "He uses his sense of smell to gauge far distances and his sense of sight for close ones. There's a point at which the scent of some animal or person becomes strong enough that he expects to be able to see them."

"How close is that?" Bolt asked.

"About two hundred paces," I said.

"That would work," Bolt said. "As long as we don't try hunting him down at night."

I nodded. "There's more. His sense of sight isn't as good as ours in the daylight, but when I sifted through his memories, he could see quite a bit better at night than any of us."

"That's nice, but I wouldn't mind having an army at my back," Rory said.

I pulled the misty air coming off the river into my lungs, remembering. "You'd think that would make things better, but then you find the people you're fighting gathered an army to back them up as well. Then the swords and pikes come out and there's nothing but dying and screaming until someone retreats. It takes days or weeks sometimes, and even if you come out of it alive you come home to find your family dead from fever. It's only a bit later you notice there are calluses on your compassion and you discover you've lost your humanity somewhere on the battlefield."

I started, realizing I'd spoken aloud. Gael and Bolt gazed at me, their faces so different but both of them wrapped in expressions of pity. Rory gaped at me, his eyes wide, but not in shock or surprise. He understood all too well.

"My apologies," I mumbled as I busied myself with my gloves. "Sometimes they . . . the memories . . . come at me out of nowhere."

CHAPTER 44

Directed by Wag's vocabulary of growls, yips, and barks, we came back to the nobles' section, where we stood looking over the blackened stone of Gael's estate. "We could have saved ourselves some time and come here first," Bolt said.

"No, we needed to be downwind to be sure," I said, but my eyes were on Gael. She sat mounted atop her horse, devouring the signs of fire that had destroyed her uncle's wealth.

"For all his clutching avarice, it all went up in flames and he with it," she said.

The sentiment surprised me. Gael's uncle had been one of the most ambitious, grasping nobles I'd met in my short time at court, and that was saying something. Still, he represented the last of her family. I reached over to squeeze her hand. The gesture lost something through the thin leather of my gloves. "Aer willing, we'll find the man who murdered him."

"I have a better idea," she said. "Let's find the man who killed the servants, the men and women who returned Uncle's arrogance and disdain with kindness. If my uncle were here, he wouldn't spare a thought for them; he'd be crying and screaming over the possessions that went up in flames."

"He was all that was left of your family," I said.

She nodded. "And he was more than willing to drug me and marry me off to someone I didn't love so that he could acquire more wealth.

I'm not going to weep for a man who held the lives of others in such low esteem just because we share bloodlines. I might shed a few tears for the man he should have been."

Bolt nodded his approval from his perch on her far side.

"All right, Wag," I said. "Let's find your littermate."

We rode out of the nobles' section and crossed over the branch of the Rinwash leading into the upper merchants' quarter, the homes nearly as grand as those just north of them but without the land or cultivated gardens. The population grew more dense and the homes poorer the farther we moved south from the queen's tor.

We had just crossed over when a wisp of smoke caught my attention and the hackles on the back of my neck stood up. I pointed to the gauzy haze drifting upward. "Gael, was there more than one fire that night?"

She looked at me and nodded. "The merchant's house where you were taken went up as well."

I believed her. There wasn't a reason on earth for me not to, but a sense of something out of place, an occurrence that didn't quite fit, settled into my gut. I twitched the reins to the side and nudged Dest into a canter until the ruins of Andler's mansion stood before me. Unlike Gael's home, Andler's exterior had been fashioned from wood instead of stone. Charred beams and supports thrust their way upward out of the smoking ash like blackened fingers begging the sky for mercy.

The others rode up beside me, but I hardly acknowledged them. Puzzle pieces were rattling around in my brain, and I needed space and quiet to get them to fit. I started with the most important question. Why burn them both?

I shook my head in frustration. No, I couldn't answer that one yet. When? That was easier. I glanced at Wag. He wouldn't have made a mistake. Our enemy had come to Andler's house first, burned it, then went to the house of Gael's uncle, Count Alainn, and did the same thing. Then he backtracked along the same route out of town and supposedly left Bunard by the southern road.

I turned from my study of soot and ruin to face Gael. "Was anybody inside Andler's house when it went up?"

She shook her head. "I don't know, Willet, but none of the reports to Queen Cailin from the city watch mentioned anything about bodies."

"He didn't need anything else," I muttered, looking at the ruins again. "Everything was right here."

Bolt must have dismounted while I was musing. He appeared at my side, watching me, waiting while I stood there gaping at the ruins of Andler's ambition, hardly daring to breathe for fear of losing the answer that came limping toward me.

"Did any other buildings catch fire around the same time?"

"No," Gael said. "Just the two where you were."

I hadn't expected any other answer, but I needed to be sure.

"Why are you here, Willet?" Bolt asked. "We already knew he would be hunting for you."

I nodded absently. The pieces were in place. I knew when and I knew why, but now I had to decide what to do about it. I turned to Gael. "I want you to go back to Queen Cailin. Stay there. Be safe."

She jerked as if I'd slapped her, though nothing but surprise showed on her face. Yet.

"If the north falls," I went on, "if whatever has gotten loose from the Darkwater manages to kill the rest of the Vigil and me, get on the first ship headed to the southern continent and don't come back."

Her expression closed, turned calm the way the wind dies just before a storm breaks loose. "No. You knew it would be dangerous when we set out."

I shook my head. "Not like this. This is a roll of the bones, and we need double fours—and that's an understatement." I willed her to listen for once. "Please."

Her eyes darkened to slate. "I don't care how much danger you're in, Willet, I'm not leaving. You have a better chance of surviving with me than without me."

I sighed and closed my eyes, pointing at the ruins of Andler's mansion, knowing I'd already lost the argument. "He's not after me. If he was, there would have been no point to burning down your uncle's house or killing all the servants." I turned to Bolt. "He's after Branna."

"The girl you asked me to hide?" Gael asked.

I nodded. "The freshest scent was at your uncle's. Wag said so. That means he came here first. If he wanted my scent, it was all over the cave next to Andler's wine cellar. It couldn't get much easier than that—my blood is still on the floor where they held me." I shook my head. "He came here to pick up Branna's scent. Then he tracked her to your estate and I'll bet that was the last place she went to before your servant, Marya, got her out of Bunard. The only reason to do that is for him to find Branna. She's the only one besides me whose scent would have been at both houses."

I watched Gael take all that in, her gaze sliding from mine as she put all the pieces together for herself. Smart girl.

Even so, Bolt was quicker. He knew what we were up against. There wasn't anyone within twenty paces of us on the street, but he put his hand on his sword anyway. "Branna is the only one who can identify Robin's killer. That means the Vigil knows him."

"And somehow that presents a threat," I said.

"She could already be dead, Willet," Gael said.

"Yes," I agreed, "but if she's not, we have an advantage over our enemy." The three of them stared at me while I stood there hoping they'd make the connection and I wouldn't have to put my voice to what I was thinking. It was going to sound even more insane out loud than it did in my head.

They just waited. It figured.

"He can't travel during the day," I said. "Our speed will be hindered, but we don't have to stop at night."

For a moment, no one said anything, but Gael's eyes lit with comprehension. Now she knew why I wanted her to remain here in Bunard. Rory might have twitched his shoulders. He didn't care or object. The hours of darkness were his accomplice after all, and he was the only one of us who could see the dwimor clearly.

Bolt shook his head. "I can't keep you safe."

"No, you can't. We knew that already."

"That's not what I meant and you know it."

"We have to know who it is," I said.

He sighed, and the muscles in his jaws bunched. I could almost hear his teeth cracking. "Knowledge gained isn't the same thing as knowledge kept. If we can't live long enough to get the information to the rest of the Vigil, it's useless."

"All right," I shrugged. "Let's play it your way. Tell me what happens if we don't get there in time."

I watched him run through scenarios in his head. He even went so far as to draw breath and open his mouth to speak before he settled back on his heels, his eyes narrowing in annoyance. "The girl dies, but we still might manage to run him to ground and kill him before he can track down Pellin or anyone else."

"The girl dies," I said.

He grimaced. "We've talked about this, Willet. You can't save everyone."

"But he has to try, or he betrays who he is," Gael said.

Her eyes held something that was too intense for me to look at for more than an instant. I had work I needed to do. I stepped over to Rory's horse, where Wag was perched atop it like a furry gargoyle. "Which way did your littermate go?"

He licked me with a tongue broad enough to wet half my face before he craned his neck so that his head pointed south, his nose twitching. I went back to Dest, put a foot in the stirrup and mounted. "When we get outside of the city, we'll let Wag lead the way."

We were just about to cross the bridge into the poor section, the only part of the city open to the rolling hills and the plain to the south, when an obscure impulse brought me to a stop. I could just see the ruins of Ealdor's abandoned church some two hundred paces away. "Stay here," I said.

All three of them twitched their reins to follow me anyway, and I held up my hand. "It's broad daylight, and this has to be done alone." I licked my lips. "Please."

"There's nothing there, Willet," Bolt said. "What good can come of this?"

I didn't have an answer, at least no answers that would make sense to him or Gael or Rory, but I needed to get back to that little church and talk to my friend. When I reined in at the front door, I couldn't help but gape at the state of Ealdor's sanctuary. My mind couldn't reconcile the image it still held with the derelict church in front of me.

It wasn't important. I stepped inside and beneath a roof that allowed almost as much sunlight as it created shadow. My boots crunched through the debris on the short walk up to the altar, but I stopped just short. To the right, there was a door hidden in the shadows. He would come from there, as he always had, walking toward me as he draped his stole around his shoulders.

I had only to wait.

"Greetings, Willet." Ealdor stepped into the light. His stole rested on his shoulders, fluttering a little in the air, but his steps made no sound and left no marks in the accumulated dust.

I looked around the interior of the church, but nothing had changed. It still looked as though it might come crashing down on me at any moment. "You left it the way it was."

He laughed. "I don't do anything, Willet. It looks as it truly does because you know the truth of it now. Would you like to officiate over the haeling?"

I shook my head and his smile diminished. "Confessional, then?"

"No," I said. "I came to ask you a question."

He looked at me with a gaze that suddenly seemed old enough to make Pellin's appear youthful by comparison. "I'm only in your mind, Willet. I can only tell you what you already know, but oftentimes a man just needs to hear himself think out loud. How goes your battle?"

I shook my head. "No, that's not true and I won't be lured into a discussion, Ealdor. I don't have time for it." I paused, swaying a bit to the pounding of my heart in my chest. "You can't stay in the shadows forever," I said. "Sooner or later, you're going to have to tell the rest of them you're real."

He shook his head and walked toward me.

And then right through.

I never felt a thing, nothing cold or clammy the way some of the veterans described the ghosts of strangers they'd killed on the battle-field. Ealdor walked through me with as much fanfare as he would have stepped through a doorway.

"You made a mistake," I said as I turned to face him. "You told me something I didn't know, couldn't know."

He stared at me, all expression removed from his face, but his eyes, his eyes might have held anything and everything.

"What are we fighting, Ealdor? We can't win fighting in ignorance."

Dust from my steps, only my steps, circled in the air around us. I blinked, trying to clear the irritation away, and in that instant, he disappeared.

I stood in the church for a handful of heartbeats before I left. When the others saw me coming, they mounted up and we rode south over the bridge that would take us through the poor quarter and out of the city.

"Well?" Bolt asked.

I shrugged, but inside I seethed with frustration and doubt. "He wasn't in the mood to talk."

CHAPTER 45

Pain lanced through Toria's neck, and she snapped her eyes open to the sensation of falling only to close them again a moment later as her head banged against thinly padded wood. Her hands were still bound behind her, but her arms had fallen asleep and she couldn't tell if her fingers were bare or not.

When she struggled to right herself, hands clamped onto her shoulders, pulling her upright. The interior lines of a carriage slowly came into focus, and by dim sunlight that leaked through the covered windows she made out the still form of Lelwin across from her and two men, armed and stoic.

The smell of lemongrass mingled with averin syrup drifted up to her from the gag she still wore, and she struggled to remain conscious. The carriage swam in her vision in a way that had nothing to do with the bumps in the road, and she fought the nausea from its swaying and the drugs to keep from vomiting.

The man to her right, the speaker for the Clast, gazed at her with as much feeling as one might concede to an inanimate object before speaking. "We're between villages, but I have no desire to be betrayed by chance, Toria Deel. That leaves me with two choices. I can leave you gagged for the entire trip to the Darkwater Forest . . . or," he said, taking out a wicked-looking hooked dagger, "I can kill your companion at the first hint of alarm you raise. I was given no drawings of her. Do you understand what I'm saying?"

She swallowed and nodded. As far as these men were concerned,

Lelwin's life was inconsequential. The moment either of them became an inconvenience, her apprentice would die.

"Are you thirsty?" the man asked. When she nodded, he held out his hand without looking away from her, and the man sitting next to Lelwin put a waterskin in it. Then he leaned forward to untie her gag. She stretched and rolled her jaw and took an unencumbered breath.

The speaker for the Clast lifted the waterskin and she drank, surprised that he allowed her to have her fill before taking it away.

Desperation burned the back of her throat, but she envisioned herself grabbing the panic that threatened to reduce her to begging and shoved it behind a door within her mind. First and foremost she needed to discover how much these men knew about her. "Why is the Icon interested in me?"

The man looked at her for a moment in consideration, neither giving an answer nor appearing unwilling to. "The Icon's decisions are the Icon's alone. Your appearance was made known to us and you have been taken. That is all you need to know."

She nodded, trying to show acquiescence, but inside she railed. The speaker's response hinted at his ignorance but didn't confirm it.

"The portrait was well done," she said, "not gifted, but even so, the person who drew it must know me well. There were subtleties within it that casual acquaintance would be unlikely to capture."

The speaker refused to respond, and no hint of knowledge or recollection showed in his eyes. Her comments had not been idle ones. In the portrait, the artist had managed to capture the fact that one of her eyes was slightly smaller than the other, a whisker's worth of difference between them that no one who hadn't studied her face would notice.

Unless of course, they were gifted. But while the strokes on the portrait were masterful, they lacked the ineffable grace that pointed to giftedness. She checked her logic, going through it point by point, like one of the king's engineers checking a sum, and found no flaw within it—but that led her to an impossibility. Few knew her well enough to craft such a portrait and since it was one of many that had been produced, it had to have been done entirely from memory. Only one of the Vigil could have crafted it.

She ran down the list: Pellin, Bronwyn, Laewan, Jorgen, and the rogue, Willet Dura. Pellin and Bronwyn were beyond reproach, and

Laewan was dead. She'd seen his body riddled with dagger strikes with her own eyes. That left Jorgen and Lord Dura. As tempting as it might be to think that Dura might have betrayed her, she dismissed the possibility. She'd delved him, and in his entire history, all the way back through childhood, he had no artistic training. Though the thought of one of the Vigil carrying a vault still made her nauseous, she had to admit it was unlikely to the point of being ridiculous that his vault was hiding art lessons.

That left Jorgen, but in its own way that was even more unlikely. Arthritis had left Jorgen's fingers a swollen mass of digits that couldn't point in the same direction, much less craft a series of portraits that could capture her likeness.

The speaker leaned forward to gag her once more, and she recoiled. "However much you've been promised, I can triple it."

"Nobles," the speaker said as he shook his head. "You think you can buy everything."

"I'm not a noble."

"You belong to the church, then," the speaker said. "The Icon has wealth you cannot imagine."

"You believe the Clast has sole ownership and access to truth?" Toria asked.

The speaker's brows furrowed for a moment, and his expression became clouded. Then he laughed. "Ah! I see now, but you misunderstand me, Toria Deel. When I said the Icon had wealth you could not imagine, I was not using your church's doublespeak to refer to truth or wisdom or any of those other intangibles you spout to keep people poor and satisfied. I meant real wealth, wealth enough to buy and rule the world, both the northern and southern continents."

Despite her efforts to keep her breathing steady and her face expressionless, she must have given him some sign that he'd given her information she could use. Jerking, he retied the gag in her mouth and doused it again with that concoction that robbed her of consciousness.

When she came to, the carriage was still and empty except for herself and Lelwin, who gave her a steady brown-eyed gaze. Toria still wore her gag, but red marks on Lelwin's face indicated how she'd managed to force hers down until it hung about her neck.

"We stopped about half an hour ago," the girl murmured. "I've heard sounds of a minimal camp being made, but nothing in the silences between indicate any village."

Toria struggled to reach a seated position, flailing with her arms still tied behind her. Lelwin extended her right leg, wedging it between Toria and the carriage seat, and lifted her to an upright position. Then she leaned forward, took Toria's gag in her mouth, and pulled it free.

"Tastes terrible," her apprentice said in the same soft tone that wouldn't carry past the two of them.

"Thank you," Toria said. "How long have you been awake?"

Lelwin shrugged. "I got bored and took a nap after our guards put you out again, but I've been awake for most of the trip. We're headed northwest."

"How did you manage that?" Toria asked. "I saw them drug you."

Lelwin nodded. "One of the advantages of looking young and weak is that when I pretend to be helpless, no one suspects otherwise. As soon as they put the cloth over my face, I held my breath and went limp. I hid my face so that I could get my nose free of the gag and its drug." She pursed her lips. "I'll need to devise new strategies for dealing with people in a few years, when I start looking my age."

"They know who I am," Toria said. Try as she might, she couldn't keep the statement from sounding like a death sentence. "More accurately"—she pushed on in an attempt to redeem it—"they know my name and enough about me to keep my hands covered. If I could get free, I could delve them and break their minds."

Lelwin's eyes widened until the whites showed all around. "You can do that?"

She nodded. "It's similar to breaking a vault, and it's forbidden, but I think our circumstances warrant exceptional responses."

"How many times have you done that?"

She shrugged. "Only once, but the process is simple enough if I could just touch them."

Lelwin shook her head. "I don't think you'll get the opportunity. They spoke a bit when they believed both of us to be unconscious. They fear your touch, even though they don't speak of it with any knowledge."

"If I turn around, can you get to my bonds and untie them with your teeth?"

Her apprentice nodded. "It's possible, Lady Deel, but is this the best time? Look outside."

Toria leaned toward the slit of light that remained of the covered window, squirming around until she could just make out the sun kissing the western horizon like a parting lover. In half an hour it would be dark, completely dark.

"We're nearly out of time," Toria said. Panic squeezed her throat so that her voice came out as a hoarse whisper.

"I don't think they have vaults," Lelwin said. "Nothing about them appeared different as we rode away from the city last night." She licked her lips, and the fear that had been lurking behind her eyes broke free. "But they're men with two women captives. Men don't require a vault to conjure evil. I heard the speaker—you matter, I don't."

The sound of footsteps outside the carriage and coarse laughter turned Lelwin's expression frantic and wild. "I swore I'd never be taken that way again."

Toria watched the fear and rage build within her apprentice, saw it break free of any control she might have tried to exert over it. "Lelwin," she hissed. "Stop it."

The girl's gaze swept past her, and Lelwin bared her teeth as if she meant to tear the throat from her imagined attacker. Toria lashed out with her foot, catching her in the shin with enough force to make her gasp.

"Listen to me," Toria said. "For over a hundred years I've delved the worst humanity has to offer. I know from a score of memories what a man is capable of and a woman as well for that matter. We do not know their intent, but if they're determined to take you, you cannot fight it."

Lelwin's gaze flashed to the door of the carriage. Toria kicked her again. "You must live!" she hissed.

"I will not bear it!" her apprentice hissed back. "I still have one of my daggers."

"There are at least three men guarding us. You don't have to bear it," Toria said. "Make a door within your mind and place everything within it. Lock every touch, every sight, every sound and smell away as if they belonged to someone else."

Voices whispered outside the carriage door, and Lelwin's expression became feral. "I don't have your gift."

"You don't need it, not for this. I taught Peret how to do this same thing."

The door opened, and a man Toria hadn't seen before stood outside, the setting sun at his back, his face hidden in shadow. Without a word he reached into the carriage, grabbed Lelwin, and pulled her outside, but not before Toria saw three other men standing in the fading light of the sun, their expressions twisted, hungry.

Lelwin curled into a roll as her feet hit the ground, and she ran, nimble as a goat. But the men standing outside were faster. With a look that might have carried threat or amusement, the man who'd pulled Lelwin from the carriage shut the door.

Toria squeezed her eyes shut and tried to close her ears against the sounds that came from outside.

But she couldn't, and worse, she couldn't lock them away so conveniently as she'd counseled Lelwin to do, not if she wanted to aid her. The sounds of the men, stripped of their humanity, devoid of compassion or pity, continued well into the darkness that descended after sunset. Through anger that painted every detail of the interior of the carriage in crimson, she fought to think.

Yet the sounds of laughter and jests that covered Lelwin's whimpers filled her with rage that threatened to break her control over the doors she held within her mind. *No!* She needed to think!

Depravity had been known to her since she'd taken up the gift a hundred years before. It was more immediate now, more personal, but it was no more brutal now than it had been a century ago.

Think!

She forced herself to listen to the nuances of their conversation, parsing their words as she searched for some scrap of information that might help them. A surge of pride for her apprentice flared like a spark from flint and steel. Lelwin was most likely correct. The men didn't seem to have vaults within their minds. Their conversation and behavior gave no hint that they were anything more than underlings within the Clast. That, coupled with the fact that they had stopped for the night, meant her captors were limited by the same need for light as normal men.

But just as sparks died without tinder, so hope sputtered and vanished within her chest. They still had no means of escaping.

She needed her hands.

First she tried to curl and slip them down over her hips. If she could just get the knotted rope in front of her where she could get her mouth on it, she could pull them free with her teeth. She squirmed and bent until the muscles in her abdomen cramped with the effort. Each time she thought of giving up, she opened her ears and listened, flaying her soul with the noises that came from outside.

Later, sweating and panting, with her shoulders aching as if they'd been popped from their sockets, she surrendered. They'd tied her wrists too tightly to allow for any such maneuver. Despair washed over her, followed a moment later by impotent anger. Helpless.

"What good is this gift you've given me if I can't help her?" she prayed at Aer. "I'm supposed to be the instrument of justice for you when all else fails. How is this just?"

Her clerical training, a mixture of all four of the orders after her childhood exposure to the forms of the Merum allowed for such conversations with Aer, but none of the orders had ever taught her how to force Him to answer.

CHAPTER 46

Sometime during the night the men opened the door to the carriage and shoved Lelwin inside, where she fell, discarded, onto the floor. A sliver of moonlight illuminated her apprentice, caught the glassy stare of her eyes that refused to blink or focus. Toria waited until the sounds of the men walking away stilled before crouching to whisper in Lelwin's ear. "I'm here."

Her apprentice responded by curling into a ball on the splintered boards of the floor until her face disappeared behind her curtain of hair.

"I can help you," Toria pleaded, "if you'll just remove the cloth from my hands."

Lelwin curled tighter.

For an hour, Toria wept and pleaded for Lelwin's aid, but no response came from the figure on the floor, not even weeping. So she straightened, resolved to remain awake, to stand watch against the night and possible return of their captors. But against her will, sleep took her, turning her surrender to exhaustion into condemnation. Even in this, she was powerless.

The next morning the door opened again, and the speaker stepped up, ducking to wedge himself to one side before lifting Lelwin from the floor and depositing her on the end of the bench seat opposite Toria. Lelwin gave no sign of awareness other than to turn her head, hiding her face.

The speaker inspected Toria for a moment, as if searching for weapons. Then he grasped her shoulders and swung her around as if she were a sack of grain and inspected her bonds. Turning her back, he reached behind her to untie the gag that lay useless around her neck. For a moment she considered attacking him, imagining the lunge and snap of her jaws that would bury her teeth in his throat. Though choosing to do nothing, she immersed herself in the image as if it were balm for her soul and Lelwin's.

Then the cloth was back in her mouth and a sickly sweet scent filled the carriage. She slumped sideways to lie on the seat, the cushion rising up to meet her as the interior of the carriage spun in her vision. Just before she lost consciousness she saw the speaker leave, heard the sound of the door being shut and locked.

When she woke it was still light, and the rocking of the carriage told her they were moving. She looked across the narrow space of the carriage to her apprentice. Lelwin still sat with her face hidden, tucked away from light and awareness.

The smell of drugs and bile from the gag filled Toria's nose, and she retched helplessly, filling the small space with the twin odors. Lelwin remained unmoving.

Thirst burned her throat, and hunger gnawed a hole in her middle. Bound and helpless, she retreated into her memories, turning her attention inward until all sight and smell and sound dwindled and faded to the merest pinpoint.

She stood in her room—the construct she'd made in her mind over a hundred years earlier, where she stored the memories she gleaned from the use of her gift. It had little in common with Dura's, which was modeled after the sanctuary within the Merum library in Bunard. She'd fashioned hers after the library in Cynestol, a grand hall, almost square, with dozens of soaring arches that met at a single point overhead and stained-glass windows that diffracted the sun into a thousand different hues of light. Where the real hall held delicate works of marble in each alcove between the arches, hers held doors, each barely big enough for her to enter, so many were there within her mind. Someday, if she survived, she would have to rebuild the hall, make it larger to accommodate new memories she stored here, but for now it sufficed.

She lifted her arms as she walked, letting hues of crimson, viridian, and cerulean wash across her skin. With a sigh, she turned toward the north end of the hall, bemused that even within her mind light failed to reach those shadowed recesses. She stopped before an array of doors that held her own memories, recollections she kept stored away from herself so that they would not, could not, interfere with her work. She shook her head, surprised that there would be so many. She stepped forward to brush her hand against the polished wood of the most recent door, not even a year old, where she'd put her love and affection for Peret Volsk after his betrayal of the ideals of the Vigil had become plain. Someday she would let loose those memories, allow them to wash over her and fill her with the grief she'd set aside just before Bas-solas. Someday. If she survived.

She turned to her left, passing one narrow door after another until she came to a paneled door, incongruous in its lack of decoration. Fashioned decades ago, she'd made it plain so that she might more easily ignore it. She paused, hesitating. Using the memories behind this door carried more than the peril of judgment from the rest of the Vigil—this use of her gift, powerful and seductive, held threats of damnation from Aer himself.

Here, as the newest member of the Vigil, she'd stored the uses of her gift that had been denied to her, inferences of power that Cesla and Elwin and, to a lesser extent, Pellin, had taught her to avoid lest she come under judgment.

She put out her hand and opened the door into memory.

"Here," Cesla said, stopping the prison guards who accompanied them through the cells in Cynestol. A hundred feet below the ground, the heat of summer lived on as nothing more than a distant memory in the minds of the inmates. The granite wept with the cool, and the guards wore cloaks against the preternatural chill.

One of them stepped forward to unlock the heavy door. The other preceded them, torch in one hand and sword in the other, though the wretch beyond could hardly pose a threat. The prisoner sat on the stone floor, his head resting on his folded arms, which rested in turn on his knees.

"You may leave us," Cesla said to the prison guards with a nod toward their Vigil guards, Axa and Bracu. "We are more than safe."

The guards retreated with a lift of their shoulders, leaving them with one of the torches to find their own way out.

Inside the cell, Cesla removed his glove and with the air of a surgeon placed his hand on the prisoner's neck for the duration of a dozen heartbeats before taking it away.

He motioned her forward, and she moved toward the prisoner, her steps timid, cautious despite the protection afforded her by two of the most dangerous men alive. Some instinct must have roused the condemned man from his stupor for he shifted enough to gaze at her in the torchlight, his eyes clear and green.

"Have mercy." His soft laughter filled the cell.

She faltered, stepping backward in the confines of the cell until she felt Cesla at her shoulder. "His mind is broken."

"Not yet, daughter. You misunderstand him. He's not begging," Cesla said, his voice flat. "He's quoting."

It took her a moment to fully realize the import of the Eldest's statement, but when understanding came, he nodded in approval at her expression. "The deeper you place the memories within the wellspring of his mind, the longer it will take for some chance sound or smell to bring them into realization for him. Shallowly, daughter."

She stepped forward and put her hand on the prisoner's neck. A flood coursed through her as she fell into a river of threaded memories imbued with color and sound. She shifted, as she'd been taught, to avoid being swept up in any of the black-tinged recollections, but there were so many, so many.

Within an effort of will, she fought the allure of living another's life, no matter how stained, and forced herself to float above the stream of memories that flowed past her. She pushed herself forward in the opposite direction of the flow until she came to the wellspring within the prisoner's mind that resembled a hole in the ground from which a stream that would become a river emanated.

She'd never seen one before, had never had the need to see one; memories were sufficient. Cesla had told her how to find it. She stood over it, unsure, but then the prisoner's words came back to her. *Have mercy.* Her resolve firmed until it became as indomitable as iron. How many of the threads had held those same two words uttered by this man's victim? She held the gift of domere, the right to judge innocence and guilt, and she would not quail.

Thrusting her hand deep within the wellspring of the prisoner's memories she touched bottom, the origin, felt its spongy surface, let the cool wash of emotions that would become memories flow over her skin. Shallowly. She pulled her hand back from the bottom of the well without pulling out.

Without remorse or pity she opened the doors within her mind to let the memories of this man's victims loose, those he had allowed by purpose or chance to live, those she had delved. One after another, she threw those doors of pain and suffering and horror open, forcing the man she now delved to take those emotions and memories as his own. There were four, only four, though Cesla had told her the man's victims numbered a dozen or more.

The memories discharged, she pulled her hand from his wellspring and waited until the first implanted memory came forth, a small liquid thread of black that lengthened and thickened as it flowed. Nodding to herself, she stood and broke the delve.

And jerked as screams resounded from the walls of the cell.

She blinked to clear her vision, saw Bracu's arms around her, pulling her away from the prisoner as Axa closed the door. But not before she caught a vision of the prisoner, eyes wide and staring, screaming as if he wanted his lungs to burst and running back and forth, uncaring that he slammed into the walls of his cell over and over again.

The door clanged shut, and Axa locked it with the air of a man shutting a clothes closet. The man's face appeared in the barred window for an instant as he clashed with the door, and a hollow boom echoed through the prison. She heard the hoarse intake of breath before he screamed again. Already his voice had become rougher and softer than before.

"How long will it last?" she asked.

Cesla shrugged, and she interpreted his gesture as saying her question was not difficult to answer but held no significance either. "Until he dies. You planted his victims' memories in his wellspring. His mind cannot reconcile the memories from two vantage points with such different emotions. Just as oil and water do not mix, neither can his pleasure and his victims' pain. Had you remained in his mind, you would have seen the memories you unleashed, black as midnight, cling to his own. Even the colors are incompatible."

She shook her head, not understanding. "But his memories were black as well. I saw them in the stream."

Cesla, taller than either of his brothers, turned to her and his eyes softened. "The darkest memories you saw in him were recollections of his pain, my daughter. They would have hurt you had you touched them, but not nearly so much as the brightest colored memories you saw. Those strands of gold and silver, flaring like shooting stars in the night, were the memories of his greatest pleasures. And they would have hurt you far more."

Her stomach roiled, and she fought to keep from retching. "Was he ever anything other than evil?"

Cesla nodded, pointing toward the prisoner's cell. Muffled thumps came through the door, the sound of the man running back and forth into the rock walls, trying to escape the memories she'd implanted. "No man or woman is born evil, but the gift teaches us just how thin the dividing wall between you, me, and that prisoner really is. The civilization of mankind is often nothing more than an illusion that crumbles at the first test. Ask any soldier and he will tell you the same. Touch those who've survived famine or pestilence and see what people will do to survive. Those of us who have been in the Vigil the longest know it best, though we do not speak of it often."

The sounds from the cell grew more frantic, scaling upward. "Why would you have me do such a thing?"

Instead of answering directly, Cesla continued as though she hadn't just begged him for an explanation. "With a few notable exceptions—mostly those who hold their humanity in higher esteem than their life—men and women are only one unfortunate circumstance from the animals. There may come a time when you will have to use your gift as a weapon."

The prisoner screamed again, wetly.

"Never!" she panted. "I will never take a life again."

He nodded, but clearly not in agreement. "That is your decision, of course, but you may find others will die if you do not."

Toria Deel opened her eyes in the confines of the carriage, mentally stepping away from the room where she stored her memories before that conversation with Cesla fully played out. She knew how it ended, had no desire to relive circumstances she couldn't change.

The more she pondered the incident, decades old, the stranger it became. Cesla, Eldest of the Vigil, had commanded her to plant conflicting memories within that man's wellspring, ostensibly to demonstrate just how far they could go with their gift. But such a horrific example was hardly necessary. Just as easily, they could have implanted a pleasant memory into someone whose life and circumstance needed light.

She shook her head. With the distance of a hundred years, the memory gathered less clarity instead of more. Cesla's mind had been a labyrinth even then, and the rest of the Vigil had joked that if he couldn't see to the end of days it was because he hadn't bothered to look yet.

Even now it was impossible to determine all of his reasons for what had happened that day.

CHAPTER 47

Toria rolled to the floor of the rocking carriage, her hands covered by leather and her wrists and arms bound behind her with a multitude of thin strands of rope. Tears ripped their way free from her eyes as regret filled her. She couldn't afford grief, but as she fought her way to a kneeling position, turning so that Lelwin—still sitting on the opposite bench—could see her bonds, accusations rose in her mind.

How many justifications had she espoused when others had to pay the price?

Savagely, she thrust those denunciations away as she struggled to work the gag from her mouth. Of course death would be less painful than living. When had it ever been otherwise? The carriage rolled north toward the Darkwater with the relentless momentum of an approaching execution, and finally, after what seemed like hours, the gag slipped to her neck.

"Lelwin, you have to free my hands," she insisted, loud enough to be heard inside the carriage but not outside. "I can get us free, but I need access to my gift."

She heard nothing behind her that might have indicated acknowledgment, so she waited and beckoned again. "Lelwin, please, I can't help you if you don't free my hands."

Nothing.

Shifting onto her knees so that she faced her apprentice, she bent and clamped her teeth on Lelwin's shirt, pulling and tugging until she'd managed to expose Lelwin's face. "Do you want vengeance?" she said to her unblinking stare. "Help me."

Frustrated, she bit the cloth of the young woman's shirt and pulled once more. Lelwin slid from the bench to land on her, and they lay on the floor of the carriage in a tangle.

"Leave me alone." It might have been nothing more than the whisper of the wind outside the carriage or an echo of hooves that her ears and mind had twisted into speech.

"I can't. Lelwin, they're taking us to the Darkwater. If we spend a night there, our minds won't be our own."

"Good. I don't want to remember." Her voice sounded hollow, dead.

"But you will," Toria rasped. "I've delved enough of them to know. You'll live each day with your memories, and at night you will rage. You won't even be human anymore."

"Do you have any idea what they did to me?"

"Yes."

She felt Lelwin shake her head. "Has it ever happened to you?" Challenge and anger filled the question.

"No."

"Then you don't know what they did to me."

She pulled the stuffy, stale air of the carriage into her lungs. "Lelwin, do you know how old I am?"

"You've told me."

"I am over a hundred years old. In the history of the Vigil, only two others have come to the gift at a younger age than I. During my time in the Vigil I have delved any number of women taken against their will, some of them so physically broken they died soon after. But it's worse than that. I've also had to delve the men who betrayed and killed so much of their humanity that they would do such a thing and find pleasure in it. I've lived every detail of their crime, Lelwin, submersed in their twisted pleasure until I thought I could never be clean again. I know."

She waited, watching Lelwin's heart-shaped face for some sign of fight, but for long moments her apprentice did nothing more than continue to stare through her surroundings. Then a sob, solitary and alone, so that it might have been nothing more than the swift intake of breath, broke the silence. Another followed it. By the time Toria bent enough to rest her forehead against Lelwin's, tears poured from her eyes. "It hurts when I move."

After a moment, but far too soon, Toria straightened. "I know. Can you help me fight?"

Lelwin met her gaze and nodded. "What can you do?"

Behind her back, Toria flexed her hands, but she left the door to Cesla's memory closed. She had the information she needed. "Something just. Something I've done before. Something forbidden."

They spent the next few moments trying to disentangle themselves from each other and more time after that positioning themselves so that Lelwin could get her teeth on the leather that covered Toria's hands.

Toria bent double and pushed her legs against the sway of the carriage. "Chew a hole through the leather at the bottom, so that when I'm upright they won't see it." She felt a tug from her apprentice's teeth. "Make it just large enough for my smallest finger."

The steady pull paused for a moment. "Why?"

"I have to be able to touch each of them without the others knowing."

The leather proved durable. The tugs and jerks on her arms as Lelwin tried to chew her way through it continued for an hour. Not until the carriage slowed with the russet light of impending sunset discolored by dust did the faintest sound of tearing reach Toria's ears.

"I have to delve you, Lelwin."

Her answer, when it came, hardly stirred the air in the carriage, but it was no less emphatic for that. "No. You'll see what they did to me."

Toria would have used her authority or appealed to friendship if she thought either of those had a chance of working, but Lelwin, like all of the urchins, hardly acknowledged authority existed, and their friendship was still too new, too tenuous. With no other recourse, Toria appealed to vengeance.

"Your memories will be the executioner's axe."

"How?"

Toria sighed. Days of riding in the carriage with her hands constantly bound had forced her to soil herself. Now that feeling of being unclean worked its way into her heart. Instead of grieving with Lelwin and looking forward to a time when she might forgive her assailants, Toria had instead stoked her need for revenge. Now she was about to enlist her apprentice's aid in something forbidden.

"I'm going to take your memories and place them in each guard's wellspring."

"What's a wellspring?"

Toria sighed again. "It's aptly named. Within the mind is the origin of thought and memory, the beginning of recollection and comprehension. The stream of memory that members of the Vigil enter is circular, returning to the wellspring before it issues forth again. Our gift is that we can enter that stream, pick a memory and follow it like a thread in a tapestry to its origin. If we go far enough, we come to the wellspring."

"I don't understand."

Toria nodded. "It's a difficult concept to explain. Why do you remember?"

To her apprentice's credit, she took time to frame her answer. Twice, she began her reply before cutting her response short. "I don't know."

"Neither do I," Toria said. "Not in any absolute sense. But I do know where memory comes from, and my gift allows me access to it."

"What will happen?"

Toria nodded in approval. Better to focus on the immediate concern. "Their minds will be unable to reconcile the same event from two different perspectives. Your pain will serve to awaken their consciences."

"How can any of them have one?" Lelwin spat.

She sighed. "I have encountered men who fit that description, but rarely. The conscience of even very evil men still exists in some twisted form that allows them to do what they do. They will go mad."

"You swear?" Lelwin said.

"To the very best of my knowledge and ability," Toria said.

Lelwin leaned forward like a supplicant at the rail.

By the time the carriage jerked to a stop they had resumed the positions from hours before—Toria lying across one bench with her arms behind her, and Lelwin curled into a protective ball with her face tucked out of sight.

The sound of hooves thundered away from them to the north just before the door opened and one of the guards, not the speaker, climbed in, smiling in Lelwin's direction. "We've stopped for the night."

When his gaze shifted to Toria, his expression went flat. Roughly, like a man handling a piece of firewood, he pulled her up to a sitting position on the bench and turned her around to inspect her bonds.

Staring ahead, she waited as time inched forward, felt his hands slide down over the ropes that kept not just her wrists bound, but her arms as well. Then she felt what she'd been waiting for, pressure on her hands through the leather for a cursory check. She would only have this instant. As quickly as she could manage without jerking or startling her captor in any way, she thrust the smallest finger of her right hand through the hole in the leather and reached for his skin.

The interior of the carriage disappeared as she fell into his mind. She would have to be quick, quicker than she had ever been. She lashed out against his will, attacking the strands of thought and feeling that comprised his actions in the carriage, holding him still.

She raced backward in time, his memories washing through her, filling her with filth, until she came to the memory of him standing with the speaker in front of a taller man, hooded, who gave the speaker a sheet of parchment with her likeness and orders in a resonant voice she knew.

Jorgen.

Before she reached toward the guard's wellspring, Toria took just enough time to wonder what had happened to corrupt him, to consider how he and Laewan could have both been turned from their duty. When she found the wellspring she slowed, thinking. If she placed Lelwin's memories too shallowly, his transition to insanity would put the rest of the men on their guard, but if she planted them too deep, they would arrive at their destination before they had a chance to escape.

Reaching into the shadowed recesses that composed the origin of his thoughts and memories, she opened the door in her mind where she'd stored Lelwin's memories of violation. The black strands poured forth, thick and tough as pieces of boiled leather. As soon as the memories were released, she concentrated on pulling her fingers closer to her in the real world, balling her hands into fists.

The interior of the carriage appeared in her vision and she waited, hardly daring to breathe, to see if the guard had detected her touch. She gave her head a small shake. Nothing could save him now. He was dead, his mind broken beyond repair, as surely as if she had dosed him with a gallon of averin sap. But if he suspected he'd been touched, she would never get the opportunity to touch the others.

She tried to still the sudden thunder of her heart. Opportunity needed to present itself soon, or she and Lelwin would find themselves either at their destination or within the Darkwater Forest.

Her guard stilled for a moment, and then her world spun as he shoved her away. She landed on her back, saw him reaching for Lelwin, who tried to back away though there was no place to go. Her legs kicked out, pushing, as she tried to become part of the seat that held her.

"Leave her alone!" Toria cried.

The guard smiled at her. "Do you want to take her place, yah? You with your highborn ways?"

Horror etched itself across her face, but she forced herself to nod. "Take me instead."

He laughed, the sour stench of his breath filling the cabin. "I've a better idea, yah? How about I take you as well?" He leered at her apprentice. "The speaker won't be back 'til morning, and what a man doesn't know . . ." He shrugged. "You're a bit old for my tastes, but seeing as how you're willing . . ."

Somewhere deep in her chest lay the twisted hope that his end would be particularly painful. Inside her thoughts, a vengeful version of herself waited, hoping circumstances or Aer would allow her to witness the guard's descent into the insanity that would kill him.

Her offer had its intended effect. He reached out, clamped his hands on her shoulders, and backed out of the carriage, turning to shove her toward two other men who stood next to packs. She tried to prolong the fall, strove to keep her balance—her intention to land in the arms of the men and touch one of them, masking the use of her gift in the confusion.

But the ground betrayed her and she fell short. Springing to her feet she ran, her shoulders swinging back and forth as she tried to negotiate the uneven footing without the use of her arms. Curses, more annoyed than angry, filled the air behind her. When she looked back, the man who'd entered the carriage plowed after her, gaining with each stride.

She ground her teeth in frustration. With the speaker gone, only three men guarded them, and she'd already disabled one. When the sounds of his panting came from just behind her, she dropped to the ground, curling into a ball. The ruse, as old as time, worked. The man, caught by surprise, tripped over her, kicking her in the ribs before he went tumbling down the hill.

She gasped for breath, pulling air against the spots that swam in her vision, and ran along the ridge. Curses from the direction of the carriage fell on her ears like benedictions. In less than a minute, hands grabbed her from behind, and she squirmed, pretending to try and break free but fighting to reach the bare skin of the man's arm with the finger she'd poked through the hole in the leather sack.

He lifted her from behind by her wrists, and she gasped in pain, fearing her shoulders would pop from their sockets. Straining, she reached.

And fell into the man's mind. She ignored the allure of his past, rushing along the stream until she came to his wellspring, where she thrust the memories of Lelwin's rape in among the man's own.

And came to herself, kicking and screaming until the man punched her hard enough force the air from her lungs. She collapsed, curled around the pain in her middle as she strained to breathe. When the spots cleared, the man stood above her with his hands balled into fists.

"Get up. If you make me carry you back to the carriage, you'll regret it." He aimed a kick at her side that sent her rolling, trying to dodge. She ended up on her stomach. With awkward jerking motions, she pulled her legs beneath her and stood.

The first guard crested the hill, but the second waved him away. "You heard the speaker, Lemm. We don't touch her, and we don't let her touch us."

"I'm not going to touch all of her, Kruin, just a few bits here and there, yah?"

The man who stood over her, Kruin, pulled a wicked-looking hooked knife and gestured toward the first man with it. "Wrong answer."

Lemm gave a curt nod and a glare for Toria that carried threats. "When the speaker's done with you, I'll make your acquaintance, yah? Then it won't matter what Kruin says."

She walked toward the carriage, angling for the third man, who busied himself with the horses, working to get them unhitched. She pretended to stumble then regain her balance, carrying her a few paces to the right. If she could fall his way, she might be able to touch him before they bundled her back into the carriage.

Five paces from her goal, the third guard shifted, moving to the other side of the horses without ever looking in her direction. She watched him shift beyond her reach with her heart falling into her stomach. Kruin shoved her toward the open door of the carriage.

She stopped, playing for time. "I need water."

Instead of answering, he pointed to her prison with his dagger. She clambered up and in, seating herself between the open door and Lelwin. Anyone who came for her apprentice would have to move her first. She prayed it would be the third man.

But Kruin closed the door, and no one came.

Lelwin looked at her expectantly. Toria shook her head. "I managed two but couldn't touch the other." Lelwin's eyes widened, and Toria sighed. "We shall see."

The sky darkened, and they waited, listening for any sound from outside the carriage that would signal Lemm's or Kruin's insanity.

"How long?" Lelwin whispered.

"I don't know. I've only done this once before, and that was a long time ago. From what Cesla told me, it's more of an art than a science."

Screams jolted Toria awake, pulling her from dreams where she tried to run but couldn't seem to lift her legs. The cries outside the carriage scaled upward in pitch and volume until Toria sought to cover her ears. Other voices screamed in response, calling, but Lemm ignored them. A crash into the side of the carriage brought her heart to her throat, but a moment later the screams receded.

Then she heard the scream fall away, the cry of Lemm's insanity interrupted at intervals as he fell down the hillside for the second time that day. Then they grew fainter still. Cursing outside the carriage accompanied the approach of light, and she blinked against the sudden glare when someone flung open the door.

Kruin stood glaring at her, torch in one hand and knife in the other. "This is your doing."

She shifted, turning on the bench so that she could defend herself with her feet at need but knowing the gesture was pointless. Kruin could simply grab her and beat her into submission.

"Think carefully, Kruin," she stalled. "I'm still bound. You've been told not to let me touch you, but Lemm is out there screaming and he'll scream until he dies. Do I have to touch you? Choose your next course of action well. If you let both of us go right now, perhaps you will survive."

He blinked, his face compressing like a man experiencing a sudden and unexpected pain.

She shifted, moving to the side so that Kruin could see Lelwin's face behind her. "Perhaps not," Toria said as his mouth opened, stretching in horror at the sight of her apprentice. The torch fell, guttering on the ground, but Kruin was no longer there to pick it up. A second set of screams broke the silence of the night into shards.

Freedom beckoned to her beyond the open door. The last guard would be chasing after his companions. She and Lelwin could slip away under cover of darkness. South. Yes, they would head south. The farther they got from the forest, the better.

The last guard appeared in the doorway of the carriage, lit from the side by his torch. The play of shadows and light across his face gave him the aspect of a ghoul. He put the point of his sword to Toria's chest. "This is the end of the road. When the speaker returns, we ride on horseback from here. If you speak, if you run, if you try to touch me, I will kill you."

CHAPTER 48

Pellin rode between Mark and Allta, the two men sworn to guard him, contemplating his tenure as Eldest of the Vigil. How could one man accumulate so much trouble in such a short period of time? But as soon as that thought entered his mind, he rebuked it. Assuming culpability that didn't belong to him was no different than trying to absolve himself from all blame. It was a snare and a temptation that carried its own peril. No, the events since Elwin's passing could not be laid at his feet. Whatever had escaped the forest had done so before he had become Eldest.

Still, that was not to say his short term in leadership had been without mistakes. Even now, he had no idea what to do about the newest member of the Vigil. Willet Dura's blundering ignorance threatened himself and those around him, but at the same time his intuitive and innovative use of his gift offered glimmers of hope for their situation.

He darted a glance at his guard. Allta rode with one hand on the reins and the other pressed against his side, protecting his cracked ribs. The yards of cloth that bound them couldn't keep the pace they set from aggravating the injury. "Can't we go faster?"

Allta shook his head. "Another mile or so, Eldest. Even with the extra horses, we have to give them occasional rest or we'll lose them."

Pellin ground his teeth at the delay. They'd looped around to the southeast away from the Darkwater, moving as fast as their horses would allow, until they'd reached the next village. After finding no sign of Bronwyn or Toria, he'd delved a couple of the villagers and found no taint of the Darkwater.

"Where are we going, Eldest?" Mark asked.

Pellin pulled himself from his frustration long enough to notice that his apprentice rarely addressed him without the use of his title since the village. What had happened to soften Mark's cynicism? "We're going to the farm."

Even without looking he could feel Allta's gaze upon him. "Eldest, the growth of the Darkwater or some other enemy must have overtaken them."

"We have to be sure," Pellin said, "and if not, they may have information for us, but if the forest has taken them then at the very least we owe them a quick death."

Mark shook his head in obvious frustration at their exchange. "Who's at the farm?"

Pellin looked to his guard. "Allta, tell him. He should hear it from you."

With a nod, Allta slowed his horse until he fell in next to Mark. "Vigil guards aren't like those they serve," he began. "We don't live any longer than normal, and most of us don't die in the service of the Vigil."

"You live for it," Pellin said. "That's more important."

Allta dipped his head at the compliment. "Vigil guards do not pass on their gifts to ready-made apprentices as members of the Vigil do. Instead, we retain our gift until we die, trusting that when it goes free, Aer will direct it to its proper destination and provide us with a replacement. We look for those with pure gifts and a certain turn of mind."

"Apprentices," Mark said.

"Just so," Allta nodded. "Not every apprentice works out, but once in a great while we find someone unexpected to take up the mantle. Rory is one such. Vigil guards who have retired usually return to the village or city of their youth, but often, by the time our task is over we have no family or friends to return to. Though we are too old to render our former service, we find the habit of duty has been too deeply ingrained to surrender it."

"You have them farm?" Mark asked. "You can get food anywhere."

Allta smiled. "The farm is at the edge of the Darkwater. The duty of those who have retired is to watch the boundary and report any change to the Vigil and the heads of the church."

Pellin watched his apprentice, waiting to see if he would make the connection between Allta's words and their flight from danger. Above all, those in the Vigil had to be able to think.

"But the forest has already leapt its boundary," Mark said, looking to Pellin. "That means something may have happened to the men at the farm."

His apprentice eyed the ground beneath his horse's feet. Generous distributions of silver had procured two horses for each of them. They'd ridden without ceasing, skirting the edge of the forest, hoping for some sign of the rest of the Vigil. Mark peered at the scrubby grass here at the eastern edge of the Sundered Hills with concentrated focus. He shook his head. "Do you see a sign, Eldest?"

"No. It's easier with trees. The discoloration of the leaves is immediate and obvious against a backdrop of healthy green. Grass can be a dozen different colors and perfectly healthy." He lifted his head, squinting in the distance where the Sundered Hills dropped toward the rolling plains at the southern tip of the forest. "Losing the men at the farm would be bad, but Aer help us if Bronwyn or Toria has spent a night within the boundary of the Darkwater."

Mark cocked his head with the exaggerated curiosity of youth. "Has anyone ever been healed from a vault, Eldest?"

"N . . . only one," he stuttered, remembering. "Queen Cailin survived the breaking of her vault."

Mark's eyes widened. "Queen Cailin? Out of how many?"

"Across the entire history of the Vigil it would be only in the hundreds"—he shook his head in disgust—"but we've easily matched that in the last few months."

"I wonder what made Cailin different," Mark said. "How were you able to break her vault without destroying her mind?"

"Not me," Pellin said with a shake. "Dura."

"He must have done something different," Mark said.

He sighed. How many levels of failure would he have to endure as the Vigil's Eldest? "I don't know. That Cailin survived the breaking of her vault may have nothing to do with Willet Dura at all."

A thought struck him, and he straightened in his saddle. "In fact, it's much more likely that Queen Cailin never had a vault and that Dura only thought he saw one."

Mark cocked his head. "Is it that easy to misread what you see?"

"No, but Willet Dura has his own vault. And even outside of that . . . " He stopped, groping for words. "There is something within Lord Dura's mind that at times skews his perceptions. He sees things and people that aren't there."

"Because he has a vault?"

Pellin shook his head. "No, thank Aer. I think this behavior has a more prosaic cause. I have met a few men like Willet before. What he feels, he feels deeply. I have no way to characterize such a trait within the boundaries of the exordium other than to ascribe it to a temperament of passion. Yet even that falls short because those who possess it often display it as compassion. Such men or women, with the right gift and talent, have marked the pages of history with their presence. They are our greatest healers and monarchs."

Mark caught his gaze. "But not soldiers."

"No," Pellin said, "not soldiers. Dura came back from the war as broken as any man and probably more so. There are many traits I admire about him, but there is a glamour within his mind."

Mark's brows furrowed over his youthful face. "A what?"

Pellin shook his head with a soft chuckle. "My apologies, Mark. I'm an old man and sometimes I use old words. A *glamour* is a vision or enchantment. For Willet, it's a protective mechanism that allows him to function in spite of the horrors war inflicted upon him."

"Eldest," Allta called, "I think we can run them a bit before we switch mounts."

His bones ached with every year he'd gathered over the long centuries, but he nodded and dug his heels into his horse.

An hour later, they rode down a long gentle slope that began as hardy scrub belonging to the Sundered Hills and ended in the verdant green of pasture. To the northeast, a thin stream meandered through the softly rolling landscape, winding its way toward a farmstead tucked into a notch where the pasture and the hills met.

Mark pointed to a smudge of black that lay like a bank of storm clouds where the sky met the earth to the north. "Is that . . . ?"

Pellin nodded. "That's the forest. It's a bit deceptive. There's at least a mile of perfectly healthy woods before you come to the true Darkwater . . . or there was." He pointed down the slope toward the farm where a pair of men pitched hay into a broad, low barn, their movements deliberate with age. "Let's see what they can tell us."

Allta nodded. "They look hale enough. I hope it's so."

A hundred paces away, the men looked up to see them coming. One of them departed, moving with a pronounced limp to return with a pair of longbows.

Mark cleared his throat. "Um, Eldest?"

"They're concerned," Pellin said, "and rightly so. Their farm is somewhat isolated, after all. And they don't recognize us yet."

The men nocked arrows and drew, but at twenty paces the man on the left shifted his bow to peer at Allta, squinting with rheumy eyes. "Is that you, boy?"

Allta's mouth pulled to one side. "Aye, Etgar, it's me."

He lowered his bow, then nudged the man next to him. "It's Pellin—he's Eldest now. Put your bow down, Orin."

Orin tensed instead. "How do we know we can trust him?" He waved the bow. "How do we know we can trust any of them?"

Etgar reached out to put a hand on Orin's shoulder, but the other man jerked away, his eyes wide and darting. His draw hand started to tremble with the effort of keeping the bow drawn. Without seeming to move, Allta positioned himself in front of Pellin, his sword drawn.

With a snarl, Orin pulled and loosed.

Pellin had just enough time to hear the twang of the bow before a weight hit him from the side. Allta's sword flashed and the world tilted in his vision as he fell. The earth rushed to meet him, and air exploded from his lungs with the impact. He blinked, struggling to focus, and saw Etgar and Allta wrestling Orin.

A knife appeared in Allta's hand. Pellin pulled enough air into his aching lungs to croak, "Wait."

Allta reversed his grip on the dagger and struck Orin across the temple hard enough to stun him.

Pellin rolled to his knees, blinking against the spots in his vision. The muscles in his gut finally relaxed enough for him to draw a decent breath. Mark offered him a hand, which he accepted with a nod and pulled himself to his feet.

"I'm sorry, Eldest," Etgar said. "I don't know what's gotten into him."

He nodded, but his attention remained on the old man on the ground. "How long has he been like this?"

Etgar shrugged. "You know he's always been—"

"No," Pellin interrupted. "I know what he was like, and it was never like this. How long?"

Etgar swallowed. "A week or so . . . He came back from scouting the forest, mumbling to himself and starting at every noise like a thief."

"Professional thieves don't actually do that," Mark said.

Pellin waved a hand at his apprentice. "Not now. Let's get Orin into the cabin." He looked at Etgar. "Tie him up."

Pellin and Mark followed as Allta and Etgar half-carried, half-dragged Orin across the hard-packed earth of the barnyard toward the small cottage. Inside, they pulled a chair from the simple trestle table and poured Orin into it. Allta stood guard while Etgar fetched rope. A few moments later, bound hand and foot to the chair, Orin rolled his head back and forth as he struggled toward consciousness.

With a gesture, Allta brought a stool and Pellin seated himself in front of the former Vigil guard while Allta and Etgar took up positions at Orin's left and right. "Orin, can you hear me?"

"Aye," the man said through a squint. "I told you we couldn't trust them. We can't trust any of them."

"Orin," Pellin said. "How long ago did you last scout the boundary of the forest?"

As if the question had the power to return a portion of his sanity, Orin stilled, regaining a bit of the stoicism Vigil guards were known for. "Three weeks ago."

Pellin looked to Etgar, who nodded. "That's about right. Here on the farm the days have a way of running together."

"What did you see?" Pellin asked Orin.

Orin's face closed, twisting until his eyes were slits. "What do you care? What do any of you care?" He strained against his bonds until veins stood out on his age-spotted skin.

Pellin sighed as he stood, circling around until he stood behind the guard. The air of the cabin flowed cool across his palm and fingertips. He had just enough time to register the warmth of the weathered, creased skin on the back of Orin's neck before he fell headlong into the delve.

Centuries of experience had honed his ability to sift through a person's memories and emotions to a razor's edge. Though Bronwyn's skill at delving inanimate stone for traces and hints of memory surpassed his, none now living approached his skill in this arena. He picked a thread of Orin's memory, one of the most recent, and stepped into its flow, becoming one with the withered guard.

He stood, one leg crossed over another, leaning against the trunk of an ash sapling as he looked out from between the trees that bordered the Darkwater. Early dawn light lit the landscape with almost horizontal rays from his left, lighting yet another campsite on the banks of the river. Packhorses, short and sturdy, built for work rather than speed, grazed without concern.

He stood, musing for nearly half an hour as the men below roused themselves. Moments later they were panning the stream where the water tumbled over a series of shallow rapids. After mere minutes had passed, one of the men thrust his fist aloft, yelling his excitement over the find he clutched in his hand.

"There's never been gold in the Darkwater," he muttered to himself.

Across the field, the men scrambled, panning the stream with the energy only men taken by gold lust could know. He shook his head in resignation. Too many people had started to come to the Darkwater what with the sentinels gone and only their rumor left to keep the curious at bay. Now he would have to hurry back to the farm and send a carrier bird to Cynestol. Another one. His last had either gotten lost or Pellin had yet to see the message.

With his free hand he rubbed his backside in anticipation of the long ride back, his glance falling on the leaves of the sapling that helped him stay upright.

For long, long moments he couldn't breathe. Then, with a savage ripping motion, he stripped the nearest stem of its leaves. They fell through his trembling fingers, drifting downwind on the breeze to land on the wet ground where they mocked him.

"No, no, no," he pleaded. "I checked last night. I always check." He stepped away from the trunk, grasping the nearest branch and pulling it down to eye level, but his petitions died on his tongue. Spots of black discolored every leaf. He moved to each tree around his meager campsite to find all of them similarly diseased.

Pellin released the memory and searched through the rest of the old guard's mind for the vault created when the Darkwater swallowed Orin's camp, but when he found it he paused. Orin's vault, the black scroll that infected all taken by the Darkwater, wavered in his vision. When he reached out to take it, the edges of the scroll glided across his touch like threads of gossamer.

With a thought he grasped it, prepared to rip it into smaller and smaller pieces until it no longer existed, but at the last he paused. Perhaps the guard who had served them so long and so well could be saved. If Etgar took him south, away from the threat of the encroaching forest, maybe Orin would return to himself. Pellin had seen his thoughts. Even now Orin's mind fought to rid itself of the Darkwater's poison.

But would he win? He waited, watching the scroll he held. Within Orin's mind time moved at the speed of thought, the space between heartbeats stretching until the pulse of his blood surged like an incoming tide to recede later. He had all the time he needed. In the world outside the use of his gift time passed far more slowly. A half hour in the guards' cabin would seem an eternity here.

After a time in which Pellin could have read Orin's entire life twice and more, the black scroll of his vault pulsed then pulsed again, growing more defined, moving from ephemeral insubstantiality to material definition. Hardening.

He sighed. With a blaze of thought, he tore the scroll into four parts, then ripped those into still smaller pieces, repeating the process until nothing, not even dust, remained.

Pellin lifted his hand and stepped away from the guard who had served him so faithfully and so well. He tried to pray, to intercede with Aer and beg for Orin's life, but the words wouldn't come. Centuries of breaking vaults had taught him hopelessness. Yet Orin deserved better than his mute surrender. With no words of his own, he recited the penitent's appeal from the liturgy.

Orin's head had dipped, and though his chest rose and fell with mechanical regularity, his eyes were closed and his mouth was slack.

"I'm sorry, Etgar," he said. "He camped on the edge of the Darkwater."

Etgar nodded, the bare skin on the top of his head catching the light. "So he said."

Pellin nodded, knowing as well what Orin hadn't said. "The Darkwater grew during the night, enveloping his camp. When he woke the next morning, the leaves on the trees around him bore marks of the disease."

Etgar put his other hand on Orin's shoulder, the gesture protective, even defiant. "That's not possible. The Darkwater doesn't grow."

"Not often," Pellin agreed, "but it does and it has again."

"It's true," Allta said. "We came from a village in the Sundered Hills that had been engulfed."

"I delved a half dozen of the villagers, Etgar," Pellin said. "Every one of them had a vault, but not one of them had any memory of going to the forest."

He turned to Allta. "We have to ride the boundary west. We need to find Toria and Bronwyn and warn them of the forest's growth."

Orin's head lolled to one side, and his eyes opened, the stare glassy, the same as every other soul Pellin had broken.

CHAPTER 49

For three days Bronwyn tracked the men from the marketplace, which was to say Balean and Fess tracked them—searching them out each evening in the villages where they stopped, careful to avoid being seen, while she waited for one or the other to return. Each night, Fess kept watch over whatever inn the men chose to frequent, waiting until they left at dawn, making their way north toward the Darkwater.

She sighed. All of which meant her apprentice spent each day sleeping in his saddle. She glanced to her right to see a thatch of windblown blond hair ruffling in the breeze, as though Fess's head were waving to her while he slept. He never complained, but she could tell the long nightly watches were taking their toll.

A flare of light flashed across her vision, and unbidden, a door into memory opened, flooding her with memories that mingled with her own and confused her sense of self. "No," she breathed. "Not now. Not yet."

Balean looked at her, his expression stoic but resolved.

She tried to wave his concern and the memories away, but they washed over her, uncaring of her pleas or needs, and her mind became a maelstrom of conflicting emotions. A man, her husband of twenty years, lay in a sickbed, and she stood accused. She lifted hands so scarred they resembled claws, thrust them at her accusers, forcing them to see.

"No!" She thrust the memory back behind the door. "That's not me!"

As soon as she did so another memory took its place, a recollection that bloomed in her consciousness from that same long-locked door, an image that carried fire and agony. With a scream she threw her arms up

387

to ward off pain from hundreds of years before. Falling. She was falling, but the sensation warred with the memory that painted a picture of her husband, jealous and raging, forcing her hands to hold burning coals for touching another.

Bronwyn forced her eyes open, saw her guard, Balean, and her apprentice, Fess, gazing at her in helplessness.

Their mouths were moving, working to make themselves heard, but she couldn't untangle their words from the wash of memory and pain. She gazed at a blue autumn sky past Balean's face and lifted her hand to block the light. She curled and opened her fingers, searching for scars and burns, but they were merely old, wrinkled and veined. She clutched at their reality, forcing the memories back behind the door.

Within her mind she slammed it shut, then locked it. She became conscious of her guard holding her, and with the feeble struggles of an old woman she made her intentions known to him.

He placed her feet on the ground, and the touch of earth beneath her feet served to further steady her mind and thoughts. She drew a shuddering breath and paused to survey their surroundings. Rolling hills stretched away to the north, east, and west, flattening somewhat to the south, and copses of cedar and pine dotted the hollows where wind had gathered the seeds over the years. "Where are we?"

"Some leagues yet from the southernmost tip of the Darkwater, Lady Bronwyn," Balean said, pointing to the north. "Our prey seem to be exercising more care in their movements the closer we get to the forest."

Partly out of intent, but more out of necessity, she lowered herself to sit on the ground, motioning Balean and Fess to join her. Her guard paused to stake the horses, ever conscious of the practicalities of their mission.

"Are you well, Lady Bronwyn?" Fess asked.

She smiled. One of his teeth had a slight chip to it. Strange that she hadn't noticed it before. And his eyes, blue, had a way of catching the reflected light from the grass to cast a greenish tint. "No, child, I'm not."

The horses secured, Balean sat with them, completing the triangle but still managing to convey the impression of watchfulness.

"My doors are weakening, Balean," she said.

He nodded, his face so still it sent a foreboding chill shooting down her spine. "How long?" he asked.

"I don't know, but not long. They're coming faster and harder than they usually do."

"Is it the splinter?" Fess asked.

She nodded, though she would have saved Balean from the admission if she could have. "Yes. I can sense it drifting through my mind, weakening the doors and walls I've spent centuries building to keep the memories at bay, but I can't grasp it." She lifted her hands, grateful to see them unscarred. "It's like trying to grip water."

"What about Pellin?" Fess asked. "Could he go into your mind and destroy the splinter?"

"Possibly," she answered truthfully. "But we may not be able to get to him in time, and we've never had to fight the taint of the Darkwater in ourselves before. He might not know what to do." She focused her attention on Fess. As a Vigil guard, Balean had been trained, taught from his first day the necessity of what might come. "There might not *be* anything he can do." She leaned forward to place her hand on the boy's knee, grateful for the fabric of his trousers that kept her gift at bay. "Fess, do you truly wish to be one of the Vigil?"

To his credit, he didn't answer right away. He stilled until he might have been one of their guards. Yet even motionless as he became, his eyes conveyed the energy of his thoughts. "I don't know."

"If we cannot reach Cynestol in time, you must," Balean said with finality.

Bronwyn stared at her guard in shock. Though he had never been as stoic in his demeanor as Allta, Balean had come close, speaking rarely, and he had never presumed to issue orders to anyone in her presence. His deference to her had become the bedrock of their relationship.

Fess's mouth twitched, but his ever-present smile failed to materialize. "Must? Is it not the right of any apprentice to relinquish his trade if he so desires and seek a new one?"

Balean cut the air with one hand in denial. "Word games will not avail us," he said to Fess. "The Vigil stands at four, perhaps less. If another of the gifts goes free, how will it ever be found? You *must* take it."

Bronwyn suppressed another shock. Not only did her guard repeat his command, but he had done so without a single glance in her direction.

Fess's smile manifested itself at last, but his eyes hardened until they became agates. "What if I have no wish to live for centuries? What if I am not willing?"

Again Balean refused to look at her, and with a start she realized her guard considered her passing to be a foregone conclusion. "Do you think you have the right to refuse? The gift came to Willet Dura in his ignorance."

"Balean." Bronwyn lifted her hand for silence. Even to her own ears her voice sounded weak, but it was loud enough, for she saw Fess begin to turn to her before Balean gave a savage jerk of his head, dismissing her interruption.

"The Vigil must endure," he said. "Lady Bronwyn has accumulated hundreds of years of wisdom and a thousand lifetimes of knowledge. What is your willingness compared to that?"

Her apprentice's face hardened, an expression that didn't—and never should—appear natural on him. Deep in her chest, her shock at Balean's behavior changed into anger on her own behalf and Fess's. With a lurch she leaned toward her guard and struck him openhanded.

He saw the blow coming, had to have seen it. He held a physical gift that few could match, and the struggles in her mind had left her weak. She saw his eyes widen a fraction and follow the path of her hand all the way to his cheek. Both men stared at her in shock, especially Fess who lifted a hand to touch his face.

"I'm not dead yet! Listen to me!" She hadn't meant to cry, but tears choked her words. She shook her head, scattering them to the ground as if they opposed her. "I will not force the gift on another." She spat the words at her guard, who sat before her with all the response of a statue. "The road is too long and difficult for one to take it up unwillingly." She turned to Fess. "To you, Fess, the gift is offered freely. It is your choice to accept or reject it. It is much like the gift of Aer himself."

Fess saw through her argument as soon as the words left her mouth. "I don't think Willet would agree with you."

She straightened. Even when he wasn't present, the reeve had a way of turning her accustomed beliefs on their head. "There have been other exceptions in the Vigil's long history, Fess. I can only attribute them to the hand of Aer."

He smirked. "The books you gave me to read say that Aer regards all His children equally."

She nodded. "Yes, they say that, but that is not all they say. The rules contained within the exordium of the liturgy apply to all men and women, but that doesn't mean they apply to Aer. Does the craftsman require permission of his work to display it with honor or use it for some more humble purpose?"

Fess reached out to cup her cheek, the touch soft as a brush from a feather. "Or destroy it, Mother?"

The use of the name for her that he'd kept locked away in his mind brought fresh tears to her eyes, and she swallowed, struggling to control her voice. "Does the creator need permission from his creation to say that he's done with it and must craft a replacement?"

His hand came away from her face, leaving her skin exposed to the chill of the wind. "He sounds like a hard taskmaster. I don't know if I want to serve Him."

Grief caught her unaware. Her stomach and chest ached to hold the boy, beg him to change his mind, not about receiving the gift, but about the nature of Aer. Instead she nodded, though every muscle in her body cried out to enfold him. "I understand, and many times through the long years, I have thought the same, my child." She could see his surprise at her words by the way his eyes widened and he gaped at her.

She cupped his face in return and nodded. "Sometimes the task is hard, Fess, but I don't believe the taskmaster to be." She struggled to rise to her feet. "In the end, there is little choice. If we cannot find grace from our creator, where shall we find it?"

Even to her own ears, her logic sounded weak. Was her sole reason for serving Aer because there was no alternative? The doors in her mind holding countless memories locked away threatened to burst and drown her identity. She reeled with the effort but forced herself to hold on a little longer, if for no other reason than in the hope of finding a better answer for Fess.

"Come," she said as she pulled her shoulders back and forced a measure of steel into her spine. "My infirmity has cost us too much time already. If we are to discover the purpose of our enemies, we must track them to their destination first."

She walked back to her horse with the stiff-legged strides of a marionette and climbed into the saddle, refusing Balean's aid. Her affliction would countenance no show of weakness. She clutched the reins as if she could wring strength from them.

They rode through the rest of the day, careful to keep at least two hills between them and those they tracked, but as the sun descended, misgiving filled her heart. They were nowhere near the next village. "Balean!" She barked his name with as much authority as she could muster. "Fess will remain with me as my guard. Track them as closely as you dare without being seen. I want to know if they intend on camping or continuing in the dark."

She held her hand out, palm forward, as he began to object. "I need to counsel my apprentice." The weight of her collected memories pulled at her so that she longed for the oblivion of sleep. "Time is not our friend here." When he still made no move to obey, she allowed her head to dip a fraction. "Please."

Bronwyn waited until the muted sound of hooves on thick turf faded behind her before she released enough of the iron she'd forced into her spine to sit as Fess staked the horses. Then he came and sat before her, his expression open and expectant but not demanding, content to wait. A warm breeze from the south ruffled his hair, and from long ago in her own past, far enough back that the memory came from her own youth, she recalled another young man who favored Fess in both looks and demeanor.

"Are you well, Lady Bronwyn?"

She smiled at him and her memory, but sadness touched it and her eyes welled. "Do you want to know something strange, Fess? I have lived so long that everyone I meet reminds me of at least a dozen other people I've met before."

He grinned, the expression bright and clear as spring wine. "Even urchins like me?"

She laughed softly. "They weren't urchins, but they were like you, young men or women who reveled in each breath life had to give them no matter their circumstances. Most of them had your smile." As soon as the words left her mouth, she knew what her decision must be. Aer forgive her, she would not go into eternity with this on her conscience as well. "When my time comes, I want you to get as far away from me as you can, Fess. Run. Hide so that Balean cannot bring you within arm's reach. Let the gift go free and pass to someone else."

He started, rocking back where he sat. "Lady Bronwyn?"

Unexpected grief, centuries of it, wracked her where she sat. She never saw Fess move, but the clasp of his arms enfolded her and she buried her face into his neck. Even in this, she did not feel awkwardness in his embrace. Even now, he remained perfectly comfortable in her presence.

"I can't!" she sobbed. "I won't let the gift take the light from your eyes, turn you into me." She knew her words didn't make sense. "The world needs people like you. We need men and women who light the room with their smile. We need to see people who remind us that life can be joy. You greet each moment as a new friend. We need that. Aer have mercy on us, we're desperate for it!"

He never answered but held her until the storm of her grief ran its course, gales of weeping that finally subsided. Fess waited until she pushed herself away and helped her to stand. When she scrubbed her eyes so that she could see, the light of day had gone, replaced by the deep charcoal of dusk.

Fess pointed to the hillside north of them. "Balean is coming back."

Her guard topped the hill and came toward them at a canter, his face grim even by Vigil standards. He flowed out of the saddle before the horse had come to a stop. "They've made camp, Lady Bronwyn, but their behavior is puzzling. While the light of day lasted they did as one would expect, staking the horses and readying a small fire, but when the last ray faded, a change came over them." He stopped, searching for words.

"What sort of change?" Bronwyn asked.

He shook his head. "It's hard to describe, but their movements appeared different—quick and jerky, and then lithe, almost as if they were gifted."

"I think you witnessed the transition between their waking mind and their vault." She pulled in a breath, her former grief displaced by frustration.

Fess stepped away from her, moving to his horse with decisive strides. He donned a dark hood and cloak, pausing to wrap a strip of cloth over one eye.

"You need eyes in the dark, Lady Bronwyn," he said as he rejoined her and Balean. Then he grinned, pointing to the eye covered by the strip of cloth. "I can give you one, anyway."

Her heart lurched in her chest, but she stifled the order that would have kept him safe. The world could not afford her timidity, and Fess, as an experienced thief, would have a better chance of scouting their prey while remaining unseen than she or Balean. "Keep your distance, apprentice. That's not a request."

He smiled as if she'd paid him a compliment. "Yes, milady." He turned to Balean. "Where are they?"

Her guard nodded. "Three hills over, in a valley where a river branches into two smaller streams."

Fess was barely out of earshot before her guard turned to her. "Will he accept the gift?" His tone carried the resolution of a man prepared to enforce his will.

She met his gaze without flinching. "We spoke and my instructions were clear. Fess knows exactly what to do when my time comes." She turned away then, unwilling to endure his scrutiny. "I need to rest. Wake me when he returns."

CHAPTER 50

A hand on Bronwyn's shoulder brought her from sleep, and she rose, searching for the familiar surroundings of her home in Caisel before she managed to pull the threads of memory together. Balean and Fess knelt by her in the first wan light of predawn, their faces somber.

"It took us a while to wake you, Lady Bronwyn," Balean said. "Are you well?"

She checked the doors within her mind, found them closed for the moment, though she could sense pressure building behind each of them, as though the memories contained within had at last grown restless with their long imprisonment. The mental fatigue that had weighed on her since they were attacked in Havenwold and she had been infected returned, and she longed for strong tea. There would be none. "Well enough," she said.

"You spoke strangely in your sleep, milady," Balean said.

She had no response to give him that would ease his concern or her own. "What of those men?" she asked Fess.

"It's strange, Lady Bronwyn. They're sleeping now, at the exact spot I found them when I first set out last night."

"Why strange?"

"Because during the hours of darkness they roamed all through the valley with their horses." He gave his head a little shake. "I don't know how many leagues they covered, but they led me a merry little adventure. We might have gone north another four or five leagues before they returned." He leaned forward. "Lady Bronwyn, they returned to the exact same spot of ground they left."

"Did they see you?"

His blond hair fluttered a bit with his denial. "No. There was enough moonlight for me to see by without getting close. I kept to the ridge to the west. Even in daylight anyone would have been hard-pressed to see me lying on the ground."

"With their vaults open, they would have killed him if they had," Balean added.

"Curious," Bronwyn said. "What did they do?"

"I'm not sure," Fess said. "There wasn't enough light to see clearly, but they stopped at various spots along the river for a few moments before continuing on toward the north."

A suspicion grew in her mind. "Do you remember these locations?"

At his nod, she glanced east to where the first hint of orange showed on the horizon. "Then let us ride north as quickly as we can."

They circled around the valley where the men slept and rode at a canter that ate up the miles until they came to the most remote spot the men had visited the night before. From her vantage point atop her horse she could see past the broad plain and the shallow streams that wound their way through it to the horizon.

"I didn't realize we were so close." She pointed to a smudge of charcoal at the limit of her sight. Doubtless Balean and Fess would be able to see it more clearly. "There lies the Darkwater—the forbidden forest." She sighed. "Lead on, Fess. I have a suspicion of what we will find, but we must be sure."

Fess took them to a spot on the bank of the westernmost stream, his gaze fixed on the ground. "There," he said after he'd backtracked over the same ground twice. "That's where they stopped, but I was too far away to make out what they did here."

She nodded, then shifted her weight in preparation to dismount—but dizziness hit her like a wave. The doors in her mind wavered, became nearly insubstantial before firming again.

Clenching the barrel of her horse, she pointed instead. "Look for silver or gold in the stream. They may have thrown it, but it's shallow enough here to see."

Balean and Fess dismounted and separated, one moving south of the hoofprints, the other moving north. Silence descended and lasted all of two minutes before both men waded into different parts of the stream to thrust their hands into the water. They brought their finds to her, depositing heavy yellowish lumps the size of her thumbnail into her palm. The morning light hit the nuggets, revealing a slight bluish tinge, and weight matching the metal in her palm descended on her heart.

"Gold." Fess breathed the word almost as if it were too holy to be uttered. "The forbidden metal."

"No," she corrected. "Aurium is forbidden, gold is not. Though few outside the nobility would know the difference." She shook her head in disgust. "It's just very rare. Our enemy is more subtle of thought than I imagined."

"If there's gold in the Darkwater streams, Lady Bronwyn, why would those men hunt for it at night?" Fess shook his head as he saw the flaws in his own question. "It's stranger than that. Why would they hunt for gold only when their vaults were open when it was obvious that this was their intention even during the daytime?"

"Your experience as a thief is keeping you from the most obvious conclusion," she said. She tried to muster a smile, but the proximity of the forest precluded it. She held her hand out toward Fess, tilting her palm so that it caught the early morning light. "See the bluish tinge to the nuggets?" She hefted the gold in her palm. "This came from the mountains north of Frayel. They weren't hunting for gold, they were planting it."

"Why?"

She took in both of the men with her glance. "You're too young to have witnessed a rush. The last one happened two hundred years ago in the wastes far north of Collum. Silver and gold carry madness with them, Fess. The idea that wealth can be had for the effort of picking stones out of a stream spreads like a fever, and tales of riches that grow with the telling infect the continent."

She paused to look at the forest. "Thousands upon thousands of people flood into the area, searching for it. Our enemy understands human nature quite well, it seems. To overcome the fear of the Darkwater he must pit it against an even stronger emotion, and there is none more powerful than the lust for gold."

"But why are these men throwing away the gold they've already got?" Fess asked. "It's pointless."

"Oh no," she said. "It's fiendishly brilliant and only the evil of the Darkwater could accomplish it. There is no gold in the forest, Fess, and even in the far north of Collum and Frayel it's rare. If those men we followed simply found the gold and spent it in secret, there would be no gold rush." She turned to face him squarely. "Whatever is in the forest is trying to lure thousands of people inside."

He frowned, still unable to put the pieces together. She waited, watching as confusion flitted back and forth across his features.

When he looked up, exhilaration and horror fought for expression. "Those men don't know they're planting gold they already had." His brows furrowed. "But that means they traveled all the way here without realizing they had the gold with them."

"Their minds are split," she said. "The vault within their minds allows the evil to use them to its own ends." She nodded. "My guess is that each time they return to their village, they spend a little bit of the gold they've found. In time the secret will surely leak out and the flood will begin." She pointed. "By then the gold will lead them and everyone else like a beacon into the forest." She saw her guard and her apprentice gazing at her—one stoic as always, but horrified fascination filled Fess's face. "In a single night, the evil of the Darkwater will own a hundred men, perhaps a thousand. In a fortnight there will be an army to dwarf the one we fought during Bas-solas, men and women who will move as if they were gifted."

"We have to stop them," Fess breathed.

A weight of despair settled into her chest. Fess was right, of course, but he had no idea the breadth of the task he'd announced on their behalf. The south side of the forest spanned nearly a hundred leagues and the rivers flowing out of the Darkwater split into dozens upon dozens of streams in the six kingdoms.

As if she were lifting a weight, she squared her shoulders and pointed to the stream. "Then let us begin where we can. Scour this stream for any more gold and then we will move to the other spots. If we take away the gold, the enemy's schemes will fail to take root. You remember them all?"

His hair floated in the breeze as his head bobbed with the earnestness of his assent. "Won't we run into those men?"

398

"Assuredly," she said, turning to Balean. "In the daylight they will be no match for you. Be quick."

When she looked back to Fess, she wanted to weep at the expression in his eyes, a look alloyed of necessity, repulsion, and regret in equal parts. She had no solace to offer or justification that would sound sincere. As a member of the Vigil, she'd worn that same expression more times than she cared to remember.

Unwilling to endure his regard, she took a step toward her horse, perhaps a second, when a lance of pain through her skull brought her to her knees. Balean had his hands beneath her arms before she could pitch forward onto her face.

CHAPTER 51

She blinked, struggling to merge the twin suns that shone in her vision, but the sky spun like a child's pinwheel. Closing her eyes didn't help. When she did, a dozen different sets of memories assaulted her, clamoring for attention.

Who was she?

A face appeared, blocking the sun, and she locked her gaze onto it as she fought to find the surface in the flood of memories.

"Lady Bronwyn."

She struggled to pull the owner's name from the maelstrom that swirled in her head. It wouldn't come.

A dagger appeared in his hand. She twisted, trying to escape, begging her arms and legs to obey her, but they wouldn't move. Her hands and feet twitched in response to her commands. Too many voices in her head vied for their control.

"Lady Bronwyn," the man said in a voice like iron, "what is my name?"

Without knowing why, she knew that to fail to answer meant her death. The man jerked and flinched. The cacophony of the memories subsided enough to allow her to see the blond-haired youth struggling to free himself, his wrist held in a viselike grip in the man's other hand.

"No," the boy yelled. "You can't."

The man shook his head, his face locked in an expression of implacable necessity. "The Vigil must survive."

The boy rained blows on the man as he grappled for the dagger, but his efforts were no more than raindrops striking rock.

"I'm sorry, Lady Bronwyn." He shifted his grip on the dagger, moving with the precision of a surgeon.

"No!" the boy screamed again.

Memories swirled in her head. All of her would die. She could do nothing more than whimper as the man laid the edge of the knife against her neck. Dimly, she became aware of the boy's hand on her, warm and comforting as a summer breeze in winter. Fess. The boy's name was Fess.

The man held his hand there while he struggled, a pup fighting against a wolf. Fess grappled for the dagger at her throat but he might as well have tried to uproot a tree for all the effect he had.

Somewhere in her mind came a memory of being attacked with a dagger, of feeling a hint of cold pressure before a wash of warm blood. The man shifted, not much, but enough to allow her fingers to brush against his skin.

Her mind lashed out as consciousness faded.

She came to, the man still on top of her. Now she would die, but the wash of blood never came. Slowly, the man's eyes emptied, losing their focus.

The clamor of voices in her head subsided enough for her to pull her gaze from the man's empty stare to the boy beside him, his face stricken. With an effort, he pushed the man away, prying loose the fingers that had clamped on his throat.

He was covered in blood.

"Bronwyn," she said, her name coming to her at last.

Sobs racked the boy as he bent to retrieve the blade that had sliced through the arteries of the man's throat. "Fess," she said aloud. "Your name is Fess."

"Are you all right, Lady Bronwyn?"

Somewhere deep inside her mind, she knew he called her by another name. The voices in her head receded a bit more. "My pack. Chiccor root."

Fess disappeared from view, and she resumed her contemplation of the sun. For some reason that seemed like it should be important, the fact that its light kept the voices away comforted her. Fess returned and placed a stick of chiccor root in her mouth. Eating it proved a challenge at first, but as the juice trickled down her throat she found she could chew and swallow more easily. By the time she finished the stick, she found she could sit up.

"Another," she ordered.

"Lady Bronwyn, are you sure?"

She managed a nod, and he surrendered another dose of the stimulant. After the second stick her hands shook and her stomach roiled, threatening to vomit the strong root. She turned her attention inward to the memories that still swirled in her mind, separating them from her own so that she could lock them away.

And failed.

Unbidden, memories of another woman overwhelmed her, and she looked at Fess as blood surged into her cheeks. "You know, you're quite well-favored." She lifted her hands to undo the clasp of her cloak and her next sentence died on her tongue at the sight of the skin covering her hands. How could she be old?

She sifted through the swirl of memories, gathering those that belonged to Bronwyn, clutching them and letting the others continue their mad dance through her mind. "Move," she whispered. "You're blocking the sun."

Fess shifted, and a bright yellow shaft struck her eyes, causing her to squint, but it brought blessed relief. The voices of those she'd delved didn't cease clamoring for her attention, but in direct sunlight she found she could ignore them. For now. With an effort, she pulled her legs beneath her. "Help me stand."

Fess put his hands beneath her arms and lifted her as easily as he would have a child. When had she become so withered?

Her eyes fell on Balean, where he lay on the ground. "Thank you, Balean, for serving me so long and well."

"I didn't mean to kill him," Fess said in a hollow voice. "I didn't, but I couldn't move his hand, and then he just went slack and the dagger hit his throat. I didn't mean to. He was going to kill you."

She nodded. "The Vigil guards call it the last duty, though I doubt Balean ever expected he would have to do it. It's rare, but not unheard of for one of the Vigil to lose control over the memories they've gathered.

When that happens, they are no longer capable of fulfilling their duties, but they can live in such a state for weeks." She shook her head. "I'm dissembling. The truth, Fess, is that my walls are breaking, and soon I will have so many different people running around my head, I won't be able to feed myself. Death is a mercy. Balean knew this, and tried to force you to receive the gift from me."

"What will they do to me, Lady Bronwyn?"

She wanted to tell him she would protect him from the consequences of his actions, but even now she couldn't bring herself to lie. "Don't borrow trouble from the future, Willet."

She shook her head. "I mean Fess. Your name is Fess." She tottered over to her horse, where she rummaged through her pack with trembling hands until she found a collection of small stoppered bottles.

Fess eyed her with suspicion, and she managed a smile. "I have no intention of finishing what Balean tried to start. The chiccor root is effective for now, but I'll need something stronger, especially at night." She lifted a small bottle with a thick brownish liquid inside. "This is much the same, but the distillation is far stronger, if harder on the body."

She glanced upward. The sun hung in the sky toward the south, close to its zenith. "Go, finish gathering the gold those men sowed in the stream." He shook his head, but she waved his objection away. "Let us do what we can, Fess, instead of worrying about what we can't."

Clearly uncertain whether he should go or stay, he finally mounted and rode away, looking back every few seconds. She clung to her horse's saddle for a while before she surrendered to fatigue and sat, letting the sun warm her. A shadow on the ground warned her, and she looked up to see a cloud passing in front of the sun. Then the past took her.

CHAPTER 52

Toria watched daylight fade like the fall of an axe as they continued north. With her hands tied, and her and Lelwin's horses being led by one of the speaker's men, their pace was as slow and deliberate as the march of condemned men to the block.

With the return of the speaker, and with him more men, escape—however unlikely it had been before—was now impossible.

Lelwin, who had not spoken since beginning their journey on horseback, leaned close and asked, "What's going to happen to us?"

For a moment Toria considered dissembling. In truth, she didn't know what would happen to them, but she felt certain their fates would likely be quite different. Any of the possible outcomes seemed to her a living damnation that made death the most hoped-for option.

But she had never shied from the truth, however horrifying she had found it to be, whether within herself or within those she had delved. She could treat her apprentice no differently. "They will try to turn me as they did Laewan. If you had a dagger I would ask you to kill me, but that would be dangerous for you."

"How could I be in any greater danger than I am now?"

Toria sighed. "The gift of domere doesn't want to go free. With my last breath I would pass the gift to you. The evil that has escaped from the Darkwater would turn you through the gift, forcing your service until you died of old age centuries from now or were killed."

Whatever Lelwin might have said in response was cut off as the speaker brought his horse around to ride beside them. "Another day,

404

Toria Deel." He smirked at her, his face bright in the ruddy light of sunset. "You will soon have what you desired. Soon, on the edge of the Darkwater, we will meet the Icon."

Bronwyn drifted in a whirlpool of memories, only occasionally recognizing some of them as her own. During those times she sought to strengthen the rooms within her mind, shoring up walls with stone and banding the thick wooden doors with iron, but as soon as she'd rebuilt one, another would fade into wispy transience. Repairing it, she would return to the first door to find its edges unexpectedly decayed, as though the neglect of thousands of years had eaten away its definition.

The swirl of memories took her again, and she lived the lives of dozens of nobles, merchants, and commons whose guilt or innocence she'd been called upon to confirm. Male and female, old and young, she lived them all. At times one of those she'd touched had been found innocent. She clung to those memories the hardest, finding in their relative innocence an escape from the twisted joys the guilty had experienced.

Light and warmth returned, and with them the ability to reclaim herself. She looked down to see the vial of syrupy brown liquid in her hand. Before time or darkness could undermine her purpose, she pulled the cork and let a small sip flow over her tongue and into her stomach. Her heart shuddered under the onslaught of the drug, fluttered within her chest before finding a quicker rhythm.

The doors in her mind strengthened enough to allow her to reclaim her identity and she stood. How long had she dozed, living other lives? She lifted her eyes, searching for light.

She wasn't alone.

Mounted men surrounded her, still and quiet, as if they'd coalesced out of thin air. She looked for Fess but couldn't see past the horses. Thoughts of fleeing beckoned. Panic put a surge of energy into the muscle and sinew of her legs, but she was in no condition to run or ride at more than a walk. It was doubtful she could even mount up before they were upon her.

Working against her shimmering vison, she tried to count the men but never made it past three. Then she noticed two women behind the others, their hands bound behind them. She pulled her dagger from her belt, holding the pommel against her palm with her thumb and hiding the blade behind her forearm.

Then the women came into focus. *No.*

One of the men dismounted, smiling as though he'd been given an unexpected gift. "Greetings, Lady Bronwyn. I see from your expression you've already made the acquaintance of at least one of my companions." The dying light caught his feral grin, casting it in lurid shades of red, as if his skin could not contain his malice. "All your power has availed you nothing. You who bent kings and queens to your will now find yourself kneeling in the dirt before me, a mere servant of the Icon."

The smile slid from his face, and he snapped his fingers to a man behind him who fell back to hold the point of his dagger to Toria's throat.

"If you do not surrender to me of your own will, I will kill her now and then the girl and then you," he said. "My orders were to deliver any of the Vigil I found—alive, if at all possible, but to deliver you in any case. Toss the knife you're hiding to the ground."

She nodded, making a show of discarding it, and hooked the thumb of her left hand under the glove on her right. "Who are you?"

"I am a speaker for the Clast." His gaze fell to her hands, and his eyes disappeared into the shadow of a scowl as he drew his sword. "Understand this, Lady Bronwyn. I will not allow you to touch any of us. Leave your gloves on and kneel with your hands behind your back."

Toria shook her head, whether in warning or apology, Bronwyn couldn't tell. Where was Fess?

"I said kneel."

She lowered herself to one knee, then noticed the vial of distilled chiccor root in her hand. Quickly, before he could object, she unstopped it and swallowed its contents, emptying the bottle.

His sword trembled with tension. "What did you just swallow?"

A full score of doses hit her system, and her heart hammered drum strokes within her chest. When she tried to wave away his threat, her hands trembled like stalks of grain in a whirlwind. "Only medicine for a very old lady."

One of the other men dismounted and approached her with a leather bag and stout cord. These he used to cover her hands, pulling the cord so that it cut into the flesh around her wrists.

"You see?" the speaker said as he walked over to haul her up to her feet. "I am aware of the threat your touch carries." His face split into a smile, but his eyes glittered. "But as I told your companion, I am in a position to grant you your desire. You wished to meet the Icon of the Clast, and so you shall." He looked north. "In fact, we have but a few miles to journey."

A hint of motion to the south pulled her attention, but she couldn't bring it into focus. *Not Fess*, she prayed to Aer. *Let him escape.*

But the speaker caught her glance and pointed. "Her apprentice. You know what to do."

Then he hoisted her atop her horse and tied it to the others. The last indignity they visited upon her was a foul-smelling gag they tied in place. She couldn't even scream. Overhead, the sun disappeared behind another cloud. On cue, the memories in her mind she could no longer force back behind their doors clamored for her attention. Memories of a thousand men and women tried to break loose from their doors, but the doors held.

For now.

She gripped her horse with her knees as they started forward. The chiccor syrup allowed her some control over her mind, but the splinter from the Darkwater still worked to weaken the other doors. Soon she would be overwhelmed, and no elixir in any amount would afford her relief.

Her heart fluttered, forced past the limits of age and fatigue, struggling to find its rhythm. How long did she have?

It was still night when they stopped. Toria clenched her teeth as she was pulled from her horse and pushed to the ground. But she would not face the Icon, whoever he might be, on her knees. She levered herself to her feet, her eyes hoping that Bronwyn, still on her horse, might acknowledge her, but in the dim moonlight, her friend stared at and through Toria, unseeing, her gaze darting to movement that wasn't there.

The speaker snapped his fingers, and one of the men lifted Bronwyn from her saddle and led her, stumbling, to stand by Toria's side.

"Are you well?" Toria whispered to Bronwyn.

Bronwyn turned to her, her face barely discernable, but Toria could see that her gaze was filled with countless scenes that only she could see.

For a fleeting instant her eyes came into focus, latching on to Toria's face. "My doors are nothing more than mist now."

Toria wanted to weep. Only the wonder of how Bronwyn kept herself upright stopped her. They were undone. She prayed the forms from every order for protection over Pellin and Willet, but doubt and hopelessness ate the words within her mind.

Though clouds moved in to block what little light the moon provided, the speaker made no move to order a torch lit.

"How will your Icon find us if he can't see?" She waited with her eyes closed, listening for some sign to see if the speaker and the men who guarded her were under the influence of a vault.

"The stars of heaven have seen fit to guide him," the speaker said. "He has no need for the sun or moon to light his way."

Toria again detected no tenor within the speaker's voice that indicated the presence of a vault in his mind, but it hardly mattered. Whether he was sane or not, she could not escape.

They waited for perhaps half an hour before she heard a sound like a distant rumble of thunder coming from the direction of the forest. Closer it came, until it resolved into the distinct beat of hooves against the ground.

When the horses stopped some ten paces from her, she heard the jangle of four different bridles. For an instant she took heart at the small number, but her heart sank almost immediately. Though the Icon had no army at his back, neither did she.

"Well met, speaker," a voice came from in front of her. "You've brought an unexpected gift to accompany one expected."

"Icon," the speaker said in tones of reverence, "my men and I came upon Bronwyn and her servant along the way. His saddlebag is filled with gold."

Laughter filled the darkness. "Well done, speaker. I am pleased. But where are my manners? Speaker, go some twenty paces from us and light a torch. Our guests cannot see."

Toria waited until the torch flared, but the Icon's voice was known to her, as familiar to her ears as any other member of the Vigil. By the flickering yellow light she could make out the hooked nose and jutting chin of the man she'd named ally for decades.

"Greetings, Jorgen."

Toria jerked at the sound of Bronwyn's voice, then fought to hide her surprise.

"Well met, Bronwyn," Jorgen smiled. "Well met, indeed." He turned, and Toria felt his gaze land on her like a weight. "Well met, little sister."

"Hardly," she spat. "You are banished from the light, Jorgen, doomed to spend the rest of your days scurrying about in darkness. How appropriate."

He smiled, his amusement obvious even in the diminished light of the torch. "Fiery as always, little one, but I shall not repay like for like. Come, sisters, there is no need for this discord."

"Join or die? Thank you. No. We received the same offer from Laewan just before we killed him. Perhaps, if you run now, you will escape his fate."

Jorgen threw his head back and laughed. "Well struck, little sister. I shall enjoy our time together."

"We aren't going to have time together, Jorgen," she snapped. "You're going to kill me or Aer is going to find a way to kill you. I have no intention of accepting your offer."

"You misunderstand me, sister." He stepped closer. "I'm not offering."

By intermittent flickers she saw horror behind his eyes, an infinite terror that had seized him and refused to let him go. What hell lived inside his mind?

"Just as no choice was given to me, none will be given to you."

Bronwyn, the part of her that she could still refer to as such, watched her doom play out in front of her, narrated by Jorgen's threats and Toria's defiance. Much of it went past her. The swirl of memories she'd been unable to lock away kept her from being fully present, and she watched the torch-lit scene around her in a state of abstraction, as though her imminent death was nothing more than charcoal sketches, scenes from a story she should know but couldn't quite remember.

But that same abstraction provided one benefit. The fear of dissolution no longer carried the terror it had. It was as if the innumerable strands of memory had dulled her ability to be afraid. Her end approached. She could feel it in the maelstrom of her thoughts and the labored beating of her heart, driven past its limits by the drug. Yet some indefinable need kept her upright, awaiting the proper moment.

Something tugged at her memory, some task or instruction that she was supposed to perform, but the whirlwind of colored memories within her mind grew every second. Only the vestiges of the chiccor root syrup allowed her some measure of functionality.

With a shrug, she gave up, allowed the chiaroscuro of memories to continue their dance. Her body, wracked and ruined by the concentrated stimulant, needed only to serve her one last command. Hopefully, it would become apparent.

"I'm going to have my guards remove your gloves, ladies, but I warn you, any attempt to use your gift on my men will displease me." He pointed to Lelwin. "I will visit pain upon her that your shallow experience can hardly conceive."

She felt a tug as a dagger sliced through the ropes binding her arms behind her. The sword point at her back kept her upright as the guard hooked a finger into first one glove then the other, stripping them off. Next to her, a woman with dark skin and dark hair flexed her hands. She knew her, hunted for the name, but there were too many swirling in her head and none of them seemed to fit.

A man stood in front of them, speaking. His name, she could summon. It was interspersed with all the strands of memory swirling around her head. *Jorgen.* A pinprick of warning floated past her, telling her she should be afraid, but the emotion held no more power over her than the ephemeral memory of his name.

"Now," Jorgen smiled, "I will give you what you in your pride thought you desired. I will let you delve me, and the truth will be yours."

He glanced back and forth between them. "Come, ladies, where is your courage? Show me the evidence of your certitude. Does not the liturgy say that Aer watches over His servants?" He held his naked hands out before him. "Which of you will put Him to the test?"

The moment she'd awaited jolted her mind, bringing an instant of clarity to the maelstrom she could no longer control. The chiccor syrup ebbed within her veins, its effects fluttering and dying. She tried to take a step forward, but her legs refused to obey. Tremors, the merest quiver that prefaced her collapse, began in her knees. Jorgen smiled, seeming not to notice.

"I will." She forced the words and, thank Aer, managed to raise her hand.

"Boldly struck, Bronwyn." Jorgen smiled, stepping toward her. "Let me welcome you to a new company."

He reached out to take her hand.

A tremor went through her arm, and she breathed a silent prayer. *Please, Aer.* Jorgen didn't seem to notice the shaking that had taken her legs or her inability to focus. Perhaps he attributed it to fear.

"No!"

She heard Toria's scream, would have offered some last comfort if she could have vocalized it, if it wouldn't have warned Jorgen of some portion of her intent.

"Bronwyn, please!"

Heedless of the sword, Toria threw herself forward, but the man guarding her flicked his wrist and the flat of his blade caught her across the temple, sending her sprawling.

At the last, Jorgen hesitated, possibly sensing something within her surrender he couldn't attribute to fear. She could have wept with relief when she felt his hand, surprisingly warm, almost comforting, take hers.

By the light of the torch, she watched Jorgen's eyes widen in rage and anger as he picked up the most recent thread of memory within her mind and realized the depth and intention of her deceit. He would have pulled back, but the delve he had forced upon her had taken him as well.

She might have smiled, but she couldn't be sure her mouth obeyed her command. With her last conscious breath she released the tenuous hold she'd kept on thousands upon thousands of memories, let them flood through the bond with Jorgen. She watched as the memories caught him, not as a river or even as a flood, but as a wall of multi-hued water, a crashing tidal wave of emotions and memories stored over the course of centuries.

For a moment, perhaps no more than a heartbeat or two in the real world, Jorgen disappeared, but the crashing cataclysm failed to sweep his consciousness from her thoughts.

In truth, she had expected no less, though she had hoped for more. Somewhere within her mind she pulled a stray thought, one of the few left to her, a request of Aer. Then it was lost, taken by the fading beat of her heart. Nothing more could be asked of her, but as she stepped through death's door to eternity, she couldn't help but wonder. Had she succeeded?

CHAPTER 53

Toria squinted through the pain that made the world jump in her vision, as though the entirety of creation had become nothing more than flames and shadows of a torch. She pushed herself to a sitting position, but none of the guards moved to intercept her, their attention captured by the silent struggle unfolding in front of them.

Jorgen rocked on his heels, his gaze stretched wide in horror even as Bronwyn's eyes emptied and she surrendered herself to dissolution and death.

The hiss of displaced air that began over Toria's shoulder and flew more quickly than her eye could follow was her only warning. Startled, she blinked. There was something wrong with Jorgen's face, but she couldn't decipher it by the flickers of torchlight. A soft moan escaped his lips and he turned, one hand slipping from Bronwyn's as the husk of her body collapsed, the other groping for the hilt of the dagger protruding from his eye. Then he fell.

Toria struggled to her feet, searching, but light flared, blinding her. The sounds of blows she couldn't see and the screams of men around her put her head on a swivel. Each time she turned, she caught only glimpses of chaos in the darkness. Then all was silent.

The bobbing of a light finally gave her gaze a place to rest. Fess stood holding a torch that licked at the darkness, smears of dried and fresh blood covering his face like a mask. As she stood in shocked silence, he handed her the torch and, in what seemed like minutes, quickly dug a grave.

He knelt beside Bronwyn's body and in a perfect, clear tenor recited the antidon for the dead, each word in perfect time and cadence from the liturgy. "'Forasmuch as it pleases Aer to receive the souls of the departed we therefore commit their ashes to the earth, time without end, knowing . . .'"

When he finished, he bowed his head. "Good-bye, Mother. You knew how much I loved you. Every time you touched me, it was there for you to see." He took a deep shuddering breath. "I wish I had told you anyway."

Toria stepped behind him, put a hand on his shoulder. "What happened to Balean?"

He didn't bother to look at her. Instead, he held out his bare arm. "You need to know what I've done."

She shook her head, though the gesture was lost on him. "Later. We can't stay here. We're too close to the forest."

He nodded and with no more feeling than a farmer harvesting grapes pulled the dagger from Jorgen's eye, pausing just long enough to wipe it on the dead man's clothes before he moved to retrieve daggers from the other men. Then he moved to where Lelwin had curled into herself on the ground.

When he cut her loose from her bonds, she blinked, turning her head first toward Toria, then toward Fess. Her eyes came into focus, and she peered at each of the dead men, searching. She stood, her hand held out in expectation.

"I need to borrow your knife."

Fess handed it to her, then took an immediate step back, unsure. But as soon as the hilt slapped into her palm she turned from him to approach Toria. "I'll need the torch as well."

She moved to one of the dead men, her expression unreadable, then knelt and placed the edge of the dagger beneath his belt. Toria watched as she sawed at the thick leather, the muscles of her arm straining until it gave way.

Aer help her, she was too tired to fight Lelwin's grief, too tired to do anything except curl in the grass and mud and escape her waking life for a while, but she fluttered her hand, signaling Fess to follow. "I may need your help. She can't be allowed to do this."

Flickers from Toria's torch did nothing to warm or soften his expression. "I don't think those men will mind. I can guess what happened. The Vigil is supposed to be about justice, not mercy. Isn't this fitting?"

She brushed his argument away, moving to stop Lelwin before she could remove the man's breeches. "It's not the men I care about. If you want to castrate them, you're more than welcome. But Lelwin cannot be allowed to do this."

"What's the difference?"

She nodded. *Better.* "If I allow this, it will take her longer to heal, perhaps too long, and Lelwin will never be part of the Vigil." She knelt next to Lelwin, covering her apprentice's hand with her own.

So intent was Lelwin on her task that she continued cutting through the thick cloth of the man's clothes. But when Toria tightened her grip and forced the knife away, Lelwin's eyes widened as if she'd been struck.

Her voice came out as a growl, threads of rage and pain and loss filling it. "He owes me."

Toria nodded. Behind Lelwin, Fess stood coiled on the balls of his feet, ready to move in case Lelwin tried to turn the knife on her. "No one can gainsay you that, but this won't help you."

"You can't know that!"

"I can and do. I have the memories to prove it."

Lelwin shook her head, but her hand lay still beneath Toria's. "You're not me. None of those women were me. I'm just an urchin, and no one looks out for us but us." She whipped her head toward Fess. "Isn't that so?"

For a moment he regarded her, and Toria thought he might agree, but he turned, his eyes searching within the limits of torchlight. He pointed to the freshly turned earth of Bronwyn's grave. "No," he said. "There are others who will look out for us . . . if we let them." He knelt. "Give me the knife, Lelwin."

Lelwin's head jerked back and forth between them for a moment, like an animal caught in a trap. Then she stood so abruptly Toria fell back on the grass.

She scrambled to her feet to stand next to Lelwin as her apprentice put the knife through her belt. Lelwin shifted to leave, the torch held high over her head, when some impulse took her and she turned to kick the dead man in the side, the sound of her boot against his flesh unexpectedly loud.

His body jerked with the impact, and his head wobbled and lolled away from them before rolling back so that his blank stare landed on Lelwin. Somehow, it appeared accusing.

With a cry of hurt and rage, Lelwin dropped the torch and buried herself in Toria's arms.

"Praise Aer," Toria whispered.

Fess lifted the torch from the earth before it could die. "There are more torches with my horse. We can gather what we are able, and then we must leave."

They retrieved their possessions, taken when each of them had been captured, and half a man's weight in gold that held a bluish tinge even by torchlight. Then Fess led them south.

Toria waited for him to speak, could sense the weight of unconfessed secrets upon him, but nothing disturbed the night air save the soft thud of hooves hitting the turf. Two hours and three torches later they crossed a road, and Fess twitched his reins to follow it.

"When did the gift come upon you?" she asked.

"Gift?"

"Come, Fess." Any other time she would have laughed, but two more of the Vigil lay dead, and the pair of urchins who now accompanied her south appeared to have lost most of themselves. She pulled even with him, noting he kept one eye covered in case he required night vision.

"You killed seven men in about as many seconds, and you've held a torch aloft with the same arm for hours now. Any normal man or woman would have switched hands at least."

He acknowledged this with a small nod, but when he spoke he skirted the question. "Men attacked us in the town of Havenwold. They all had vaults. Lady Bronwyn delved one of them, said something came out of the darkness of his thoughts for her. She got loose before he died, but it left a splinter behind that ate at the doors she'd created in her mind.

"We followed them, and I saw them sowing gold into the streams at night and then harvesting that same gold in the daytime."

He paused, waiting.

"Someone wants to create a gold rush," she breathed. "Even the fear of the Darkwater can't withstand the lure of gold."

Fess nodded. "That's what Lady Bronwyn said. She started eating chiccor root to fight the splinter. Then she sent me to gather the gold. I had to leave her behind."

"Her and Balean," Toria corrected.

But Fess let the obvious prompt go by, instead picking up the narrative of his story without explaining Balean's apparent death. "I got careless. I didn't think we were in danger. When I returned, you and the others were standing over her. Two of the guards found me and ordered me to surrender or else Lady Bronwyn would die. I did, and then they knocked me over the head. When I came to I was tied to my horse. I'm still not sure why they didn't kill me."

Something, a hitch in his voice or the way he changed the cadence of his words, gave the lie to his story, some omission, but she answered the implied question anyway. "They wanted to turn you. They likely saw you as too young to be gifted."

He nodded, but the gesture carried no conviction. "During the ride to the Darkwater, Lady Bronwyn kept mumbling, but the words didn't make any sense. They were just a jumble. But once, I heard my name and two words. *'Be ready.'* Then it was just more noise." He sniffed. "After the splinter took her, it was like she slowly faded away. What happened to her?"

Toria pulled the night air into her lungs, felt the cool of it like balm for her mind. "It's called dissolution. We lose the ability to keep the memories we've gathered partitioned away. Imagine multiple sets of memories filling your head all at once." She paused, unsure whether she should push his confession. "It doesn't occur often, thank Aer, but within the Vigil we fear it the way most people fear the wasting disease. When we take a guard, we make them swear to release us from life if it happens."

He might have nodded or it might have been nothing more than the stride of his horse that made his head dip. "When that man, Jorgen, touched her, I knew the time had come. The guards were too distracted to notice my approach." He paused. "In the space of a heartbeat the first guard was dead. Then I threw his dagger at Jorgen. I might have been able to make a throw like that maybe one time in ten when I was with the urchins. I'm good, but Rory and Lelwin are better, and the Mark as well, for that matter." He shook his head. "It seemed so easy, almost like I was placing it with my hand instead of throwing it." He searched the darkness, his eyes wide in the torch's guttering glow. "And then the rest were dead. I have no idea how . . ."

The torch flickered, its fuel spent, and Fess reined in his horse. "That's the last one. We'll have to wait for dawn unless you want to risk a fall."

She craved light along with a bath and clean clothes as though she were starving for them. "How far away is sunrise?"

"Two hours." He dropped the spent torch to the road, where it hissed against the damp earth. By its last flickers he dismounted. Toria copied him, and Lelwin as well, though she didn't speak. "How do I know that?" he asked her.

"It's part of the gift. Those who have it seem to keep track of time with the rhythms of their body. Elory . . ." Her voice caught.

"Where is he?"

"Dead. The speaker of the Clast said he was killed trying to save me. That was days ago."

They waited in the darkness for sunrise.

CHAPTER 54

By almost imperceptible degrees the sky lightened to the east, and Toria saw indistinct outlines—her horse, Lelwin clutching her knife where she sat, Fess patrolling around them in a set pattern. Half an hour later muted colors became visible and Fess pronounced himself able to guide them south.

They came to a village halfway between dawn and noon—she wasn't sure she wanted to know the name of it or its inn. Bronwyn's death pressed on her mind like a weight she couldn't escape or shift.

The pounding of a smith's hammer beckoned them onward, and they passed by farmers and street merchants, without response. They turned a corner, and Fess pointed at a squat two-story building of cut stone with a slate roof and a broad porch that ran the length of two sides of the building.

"We should enter from the back, Lady Deel," he said.

She nodded, though she wanted nothing more than to dismount, run through the front entrance, and dive into the first available tub. Part of her wanted to weep at the distant tone in Fess's voice—respectful, calculating, and so unlike the overgrown boy who'd left Bunard with Bronwyn—but she had no comfort to give him.

They dismounted in the stable yard behind the inn. Toria watched Fess speak to the stable hands, a pair of grizzled men bearing scars who wore their disdain for life in twisted expressions and narrowed gazes. Something he said, or the deadly grace he now wore, caught their attention. Their eyes widened, and each man dipped his head in acknowledgment, careful not to give offense.

Off her horse, Lelwin moved to put the wall of the stable yard at her back, her right hand still clutching her dagger. When Toria and Fess moved toward the entrance of the inn, she darted from the wall toward them, positioning herself in between, searching for threats.

They entered a broad hallway that led from the stables past the kitchen to a taproom that occupied most of the bottom floor. Fess caught the arm of a serving girl carrying a platter of used dishes back toward the kitchen. She turned, her expression a prelude to voicing her indignation, but stopped when she saw his face.

Fess pointed to where Toria stood with Lelwin. "We need rooms and baths," he smiled, lifting his hands. "As I'm sure you can see."

She nodded. "I'll fetch my ma. The baths are out back."

Fess nodded. "That will be fine for me, but my lady"—he nodded to Toria—"and her attendant desire a greater amount of privacy. Do you have a tub you can bring to their room?" He pressed a silver half crown into her free hand.

"Aye," she nodded, staring at the coin. "Take the two rooms at the end of the hallway."

Fess caught her arm, depositing another coin in her palm. "We'll need changes of clothes as well—nothing fancy, just clean."

"How long will you be staying?" the girl asked.

Fess turned, deferring the question to Toria.

"A few days, no more," Toria said. "Just enough to rest before we continue on."

As soon as she left, the smile dropped from Fess's face. "The village is too busy. The stable here is filled with pack mules. We're still too close to the forest."

She nodded. "I have to rest, Lelwin even more so." She didn't want to think about the problem of the Darkwater. There were no solutions.

"I'll stand guard while the two of you bathe. Then Lelwin can stand watch while I get cleaned up."

Thirty minutes later, Toria slipped into one of the two copper-lined tubs in her room with a sigh. Wisps of steam rose from the scented water, and she tilted her head back until it soaked through her thick hair to warm her scalp. Next to her, Lelwin assaulted her skin with a lathered brush, her motions frantic.

Two days later Toria was contemplating their next step as they huddled over a breakfast of bread and hot sausages—Fess already eating in that way Vigil guards did, facing the door with one hand on his sword, lifting his food to his mouth without ever looking at his plate. Lelwin ate, still clutching the dagger she carried with her everywhere.

Toria saw Allta first, despite the fact that he followed Pellin into the inn. Then she was in Pellin's embrace and wishing she could stay there forever.

"We found bodies, so many, close to the edge of the forest," Pellin said. "We tracked you here. I didn't know what to think or who I'd find."

Sobs tore their way loose from her throat, and they stood with the other patrons of the inn eyeing them or ignoring them according to their temperament. "Bronwyn and Balean are dead—and I fear Elory is too."

His arms tightened, but there were no condemnations. "I'm sorry, so sorry, daughter of my heart. I was too slow to save them." Too soon, he released her in stages, his arms slipping from around her shoulders, until they stood separated once more. "Come, your table will accommodate three more"—he waved Allta and Mark over from where they stood at the door—"and it's isolated enough for our purposes."

Pellin pulled a chair from the empty table next to them, and Allta placed one against the wall, where he had an unobstructed view of the door. Mark stood beside Lelwin.

Toria watched as Lelwin shifted away from both Mark and Allta, her eyes shadowed. The girl needed a healer and time. A lot of time. What to tell Pellin—there was so much.

But it was Fess who spoke first. "Eldest," he said softly, "you will want to delve me." He glanced around the room, extending his arm casually across the table as though he was reaching for the salt. "It will save time explaining Lady Bronwyn's death."

Pellin nodded. "Thank you, Fess. I'm sure Toria Deel has already done so. I think I can shortcut the process by doing this just once, on her."

"No," Fess said before Toria could answer. "She has not." For some reason he didn't look at her as he said this, but at Allta.

"Very well, Fess," Pellin acquiesced with a sigh. "I will delve you after Toria Deel. I'm tired, but only in body."

Pellin removed his glove as he turned toward her, his gaze filled with questions.

She sighed. Even now the thought of using her gift brought an ache to her mind, a dull throbbing whenever she tried to think. "I have suspicions, Eldest, but events . . ." Her shoulders lifted. "I was too tired to delve him. You will know most of what happened." She mimicked Fess, pushing her arm toward the Eldest. He knew of her past, of course, of Cesla's forbidden lesson in the prison beneath Cynestol.

He just didn't know she'd used that instruction as a weapon.

His hands were always so warm, regardless of weather or circumstances, but when his fingertips lifted from her arm, his gaze turned cold, sorrowful. "Oh, my daughter, what have you done?"

She thought he would say more, offer some solace or condemnation, but he folded in on himself in silence. Cesla, even Elwin, had understood her better.

"Eldest?" Fess prompted. He shifted, pushing his arm farther across the table.

After a hundred years in the Vigil, it still surprised her that the exercise of domere took so little time, while inside another's memories, hours seemed to pass. Pellin's fingers brushed the back of Fess's arm and mere seconds later he started, jerking his hand back.

"I submit myself to your judgment, Eldest," Fess said. He turned, shifting in his seat so that he faced Toria squarely, his back to Allta and Mark. "I killed Balean."

Mark drew a sharp breath, and Allta shifted, using Fess's body to hide his hands from the view of the other patrons, but Toria could just see the point of his dagger at the base of Fess's neck. Fess straightened, sitting with the air of a man being careful with each breath.

"Eldest," Allta said in a low voice, "move back. You are within his reach."

For a long moment, as long as it would take to delve everyone else at the table, Pellin gazed at Fess without moving or thinking. "You will make recompense for Balean's death, but as it so happens, Bronwyn's death has deprived the Vigil of its expert on church law."

The boy nodded, the lines of his face as stark and stoic as any guard's. How could he have lost every vestige of his youth in such a short time? "I've read the most applicable documents, Eldest. Lady Bronwyn insisted on my education."

"Yes." Pellin nodded. "She would have."

Allta still held the blade of his dagger against the boy's neck.

"I know the price, Eldest."

"Doubtless, you've read through the main points," Pellin said. "It rarely applies to members of the Vigil."

"It sounds like you're trying to find a loophole, Eldest," Fess said, his voice strangely accusing.

"The circumstances of Balean's death were exceptional, even accidental," Pellin said. "There are, of course, consequences." He sighed. "There always are."

Fess stared at the Eldest, his face inscrutable. Surely, the boy understood Pellin had no intention of executing him?

"There is more, Eldest, that you should know," Fess said.

Pellin shook his head. "There can be no more, Fess. Delving is quite thorough."

"Bronwyn told me to run when she passed," he said, ignoring him, "that the gift would want to be passed on."

Pellin nodded. "I know, and I know why she said so. I saw it, Fess. She loved you."

Slowly, Fess lifted his arm from the table, but instead of placing it back in his lap, he reached up, past the blade at his throat, to touch the back of Allta's hand.

Toria watched, shaking her head in disbelief as his eyes widened, as someone else's memories coursed through him.

"There was a boy in your village, the son of the mayor," Fess said. The knife kept him from turning, but he cocked his head to look at Allta out of the corner of his eye. "He wouldn't look anyone in the eye, but he couldn't seem to keep his hands off the melons."

Allta's eyes widened, and he stepped back, sheathing his knife.

"You see, Fess?" Pellin bowed his head and sighed. "We can dispense with trying to determine your punishment. Aer has already decided."

CHAPTER 55

I rode as close to Bolt as he would allow, with Gael beside me and Rory behind. My horse, an unfamiliar palfrey stallion with few years and less sense, kept trying to overtake the lead horse, and I felt an odd pang at not having Dest beneath me. Out of habit, I wondered how much silver and gold we were burning through to keep ourselves mounted and moving at this pace.

But money and horses weren't the problem. With Wag's nose and nearly tireless pace we'd cut the lead our enemy had on us until he was no more than half a day ahead. Bolt turned in his saddle with the same question etched into the crags on his face that had been there almost from the moment we'd left Bunard.

I nodded, and he reined up as I rode past him.

"Wag."

The sentinel stopped, then trotted back to sit and peer at me with his head cocked. With any other dog, its owner might make a joke about the quizzical look. They might offer some explanation that, of course, the dog would never understand. I laughed as I dismounted. The intelligence some dog owners pretended to bestow on their animals, Wag actually possessed.

I pulled a glove and put my hand on his head long enough to confirm that the scent of the other sentinel and the man who had taken it had, indeed, grown stronger. I looked back at Gael and Rory before turning to face Bolt with a shrug. "Distances don't translate exactly, but directions do. The scent is strongest to the south."

Bolt pointed to the rolling hills in that direction. "We crossed the boundary into Owmead two days ago. He might be making for Andred, but that's at least four days away."

I looked at Gael. "Would anyone in your household have sent Branna there?"

She shook her head. "I don't think Marya knew of anyone, but it's impossible to say, Willet. If it were me, I wouldn't stop running until I had my feet planted on the southernmost tip of the southern continent where the sun never sets."

I almost laughed. "And yet here you are, chasing after this thing."

She rolled her shoulders in a way that showed the graceful lines of her neck. "Women do foolish things when they're in love."

Bolt snorted. "Yes, well, that doesn't really help us."

I thought of Laidir and how he'd given his life rather than believe the truth I'd told him about his queen. Despite his foolishness, I saw something noble and pure in his actions. "It might," I said, looking at Gael. "Love is capable of wonderful and ludicrous sacrifice."

"It scares me when you get that look, Willet," Gael said.

I nodded. "I'll try not to wear it where you can see."

The wind kicked up, blowing from west to east, and I caught the faint scent of salt on it. "We're close to the ocean. Maybe Branna did the smart thing and took ship. Not even a sentinel could track her across the Western Sea."

"If Aer and luck are with us," Bolt said.

I rubbed my backside and climbed back in the saddle. "He can't move during the day."

"But he's moving faster than us during the night," Rory said.

"Even so, Wag's perception of the scent indicates we'll catch up to him tomorrow," I said. "We can only hope it won't be after dark." That would be bad. "How hard can we run the horses?"

"We can alternate a canter with a fast trot without hurting them, and they'll rest when we slow down for the night."

He looked around, as if gaining his bearings. "There's a sizable city ahead, at the mouth of the Havilah River—Vaerwold. I would guess it's less than a day's ride. That might be his destination. In any case, we'll probably catch up to him there."

The saddle hit my thighs like a blacksmith's fist. Unless she had escaped to who knows where, tomorrow we would either find Branna dead or we'd find the man who wanted to kill her, the man who'd forced Robin to kill Elwin. "Let's go, Wag."

He resumed his placid trot, his nose twitching as he sifted through a thousand different scents carried on the breeze.

"Faster," I called to him, a word he knew well now.

He broke into a lope that ate up the ground, and the horses cantered to keep pace. Three hours later we hit the coast road, the sound of waves pounding the chalk cliffs below us loud enough to necessitate yelling whenever we needed to communicate. The sun vanished beyond the sea so fast I could feel time slipping away. Then the wind swirled, alternating between the four points of the compass. It was the first time since we'd left Bunard that it had blown north to south.

Bolt felt the change the same time I did. "In a few minutes we're going to turn from hunter into prey," he said. "The other sentinel is going to pick up Wag's scent."

I threw one leg over the saddle and dismounted, taking my glove off in the same motion. Wag licked my face with a tongue that should never have been able to fit in his head. I put my hand on his shoulder and closed my eyes, drinking in each scent as it came to him. The wind dried his slobber from my face as I waited for it to change directions and back again. Within Wag's mind, I could pick up no trace of the other sentinel, only the smell of seaweed and salt and fish. Then the wind shifted, coming at us from the south, the direction of Vaerwold, and an untold number of canine scents came to me from the city. But one brought an image of Wag's littermate to my mind. Layered beneath it lurked the smell of the men who'd taken her. They were there.

I straightened. "How far are we from Vaerwold?"

Bolt shook his head. "I don't know exactly where we're at, but maybe ten miles."

I tried to figure the sums in my head, but I was a reeve who'd been an aspiring priest. If there was a talent for the mathematicum, I didn't have it. Giving up on the problem, I said, "We have to make a run for it. It will put us in the city in the middle of the night, but we don't have much choice."

I mounted, and we rode at a gallop as the light turned from orange to crimson to charcoal. I couldn't see more than a dozen feet ahead, and Bolt still ran the horses, chasing after Wag, who bounded along the road on padded feet that never made a sound and barely kicked up dust.

Then Bolt's horse stumbled, the head jerking downward in a prelude to the roll that often crushed the rider. I yanked back on my reins with my heart in my throat, watching Bolt's horse fall and knowing I could do nothing to stop it.

In the space between one panicked heartbeat and the next, I saw Bolt shift his weight to the hindquarters of his horse, hauling on the reins to lift its head. The sound of his mount's hooves striking the road sounded like the breaking of bricks as the horse fought to regain its balance—and it worked. After another clumsy stride, it righted itself and Bolt brought it to a stop, its breath blowing through its nose like a bellows.

Wag came out of the darkness to stand, peering at the four of us as if to ask why we'd stopped. "We can't see as well in the dark as you can, my friend," I said. I didn't know how much of that he understood, but he sat back on his haunches and waited, his tongue lolling out of one side of his mouth.

"How's your mount?" Gael asked.

Bolt didn't bother to dismount but nudged the horse forward a few strides and back again. "Well enough, but we're going to have to go slower."

Rory pointed to Wag. "Since he can see in the dark better than we can, why not have Willet use his eyes?"

The three of us looked at Rory, then back at Wag.

Bolt looked at me. "Can you do that?"

I started to nod then thought better of it. I settled for standing there like I was lost and needed directions. "I don't know. Has it ever been done?"

He shrugged. "I don't think anyone has ever needed to."

"Why can't you do it?" Gael asked.

I caught an undercurrent of something else in her question, perhaps a desire to understand just what Elwin's gift had done to me, but we couldn't afford the time I needed to answer all the unspoken questions so I settled for the one she'd asked out loud. "Delving someone is like becoming them," I said. "I'm sure any of the others could do this better, but the memories and the feelings become my own and I retain just enough of myself to pull out when I'm done." I shook my head. "Wag would have to ride with me, and I would have to delve him and guide my horse at the same time."

The sentinel looked at me with his tongue dangling in the breeze as if the entire conversation were for his personal amusement.

"I'll try," I said, "but he's put on a bit of weight since we found him." I dismounted again and went from horse to horse, putting my hand on the head of each mount.

"What are you doing?" Rory asked.

"Braben's stable hands can tell more about a horse with a glance than I could if I had all day, but I'm trying to decide which of them is best suited to carry both Wag and me." It didn't take long. All of the horses were blown. Bolt's horse wasn't favoring the right foreleg yet, but it wouldn't be long. Of the three remaining, Gael's was in the best shape to carry a double load.

We swapped and I whistled to Wag, motioning. He took three light bounding strides and alighted in front of me. My new mount tossed his head and shifted, but settled quickly. "All right," I said. "Let's see if this works."

I gripped the reins in one hand and buried the other into the thick fur just behind Wag's head. As before, the world shifted from one dominated by sight to one defined by smell. I could see the flow of his memories, short strands of differing colors that flowed past me, but I knew them as well as my own. I ignored them to concentrate on Wag's sense of sight.

And nearly fell off my horse as two sets of vision jarred and clashed with each other in my head. I gripped my horse's mane and squeezed my eyes shut so that only Wag's remained. The world at once appeared brighter, but less colorful, the tones muted so that only blue, yellow, and gray remained.

"Wag, look at the road." I spoke out loud for the benefit of my companions, but I thought the command as well, planting an image within his head of what I wanted. His vision in my mind dipped until I could see the hard, dusty trail beneath our horse. Directly beneath our horse.

"That's too close. Look up a bit."

His vision jumped to a spot about fifty paces away. "That's too far."

"Maybe we should all dismount and walk," Rory said. "It might be faster."

"Give him a moment, boy," Bolt growled. "As far as I know, no one's ever done this before. We can spare a few moments if it allows us to push the horses to a trot."

Wag's head swung back and forth, and my stomach rolled over as my vision kept changing while I remained perfectly still. When we settled on a spot in front of the horses about fifteen paces away—enough time and distance so that we could stop if needed—I breathed a sigh of relief. I nudged my horse into a trot, my mind filled with the world as seen through Wag's eyes.

Night slipped past in a timeless focus on the road as we tracked the scent. When the waning moon rose, the road in front of us sharpened into greater clarity and we increased our pace. And soon we rounded a broad promontory and began the descent toward the lights of Vaerwold.

The port city lay tucked into a natural harbor, a broad circle of water miles across, with an outlet to the sea no more than half a mile wide. Piers filled the expanse of its arc, and hundreds of boats and ships thrust their masts into the air. Time and weather had contrived to carve out a broad shelf of land a few hundred yards wide next to the harbor, and every inch of it had been claimed by the city.

From our vantage point on the road we looked over a massive keep that had been carved out of the heavy rock cliffs that overlooked Vaerwold. Its catapults stood ready to defend the harbor. A chasm hundreds of paces wide and nearly as deep separated the keep from the back side of the cliff.

"The hold of Duke Marklin," Bolt muttered to me. "If you think the Orlan family is ambitious, you haven't traveled enough."

We nudged the horses forward and came to a fork in the road. To the right, the road, paved with bricks on the slope, led down to Vaerwold. The road to the left tracked the cliffs, looping around the keep before it continued south.

I felt the change in Wag at the same instant the image of his littermate snapped into focus. The fur on his neck stood on end, and he growled.

"They went down there," I said, "and they're close, almost close enough to see."

Bolt sighed. "I'd really prefer to have encountered them during the day. It would have been so much easier to find him hiding in a building or cave. That way we could just burn it to the ground and watch what happens to him when we force him into the light."

I nodded, even though Bolt probably couldn't see my agreement. "We have a bigger problem."

"I'm not sure how that's possible," Bolt said.

"We're counting on our enemy to lead us to Branna, but I doubt he's going to give us much of an opportunity to stop him before he kills her."

"I would have thought going into a strange city at night when he knows we're coming would have been the bigger problem," Rory quipped.

"Boy," Bolt growled, "one of the things you'll get used to as a Vigil guard is the fact that circumstances will almost always work against you. 'Never ask how things might be worse . . .'" he quoted.

"'Because you'll find out,'" Gael finished.

Rory lapsed into silence, and I grunted my disgust. "That's not one of my favorites."

"Probably because you get to live it all the time," Bolt said.

"Willet," Gael said softly, "you can't wait for him to find her. That's like using her as bait."

I sighed. "I agree. He's not going to find Branna and then take his time about killing her." I looked over my shoulder to the east, but the sky remained resolutely dark. "Aer have mercy, I wish the sun would come up. Let's go, Wag. Find your sister." I put my hand back on his neck and closed my eyes.

We descended the road, a sandy cut in the hillside that switched back and forth on its way to the harbor. At the edge of the city, the road leveled out, and beneath my hand I felt Wag bristle, then start trembling. I looked around with his vision, the world awash in barely perceptible blues, yellows, and grays.

"He's close," I said. I pulled my hand away to check the east, but stars still shone overhead.

The city of Vaerwold didn't have branches of a river to separate its classes, but the wealthiest merchants had congregated at the edge of the water in the center of the city in massive well-lit stone keeps. Farther inland were the smallest dwellings for the city's poor. The wind coming off the bay swirled, and my mind filled with Wag's frustration as the scent of his littermate came at him from every direction. I breathed a sigh of relief. That swirling wind might be the only thing keeping us safe.

Lights dotted the city in clusters, like fireflies in the summer. I offered a prayer dredged up from my days as an acolyte.

"I hope the girl has sense enough to be someplace well-lit," Bolt said.

"Wag can find her," Rory said.

"I wish he could, lad," Bolt said, "but not even a sentinel can find what he hasn't smelled."

"But he has," Rory said. "He had to. He just doesn't know it's her scent."

Wag turned his head to look at the young thief, and his face, blurry and overlaid with his earthy scent, appeared in my vision. "Tell me."

"Wag's been following the scent of his littermate the whole way out of Bunard," Rory said. "But his littermate has been following Branna. Wag's been smelling her the whole time."

Bolt sighed his disappointment. "That's a good idea, boy, but thousands of people must have taken the road over the past few months. Wag has her scent, but he doesn't know which one is hers."

"But he can," Rory said. "Out of the thousands of scents in his mind, how many of those has he smelled here in Vaerwold, on the road, and in the city of Bunard?"

I looked at my guard. "'Never ask . . .'" I said.

"'Never know,'" Bolt finished.

I didn't have any idea how many people might have trekked from Bunard to Vaerwold in the past few months. I put my hand on Wag's head and waited for his enthusiasm to subside. To Wag, a two-minute absence wasn't much different than two weeks. He seemed to like having me in his thoughts.

It took some coaxing and explaining for me to tell him what I wanted, but less than I feared. His canine instinct to catalog the world according to smell was exactly what I needed. When I pictured Bunard, the road we traveled, and then Vaerwold, his mind brought forth the memories of scents in each, overlaying them.

"How many are in all of these places?" I asked.

Wag's thoughts jumbled before he gave me the answer. He didn't understand numbers in the same manner as a man, instead dividing the world according to life in the pack. One, he understood as a lone sentinel. Two, he pictured as a male and his mate. After that, his thoughts tended to think of numbers in terms of "small pack" and "large pack."

"How many?" Bolt asked.

"Large pack," I said and then shook my head. "Sorry. That's his way of counting. As best I can tell, something more than ten. Probably less than fifty."

Bolt shook his head. "That's not real helpful. It's going to be difficult to be discreet."

After a moment, I heard Gael laughing softly. "It's less. Far less."

She looked at me. "It's odds or evens that a merchant might be a man or woman," she said. "At least in Collum. Roughly half the merchants are women."

"I don't see how that helps," Bolt said. "That still leaves us with two dozen possibilities. The city watch isn't going let four armed strangers do a house-to-house search in their city. This is Owmead, girl. King Rymark sees threats everywhere, and he makes sure his soldiers hold the same viewpoint."

She shook her head. "A merchant might be a man or woman, but the porters are all men. I haven't seen a dog yet that couldn't smell the difference between male and female."

I put my hands into Wag's ruff and pictured Branna, Gael, Constance, and every other woman I'd ever known. It could have been coincidence, but I thought I detected a definite note of amusement in Wag's thoughts. I focused on the large pack of scents we'd culled before. "How many are women?"

Within his mind, scent after scent dropped away until only the picture of a male sentinel and his mate remained, the scents here in the city fresh. I stood, smiling at Gael as if Laidir had raised me to the nobility all over again. "There's only two. I chose so very well."

"We don't have to wait, Willet," Gael said.

I stared down the curving road that led into the city, waiting for the wind to settle, straining my eyes for some hint of dawn. "I know. How can one night last so long?" I muttered. I didn't get an answer, but I didn't really expect one. Beneath my hand Wag still shook as if he might launch himself from the back of my horse any second.

Then the swirling breeze died before coming steadily out of the west and the other sentinel's scent came to me, strong and clear, from the center of the city, near the harbor.

"This way," I said. Of the four of us, I would be of the least use in a fight, but I pulled a dagger anyway. Steel whispered against leather all around me.

CHAPTER 56

Small hints of movement from rats and other vermin drew Wag's attention, and I kept jerking my head in sympathy. The towers built to protect the city loomed over us, cutting off the sparse moonlight.

I heard the whistle of wind through fletching, the sound of air being shoved aside by an arrow coming straight for my heart, and knew I didn't have enough time to get out of the way. I tried to move anyway, hoping I might take it through my shoulder instead of my chest.

A blow like the punch of a hammer hit me from the side before the arrow arrived, knocking me sideways. Fire raced across my shoulder to the sound of cloth and flesh tearing. The ground raced up to meet me, and I hit my head.

Lights twirled and spun behind my eyes.

"Get behind the horses!" Bolt's scream echoed back from the keep. "Wag, keep him down!"

Another arrow struck sparks inches from my face, and a splinter of stone tore across my cheek. I tried to stand, pulling my way hand over hand up the reins of my horse, but even upright, the world wouldn't stop spinning. Teeth clamped onto my arm and pulled me back down and a small mountain of fur and muscle lay on top of me. I heard sounds from the last war, the meaty chunk of arrows finding their mark and the screams of horses.

Bolt stood over me, wrapping the reins of my horse around his free hand, keeping it from fleeing. It screamed again as an arrow took it through the lungs. It shuddered. Any second it would go down.

"Rory, get the archer!"

I shook my head, trying to focus, but my thoughts scattered like dust in the breeze. For some reason I could only express as instinct, it was important to keep Rory close.

But it was too late, he was already gone, fading into the darkness to try to get to whoever stood on top of the keep shooting arrows at us. "Bring him back," I said, or tried to. My tongue didn't want to cooperate.

"Rory," I said more simply.

"Stay down and behind the horse, Dura," Bolt growled. "Rory will take care of the archer in a moment."

As if he had the power of prophecy, the arrows stopped. Gael darted away from her horse, and I felt more than saw her touch my face. "Willet, are you well?"

There was no way Rory could have gotten to the roof so quickly. "Too soon," I struggled to pull the words together. The pounding in my head wouldn't let me speak. I rolled under Wag's weight, belly down in the dirt and sand, reaching.

I scooped it into my hands and threw, broadcasting sand all around us.

Bolt stared at me. "What—" he began before oaths spilled from him. Lurching toward me, he wove a blur of steel that whined in the air. "Gael! What do you see?"

Wag went on point, but his head swept back and forth as he tracked the scent. I kept throwing. My hands slid across the dirty sand, and I felt pebbles, lots of them, roll under my skin.

"There's nothing," Gael said from the other side of me. Her sword wove a series of figure eights in the air fast enough to create a dissonant harmony. "Wait."

I saw her head jerk to the left, behind us. Clenching my hands in the pebbles, I threw, heard the sound of gravel hitting something other than the ground.

Her sword broke from its pattern to lash out at the same time a dagger flashed over her shoulder, finding its mark. I winced at the sound, but Gael flicked her wrist and riposted from the other direction as another dagger hit her opponent.

I heard a muted thump followed by the crack of someone's head hitting rock. My knees might have belonged to someone else for all the control I had over them, but I made it to a standing position.

Torches sprouted in the distance, bright glowing flowers against the night. They gathered together, then started toward us.

"We can't stay here," Bolt said.

I looked at the dead man. Dressed in nondescript clothing, he had the thick shoulders and neck of a soldier, but his features were completely ordinary. Even before he'd been turned into a dwimor, there was nothing remarkable about him. There was just enough light here between the buildings to see his eyes and the hooded stare that had taken them in death, but I was uninterested. I had no compulsion or desire to ask him what lay on the other side of eternity. What had he surrendered to obtain his near invisibility?

Rory came running up from the side just before the men with torches came into view. "I never even caught a glimpse of him. No one was up there."

The sky overhead might have lightened from black to charcoal. I couldn't tell. "Are we in time?" I asked.

"I don't think he'd waste time on this attack if he'd already found the girl," Bolt said.

Rory pointed. Reflected light showed beyond the arc of the street. Any moment the men holding those torches would come into view. Even now I could hear the heavy-heeled stomp peculiar to annoyed soldiers.

"I think we should leave."

Bolt nodded. "Come quickly. Leave the horses. Now, before they see us. Soldiers are like boys and dogs. Nothing arouses their instinct to chase more than seeing someone run away."

Gael ran to her mount to dig through the packs at the back. She pulled out a pair of unlit torches wrapped with thick black cloth held in place by wire and tucked them under her arm. "A gift," she said. "We'll need them."

We backtracked along the arc of the road until we came to an alley that intersected, leading inland toward the cliffs and the duke's keep that overlooked the city and running the opposite direction toward the docks.

"This way," Bolt murmured. "The soldiers will head toward the docks."

I followed, trying and failing to make my footfalls as silent as everyone else's. "Why?"

"The lifeblood of this city is the shipping trade," Bolt said. "Above all, the duke is supposed to safeguard the merchants."

We ran another two hundred paces, the buildings quickly transitioning from wealth to squalor as though the five sections of Bunard had been condensed. Bolt took another alley to the right and the smell of too many people in too small of a space hit my nose like a blow. I wondered how Wag managed to stand it.

We stopped when Bolt held up a hand, calling for silence, but no sounds of pursuit came. He turned to me. "Which way?"

I shook my head. "I don't know."

He pointed to Wag. "We're out of time, Willet. If we don't hurry, he's going to find Branna before we do. There are only two possibilities. Which one is her?"

I thrust my hands toward Wag, fell headlong into his thoughts, conjuring an image of two faceless women along with the scents he'd detected earlier. *Where are they?*

His head moved, and I followed the motion, my eyes open to see him sighting toward the docks and the sea, the scent of one of the women overlaid with the smell of the sea. Then he turned toward the interior, his head angled up, looking toward the massive keep that guarded the city.

I stood as my mind and heart tried to outrace each other. Where would she have gone? A snatch of liturgy fell from my tongue, more pleading than prayer, and I set off at a run toward the keep. "This way."

"How do you know?" Bolt asked. I pounded up the incline toward the keep, tried to ignore how easily everyone else, with their gift, kept up with me. "She's a child of Bunard," I panted. "Stone is her friend."

Fatigue burned through my legs and lungs, and I stumbled, still hundreds of paces from the keep's entrance. "Go," I said to Wag and the rest of them. "Find the girl. I'll catch up."

Bolt turned to Rory. "Stay with him."

Wag's strides lengthened, and he flew ahead, Bolt and Gael racing behind him, their legs blurring. They disappeared ahead of me, rounding a turn in the path. I heard Wag's challenge, deep and angry, just before Rory and I rounded a broad outcropping of rock.

Fifty paces in front of us, I saw a guardhouse at the near end of a bridge leading over the chasm. Four bodies, lit by the dim torchlight, lay scattered in postures that living men would never assume. Halfway across the bridge a figure raced toward the keep with a sentinel by his side.

Gael, Bolt, and Wag raced down the path but stopped at the guard-house. I heard Gael's voice on the wind, high and strident, but I couldn't make out the words. Bolt and Wag skidded to a stop as Gael thrust one of the two torches she carried into the embers of a guttering torch that lay next to one of the dead guards.

Light like the sun flared, and I shut my eyes against the glare. When I opened them again I saw Bolt's arm outstretched, the torch spinning end-over-end above and beyond the dark figure and the other sentinel. It landed by the doors of the keep, burning like a star come to earth, and the man skidded to a stop with a roar of anger, his arm over his eyes.

I ran to catch up, arriving with Rory at my side as the figure rounded on Gael and Bolt, his strides eating the distance between them. Malice poured from the hood of his cloak, and a sword and dagger appeared in his hands as if by magic.

Casually, almost disdainfully, Gael thrust her remaining torch down into the embers.

"Come then, if you dare!" She raised that flare of sunlight aloft. "Face the light!"

I came alongside, my legs and lungs begging for respite. "How long will they burn?" I panted.

Gael's voice came out in a growl. "Long enough." She took a step forward. "He's pinned between the two torches."

With a cry of rage, the figure scooped his sentinel under one arm and ran toward the keep. We raced after, following the light of Gael's torch. Ten paces from the massive doors, he took two steps, bounded off the parapet and upward into darkness.

I waited, listening for the fading wail of someone falling to their death or the impact of the figure against the rocks below, but nothing came. Gael thrust her torch forward. By its fading illumination, I could just make out a figure against the dark keep wall, clinging absurdly to its face. Impossibly, with the sentinel in his grasp, the figure started to climb, inching toward a window twenty paces above.

The doors of the keep opened, and a dozen soldiers poured out. "Stand where you are."

"We can't wait for this," I said.

"Keep Wag with you," Bolt murmured under his breath. He looked to Rory and Gael. "These men aren't our enemies. Put your hands up and let them close, then use the flat of your blade."

Dark-liveried soldiers surrounded us, sword points forward. Bolt, Gael, and Rory formed a triangle around me and Wag.

"Now," Bolt said.

I didn't see most of the blows, but I heard them along with the clatter of swords and bodies hitting the stones. We raced into a high-vaulted hallway.

"Wag," I said. "Find her."

We raced up the nearest stairwell as more soldiers poured from a corridor leading back into the cliff. Cries of alarm trailed us as Gael and Bolt dispatched squads of soldiers that blocked our way.

"How are we going to get out of here?" Rory asked. "They're going to bottle up the entire keep."

"One thing at a time, boy," Bolt said. "Let's get to where we're going first."

We raced up another staircase, and Wag stopped before a door, growling. Bolt hit it at a run with his shoulder, and it flew inward, the lock splintering through a handsbreadth of solid oak.

Gael tossed her torch into the room and star-white light illuminated the surroundings. A cry outside a broad arched window keened through the keep with madness.

My scream of jubilation died in my throat as a massive furred shape vaulted through the open window, scented the air once, and launched itself toward a bed along the far wall.

Hope died in my chest as Bolt and Rory threw daggers that missed their mark, piercing the air where the sentinel had been. So close. We'd come so close.

Inches from impact the sentinel hit a wall of muscle and bone and sinew, and the room erupted in violence.

Wag.

Growls of rage rebounded from the walls as Wag and the other sentinel fought, rolling across the floor, each working to cripple and kill the other.

By the light of Gael's torch, I could see just what Wag's injury had cost him. Quick and heavy as he was, the other sentinel was bigger and faster. Bolt moved toward the melee, his sword drawn to put the other sentinel down, but they were moving too fast, their positions switching in the blink of an eye. Blood spattered the floor, and I heard a high-pitched yelp to accompany the crack of bones in Wag's leg.

Bolt's indecision was all I needed.

Stripping my gloves, I jumped toward the sentinels, both hands extended. Bloody jaws moved for Wag's throat.

A snatch of prayer that never made it to my lips flashed across my mind. *Please.*

Just before I made contact, Wag and the other sentinel saw me coming. My hand touched Wag's mane as the other sentinel's jaws closed on my arm and then released.

I heard the bones crack before the pain—Wag's, mine, the other sentinel's—exploded through my mind in white-hot flashes of lightning, but somehow I managed to hold my grip on the other sentinel.

Howls and screams tore from my throat and filled the stone keep as two pair of eyes, one familiar and the other malevolent, leapt at me, washing all sense of self away. My mind fractured. Swept like a twig on a tidal wave, I fought to right myself, but the minds of the two sentinels, both filled with fury and pain, blended with mine.

The coppery taste of blood flowed across my tongue, and I longed for more, even as the desire to rip the throat from my enemy filled me. I lashed out with my mind, trying to still the memory, and felt the room pitch sideways as Wag released his hold on his sister and the other sentinel shook me like a rag.

For a pair of heartbeats that stretched for an eternity, I lost my hold on the other sentinel, and only my thoughts and Wag's filled my mind. Rory, Bolt, and Gael looked as if they were wading through water to get to me, they were moving so slow.

Save the Master! Kill sister! Kill Modrie!

Wag's thought blistered through me despite his pain. Despite his broken leg, he moved so that I could maintain my bond with him through my gift.

No! I thought back. *Back away!*

His growl of refusal carried all the pride and power of his breed. Wag refused to obey. "Save him," I yelled to Bolt. Then I let go and used my free hand to grab the thick ruff of the other sentinel.

Threads of memory flowed by me, the memories and emotions of the sentinel's mind. There weren't so many as a human might have, but Wag's mind and that of his littermate, Modrie, were only a few weeks old. Even so there were more strands of memory than I expected.

And all of them were black.

Then out of the darkness a strand of obsidian, sticky and barbed, latched on to me, then another, tying me to Modrie's mind. Memories of Barl came to me, the butcher who'd gone to the Darkwater out of envy and hate. His vault had been open when I touched him, and the evil that had taken him had tried to trap me in his mind as he died.

But the sentinel's mind and body were in no such distress. Though the barbed strands hurt, they carried no immediate threat of snuffing out my mind. I opened my eyes, and the room pitched in my vision as I reckoned time normally once more. My companions had hardly moved. In a fraction of a heartbeat I would hit the floor, slammed against the stones like a rag doll.

I closed my eyes, saw again the strands of black that constituted the memories of Wag's sister. Then their import became clear. Not one of Modrie's memories brought her joy. From the time her sire had placed his paw upon her head, pain and torture had been all she'd known.

Fire blazed through my mind, and I slashed at the threads binding me in place, burning them with my outrage. More came for me out of the darkness, but I ignored them. If I spent too much time in Modrie's mind, I would die, dashed against the stone floor like a squirrel thrashed by a dog.

I had no idea if it would work, but there was nothing left to try. Lashing out, I tore every black memory within her, ripping them into smaller and smaller pieces until they were nothing but dust, until nothing remained of Modrie's past at all.

I opened my eyes to find myself flying through the air, loosed by the sentinel at the moment I'd broken her mind. The stones of the wall rushed to meet me, but before the world went black I heard the beginnings of another cry of rage from outside.

When I came to I could have counted the parts of my body that didn't hurt on one hand, or might have if my hands hadn't hurt so much. Footsteps thundered along the hallway, and cries of fear echoed from the walls. Wag nosed once at his littermate who lay on the floor with her eyes open but unseeing.

"Find her, boy," I said through clenched teeth. "Find the girl." He limped, whimpering, on three legs to a bed tucked into a corner of the room, pushed his nose against a huddled figure beneath her blankets.

CHAPTER 57

Somehow I'd ended up on my back looking at the ceiling. I couldn't remember how I'd gotten there. Gael's face appeared above me, lit by the light of a too-bright torch.

"Oh, Aer," she cried. "You're a mess, Willet."

I tried to sit up, but Gael put her hand on my chest, holding me still. Across the room, Wag still nosed at the figure huddling on the bed.

"Take me to her," I said. The pain constricting my throat made it sound like a threat. "Hurry, before the duke's men get here or I pass out." Already the room was starting to spin.

Gael cradled me into her arms like a newborn, but the motion tore a scream from my throat as the broken bones in my arm shifted.

Rory and Bolt put steel around me as Gael laid me on the bed and pulled back the blanket. Branna didn't look any different from the day I first saw her, though no one with me except for Gael would have known that. I held out a shaking and bloody hand to touch her, but she recoiled.

"It's okay, Branna," Gael said. "He's here to help."

She still didn't let me touch her, her gaze darting instead to Rory, Bolt, and Wag.

Soldiers crashed into the room, armed with pikes and torches, adding their light to ours. Too many times circumstance had contrived to keep me from learning the identity of Elwin and Robin's killer. I had no intention of allowing it to happen again. When Branna made no move to take my hand, I took hers instead.

I fell through the rich green of her eyes and into the thoughts and memories beyond, recollections of fear and shame. The threads of her memories streaked past me, most in darker shades. Here and there a brightly colored strand flowed around me, but there were few of those, too few. In her river of memory I spotted a recollection the shade of pitch, and I slid into it, letting it become part of me.

I walked through the upper merchants' section of Bunard with my head down, my steps quick, but not fast enough to outpace the burn of shame that lit my face. My throat hurt with the strain of bearing my shame and rage in silence. Home. I just wanted to be home, where I could bathe and hide. Dawn was close, and the city would come alive soon.

Desires burned in my chest that bore no resemblance to those that allowed Andler to barter me to fellow merchants. I wanted a bath to wash the memory of yet another man's touch from my skin. I wanted to hide my face and body so that no one would ever see it again. But most of all I wanted Andler dead with a passion that threatened to turn my mind to ash.

I ducked away from Bunard's main thoroughfare. Too many people might see me there. Only sellers and night women returning to their own bed would be out at this hour, and dressed as I was, no one would mistake me for anything except what I'd become, what Andler had forced on me. Following the path of the Rinwash, I made my way south, my soft boots silent on the stones.

And stopped.

Voices. I heard voices. Ducking beneath the eaves of the nearest building, I considered backtracking through the market, but some early riser would likely see me. I slid around the corner, my back against the wall, wanting to flee but holding.

Pure night never fell in the city—there were too many people who worked early or late, or conducted their business unseen—and tonight a crescent moon added its own illumination. Near the flood wall, I saw three men—two facing one, each man tense.

"Come, Elwin," the lone figure said. "There is no need for doubt." Tall, but hidden in shadow, he moved like a man in his prime. He stood with his hand outstretched, expectant.

Slowly, as if in a trance, the other man lifted his hand, reaching.

"Eldest," the man with the sword said, "this is some sorcery. Let us wait for dawn."

Elwin's hand stopped, and his movements became tentative. "I saw you."

"A likeness placed there by our enemy," the man said. "I assure you, I'm alive." He kept his hand outstretched, the offer plain.

"Where have you been?"

The man took a half step toward Elwin, and the guard tensed. "Discovering the truth. The exordium, the liturgy, the forest—they are all just phantoms, mere shadows pointing to substance. There is so much more. We are so much more."

Some resolve appeared to take hold of Elwin. He stiffened, and his hands balled into fists. "Why meet at night?"

The other man stepped forward, and the guard tensed again.

"When does the truth ever come without a price?" the man said. "For uncounted days I lay in the confines of the forest, locked in a struggle to understand its power, its evil. At first I ranged through the trees, lost, disoriented within lightless shadow where the sun never hits the ground."

"Why did you go?" Elwin asked.

"I wanted to understand," he said. "For uncounted years we tracked those who slipped past the sentinels, never confronting the forest itself." He inched closer. "I grew weary of my ignorance, and I longed to strike a blow against the evil that could make a man less than he was. And I found it." He laughed an easy sound that spoke of long familiarity renewed. "Come, Robin, you were ever suspicious of me. I assure you, I am quite safe."

The sword in the guard's hand never wavered. "Where's Blade?"

"I'm sorry," the man said. "I thought I could protect him, but his mind broke after the third day."

"You left him," Robin said.

The man shook his head. "No. I was taken from him. I fought the insanity of the Darkwater, felt its poison rage within me. Time ceased, and when I came to myself, Blade was gone."

"That was ten years ago," Elwin said.

"So long?" the other man asked.

"Eldest," Robin said, "let us wait for dawn."

The man shifted, no longer reaching, his posture relaxed, diffident. "My knowledge is not without cost. My long struggle in the forest has damaged my eyes. I can no longer abide the sun. But if you wish, we can meet again after sunrise."

"Tell me what you saw," Elwin said, his voice almost pleading. "What is the Darkwater?"

The other man shook his head. "Words can't describe it. I descended into that place that denies sun and time and came to water that stretched away from me in the darkness. Massive trees rose from its banks. I stood on the shore of a lake whose boundaries are shrouded in perpetual night. Desperate to understand but fearful of what might be lurking within their depths, I remained for a time beyond reckoning.

"Finally, I stepped into those waters." He raised his arms, palms up. "And I was reborn." Figures materialized, separating themselves from the shadows, moving with soundless footsteps and the grace of the gifted. "Sinking through mud, I felt something unexpected. I cast off the strictures of unthinking obedience and plunged my hands through the water and ooze, striking not stone but metal." His voice lowered. "I knew."

Elwin shook his head in disbelief or wonder. "You delved the forest." He looked as if he would withdraw, but a heartbeat later he leaned forward. "What is the Darkwater?"

The other man might have moved. "If you want to know, I will show you. Touch me, brother."

"Eldest, don't," Robin said, his voice pleading. "I can't protect you."

"No," the man said. "You can't."

Elwin moved as if in a dream, his hand outstretched.

With a cry of mingled rage and loss, Robin struck.

I came out of the delve into the light of the room with Branna's face before me. Around us soldiers stood with pikes. Gael stood beside me, guarding me with the glaring light of the torch Myle had made for her, but it was Bolt's gaze I sought. The room spun, and I looked at my guard through a narrowing tunnel of black.

"It was Cesla," I said as the room and everything in it faded. "He's alive."

Screams erupted from outside the window.

EPILOGUE

Edring, Aille
Two months later

In a few more weeks, far to the north, the wind would be blowing down the length of the cut, the mountains channeling the frigid blast into a weapon that would batter the walls of the keep in Bunard. But here in Edring, the seasons were more muted, their voices blending so that the change from one to the next had to be defined by the passage of time rather than the change in the weather.

Sweat glistened on each brow at the table, but while I shifted and squirmed in the late afternoon sun, wiping the salt water from my forehead, Pellin seemed comfortable, relaxing in the heat. Toria Deel luxuriated in it, as though the sultry breeze from the south sea was the only thing she found pleasurable in our meeting. Fess and Mark, seated next to each other, endured the warmth with the stoic aplomb typical of the urchins—what they couldn't change, they simply endured.

Yet there was an emotional distance between the two I'd never witnessed before. Even their offhand exchanges carried notes of formality that grieved me. Bronwyn's gift had come to Fess despite her best efforts to prevent it. Adding that to the gift he had received from Balean—something the Vigil had previously thought impossible—the boy had already begun to pay the price.

I scratched at the bumpy scar along my right arm and tried to be grateful to be alive.

Somewhere in my mind I became aware that Bolt had finished relating the tale of our escape from Cesla and that Pellin and Toria had turned their attention to me, waiting for an answer.

"I'm sorry," I said. "I missed that."

"Why did it take you so long to come to Edring?" Toria said with that tone and expression that communicated quite clearly that this was the second time she'd posed the question.

I couldn't find it within myself to take offense. Maybe the summer heat had lulled my tongue and wit to sleep, but probably I was just too tired to care. "If you'll recall, you abandoned me in Bunard without telling me where you intended to meet. We spent almost two months trying to find you and Pellin and Bronwyn by the Darkwater. We only traveled here because I wanted to check on Custos."

Toria waved at one of the flying bugs that plagued the southern half of Aille in such abundance, and the motion served to dispel the objection in my words if not my tone. "He's ensconced within the library with . . ." She stopped short of saying Peret Volsk's name.

And that was probably the real reason she was angry with me.

"Sending the librarian with Volsk was an unnecessary risk," Pellin said, but there was no heat to his voice. The discovery that Cesla was still alive had put the expression on his face of a man who'd woken from a nightmare only to discover that the terrors from his dream had followed him into the waking world.

His fingers twitched toward my arm, the desire to delve me again plain in the unconscious gesture. "For hundreds of years Bronwyn and I have searched the contents of the library over and again. We never found anything that told us why the Darkwater was evil or how to fight it."

"What did you see at the forest?" Toria asked, splitting her question between me and Bolt.

My guard answered first. "The kings and queens have it surrounded, and the lines are drawn." He shook his head. "But they can't hold forever. Rumors of gold continue. It's only a matter of time before it sweeps through them like a fever."

Bolt let it go at that, but the news was worse, and it needed to be said. "Rymark, Ellias . . . " I threw up a hand. "Every army around the forest has caught at least one deserter returning from the forest, but none of them have gone crazy. The commanders in the field are still putting the ones they discover to the sword, but there's no way to catch them all, and that sort of discipline breeds its own rebellion."

"'Push a weapon too hard and it turns on its wielder,'" Bolt quoted.

Pellin sighed. "It would have been better if the deserters *had* gone insane. Now the rest will lose their fear of the Darkwater."

"At least we know where your brother went," I said. "With Jorgen dead, it's a safe bet Cesla's controlling those who have entered the Darkwater."

Pellin nodded, but only after he flinched at the mention of his brother's name. "He's not my brother anymore. Cesla was incredibly gifted and headstrong—a few would say arrogant."

Bolt coughed. "Maybe more than a few."

"But he was never evil."

I looked around the table at our small company. Toria had managed to find someplace for her gaze to land other than Pellin or me. We were an incongruous group, a mix of priests and urchins fighting men. Between the Vigil and the guards and the urchins we were the most dangerous people on the continent, but we were too few.

Far too few.

"I can't figure out why it was so important for him to silence Branna," I said. "What is Cesla trying to hide?"

Pellin looked at me before shaking his head. "Since we delved you, I've been through every memory I have of Cesla, but nothing within them hints at any weakness I can see."

"I've done the same," Toria said, but she spoke to her hands clasped on the table in front of her, and for a moment I saw the tendons flex in tension.

"Where is Branna?" I asked. Pellin had delved her and hidden her away within hours of our arrival.

The Eldest took a protracted breath before he answered. "I sent her and Lelwin to Elbas. The Servants there are the best healers on the continent."

A dark shadow floated across Fess's and Mark's expressions, and I saw their hands reach for their daggers. They knew what had happened to Lelwin, and though I couldn't fault their reactions, the depth of their rage scared me, because it mirrored my own.

"We can't just sit here," I said.

That broke Toria's unseeing gaze, shaking her out of whatever memory had taken her. "What would you have us do? Storm the forest?" She waved at our group. "The Vigil was never meant to fight—we were meant to guard."

I leaned back in my chair and took an ale-sized swallow of the wine in front of me until the warmth in my throat matched the sultry air of Edring. She was right. If the Vigil couldn't fight, then there was no point in going north to the forest.

I'd never been one to shy away from bleak assessments, and I didn't bother to now. "The kings can't hold forever."

Before Pellin or anyone else could answer, Wag, too big now to pass as an ordinary dog, came to his feet to stare at the door in expectation.

Custos and Peret Volsk entered a moment later, discomfited at seeing us all looking their way. Without looking in Toria's direction, Volsk managed to position himself behind one of the ornamental pillars in the room, blocking her view.

Custos looked as if he were bleeding from the mouth. Thick red liquid oozed from his lips, leaving small trails down his chin.

"What happened to you?"

He blinked, swallowing thickly as he wiped his chin with his sleeve. "Ah. We stopped by the market. They have figs, Willet, the most amazing figs! I'd read about them, of course, but the words can't convey the reality."

I let myself laugh. There would be little enough to laugh about later, and it seemed to me one of the ways to fight the coming darkness, feeble though it might be. "Your mouth looks like someone hit you."

"They're called blood figs, my boy. It's as if Aer imbued them with wine."

Volsk cleared his throat, and Custos turned to give him an owlish blink. "Hmm? Yes! I've found something, Willet. Do you remember what I told you about the Everwood?"

Somewhere in the jumble of my head were all the memories I'd gathered since Elwin had passed me his gift. "No. Remind me."

My friend's eyes brightened until they could have lit the room. "I

450

think we can call them, Willet. The clues were there all along, but it was the language—the language changed so that we didn't understand what we were reading."

I wasn't the only one who was lost. Except for Volsk, every face in the room mirrored my confusion.

"Call who, old friend?"

His smile matched the light in his eyes. "The Fayit."

Ah.

Pellin and Toria slumped in their seats, their disappointment obvious. Gael gave a musical laugh—not mocking, merely fond—but everyone else wore expressions of disbelief. Except Volsk. His mouth tightened, almost as if he were offended on Custos's behalf. I must have misinterpreted.

But Custos had surprised me more than once. Of all the people in the room, only I was in a position to fully appreciate the mind that lay behind that unprepossessing gaze. Only I had delved him, and right or wrong, my friend was worthy of respect.

"How?" I asked. "Do we have to go to the Everwood?" But I knew the answer even as the words left my mouth.

He shook his head. "I don't think so. The rhymes and stories seem to indicate that they have their favorite haunts, but the location needn't be specific."

"Are you sure it will work?"

He bit his lip, his enthusiasm visibly waning. "I think so, but I haven't been able to find any of their names."

Pellin held up a hand for silence, and Custos rocked back on his heels. "I appreciate your efforts, my friend, but I've read the texts—dozens of times, actually—and Bronwyn lived in the library whenever she could make her way back here.

"We spent decades trying to unravel the meaning behind the singsong chants, along with their games." He looked at Custos, his brows raised in speculation. "Did she ever tell you her theory behind the children's game 'the calling of the fates'? No? Well, I'm sure she would have shared it with you eventually. Odd, isn't it? No matter where that game is played, even on the southern continent, a thousand leagues from here, the rules are the same. The children form a circle of four or six or nine to chant their rhyme and ask the fates who will die."

I didn't need Custos to tell me *fate* and *Fayit* had become synonymous in our language. Anyone who'd been an acolyte to the priesthood would know.

"That's just it," Custos said. "I believe, if we can assemble a circle of nine pure talents, six gifts, or four temperaments . . . we can call them."

Pellin shook his head. "We tried. It didn't work. Bronwyn believed the problem lay in the decay of man himself. There are no pure gifts or talents or temperaments in the world any longer. Man has become less than what he was."

Custos shook his head. "I think the problem lies in the absence of the name. In the children's game, they select one of their own to be the Fayit, and then they call him or her by name. Only then do they appear in the circle."

Frustration creased Pellin's brow. "There *are* no names in those silly rhymes—not in our library or any other." He sighed at the look on Custos's face. "I mean no offense, my friend. In this time of encroaching night, you've found a way to fill me with wonder I haven't felt for hundreds of years, but rhymes and songs won't help us. We don't have the time to go chasing hints and suggestions. We need a plan and weapons. We are all that remains of the Vigil."

I stood, lifting myself out of my chair as he spoke, enamored of a strange impulse, as though the vault in my mind had opened before I could go to sleep. In the midst of the dense *jaccara* trees of the open-air seating in the village of Edring just north of Cynestol, I could have suddenly pointed north and west to the Everwood with unerring accuracy.

"A name," I murmured. "A name."

I lifted my hands, trying to ignore the looks of concern and disbelief that surrounded me. This was probably the moment Pellin and Toria and Volsk had waited for, had expected. I'd finally gone completely insane. Allta had his hand on his sword.

"Ealdor," I called. "We need you."

Nothing happened.

"Willet?" Gael asked, her voice soft, questioning.

"Ealdor," I called again. "I know you're real. You told me about the leaves, about something I couldn't have known."

Gael's hand found my shoulder. "Willet, you're scaring me."

I raised my voice. "For the love of Aer, Ealdor, we don't even know what we're fighting."

A moment passed, and I lowered my arms, angry, frustrated. "Stupid phantom," I growled to myself. "Never there when you really need him. He probably wants me to go find an abandoned church. . . ."

Then he walked out of the shadows of the pillar opposite me, his hands fiddling with the worn purple stole he always wore when we celebrated haeling together. "Hello, Willet."

I didn't need to hear the chorus of gasping disbelief to know everyone else saw him as well.

ACKNOWLEDGMENTS

It seems the making of each book is an adventure unto itself, and there's always something or someone new to thank. For *The Shattered Vigil* the feedback of my beta-readers, Jesse Tidyman, Whit Campbell, and Amelia Putnam, was invaluable. As always, my editors, Karen Schurrer and Dave Long, were awesome; and my agent, Steve Laube, was always there to talk me down whenever the business side of writing threatened the creative side.

ABOUT THE AUTHOR

Patrick W. Carr was born on an Air Force base in West Germany at the height of Cold War tensions. He has been told this was not his fault. As an Air Force brat, he experienced a change in locale every three years until his father retired to Tennessee. Patrick saw more of the world on his own through a varied and somewhat eclectic education and work history. He graduated from Georgia Tech in 1984 and has worked as a draftsman at a nuclear plant, did design work for the Air Force, worked for a printing company, and consulted as an engineer. Patrick's day gig for the last nine years has been teaching high school math in Nashville, TN. He currently makes his home in Nashville with his wonderfully patient wife, Mary, and four sons he thinks are amazing: Patrick, Connor, Daniel, and Ethan. Sometime in the future he would like to be a jazz pianist, and he wrestles with the complexity of improvisation on a daily basis.

Sign up for Patrick's newsletter!

Keep up to date with news on Patrick's upcoming book releases and events by signing up for his email list at patrickwcarr.com.

More From Patrick W. Carr

As a dynasty nears its end, an unlikely hero embarks upon a perilous quest to save his kingdom. Thrust into a world of dangerous political intrigue and church machinations, Errol Stone must leave behind his idle life, learn to fight, come to know his God—and discover his destiny.

THE STAFF AND THE SWORD: *A Cast of Stones, The Hero's Lot, A Draw of Kings*

◊ BETHANY HOUSE

You May Also Enjoy . . .

Prince Wilek's father believes the disasters plaguing their land signal impending doom, but Wilek thinks this is superstitious nonsense—until he is sent to investigate a fresh calamity. What he discovers is more cataclysmic than he could've ever imagined. Wilek sets out on a desperate quest to save his people, but can he succeed before the entire land crumbles?

King's Folly by Jill Williamson
THE KINSMAN CHRONICLES #1
jillwilliamson.com

In this highly imaginative fantasy, a reluctant hero undertakes a dangerous and heroic quest to discover his destiny and fight against the dark forces seeking to control The Realm.

The Emissary by Thomas Locke
LEGENDS OF THE REALM #1
tlocke.com